THE ELIXIR OF YOSEMITE

VERTICAL MURDER - BOOK ONE

MC BEHM

THE ELIXIR OF YOSEMITE

BOOK ONE: VERTICAL MURDER SERIES

M.C. Behm
South Lake Tahoe, California
mcbehmbooks@gmail.com
www.mcbehm.com

Yosemite Valley, to me, is always a sunrise, a glitter of green and golden wonder in a vast edifice of stone and space. I know of no sculpture, painting, or music that exceeds the compelling spiritual command of the soaring shape of granite cliff and dome, of patina of light on rock and forest, and of the thunder and whispering of the falling, flowing waters. At first the colossal aspect may dominate; then we perceive and respond to the delicate and persuasive complex of nature.

—Ansel Adams

Cover Illustration by Michael Corvin - https://corvindesign.carbonmade.com/

Editing by Randy Mundt - armundt@charter.net

Section Illustrations by Marion Frebourg -
http://cargocollective.com/marionfrebourg

Mentorship from John Hindmarsh - http://www.johnhindmarsh.com/

And spiritual support from Tahoe Writer's Works -
http://tahoewritersworks.com/

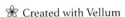 Created with Vellum

AUTHOR'S NOTES

The Hetch Hetchy Valley in Yosemite National Park was dammed in 1923 despite widely publicized eloquent petitions from America's founding environmentalists.

Electricity generated on nationally protected Yosemite land was sold illegally and in defiance of federal legislation and United States Supreme Court mandates.

Environmental activism has, in the past two decades, been systematically adjudicated as *ecoterrorism*.

To Emily, the sophomore during my second year teaching who performed the soliloquy that I wrote for a new ending to The Taming of the Shrew and wept while doing so. Ever since that audition, I have know that it was possible for me to write.

To my Grandmother, the source of my nom de plume, for belittling, guiding, disillusioning, and inspiring me.

To my muse and love, Jayme, a.k.a. Wifey.

~

As well dam for water tanks the people's cathedrals and churches, for no holier temple has ever been consecrated by the heart of man.
—*John Muir, The Yosemite*

RESEARCH

A glossary, bibliography and endnotes (designated by asterisks in the text) can be found in the appendix. All rock climbing route descriptions and locations in and around Yosemite National Park are based on actual topography and accumulated climbing data.

PART I

MUIR AND MAYHEM

Take a course in good water and air, and in the eternal youth of Nature you may renew your own. Go quietly, alone; no harm will befall you.

—John Muir, *Steep Trails*

1

TIS-SE'-YAK'S TEARS

Sunday, 2:01 P.M.

"Off belay!" Stuart's voice trailed down the length of his rope as it brushed against the massive edifice of Half Dome's northwestern face.

"Belay is off!" Abigail called up the hundred-plus-foot third pitch of the Regular Route, which Stuart had just climbed.

Putting one hand on the cordellette anchoring him to the wall, Stuart closed his eyes and inhaled the warm scent of Yosemite granite. *It happens now,* he thought. Habitually he began to pull up on the rope until it became taut to his partner's harness below.

"That's me!" Abigail yelled.

Inserting the rope into his belay device and locking his carabiner, Stuart turned his body and yelled back down, "You're on belay, Babe!"

"Climbing!"

It's been so long. Stuart slid the rope through the aluminum device and wondered how it would feel, what sensations would return to him. He gazed up at Half Dome, beautiful and uncompromising in the early afternoon light. Long black water stains gave the giant rock facial qualities; according to the Ahwahnechee people, these were the tears of *Tis-se'-yak* that fell to the reflecting lake below. These tears sculpted minute cracks and fissures that made it possible for Stuart to be here, hanging over 1000 feet above the valley floor.

My course is set. The Professor didn't allow—

"Hey, you daydreaming?" Abigail asked as she vaulted onto the ledge by his side.

"No, sorry. Are you good?"

"Yeah, I'm in." Abigail snapped a locking carabiner into the anchor Stuart had set up only ten minutes before.

"That was fast. Are you ready to lead us up this 12a beast?" Stuart asked. "This is the pitch you were stoked to climb, isn't it?"

"The Higbee Hedral. I'm more ready now than ever. I'm just glad to be out of that damn symposium."

"Easy there," Stuart said with a laugh as he began to exchange gear with Abigail. "The future of Yosemite or something?"

"Yeah, restoration and usage plans and on and on." Abigail unclipped her water bottle from her harness and took a long and careful drink.

"Sounds more heinous than this pitch."

"No." Abigail took a deep breath. "That's not it. I like that stuff; I was a speaker after all. It's just... I don't know. Creepy or something."

"Do tell."

"The people there. It was different."

"I thought it was all hippies and scholars and shit."

"Yeah, it usually is, but not this time. There were these two suits in the back of the room."

"Did they say anything?"

"No, but..." Abigail sighed and cast her gaze skyward.

"So, getting up the next pitch free would be like—"

Abigail smiled. "Like kicking those goons or whoever they were, right in the nads."

"Nice. You're on belay."

"No time like the present." Abigail's cheeks curled into a wily smile as she unhooked from the anchor. "The end," she said as she inspected her figure eight knot. "It feels a little sharper today."

Brushing aside his scraggly blond hair, Stuart watched as Abigail fired upward into the fourth pitch's boulder crimps and lock-offs, on lead—the sharp end of the rope. He stroked his bleached-white goatee and chuckled to himself. *Man, she looks good from this angle.*

Abigail's raven hair bounced between her shoulder blades as she shifted her weight from one foot to the other. As Stuart moved the rope to which they were both tied through his belay device, he shook his head. *She'll probably make it easy—easy for me to kill her.*

2

___

MEDITATION

Sunday, 2:56 P.M.

R*ight.*
        Thump.
        Left.
Crash.
Pivot then.
Right.
Crash, crash.
Root.
Turn.
Jump.
Rock.
Whump, whump.
Left.

Woody worked the terrain at breakneck speed as Euro Trance pounded through his headphones. At times his pace intensified, then eased off, having more to do with what was on his mind than the difficulty of the topography. His breathing, heartbeat, and cadence flowed with the symphonic E.D.M. pulses ricocheting from his eardrums into his neural chemistry.

Whenever Woody sped past a family of hikers or dodged around a mountain biker grinding her way uphill, his intensity provoked remarks: "I don't believe this," or "Nobody runs out here." The more frequent commentary was, "Be careful," or "You could hurt yourself," which Woody had become adept at lip-reading. It was these superficial I-care-about-you comments that ticked Woody off.

Out of pent-up rage, he took the next sequence of strides at a more reckless clip, incorporating Parkour—a dive roll, a backflip off of a tree, or planting his hand and leaping off one switchback to another. Trail running was Woody's way to clear his mind, to let any questions or problems find solutions in the rhythm of his feet in the dirt and the music in his head.

Buzz.

Woody snapped out of his trance, took a seat on a boulder near the ridgeline of Mt. Tallac and unhooked his phone.

R u coming? The message was from Joy.

Woody typed, *Yes,* then deleted it. Joy would be away at college soon. He did want to go back to Yosemite. *I haven't been back since—*

Yes, he retyped. Woody stood up and pressed *send*. He slammed his phone back into his pocket and broke into a run.

The trail in front of him took a precipitous fall line through a rock-strewn mountain bowl on its way toward Fallen Leaf Lake. Woody's heels made greater contact with the trail while his body's angularity shifted backward from the balls of his feet.

Thump, thump went the music.

It's not that Mom doesn't trust me. It's just—

The trail plummeted into the loose volcanic rock of Cascade Bowl. Woody took the first stride with some caution, testing to see how far he slid as the small rocks compressed into one another. Transferring his weight and thrusting his right foot forward, he planted his next step slightly farther than the preceding, causing a more prolonged skid.

It was also the older girls. He knew what his mom would say. And being away for a weekend in Yosemite. "It's dangerous there," she used to implore them when Woody and his father proposed an adventure.

Get it together, Woody berated himself.

His hips stretched and absorbed. The length of his strides expanded. The rocks hissed as they smashed into one another.

A young couple was eighty feet below, laboring their way up the trail from South Lake Tahoe to the Tallac summit. Woody saw them freeze.

"What the hell is he doing?" the girl seemed to ask her partner as she pulled him off the trail.

Woody intensified his next steps until his pressure and velocity were at the very threshold of control; the volcanic bowl carried him like the arc of a giant ocean swell. The couple in front of him cringed; he smirked as he blew past.

Joy is leaving; might be my only chance to spend time with her.

Since his father died, Woody hadn't really connected with anyone, except Joy.

I'll lie.

3

DOWN TO MIRROR LAKE

Sunday, 2:57 P.M.

Stuart reflected on the upcoming moments. He had killed many times before. He liked the feeling. Each time, he felt it reunited him with something familiar, something familial.

Take was the word Stuart hoped he would hear her say; *take* would make the kill so flawless.

The word *take* was a sacrosanct trust between the belayer and the climber. When a climber spoke the word to his or her belay partner, the mechanics of the command dictated that the belayer literally would take up the slack in the rope. Its utterance implied an absolute faith in the person tied to the other end of the rope. It meant, quite literally, *take my life in your hands.*

Stuart hoped he would have such an opportunity. He hoped he wouldn't have to pull down on the rope to get Abigail to fall, but that she would weight the rope on her own volition.

"Take!" Abigail called from above.

Stuart smiled. *This will be easy after all.*

FEELING THE ROPE BECOME TAUT, Abigail pulled her body into the wall and the nut she had just slotted into a perfect constriction. The piece looked solid. She had tackled the crux of the pitch free—without aid gear or using the bolt ladder. It was time for a break.

Pulling up on the small ledge above her placement, Abigail moved her body as close to the wall as possible, thereby reducing the amount of the climb she would have to repeat once she started climbing again. Careful not to get her harness above the pro she had just set, which would enable it to walk or move upward out of the constriction, she tensed her muscles until she felt the rope get nice and tight, loading the nut and pulling her waist into the wall.

Abigail felt the belay loop rise, the reinforced nylon leg straps squeezing into her thighs. She took a slightly wider stance on the wall, as her body angled at forty-five degrees away from the vertical surface. Abigail brought one hand down to the rope at her waist and then, confident in her stance and her last piece of pro, she removed her other hand from the wall, letting it dangle loose behind her as she stared up at Half Dome to study her next moves.

Then, something was wrong.

A high-pitched whizzing sound threw Abigail's eyelids back. She fixed her eyes for only an instant on the rope zinging through the carabiner.

Where was the pop? If she was falling, which clearly she was, her last placement, her last pro should have *popped*—a distinct sound as the steel lets loose from the granite.

It's okay. I've taken whippers before.

The air rushed by her as she descended ten, thirty, sixty feet, knowing that on the other end of the rope, Stuart was her counterbalance, and if she was falling this far, he was in for one hell of a ride.

Serves the bastard right if he screwed up his belay device.

But then that didn't seem probable.

That wasn't possible.

And then she was still falling.

And falling—way past the distance she should have fallen until her partner's end of the rope would have caught, yanking them both like elastic Gumby dolls at two ends of the same dynamic line.

And she realized at this moment that even though she had seen Stuart's eight knot, even though there was a bomber anchor from which she started this pitch, and even though she had made at least ten placements—four of which someone could hang a small car from—even though all of this was true, she was still falling.

And falling.

And it was now that Abigail understood she would continue to fall until there was no more empty space to fall into.

She panicked. Abigail flung her arms and legs out as if to reconnect somehow with the surface of the rock and arrest her descent. But as she did this, Abigail knew there was nothing to be done.

She looked up at Half Dome, *Tis-se'-yak*, her long black tears streaming in vertical shafts down the face of the rock. She didn't wonder why—why she was falling, why Stuart hadn't caught her. At this moment, what she knew to be one of her last, and while the air gushed around her free-falling body, she thought instead about *Tis-se'-yak*, about those tears that followed her. She reflected on the native legend of the valley, how the tears of Half Dome had filled Mirror Lake, how these forces of nature—rock and water—were as immutable as the force that now pulled her downward, and how this—this was a good place to be.

4

BLACK COFFEE

Sunday, 2:58 P.M.

R ick Turlock woke with a start.

There was a naked arm across his chest. He inched his way out from under the loose embrace and slid his feet to the floor.

It was mid-afternoon, lazy rays of sunshine added a soft refraction to the log walls and wavy glass windows of his cabin. Just a couple hours were left before he had to be at work. Rick padded to his closet past his easel and watercolors and began slipping on his Park Service uniform. The figure in bed stirred beneath an undone sheet.

Rick tiptoed over to his kitchenette against the far wall, poured coffee grounds into the base of a French Press and put a kettle on the two-burner stove.

"Good afternoon, Sunshine." Her soft voice, with just a hint of seduction, wafted into the kitchen.

"Hey there," Rick responded, walking back toward his bed while racking his brain to try and recall the first name of the beautiful woman smiling provocatively at him. *Shit, it was Caro-*

line, maybe Christina—definitely a "C" name.

His guest slowly sat up, the bed sheet slipping from her bare shoulders, down her breasts and rippling around her mid-section. "So this is it?"

"This is *what?*" Rick smiled sitting down on the bed.

"This is you?" A finger traced the outlines of Rick's badge.

"*Chief?*" she said with a smile. "How does someone whose people were kicked out of this valley, end up working here with a nametag like that? I can't decide if the irony is hilarious or tragic."

"Yeah. Not exactly *my* people," Rick said.

"Go on..."

"I'm Lakota, from a different part of the country."

"Rick's not your real—"

"Heyoka."

"Why Rick then?"

"Puts people at ease."

"Oh, *Ranger Rick.* I get it. But, there's more to it though, right?"

"Yup." Rick took a deep breath and stared out the window, into the branches of a blackened oak tree. "I wanted out of the reservation, to distance myself. I used to be angry."

"With...?" His guest sat up straight and stretched her spine.

"You are gorgeous, you know that, don't you?" *Now, why can't I remember your damn name?*

"Rick, I'm fifty-one years old. What I *am* is comfortable. You were telling me about anger––perhaps the reason for your abundant tattooing? "

"Oh, yeah––anger. Everyone, I was angry with everyone––the meth addicts, the social workers––everyone except my grandfather. Just him, he was different. He taught me about the outdoors; that's how I started climbing, painting, hunting—the stuff that brought me here."

"Huh. So how did you lose the anger?" His guest stood up from the end of the bed, letting the sheet fall to the floor. "Water's boiling, dear." She walked across the cabin's wood planks and throw rugs to the kitchen where she turned off the stove and poured hot water into the coffee grounds.

"I moved here in 1977––" Rick paused and observed his naked guest tiptoe around the kitchen looking for cups. "Well...that was the year Jon Scott Glisky crashed his Lockheed PV-1 Ventura in the Tuolumne high country near Lower Merced Pass Lake, killing himself and his copilot." * Rick got up and grabbed a shirt for his guest, carrying it with him to the kitchen. "You're cold."

"They're that obvious?"

"It's hard not to look."

"Okay, Chief. Thanks." She winked and slid into the shirt. "You were saying..."

"You see, the World War II vintage plane Glisky nosedived through the ice had actually been carrying six tons of baled Mexican marijuana.* Employees of the National Park Service were unable to remove much of the drugs due, I suppose, to the harsh winter storms, so they figured it could wait until spring." Rick began pouring coffee.

"Let me guess, they figured wrong?"

"Yeah. Most climbing dirtbags, like me at the time, and the Park lackeys, we might have been poor but we were pretty industrious. So when we heard there was free dope up in the high country, well... we hiked the twenty or so miles from the valley floor up to the lake with empty packs and chainsaws."

"Fun!"

"It was a wild summer." Rick took a sip of coffee. "The gear store, selling climbing and camping stuff, couldn't re-supply their shelves fast enough. We bought everything we always wanted— new ropes, new clothes, new tents, and so on. We all ate well, smoked a lot of gasoline-laced pot, and were extremely content."

"Not angry?"

"Definitely not."

"Okay, my turn for some artificial outrage––" She paused to

take Rick's coffee cup from his hands and enjoy a sip. "So, you don't remember my name, do you?"

Rick smiled and backed away toward the bedroom. "Well, it starts with a "C," has I think three syllables, and I have two names in my head, but..."

"Oh this is fun; I'd like to hear what my other name is..." She closed the distance and gave Rick a playful shove backwards onto his bed.

"Okay, either Caroline or Christina."

"Nice. I like them."

"So which one?"

"It's okay, Rick or Heyoka. You have to work, don't you? And I have to get back to real life on the other side of the country. My jeans, please?"

Rick sat up and handed Caroline or Christina the jeans from his bed. "I'm sorry."

"Rick, I'm fine. More than fine," she said as she slipped into her sandals. "You're the one who's stuck alone in paradise. It *is* the end of tourist season, isn't it?"

"Yeah." Rick shook his head. "Can I drive you to—?"

"No." His guest stood up and looked around the cabin. "So this is it?"

"Yeah."

"Is it alright if I take one of these?" she said, gesturing to Rick's stack of watercolors.

"Please."

She leafed through the top set of paintings and found one she liked. "Thank you, sincerely. I'll be going now, Chief."

Rick nodded and watched as she walked out of his world.

Well...that was oddly forthright.

Her observation, though, cut into him with uncanny precision––it was the end of the season, fewer tourists and less excitement. The three thousand-foot walls of Yosemite Valley would begin to close in, casting impenetrable winter shadows and leaving Rick alone with his thoughts.

Rick shook his head, stood up and marched back into the kitchen, quickly filling two small thermoses of coffee. Donning his forest-green Park Service hat, he strode out of his rustic cabin's front door.

A little hot today and still no sign of weather.

The extra coffee was for his assistant, Jeffrey, who would have been up most of the day. An environmental symposium was taking place most of the weekend at Yosemite Lodge at the Falls, and Jeffrey certainly would have been in attendance.

"Hmm," Rick grunted. *All these wild and scenic "plans" and occupancy impact studies.* It was clear enough what was happening—more and more people were visiting Yosemite, trampling meadows, pooping in the damn bushes. There were some obvious solutions too, and the quota on hiking Half Dome was a good start.* *They need to funnel these people into other parts of the Park—Hetch Hetchy for example.* Rick would debate this with Jeffrey.

As Rick passed Yosemite Village, he noticed another poster for the symposium. This one had a picture of an attractive young lady in a dress shirt waving with nonchalance at the camera. It read: "Abigail Edwards, Keynote Speaker." *Another know-it-all environmentalist*, he mused. Rick paused and looked closer at the photograph, studying the telltale calluses and faint lacerations on Abigail's fingers, while a smile spread across his face. *She can't be that bad. She's a climber after all.*

A PITTANCE

Sunday, 2:59 P.M.

Clinging to a rocky hillside overlooking an exclusive Sausalito neighborhood and San Francisco Bay, The Professor's estate dwarfed its surroundings. With towering brick turrets covered in ivy and narrow masonry openings containing expensive architectural windows, its four stories commanded attention. On this day, if someone studied it closely, he or she would notice smoke rising from an ornate copper chimney cap—an odd sight for sure in late August, and though there was a slight chill in the air, often the case on the west side of the bay, stoking a fireplace in summer was incongruous to say the least.

The Professor sat in the study, reflecting on the view. The Golden Gate Bridge shone in late afternoon sun, and Alcatraz gleamed pearly and alabaster on its island throne. The view never lost its appeal—fog wrapping around the hilltops, office towers and iconic landmarks catching afternoon rays, all of it proclaiming San Francisco's prominent place in the financial and cultural hierarchy of the world.

"The Leach family has worked for this," The Professor said aloud through the open window.

This house, this location, the private jet, the helicopter on call, the expensive schools, and trips—the family had been working for it all for generation upon generation.

That infernal court case, thought The Professor, grimacing. *It can't be helped. Anyway, it has been a useful nudge—a slight encouragement.*

The prosperity of the family had to be secured in a permanent and tangible way. Rather than resenting the obligation, The Professor embraced it and knew that, in the next thirty-six hours, the one Achilles heel that could threaten the Leach dynasty would be eliminated.

Staring down at the list just created, the Professor smirked.

ITEMS:

    Scuba gear $3,187

    Wiring / computers $8,022

    Range Rover $64,651

    Access/fees/reservations $1,291

    Camping gear $1,675

    Explosives NA (provided by company)

    Climbing gear $2,963

    Volkswagen bus (vintage) $25,479

    Used Ford Focus $7,570

    Payoff #1 (Capwater) $450,000

    Payoff #2 (Stuart) $2,000,000

TOTALING THE COLUMN, the Professor had only one thought: *a pittance.*

The imported mahogany coffee table on which the list now sat faded in and out of light while the fire's wavering glow illuminated the cherrywood bookcases lining the walls. Sipping a glass of cognac, The Professor then set it on top of the list and leaned back into the burgundy upholstered wings of a massive claw-foot chair.

To The Professor, reviewing the numbers seemed more comical than necessary. It was a minute fraction of what it would otherwise cost.

In the next few hours, The Professor was expecting a posting online. It would be from a "student" of sorts and would be untraceable to the poster, and easily viewable by anyone. The cryptic posting needed only one word—*Muir*. This word would mean that the first step in a process had been completed, a process destined to not only alter the physical realities of the holiest of protected lands, but upend the very nature of all that the famous John Muir sought to accomplish.

Satisfied with the list, The Professor moved the crystal snifter to the side and crumpled up the paper, tossing it unceremoniously into the fire. Slowly, irrevocably, the flames consumed this little exercise in justification.

NAACP

Sunday, 3:09 P.M.

"**Y**ou sure you don't want—?" Mojo began.

"No, Mom. I'll walk. It's not far," Woody replied.

"All right." Mojo leaned in and hugged her son. "Run fast."

"Thanks, Mom," Woody said with a laugh. "See you in a couple days." The expression "run fast" was a slogan initiated by Mojo for the cross-country team, always said after a pregnant pause as a matter of indisputable fact—"Hey guys... *run fast.*" Unlike other sports with layer upon layer of strategy and technique, competing in cross-country relied mostly on putting in training miles and then when the time came, as Mojo said, just doing it—*running fast.*

Woody glanced over his shoulder as he walked down the block. His mom stood by the window watching him in his blue-and-gold South Tahoe High School tracksuit. The nylon swished incessantly as he walked. Woody didn't like wearing the outfit, but it covered his arms and legs in front of the girls, and he figured it would help to convince his mom that he was going off to his preseason training camp and not on a weekend climbing trip.

It'll be fine, Woody thought as he hurried down the block and around the corner. He'd be back from this little adventure soon, and even if his stunt ended up restricting his liberties during his junior year, it wasn't like it really mattered—school was starting and Joy would be off to college. Joy was two years older and they were just friends, but he couldn't help how he felt. She didn't fit in the standard high school subculture boxes. She was different—and a little weird, just like him. Joy and her older sister Jasmine were Irish, but the bulk of the obvious indicators were bestowed on Jasmine, who teased out her red hair and wore her freckles with pride. Woody could barely make out a few freckles on Joy's cheeks, and when the sun caught her blonde hair in the right light, you could just see a hint of ripe orange. Otherwise, the only physical attribute of Joy's that gave away her Celtic ancestry were her blue eyes, which seemed to possess their own electric current.

"Whew—check it! *The man in uniform.*" Jasmine hung onto her open car door and wolf-whistled loudly at Woody as he turned onto their street. Woody immediately looked down at his shoes and cast a furtive glance over his shoulder.

"Hey, looks like good climbing clothes to me. Give the kid a break," scolded Rebecca, Jasmine's girlfriend and business partner, as she cinched a bag to the rainbow-painted Thule rack on top of their '85 Subaru.

In the back of the car, Joy looked at her sister and cracked her knuckles.

"Yo, Wood. Hella nice digs," Jasmine continued, unabated by Rebecca's comment and Woody's body language.

Now within reasonable speaking distance, Woody acknowledged Jasmine. "Um, yeah, my mom thinks I'm at a cross-country preseason training camp."

"Nice. So we're on a *super stealth mission.*" Jasmine winked at

Woody and clicked her head back and forth as she loudly hummed the theme to *Mission: Impossible*. Whenever Jasmine did her Michael Jackson *Thriller* head-dance, as Rebecca termed it, her frizzy, fire-engine red hair seemed to be one beat behind her face, which increased the disembodied-head effect.

"All right, all right." Rebecca laughed and opened the back door next to Joy, motioning for Woody to get in. "Load up, kiddo."

Woody gave Joy a deferential smile as he placed his backpack into the Subaru wagon, already cluttered with climbing shoes, rope, and other well-loved outdoor gear.

"You'll have to excuse my sister." Joy glowered toward the front seat. "The concept of *stealth* is anathema to her very being."

"Oh yeah," Jasmine countered, briefly feigning insult before flipping the switch back to her normal personality. "I'm like—*all about stealth.*" She turned quickly toward Rebecca, who was taking her place in the front passenger seat, and planted a kiss on her lips. "See?"

Rebecca rolled her eyes at Jasmine. "So Woody, when you become a world-famous runner, mind if we snag that tracksuit for our shop? You know—frame it with your signature next to some picture of you crossing a finish line?"

Woody smiled. "Yeah, um... I guess so."

"In any case, we're glad to have you along," Rebecca said as she gave Jasmine a derisive look.

"Well, partners, shall we *disembarkate?*" Jasmine started the engine of her four-cylinder "Blue Beast."

"Not a word, Jaz... not an actual word," said Joy.

"Oh, I like that one," Rebecca responded, shuffling through her music collection to find something for the drive.

The Subaru, ornamented with an eclectic mix of obscure political slogans and trendy outdoor stickers, groaned to life and found its way onto Highway 50, over Kingsbury Grade, and then south on Highway 395 toward Yosemite. After a brief debate between Jasmine (who wanted to listen to the Russian punk band, *Pussy-Riot*) and Rebecca (who insisted she had heard the unintelligible Russian tirades too many times in the past week) the sounds of Brazilian reggae filled the car. Rebecca cracked her window and closed her eyes. To their right, the mountains John Muir described as *the range of light* seemed to grow shadows like the roots of a thirsty aspen grove, extending gradually at first, then with sudden intensity toward the Nevada desert.

In the backseat of the car, Joy straightened her blonde pony-tail and purposefully flipped the pages of her text on differential equations. Woody was finally relaxing despite his awkward track suit and sank deeper into his seat, pressing his knees against the back of Rebecca's and resting his shaggy brown head in the nook between the window and the backrest.

"Is that... for college?" Woody asked.

Joy dog-eared the page she was on and carefully closed the book. "Yeah, I'm planning on taking physics courses and ordered some used books online, to—you know—work through the material."

"But, you haven't chosen your courses yet?"

"Precisely," Joy responded, cracking the knuckles on her other hand. "They expect us to select courses that cost thousands of dollars, based on a two-paragraph course description. I'd rather get a better idea—thank you very much."

"But how did you—?" Woody caught himself. He had quickly learned not to ask Joy how she got a hold of information over the Internet.

Woody changed the topic. "Are you going to miss Tahoe?"

"Some things—I suppose," Joy responded.

"Berkeley, huh?"

"It'll be different, that's for sure."

"Sucks that I have two years left."

"Don't look at it that way," Joy said. "I mean—you've got a chance to actually take State, either this year or next in cross-country, and then you'll be eligible for all sorts of scholarships."

"Thanks," Woody said, looking away.

"I don't know how you do it, but I've never seen anyone run as hard as you do. Last year, you were just a sophomore, and no one could touch you."

"Yeah, until I got to regionals."

"But those were seniors, Woody, the best in the State of California."

"Yeah." Woody knew his running was a gift, but he was embarrassed by what all of the exercise had done to his body. That and, though running was his way to commune with his dead father, the experience wasn't always a good one; there was just so much that he couldn't forgive.

"So, what's the backup plan when they discover you're not really at a cross-country camp?" asked Joy. "Your coach will be upset and your mom—she'll go, well... *nuclear.*"

"Um, I'm not worried about Coach Ward; you're right about my mom. I've got a friend to cover for me, but—"

The unanswered question hung in the air for a while, and Joy returned her attention to the book in her lap. Woody stared out the window, watching the sun hide and appear behind the mountains. The old Subaru continued south down Highway 395, the great thoroughfare linking the land of extremes—Death Valley, the lowest point in the lower forty-eight states, to Mount Whitney, the highest point.

"I wonder if *Mr. Sexybodilicious* Aiden Watson is going to be there tonight?" Jasmine asked.

"Even with all the hype—he's still *The Shit*," said Rebecca.

"I thought he was out establishing these super new climbs in Hetch Hetchy right now. Yeah, the last *Rock and Ice* magazine showed this sweet 5.13 climb starting from an illegal raft out on the reservoir," Jasmine said. "He named it, like—'What Lies Beneath'—or something."

"That's right. It's illegal, you know. I guess you're not allowed to even touch that water," Rebecca said.*

"You'd think it was, you know, *private property*."

"But in a National Park?"

"Sucks."

"It's good though—" Rebecca began.

"What do you mean?"

"No, it's good that Aiden and others are drawing attention to Hetch Hetchy. The focus has been on Yosemite Valley for so many years."

"*What Lies Beneath*," Jasmine pondered, as she twisted a red lock around her finger. "Yo—it's a message. Like, *what pitches of the climb are covered in water?*"

"I think so, too. The reservoir is somewhere around two or three hundred feet deep, which would add at least another three pitches to the climb," Rebecca responded.

"Too bad."

"Too bad Aiden isn't going to be there?" Rebecca said.

"Oh, who knows? Tuolumne isn't that far from Hetch. We might get a treat."

"How does Aiden do it anyway?" Rebecca asked. "I mean, most professional climbers need part-time jobs."

"He's created a different, I don't know... ethic or something," Jasmine said.

"Do tell?"

"Well... climbing and being all—*enviro-activist*, you'd think would go hand-in-hand," Jasmine began.

"Oh, right. He uses notoriety to advance causes and fund-raise for certain organizations like the Sierra Club and the Access Fund," Rebecca said.

"Yeah, even for the damn Park Service. The rangers love *all* over him ever since he got those donations for that wilderness station," Jasmine said. "What was it he said about, you know... *advocacy and climbing?*"

"That's right. He was busting on his friends who travel and climb. Something about, why travel halfway around the world, when there're undiscovered routes right here that deserve attention?" Rebecca laughed.*

"Of course, he's got that extra *something-something* that pays the bills."

"Yeah," Rebecca agreed, "it doesn't hurt that he looks good on the cover of a magazine."

"You're right," Jasmine added. "Not that, you know—I'm into that."

Rebecca just smiled.

"Do you remember that rad quote he gave some *douche* journalist who wouldn't leave him alone about being *the only African American elite climber in the world*?" asked Jasmine with emphasis.

"Yeah, Aiden told the journalist, 'Well, you know what the NAACP stands for, don't you? The National Association for the Advancement of Climbing People.'"

"That was great," Woody chimed in from the back of the car.

MOUNTAIN TEMPLE

Sunday, 3:10 P.M.

S tuart peered down four hundred feet below until the granite talus field at the base of Half Dome blurred into one gray wash of shades and textures. Somewhere down there, amongst a million years of Half Dome's debris, lay the flaccid body of Abigail Edwards.

It all happened so fast, he thought. *So easy.*

Abigail had no idea he had untied his eight; she was too consumed by the climb.

It had been so easy.

There was no struggle, no hand-to-hand combat, and no look of fear in his opponent's eyes. Like most climbers, Abigail was running on autopilot—placement here, handhold there, shifting, focusing, and ascending.

Stuart exhaled into Half Dome. *It has begun.*

Checking and double-checking his gear, Stuart connected two orange-and-silver carabiners to the belay station anchors, and then reached into his gear bag and pulled out the extra rope.

Everything needed to go really well now. The adrenaline rush could not be allowed to color his judgment.

Before escaping the rock, Stuart checked his surroundings. *How many thousands of tourists just witnessed this murder?* he wondered.

Half Dome is one of the most photographed objects in the valley. To his right was Glacier Point, on top of which hundreds of people were gathered at this moment, pointing and smiling with their friends and families as they watched Abigail fall. The valley floor below him––from locations all around Yosemite: the meadows in front of Camp Curry, the hike up Yosemite Falls, even the drive on Highway 102 into the valley—held stunning views of Half Dome. To his left was Olmsted Point in Tuolumne Meadows, another prime vantage point for photographers. Stuart smirked. He felt like a hooded executioner from Elizabethan England––lowering his axe over the condemned in front of throngs of Londoners who squealed in voyeuristic delight––only his hood, his veil of concealment, was imperceptible distance.

The only real risk was another climbing party. He knew there was a party ahead of him and possibly someone on one of the other few routes up the face.* He readied himself for his deliberate descent from anchor to anchor and checked his surroundings for anyone, anyone at all.

Clear. Stuart exhaled again into the rock.

Slowly, Stuart fed the extra rope through the two opposing carabiners. He lowered it down first one side to the halfway point, then the other side, so that below him lay a 210 foot easy rap. Connecting his belay device to the two ropes, he pulled himself into his new anchor.

Stuart gathered up all of the other climbing gear and stowed it in his pack. Now only his rope was attached to the fixed bolts on the wall in front of him, he took one more deep breath and began to rappel.

No jumping; no rapid descent.

The rope fed easily through his ATC. His hands were steady while his feet moved in long vertical steps, walking in reverse down the wall in eight to twelve-foot intervals—*right, left, right, left.*

Arriving at the next anchors, Stuart quickly tied himself into the bolts and pulled the rope through. He then fed the rope through this anchor and set up for his last rappel.

Reaching the ground, he pulled his gear together and moved across the field of rock debris to where Abigail lay. She was actually easy to locate and appeared not as horrific as he had imagined. Her body lay folded to one side, as if curling inward for warmth; from overhead, she could almost look like she was sleeping.

Stuart crouched down, careful not to leave any fingerprints and studied his kill more closely. While the upper facing part of her body was nearly whole and unscathed, the downward side was more gruesome. Clearly the impact had crushed every bone that had made contact with the ground, and the blood that congealed around her body glistened with granite bits poking up through its crimson surface.

Stuart checked his watch. *I'd better stay on schedule,* he thought. Removing his phone from his pack, Stuart opened the camera application, took one picture, and checked it in the display to make sure Abigail could be identified. Satisfied, Stuart nodded goodbye to Abigail and negotiated his way down the aptly named *death slabs* and the rest of the climbers' path to the paved tourist walkway at Mirror Lake.

Families and foreigners seemed suspended around him like marionettes. They floated past on bicycles in groups of four and six, chatting and sharing, laughing and munching on their trail bars and snack mixes. *Had it really been that easy?* He strolled down the paved handicap-accessible walkway toward the road. Passing one group of overweight tourists who gawked at the climbing gear dangling from his bag, Stuart shook his head and focused his attention toward jogging to make the shuttle bus pulling up to the Mirror Lake stop.

Hopping aboard the electric shuttle, Stuart pulled out his cell phone and typed a text message: *M-U-I-R*. He sent the text to a web server that posted his word online to a specific site. Next, Stuart glanced around the bus and scratched his white goatee. People talked to each other, shared stories, and looked out the windows; no one was paying particular attention to him. Sensing he could risk importing the image, he held his phone close and uploaded the photo of Abigail to the same website. *The Professor will be pleased.*

When Stuart arrived at the public parking by Camp Curry, he walked with a growing sense of relief across the lot and to his car. Stowing his gear in the back, he removed his wallet and car keys. The nondescript gray Ford Focus had been a good car for him, perhaps not the most rugged or macho, but it validated his disguise as just another "dirtbag climber." Soon, he could own any vehicle he wanted.

Driving out of the Park, Stuart glanced upward through his windshield at El Capitan. The giant granite hulk of rock stood sentry over the entrance to the valley, and Stuart breathed a little easier once he had passed beyond its inspection, like he had just exited onto the street, dodging one enormous security guard.

8

UNION SQUARE

Sunday, 4:10 P.M.

After speeding across the Golden Gate Bridge into the city, The Professor had felt comfortable, confident even. Stuart had completed the first task and the photo he delivered was superb. It was an image of a woman—a specific woman, Abigail Edwards, the activist—lying in a pool of her own death. A caption would soon accompany this image. This message would be the catalyst for all that would transpire in the coming hours—the tipping point.

"Ahhh..." The Professor exhaled.

Parking at the corporate headquarters on Market Street, near its intersection with the Embarcadero, The Professor walked the five blocks up Market Street to the San Francisco flagship Apple store. Walking in, The Professor found a particularly young and evidently overwhelmed associate in the requisite primary-colored Apple T-Shirt and purchased an iPad, paying cash.

With the new device in hand, The Professor sauntered up Stockton to Market Square and walked into a ubiquitous corner Starbucks to order a "medium" coffee. Referring to any of the Starbucks sizes by their branded labels—*venti, grande,* and *tall*—was an act to which The Professor refused to submit. The sound of some self-important hipster ordering a *double venti hoity-toity skinny latte with a shot of vanilla*—or whatever, was infuriating. Occasionally a barista would frown and say, "You mean like a *grande?*" The Professor would flinch noticeably and nod, waiting for the medium-sized cup of joe which today made its way to a bench in Union Square, where the iPad would have its first and only usage.

Union Square was alive in the late summer afternoon. Tourists purchased food at the overpriced outdoor cafés. Young professionals spent money on each other. And an outlandish troop of college-age kids with brightly colored hair performed a mix of juggling, acrobatics, and fire spinning, set to the rhythmic breathing of an Australian didgeridoo and the steady cadence of an African Congo drum. The Professor sipped coffee and peeled away the iPad's packaging.

Once unwrapped, the iPad easily connected to one of the numerous free-access wireless networks. Navigating to the website onto which Stuart uploaded his image, The Professor downloaded the image into the iPhoto application and admired it for a few moments. Abigail's body, though obviously lifeless, appeared serene with little indication of her brutal death.

The plan was coming together perfectly. The stalling and negotiations at the District Court in Sacramento could only last for so long. Action was required. It was not quite a crisis, but those on the board certainly described it as such.

If only they knew.

Cropping the picture and adjusting ever so slightly its exposure, The Professor saved the image and prepared for massive dissemination. Producing a small black leather moleskin notebook from a jacket pocket, The Professor opened up the Safari browser again, this time selecting a different wireless network with a slightly stronger signal. A fake mail account was set up using the name "Adams Ansel" with a fake address in Yosemite. Then, The Professor composed the first email message from this account. It read: "Here lies Muir's Mountain Temple." Attached to the email was the image that Stuart had taken. Then, The Professor typed in the recipient email addresses listed in the moleskin notebook. They included the heads and officers of Earth First!, the Sierra Club, Environmental Life Force, Environmental Defense Fund, The Alliance for Climate Protection, Earth Defense Group, Natural Resources Defense Council, and many others.

Satisfied with the list, The Professor took a deep breath and hit *send.*

The Professor then navigated to the websites of a few of the more militant environmental groups and posted the image with the same caption to the open blogs that these sites hosted.

It was done. It was now unstoppable.

This will get Doc's attention.

The Professor took another sip of coffee and smiled at the gymnastic antics of the street performers. After cleaning the surface of the device with alcohol wipes, The Professor placed it back in its packaging and slid it discreetly with gloved hands under the bench. Glancing at the San Francisco Bay Guardian, The Professor smiled at an image of a California senator. *It's too bad those persistent ecoterrorists weren't as easy to manipulate as California's politicians. If only Abigail had responded to that generous offer of a doctoral position at Princeton; then, she'd be happily ensconced in her new role on the East Coast. Instead, well...*

Glancing around to be sure no one was observing, The Professor stretched from side to side, yawning. The crosswalk sign adjacent to the park was flashing on regular intervals between *DON'T WALK* and *WALK*. It was time.

Casually, The Professor reached under the stone bench to retrieve the attaché case and shopping bag. Intentionally, the iPad remained, packaged and ready to pleasantly surprise some unwitting San Franciscan.

The Professor strode out of the square and across the street, hustling to make the flashing sign, then slipping around the corner out of view.

9

THE MESSAGE

Sunday, 4:16 P.M.

"Rick, you'll never guess what I heard at the symposium." Jeffrey looked like a kid in a candy shop. His bloodshot eyes sparkled behind his flat-black rectangular glasses. His black hair, which as usual was unkempt and beginning to protrude at various angles, also had a glossy sheen to it, an indication that not only had Jeffrey not slept since before the previous evening's shift, he hadn't showered.

"You're a piece of work, Jeffrey," said Rick. "Tell you what, I'll hold down the fort here. I know you're dying to tell me all about the meeting, but *I'll* be dying unless you take a shower and catch some sleep."

"But boss, you know that's not protocol." Jeffrey leaned in closer, setting down a pile of papers and his laptop covered with various stickers from environmental groups, like the Pacific Crest Trail Association and Greenpeace.

"Whew. I hoped the smell wouldn't intensify with proximity. Ugh. And look at yourself, man. You can't really call that a uniform."

Jeffrey's Park Service shirt was crumpled and slightly stained; he had failed to switch into his hiking boots, and he was at least three days unshaven, which for many wouldn't be a problem, but Jeffrey's facial hair seemed to escape in sudden long random curlicues rather than a more uniform scruff.

"Okay, but I'll be back in an hour. I'm sorry, Rick. I shouldn't have been so preoccupied—"

"It's all right." Rick laughed as he set down the coffees he had brought. "I'm sure I'll hear all about this *big surprise* when you get back."

"It's big, Rick. Really big. It has to do with the Hetch."

"Okay—that's enough. Now get out of here before some tourist smells you."

"Sure thing." Jeffrey walked out of the office and Rick turned, sat beside his two coffees, and sifted through the incident reports from the day.

Was that the right decision? Rick thought. *I shouldn't keep making excuses for Jeffrey. He needs to learn lessons now with the small stuff. I'm not helping him by letting him get away with these stunts.* Rick balled his fists, digging his fingernails into the fleshy part of his palm, and looked down at the tattoo barely peeking out from under the cuff of his uniform.

Where was I? That's right... incident reports. Rick cleared his head of second guesses and scanned through the papers.

There was the usual stuff for late August—some dehydration cases, a few bear encounters, a smattering of minor traffic bumps, and parking violations. *Nothing to be surprised about,* Rick thought. It looked like a pattern was developing with the bear encounters; the picnic area at Tenaya Lake was receiving more and more complaints. *Probably Wanda again.* Wanda was what the rangers had dubbed this particular bear, mostly because they saw her swimming in Tenaya Lake and someone had just watched the movie *A Fish Called Wanda.* The name stuck, which was technically against the rules because naming animals made it harder to euthanatize them. Unfortunately, for Wanda, it appeared she was getting more brazen and less afraid of humans, exactly the reason most bears were called by numbers and not pet names. Rick didn't like putting bears down, but he knew it was a reality in Yosemite until people learned to be more careful with their trash. Maybe tonight he'd send someone up to Tuolumne with the bear bazooka to try and locate and scare some sense into Wanda.

The bear bazooka, or "BB gun" in common ranger parlance, was basically an oversized shotgun loaded with a medley of alarming substances, ranging from birdshot and rubber pellets to flash powder, pepper spray, and M-80 firecrackers.* Rick's colleagues would often joke about using the BB on certain choice tourists during the "season."

About half an hour had gone by. Rick's shift had officially begun. He was going to pick up the phone and connect with the other departments, including the Tuolumne site, to discuss Wanda, when the phone rang.

"Yosemite Ranger Office. Ranger Rick Turlock speaking."

"Rick, it's Sheryl."

"Yeah, Sheryl—what's up?"

"Just got a call from some climber. Said something about an incident out by Half Dome. Thought he saw a fall; went to investigate and then, well... he wasn't really sure what to tell me."

"What do you mean?"

"Well, there's a dead body. Female. But he said that... well, there was someone, a climber, standing by the body who just took a picture and then left."

"*What?*"

"Yeah, weird."

"Did the caller approach?"

"No, he was still up on the wall, but he got... like a weird vibe or something; like the guy with the camera knew she would be there. So he just stayed out of sight."

"Hmm."

"I guess it could be homicide—either that or someone just wanted a sick photo of the body."

"Okay. We need to get someone up there right now. I'll call dispatch."

Rick chugged down the rest of his coffee, picked up the other phone and dialed. The phone rang in Rick's ear as he stared down onto his desk. *That couldn't be just any climber on the face of Half Dome. This person had to be experienced, had to know better than to make a careless mistake. And the photographer. Why? Who?*

"Dispatch, this is Paula."

Rick clicked over in his mind from questioning to commanding. "Paula, it's Rick. We've got a situation. There's a dead female climber at the base of Half Dome, appears to have fallen, but possible murder."

"Really?"

"That's affirmative. I don't want to chopper this and draw excess attention, but as it could very well be a crime scene, we need to get our people up there now to cordon off the area until we can get the Mariposa County detectives there."

"Okay, I'm on it. We'll have two officers meet you at Mirror Lake in twenty."

"Tell them to bring warm clothes. They may be out there most of the night."

"Ten-four."

As soon as he hung up, Rick immediately dialed Yosemite Search and Rescue (YOSAR) and had a similar conversation but indicated that as the light was fading, he wanted them there as fast as possible. "Find the body. Secure the area. We will come and relieve you, so don't worry about having to spend the night out there. We just need our people there before anyone else."

Next, Rick growled under his breath and dialed the Mariposa County Sheriff's Department. "This is Rick Turlock, Park Supervisor at Yosemite. We have a possible murder of a climber and request detectives."

"Hold on. Let me put you on with the chief," said the dispatcher.

"Rick, what's going on?" Chief Lorenzo asked.

"We have an 1144 out by the base of Half Dome. Possible murder."

"What? *Murder*—are you sure?"

"Not entirely Chief, but there was some suspicious activity near the body."

"Can you confirm all of this?" the chief asked.

"Our people are on the way, but regardless we're going to need some detectives. I'm securing the scene, however I really don't want to chopper in and alert any potential suspects."

"Alright, I'll send someone."

"Chief, it's not easy getting up to the base of Half Dome. Tell them to come prepared for some scrambling up a pretty steep drainage."

"What? Why don't you just get a helicopter? We're losing daylight for Christ's sake!"

"That's part of the problem; as soon as the light is gone, getting a chopper in that close to Half Dome is not advisable," rebutted Rick.

As Rick and Chief Lorenzo debated strategy and timing, Jeffrey burst through the door. "What's going on? I heard Half Dome? There was fatality?"

Rick held up his index finger to indicate that he needed a minute. Frazzled, Jeffrey sat down and opened his computer.

After another agonizing minute of debate, Rick slammed down the phone. "That idiot. He wants to wait for morning." Donning his jacket and indulging in a quick sip of coffee, Rick said, "I wish I knew what the scene looked like."

With his pupils fully dilated and his eyebrows reaching for his hairline, Jeffrey slowly turned his laptop screen toward Rick. There, in full and horrific detail, lay a dead female climber, her long black hair matted and splayed out like a geisha fan in the encircling blood. The caption under the image read, "Here lies Muir's Mountain Temple."

"Be careful what you wish for," said Rick.

"Uh, Rick?"

"Yeah?"

"She, umm... I just met her."

RESPONSIBLE

Sunday, 6:05 P.M.

J asmine's blue Beast pulled up to the John Muir Trailhead in Tuolumne Meadows as the descending sun blanketed the low-angle granite domes rising out of the landscape like gray waves in a green ocean.

To the passing motorists and returning day hikers, it may have seemed odd that three ladies and one skinny teenager were gearing up alongside the highway, strapping sleeping bags, pads, and other articles to their packs, talking and laughing as if starting a hike at daybreak.

"How's that feel?" Rebecca asked as Woody emerged from behind a few trees, no longer sporting the signature blue and gold track suit.

"Yeah, um... better. Thanks," Woody replied, glad to change his clothes without letting the girls see him with his shirt off.

"There's potable water where we're going, right?" asked Joy.

"Here we go again," said Jasmine, shaking her head at her sister. "*Classic kill-Joy.*"

"Oh, come on, it *is* the end of the summer and all sorts of bacteria could have bred over the hot months," countered Joy. "Seriously, you can go get giardia if you want, but you don't have to get the rest of us sick, too."

"Whatever, sis. This right here—" Jasmine threw her arms wide as if to indicate the entire Tuolumne region— "it's the damn Garden of Eden, hella pure and clean. That's not something you'll learn at Berkeley."

"College... again?" Joy huffed and raised her eyebrows.

"Yeah, that's right, Sweet Cheeks."

Woody tilted his head.

Joy returned fire, "Just because you couldn't *handle* anything post high sch—"

"Woo, it's just water, guys. Relax," Rebecca cut in. "We're in Yosemite. What could possibly be wrong in the world?" She took an exaggerated breath, indicating that the sisters should do the same. "For my part, I'd drink the water right here in the meadow. It meets the three rules for me: cold, fast, and clear."

"Well, I'm bringing my filter," Joy declared. "What about you, Woody?"

Woody avoided eye contact. "I... um... don't really want to take sides—"

"Sure you do, Woody." Rebecca laughed out loud.

"Yeah," Jasmine said. "You just don't want to upset your little girlfriend here."

Joy shot her sister a death scowl.

"Yeah, kiddo—so like, what do you think—filter or not?" Rebecca asked.

Woody paused. "Well, I guess if Joy wants to be careful, let her." He hoisted his pack onto his shoulders and checked the straps, trying to seem casual, as if the word *girlfriend* hadn't just been used in association with him and Joy. "But I have to agree with your sister, Joy. Um, I'm sorry. Just try to be—what did my dad always say?—selective, yeah—selective about where you get your water. Cold, fast, and clear, like Rebecca said. If... we're going where I think we might be, there's a glacier dumping minerals into the water. Talk about a great source for drinking, you know—rich and good for you—that's it." Woody looked apologetically at Joy and added, "Um... why would you want to run that kind of water through a little plastic contraption with chemical filters?" *

The three girls stared at Woody as shadows crept up his gray pant legs. Jasmine's red mop of hair glowed in the late afternoon sun—like a halo of her admiration for him.

"I knew we invited you on these trips for a reason," said Rebecca.

Jasmine giggled and knocked her backpack into Woody by swiveling her hips.

Finally, Joy spoke. "Okay, okay—you show me a freak'n glacier, and I'll drink the damn water, all right?"

Woody shook his head. Sometimes he wished he had a brother or sister, and then again—well....

The group headed up the John Muir Trail, south from the highway. Then, after thirty granite steps, they turned onto a small climbers' trail just at the crest of the hill and followed the Budd Creek drainage up and into the Tuolumne high country.

"Hmm," murmured Woody, as they turned off the John Muir Trail and onto the climbing trail.

"What's that?" asked Joy.

"Oh—uh, me? Oh, I was just thinking about the last time I was here."

"How do you know so much about this area?"

"I used to come on these camping and climbing trips with my dad. Um—he was a nut when it came to John Muir and outdoor survival. He was all about this place, you know, Yosemite and Tuolumne."

"So you've been on this climber's trail before?"

"You could say that—"

"It's too bad he's not around—your dad—to climb and camp with you now," Joy said.

"Yeah," Woody paused, "you're right—but I'm sure he'd be glad that I'm still coming here. Now—um, my mom on the other hand, well—"

"She doesn't care for me, does she?"

"No, it's not so much that she doesn't like you. She's just—I don't know—maternal instinct and all," Woody sighed. "I wish you could have met my dad though."

"Me too. I love learning about Muir and Roosevelt and the history of environmentalism—I mean, imagine being here along this stream before there was a road in Tuolumne, before there was the John Muir Trail."

Woody smiled. This was exactly the sort of thing his father used to bring up. "Makes you wonder where John took Teddy when they ditched the Secret Service and headed up into the high country."[*]

"Maybe where we're going?"

"Maybe."

The group made good time alongside Budd Creek. They hopped over downed logs and slid through fields of boulders, following the sinuous trail deeper and deeper into the recesses of Tuolumne.

Joy's comment about Woody's father initiated a kaleidoscope of memories. It seemed like any mention of him would catapult Woody deep into his unresolved feelings about his dad's untimely death. Spending time on trails and specifically trail running had become his way of sorting out his feelings. There was something about the repetitive motion, the cadence of foot after foot, the pounding of his heart, and the harsh mountain air rushing in and out of his lungs—it was as if the mantra of foot placements and the thunderous expansion and contraction of his breathing drowned the pain.

As he hiked along with the Cooper sisters and Rebecca,

Woody slipped into another reverie. This time he thought of his English cousin, Drake, at his dad's funeral. Drake and Woody had escaped from the endless stream of sweaty palms and superficial condolences. Somehow all the adults thought that a stiff handshake was the right antidote to Woody's grief. Not Drake. Drake sensed that Woody needed to come up for air, so he approached Woody and in characteristic British nonchalance said, "So, how's about we leave this bollocks for a bit, eh mate?"

Woody was glad to oblige.

They hung out, played innumerable games of pool, and Drake, who was into the club scene in London, introduced Woody to Euro-style techno and trance music.

"What are we listening to?"

Drake gave Woody a wry smile as he circled the pool table. "Yeah, you probably don't get this sort of naff on your radio here —this is Armin van Buuren."

"Armin van who?"

"Right. Case in point. This ain't your house-style E.D.M."

"Huh?," Woody said.

Drake just laughed as he leaned over for the next shot.

Woody ended up downloading loads of music off Drake's laptop, and the two kept in contact after the funeral. Every few months, Drake would send Woody a link to where he could download other albums and songs by various European techno artists. The tracks became Woody's companion on his long runs into the backcountry.

Woody's thoughts jumped now to his first big run after the funeral. It was Saturday morning. Woody and his mom were sitting in the living room, after a quiet breakfast. He got off the couch to switch on the PlayStation.

"Are you turning that thing on?" Mojo asked.

"Yeah."

"Oh great—World War III in our living room once again?"

Woody didn't want to argue. He just walked past the television and back to his bedroom.

"I'm sorry—I mean, if you want to..." Mojo stammered. "Woody. Woody, did you hear me? Go ahead and play your game. Woody?"

A couple of minutes later, Woody returned to the living room in a T-Shirt, shorts, and sneakers. He had his iPod in his hand. "I didn't really want to."

"Where are you going?"

"Out."

"Nice specifics, Wood; how about—?"

"Look, I'm not sure. I'm going for a run. That's all. I just..." Woody turned to go.

"Bring your cell phone, Wood," Mojo said. "Please."

"Fine." Woody went back to his room and grabbed a small backpack and stuffed in his iPod and cell phone, some food, water, and a lightweight jacket.

The addition of the cell phone would be lucky for Woody. He walked out his front door, hopped on a trail near Fallen Leaf Lake, plugged in his music, and started to jog. Before he knew it, he was a mile and a half into Desolation Wilderness. He turned north and kept moving, over Dick's Pass and deeper into the trails, passing hikers with large backpacks out on multi-day trips. The sun rose high in the sky and still Woody powered on. He got tired, he got sore, but he kept moving. The pain and exhaustion felt good, felt therapeutic. What his father had done, his insistence on acceptance, became the distance he was covering.

Mid-afternoon, Woody finally stopped at a small rocky plateau above Rubicon Lake. He checked his watch and his surroundings. He was not lost. He had been there before on a backpacking trip with his father, not more than two years prior. Woody removed his small pack, which had worn red abrasions on the bony parts of his shoulders. Oddly, this pain too felt good. He reached into the pack and removed a Clif Bar. Opening the wrapper, he bit in and started to laugh. His parents, John and Mojo, had gotten into the most asinine argument over Clif Bars and cabinet space. John demanded a prominent drawer be designated in its entirety as a repository for sports bars. Mojo considered the idea preposterous. They had argued with philosophic intensity about the placement of spatulas, the location of the cheese grater, and the relegation of silverware to a second-tier drawer, all to make room for John's ample supply of Clif, Power, LUNA, and Balance Bars.

Woody's laughter dissolved into tears as he remembered the three of them laughing and hurling prepackaged adventure goodies at each other as the argument erupted into a ridiculous snowball fight with his dad's prized nutrition rectangles.

When he was finished with the snack and his tears, Woody pulled out his phone, powered it on and dialed home. He had just enough reception where he was to place a call and knew that the same could not be said for where he was going.

"Woody, oh my god! Where have you been?" Mojo was beside herself.

"Sorry. My phone was off."

"Why? Where are you?"

"Look—uh, Mom," Woody began. "Just pick me up and I'll explain it all when I see you."

"Fine. Where are you?"

Woody took a deep breath. "Almost to... Meeks Bay."

"Jesus, Woody, did you hitchhike? That's dangerous, you don't know who—"

"Mom, Mom," Woody interrupted. "I ran."

No one spoke for a moment.

"Along the road?" Mojo asked.

"No."

"I'll be there as soon as I can."

Woody added, "I should be at Meeks by the time you get there. If not, just wait at the trailhead."

"That's," Mojo began, "that's a long way, Woody."

"Yeah."

Meeks Bay was over fifteen miles by car from their home, and Woody had taken a series of trails that amounted to closer to thirty miles. It was the first in a series of long cathartic runs Woody would undertake. As his body grew stronger and he experimented with the correct weight distribution of gear and tightness of his pack, Woody pushed farther with his runs.

"I STILL CAN'T GET over what Alex pulled off on El Cap last year." Jasmine said.

Woody shook his head, bringing himself back into Tuolumne and the open granite shoulder where Jasmine had stopped to soak in the descending sun.

"Yeah, that was a spectacular free-solo. I hope it's never repeated." Rebecca countered.

"What do you mean?" Jasmine asked. "It's amazing. I'm glad that people are badass enough to free-solo and not a bunch of 'manginas,' like the Clif Bar corporates.'"*

"Come on sis, it was about time someone took a stand against free-soloing," Joy said.

"What are you talking about?" Jasmine asked. "It's about purity... the essence of the thing."

"I don't buy that line," Joy said as she took a seat with her back against a large boulder and closed her eyes in the fading sunshine. "Some climbers have publicly stated their opposition to it though."*

"Like Aiden, right?" Rebecca asked.

"I think so," said Joy.

"I don't see the problem with it," Jasmine continued. "It's just—like another form of climbing. You know, we used to have a lot of first ascents and super hard route-setting. Now, many of the big climbs have been established, so people are just taking it up a notch, to the next level, by free-soloing those same routes."

"A notch? The next level?" Rebecca rolled her eyes.

"Yeah, it's hella exciting—climbing unprotected up a route. We've done it," Jasmine continued. "There's a proud history, you know—-Peter Croft, John Bachar, Dean Potter, and now Alex Honnold.* It elevates the entire sport, knowing that a route like the Regular Northwest Face on Half Dome or Astroman on Washington Column has been free soloed."

"You do realize that half of the people you just mentioned died climbing?" Rebecca responded, setting her pack down and stretching out her shoulders.

"Bachar's circumstances aren't known. Potter died BASE jumping," Jasmine retorted.

"Still—all tangential to climbing." Rebecca shook her head.

"It's almost like the cinematographers, film festivals, and magazines are, well, complicit in suicides," Joy added.

"Accidents, not fucking suicides," Jasmine yelled. "Free soloists, they climb a route many times with protection, until the route is, you know, totally dialed; then—once they are comfortable—only *then*, do they free solo."

"Yeah, but what about on-sites and those dipshits out at Matthes Crest?" said Rebecca. "And remember that scary-looking guy just exploring all over the East Wall of Lover's Leap?"

"It's just another form of climbing," Jasmine insisted.

"A dumb one," Rebecca said.

"I can't believe you guys." Jasmine was not deterred. "Fact: free soloists are good for the sport. They raise awareness, obtain donations to the access fund, it's a virtuotic cycle. Can't you see... you know, that article in *National Geographic* with Alex on the cover—it's a celebration of life and the human spirit?"

"Good slip there Jaz," Joy said. "Virtuotic, like idiotic, *National Geo* is like any grocery-store tabloid. They're just selling tripe and pushing sensationalism to make a buck." *

"You're talking about *National Geographic!*," Jasmine implored.

"So?" Rebecca said. "That was the article with this cute and uninformed little diagram that showed aid climbing on one side and free soloing on the other as if somehow there is a natural continuum from one to the other. What infantile bullshit!"

"Exactly. I'm not so worried about the soloists, you know. It's more about the other parties on the wall being responsible," Joy added. "What if some free soloist took a fall right after passing you on a climb? He could knock you off and seriously injure you, while killing himself, or..."— Joy cracked her knuckles—"what if, the more likely scenario, you fell and ran into him? Even though you were tied in and would be fine, you would essentially have committed involuntary manslaughter."

Jasmine pursed her lips and exhaled, whistling lightly.

Budd Creek gurgled and bounced around in the little canyon below and the air temperature seemed to drop with the weight of Joy's deduction.

"Yeah, I guess..." Woody spoke up. "I guess I don't really have a problem with, you know... the existence of free-soloing; there is a purity there. And... I mean, people are going to do it and Alex's reasons seem good enough for him.... I just have a problem with the pressure from corporate interests, you know—magazines, movies, and TV shows. How far is it going to go? And when it ends badly..."

"Yeah, then they'll be like, 'well, he knew the risks,'" Joy huffed. "*They* damn well know the risks too, but they keep making money on it."

MISSING

Sunday, 6:30 P.M.

"I'm going to strangle that kid," Mojo erupted into her phone. "What do you mean he's not on the bus? He's not here either—jeez, I feel like...I'm in some lame-ass 'yo mama' joke about a bus!"

"It's okay, Mojo," Colleen said. "I'm sure he's... well, *somewhere.*"

"Yo mama's so stupid, she got run over by a parked bus—"

"Mojo!"

"and her son wasn't even on it."

"Please Mojo, Take a deep breath, where would he want to go for the weekend that you wouldn't approve of?" Mojo's friend Colleen had a son about the same age as Woody who was also going on the cross-country trip. At Mojo's urging, Colleen had called her son, Doug, and asked for him to check and see if Woody needed his tent, which Mojo had found in the garage. When Doug hesitated, Colleen pounced. "Douglas, what aren't you telling me? If I find out that Woody isn't there and that you lied to me—" She didn't need to finish the sentence; Doug had cracked.

"Well, the list of already unsanctioned activities is pretty long for that kid, and it's going to be even longer as soon as—" Mojo sighed. "I bet you anything he took off with those climbers somewhere. He knows what I think about those older girls."

"They're good kids, Mojo. Joy is heading off to Berkeley, you know."

"That doesn't change the fact that Woody's going to be grounded until—like *forever*."

"They'll be fine. Relax. What have you been working on these days anyway?" said Colleen.

"Oh, I'm going to be working on that kid when I finally get a hold of him."

"Mojo, now really."

"Sorry, I know, he's a teenager—rebel without a cause and all that nonsense. It's just that I finally thought I had a good rapport, you know, a level of trust with my son and now he pulls this stunt. It's like we're back to when John died."

Mojo and Woody had struggled through a year of slammed doors, silent treatments, avoidance, and dysfunction. Woody had compensated for the loss of his father with sports. Mojo had similarly gotten lost in her work. She would spend the entire night writing and researching, then crash the next day. Unfortunately, all of her self-inflicted sleep deprivation shortened her fuse when it came to dealing with the moodiness and antics of her only child. The one thing that Woody and Mojo didn't fight over was their old Chesapeake Bay retriever, Chessie, who would lay at Mojo's feet when she worked late at night and would accompany Woody on his shorter runs, or sit patiently for him at the base of a climb.

"It'll be all right. Really it will," Colleen said. "I thought you were just telling me that those girls were part of the reason Woody finally seemed to open up to you."

"No, you're right. I shouldn't be so hard on him—I just wish he wasn't so damn hard on me." Mojo exhaled audibly into the phone's receiver and relaxed her shoulders. "So—your question, what I'm working on. I'm researching the recent developments in the Hetch Hetchy controversy. It seems like the major stakeholders are close to a deal, but—it's odd. The case is stuck or something. It seems mired in one problem after another."

"Stalling, huh?" Colleen asked.

"Maybe."

"That's too bad."

"Yeah—it's par for the course when it comes to Hetch Hetchy. They've been putting off solutions for years."

"What do you mean?" Colleen inquired.

"Well, even when compliance with federal legislation was ordered by the Supreme Court in DC—you'd think the big dudes in black robes would have the final word—but even that didn't totally stop the corporate interests here from continuing to profit from what should have rightfully been public power and public water." *

"But weren't you telling me that restoration was looking more and more feasible?" Colleen asked.

"Yeah, that's true. Ever since the State of California Department of Parks and Recreation study in 2006, there seems to have been momentum toward a solution.* But now, I just can't tell where we are."

"They'll come up with something, I'm sure."

"Something," Mojo said with a laugh. "Oh, they'll come up with *something* all right. Something genius, like a radical new way to do absolutely nothing."

"What does your contact—what's her name...Abigail—say about all this?"

"I haven't seen her post anything recently. She sent me a copy of the speech she just gave at some symposium, but it was pretty, you know, sanitized." Mojo paused. "So Colleen, do you think I should call—who is it that Joy lives with—her grandmother or something?"

"That's right, but Mojo, it's late. Woody is a big boy. He'll be fine. Why don't you call in the morning?"

"That's what worries me—Woody's delusion that he actually is a *big boy*. It's probably more like, *big boy-toy*—"

"Now really, Mojo."

"Okay. I can wait." Mojo nodded her head. "Do you think they're in Yosemite?"

"Doug said he thought Woody was going climbing."

"That probably means Yosemite—and that probably means *Joy*."

ROYAL COURT

Sunday, 6:35 P.M.

At the top of the Budd Creek drainage is a small body of water surrounded by a flowering high alpine meadow. Woody knew the area well. He had come here with his father on their way to climb Matthes Crest, one of the last adventures they had together before Woody's dad became too weak.

John had joked that he was going to be like Galen Clark who, according to California lore, told his family and doctor that he was "going to the mountains to take my chances of dying or growing better" and ended up cheating his terminal illness by nearly sixty years.

"Yeah, Woody," John said while they hiked up to the shore of Budd Lake. "Old Galen Clark, he's the one credited with the discovery and protection of the Mariposa Grove—the big trees in the southern Wawona section of Yosemite. He was diagnosed with a severe lung infection and told he had six months to live."

Woody had taken off his pack and removed his water bottle while he listened to his father.

John continued, "Rather than die in the city breathing the

same air that made him sick to begin with, Galen moved to the south of Yosemite Valley. There, as a homesteader, he stumbled upon the giant Sequoias, the largest trees in the world.* Imagine that—whoops!" John pretended to stumble and then looked skyward. "Oh, hello there."

Laughing, John had set down his pack and taken a seat on a fallen pine.

"Mr. Clark," John continued, "wrote passionately to his friends in the US Congress about preserving the big trees. I think he called them 'a great national treasure.' Yup, good ole Galen helped to shape and pass the Yosemite Grant signed into law by President Abraham Lincoln, right in the middle of the Civil War."
*

"Um—didn't they have other things on their mind—you know, the Confederacy, abolition of slavery, 'house divided will not stand,' and all that?" Woody asked.

"That's pretty good, Woodrow. You've been paying attention in history class," John beamed. "Yeah, I suppose they did have other things going on, but they still passed the Yosemite Grant, setting what was basically a new precedent in conservation and stating for all the world that federal governments had the authority and responsibility to protect natural wonder." John swept his arm out in a large arc over their alpine surroundings.

"Yup, Yosemite returned the favor, you know. She gave the old and ill Galen an elixir of fresh air, clean water, and all this here— it probably kept him alive for those fifty-seven more years."

John reached down and filled his water bottle to the brim, smiling as he did so, and said to Woody, "I expect this is the same water that Galen was drinking one hundred and fifty years ago —huh, Wood?"

"IS THAT THE GLACIER?" Joy asked.

Woody blinked his eyes to clear the daydream. "Yeah, Joy," Woody responded, "That's it; drink up."

The group crested a knoll by the side of Budd Lake and walked down to the shore. Even in August, there was still snow against the ring of eastern mountains. To their right, the lake spilled over into cascading meadows of lush greens punctuated by small purple and yellow flowers. Just beyond the meadow lay the church of rock for which the region was named. Cathedral Peak erupted out of the landscape, its main apex challenging the heavens like the tower in Van Gogh's *Starry Night.*

"Over there. Come on," Jasmine shouted as she pointed down the hill toward the lake's edge and a small clearing where ten people were milling about.

The group came down toward the circle of people gathered by the shore. Reaching the clearing first, Jasmine dropped her pack and threw her arms around one lanky redheaded guy, smiling and laughing. Rebecca too seemed to know many of the others gathered by the lake and distributed hugs and nods with ease and familiarity. Woody and Joy slowed down as they approached and waited to be acknowledged.

"Woody, is that who I think it is?" said Joy in hushed tones.

"Wow. Yeah—um, I think that's Moulden, Leo Moulden —*no way.*"

"And there's Paul Roberts."

"And, that's Jesse Bonin, and next to him is that German dude, Jonas Bauer or something."

"Gosh," Joy said under her breath.

Woody sensed Joy's hesitancy. Even though her sister had been climbing and socializing with many of these famous climbers at bouldering competitions, on road trips, and online, Joy had never met any of them.

"Yo, Woody, Joy, get over here. I've got someone for you to meet," called Jasmine.

Slowly, Woody and Joy walked over to Jasmine, not sure of how to act now that they were surrounded by this royal court.

"This is Leo Moulden, Joy."

"Nice to meet you," said Leo. "Your sister says you're close to *sending* Cajun Hell at Mayhem Cove."

Joy blushed and looked down at her feet.

Leo continued. "But I hear you're leaving climbing this fall for college."

"I'll still climb," Joy said.

"No—it's all good. You've got a lot of time to score big climbs in the future. So who's your friend?"

"This is Woody."

"I really like your story about how the fall you had in Patagonia changed your life," Woody blurted out.

"Thanks, man," Leo responded, a little surprised by the suddenness of Woody's affirmation. "You know, adversity brings out the best in us."

Jasmine reached over and tousled Woody's hair.

As the sun sank lower, Woody felt more at ease with the crowd surrounding him. Other famous names wandered into camp. There was Sean McDermit and some of his friends. Then came some woman Woody knew he had seen in a Metolius ad.

Moments before sunset, Leo and Jesse started a small fire, and the crowd began to congregate around the light and warmth. Stories were shared about three-week-long devotions to boulder problems that never yielded results. Easy laughter drifted in and out of the firelight along with marijuana smoke that seemed to grow thicker as it commingled with the fire and the descending night sky.

As the last hues of day were absorbed by the evening darkness, three figures appeared on top of the hill and stood for a moment observing the group.

"Don't you know it's illegal to have open fires of this size in the

Yosemite backcountry?" an artificially deep voice said from the hill above the campsite.

Everyone froze in disbelief. Rangers didn't usually venture out this far late at night.

Then Paul recognized one of the figures walking toward them. "Aiden, you goofball. Don't freak us out like that."

Aiden Watson waltzed down toward the impromptu camp, along with another figure that Rebecca recognized and yelled out to. "Doc, I'm so glad you made it," she said.

Aiden's big toothy smile gleamed in the firelight as he gave one of the girls a big hug. Behind Doc and Aiden came another person carrying a large log.

"Yeah, you know"—the other figure paused to make sure he had everyone's attention—"you've got to be careful with these open flames."

With that, and before anyone could stop him, the man who hiked up to the lake with Aiden and Doc, tossed the massive log into the fire. As he did so, his face lit up, revealing long unkempt blond hair, a strange bleached goatee and wild smile.

Aiden looked over his shoulder and scolded his hiking partner. "Now that—that just might be a bit too much, Stuart."

13

SPARKS

Sunday, 7:10 P.M.

I t had been a day.

"Epic," Sloan said as he readied himself for the final push to the apex of Cathedral Peak. His final move could best be described as a beached-whale maneuver. In the absence of a solid handhold on top of the final rock, climbers like Sloan had to resort to mantling with their hands on the edge of the rock until they could manage to get their torso high enough to put their weight-pivot threshold above the peak. At that point he could rock forward onto his stomach and precariously rest on the edge of the mountain.

Muir probably didn't do it this way, Sloan thought to himself. At that moment, in the final minutes of daylight, he saw the crack at the end of the tabletop peak. Laughing at himself, Sloan reached his hand forward into the granite fissure and pulled himself the rest of the way onto the summit.

Epic.

Throwing a couple of pieces of pro into the crack and using

some slings for an anchor, Sloan yelled down to his partner and newlywed wife, "Off belay!"

Nikki undid the rope from her Grigri and called up to Sloan, "Belay off. Up rope!"

"That's me!" Nikki called up to Sloan once the rope had gotten tight on her harness.

"On belay!" Sloan yelled.

"Climbing. You better be at the top!"

"I am!"

The all-day adventure was nearing completion. First, there was Sloan forgetting his belay device and having to run back to the car; then, there was the pace of their progress. Being new to multi-pitch climbing they had "stitched-up" the climb, placing protection frequently and making each pitch shorter than necessary.

"Not that bad, was it, hon?" asked Sloan as his wife rounded the sub-peak and made for the true summit.

"No—actually, it was *unbelievably bad*, but—wow. Look behind you."

All around them the gray granite domes and solitary spires of Tuolumne Meadows glowed purple and red in the setting sun. Long black shadows like vapor trails stretched across the valley floor and Tuolumne River. Deep violet and black streaks gave way to explosive greens and then faded back to deep indigos and finally, to remnants of blue sky.

"Surreal," said Sloan. "What's that quote from Muir in the guidebook? 'This is the first time I can truly say that I've been to church in California.'"*

"Every climbing party that summits probably says that," Nikki responded.

"Once I get you up here, I'll just keep you on belay and then lower you down around the corner, over there, to the hike down," Sloan told Nikki.

"You're kidding, right? *That's* not the downclimb."

"No, I'm not kidding. Wait—right there."

"Now?" Nikki sat precariously on the edge.

"No, I mean—off in the distance. I thought I saw by that lake, it looks like, yeah, it is—check out those sparks."

Sloan pointed to the southeast of the peak where a small alpine lake was surrounded by a rim of granite mountains. Alongside the lake there was an eruption of sparks through which Sloan could barely make out the shapes of many people surrounding what clearly looked to be a sizable campfire.

"No way. I see it now. Isn't that illegal?" asked Nikki after finally gaining the summit.

"That size? Yup."

"Should we call someone?"

"Yeah." Nikki reached into her pack and handed Sloan the cell phone they had brought for emergencies.

"Do I just dial 9-1-1?" asked Sloan.

"I guess so. You've got reception, right?"

"Yeah, looks like up this high we've got a couple of bars." Sloan punched in the number and put the phone up to his ear.

"9-1-1 emergency," a voice said on the other end of the line.

"I'd like to report a large illegal campfire to the southeast of Cathedral Peak."

14

GOING TO CHURCH

Sunday, 7:25 P.M.

"Abigail... Abigail E... something." Rick couldn't believe it. Jeffrey had just heard her speak at that conference. She was the same attractive woman he had seen on the placard earlier. While Rick was on the phone with the Calaveras County sheriff's office, Jeffrey had received an urgent email from another environmentalist with an image of Abigail. *Why would there be a photograph of this?* he thought.

Before leaving for Mirror Lake, Rick had tasked Jeffrey with figuring out as much as he could about Abigail. "Make absolutely sure the speaker is the same woman as the one in this photograph," Rick said as he gestured at Jeffrey's laptop.

Rick didn't like ambiguity. He liked routine and procedure, especially when it came to his job. Jumping into his Park Service Yukon, Rick hit the lights and sirens and sped away from Yosemite Village. He trusted that Jeffrey would bring some clarity to what had transpired and prepare more details for the detectives coming up from Mariposa. Jeffrey was good at that sort of thing. You could hand him a long list of objectives or an open-ended question and he got down to business, logically and sequentially. Sometimes it was hard to take him seriously, on account of his physical appearance, but you could rarely dispute the results of his research.

Rick parked at Mirror Lake and rendezvoused with three YOSAR crew-members.

"Two of you, get ahead of me and find the 1144. The other one––I'll let you decide who gets the short straw––needs to make sure I can make it up the Death Slabs."

"Oh, you'll remember the way, Chief," one said.

"I'm not worried about getting lost, it's just been years since––"

Rick's radio buzzed at his side. "Rick here."

"Rick, it's Jeffrey."

"Yeah Jeffrey, what's up?"

"We just had a call come in from climbers at Cathedral Peak. They said that they saw a fire up by Budd Lake. Sounds like a campfire, a pretty big one, and there's a group of people out there. I'd just send the rangers we have up at Tuolumne campground, but––" Jeffrey hesitated.

Rick sensed that Jeffrey was searching for his next words–– and then it dawned on him. The words were out of his mouth before he could censor them. *"Mountain temple, Muir's mountain temple.* Do you think...?"

"I don't know boss, but nobody ever camps out up there at Budd Lake unless it has something to do with climbing in the area. And it looks like we just had one climber kill another and leave a message about Muir... and a temple."

There was silence on the radio as they both contemplated the implications.

"And the most obvious climb up there near Budd Lake wouldn't be Matthes Crest or Eichorn's Pinnacle, it would be Muir's 'church', his 'temple', it would be––"

"*Cathedral.*" Jeffrey finished Rick's thought. "'This is the first time I've been to church in California.'"

"Yes." Rick stood for a moment, looking out across Mirror Lake at Half Dome, its face powerful and forlorn in the darkness before the moon.

"Rick?" Jeffrey's voice crackled over the radio. "Chief?"

"Yeah, Jeffrey, I'm here." Rick gathered his thoughts, keeping his eyes fixed on the great rock with a dead girl's body still lying before it. Nothing about this situation was protocol.

"Hrmm," Rick growled.

Jeffrey heard this and knew to let Rick have some time to gather his thoughts.

Rick stared at Half Dome. He despised making decisions on the fly. There was a procedure for everything. Speeding, here's a ticket; illegal car camping, get up and move along. Even dealing with bears, follow the procedure. This, however—a dead body... a murderer—

"Okay, Jeffrey, call up the Tuolumne rangers. Let's see . . . who's on tonight? It should be Jason and Leroy, and I'm not sure who else. Tell them there's a campfire up by Budd Lake, probably climbers, and instruct them there was a possible homicide involving a rock climber in the valley today, and the two may be connected. Then, tell them to go to the Muir trailhead where it intersects with Highway 120 and..."—Rick took a breath and closed his eyes—"we'll meet them there."

PART II

CHASING MUIR

A mile or two above the lake stands the grand Sierra Cathedral, a building of one stone, sewn from the living rock, with sides, roof, gable, spire and ornamental pinnacles, fashioned and finished symmetrically like a work of art, and set on a well-graded plateau about 9000 feet high, as if Nature in making so fine a building had also been careful that it should be finely seen. From every direction its peculiar form and graceful, majestic beauty of expression never fail to charm. Its height from its base to the ridge of the roof is about 2500 feet, and among the pinnacles that adorn the front, grand views may be gained of the upper basins of the Merced and Tuolumne Rivers.

—John Muir, *The Yosemite*

15

IT WILL BE ACHIEVED

Sunday, 7:45 P.M.

"So we're still up for a full-moon adventure tonight, right?" Stuart said, sitting down on the decomposed granite in front of a tree.

"Of course," said Leo.

Woody sensed a murmur circulating throughout the campfire as the group wondered what sort of crazy activity Stuart and Leo had in mind. In other circumstances, a slackline would be strung up between two trees and people would take turns crossing the tightrope, spinning circles, sitting, jumping, and even laying down on the narrow piece of fabric. But here, deep in the nooks and crannies of Tuolumne, something grander was in order.

"Whose idea was it to meet out here anyway?" Joy asked her sister.

"I think it was Stuart's."

After about half an hour of idle conversation while the fire dwindled and the moon climbed, Leo spoke up. "I think it's time."

"You still haven't told us, you know—*what* it is time for," scolded Jasmine.

Stuart got up and started to speak. "Should be pretty obvious, shouldn't it?"

"Nice night for it," Aiden interrupted. "Not too cold, great visibility."

"Aiden is right. Full-moon climbing doesn't get much better than this," Leo added.

"But wait a minute," Rebecca chimed in. "Climbing—you mean bouldering? I don't see much in the way of gear or ropes around here."

She was right, thought Woody. *No one has really brought gear.* He had been out with a friend doing a full-moon climb at Lover's Leap once; it was a little scary, but his eyes had adjusted and the placements were solid. The climb was pretty easy, too—Bear's Reach, made famous by Dan Osman in the early nineties when he climbed the four hundred-plus-foot route in the just over four minutes. But then, Dan, who had since died, was able to record such a fast time because he had been—

Then it hit Woody. *That's exactly what Stuart and Leo are proposing.* And before he could vocalize the phrase—

"Free-soloing. You mean you want us to *free-solo* Cathedral?" Rebecca admonished Leo.

"Why not?" Stuart countered. "It's a 5.6, straightforward—a hike."

"Muir did it in his hiking boots about a century ago," said Leo.

"That was the downclimb," Rebecca responded.

"I know, but the point is, it's easy," added Stuart.

"There are actually a lot of different ways up the peak," Aiden added. "So we could all do it simultaneously, which would be fun and a little safer."

"I thought you didn't free solo, Aiden?" Joy asked.

"Yeah, you're right. As a rule, I don't like to free-solo. I've done it and it's a rush, but why? Tonight, though—I think I could be persuaded. After all, it's Cathedral, and people have been free-soloing in Yosemite since, you know, forever."*

"Great. And everybody here is a solid climber, so just keep your head about you," said Leo. "You can either leave your stuff here for camping or take it to the base of the climb. Anybody who doesn't want to do this—"

"Get the sand out of your vagina," Stuart interjected.

Leo scowled at Stuart. "No pressure guys, seriously. If you don't want to free-solo, don't feel obligated."

"Now?" Jasmine asked.

"Sure thing," responded Stuart, standing up and stretching.

Gradually, other climbers rose too, brushing the dirt from the back of their pants, and readying themselves. A few muttered to each other, "You doing it?" and "I guess so, you?" Some sorted through their clothes to find the right top and bottom to keep them warm but not sweating as they climbed. Everyone grabbed chalk bags and climbing shoes.

A tall and slightly stocky guy, whom Rebecca had greeted earlier, joined Rebecca, Jasmine, Joy, and Woody as they discussed the climb.

"What do you think, Doc?" Rebecca asked.

"Yeah, I'm not as strong of a climber as y'all are," Doc answered, "but what the hell? I've survived much worse."

"Are you going to carry your hiking shoes up with you?" Joy asked her sister.

"Naw, I'll just take my flip-flops for the hike down and leave my shoes at the base," Jasmine responded.

"What about you, Woody?" asked Joy.

"Yeah, I guess I'll put my ASICS in my pack, but—um, I don't even know if I'm doing it," Woody responded.

"I know. I'm not sure either."

"Yeah, I've kind of got a thing against unnecessarily risking my life."

"True," said Joy. "After that conversation we just had on the way up here..."

"What were y'all talking about then?" Doc asked.

Rebecca answered, "Ironically, we were all discussing how stupid free-soloing is."

"Well, not *all* exactly," Jasmine cut her off. "We were saying how stupid it is that people try to profit from it."

"You mean like magazines, movies, and books?" Doc said.

"Yeah," Woody said. "What did you mean, Doc, when you said you're not a strong climber?"

"Well," Doc chuckled, "I'm affiliated now with this disreputable bunch through Aiden and we're into some activism stuff. Climbing is just the price you pay for hanging out with that guy. Now, which one of y'all has actually been up this monstrosity before?"

"I have—a few times," Woody responded. "It's really not that bad. In fact, it's basically as easy as they come—lots of good breaks. I guess if I were going to free-solo anything, um, I suppose this would be it. I suppose this *will* be it."

"Yeah, and ain't nobody selling magazines off us." Doc gave Woody a light punch on the shoulder.

"Is everyone going?" Joy asked.

"You can do this, Sis." Jasmine said.

Some in the group had already set off for Cathedral. Aiden toted some water up from Budd Lake and dowsed the remnants of the fire as Jasmine stood on her tiptoes and peered north toward the string of bouncing headlamps meandering toward the giant peak.

"Well, no time like the present," Rebecca said.

"Alright, I'll do it," Joy said, slapping her sides in resignation.

With Joy's consent bolstering the group's confidence, they picked up what little gear they were taking and headed toward the mountain.

They hiked efficiently from the marshy Budd Creek drainage up to Cathedral base in the crisp high alpine evening. The brief uphill through the trees went quickly and before they knew it, seventeen climbers were staring up at a fully moonlit Cathedral Peak.

"Wow," exclaimed Joy.

"Impressive at night, isn't it?" Aiden said as he switched out of his shoes on one of the rocks at the base of the climb.

"Yes it is. Aiden, how does this compare to some of your Hetch Hetchy projects?" Joy asked.

"Funny you should ask. Out at the Hetch Hetchy Dome, there are similar crystallized knobs, just like on Cathedral here. The route I'm working on will be almost all face, very little cracks, so in that respect they're totally different—but in terms of friction, it's crazy—you just stick."

"Really?"

"Yeah, we thought at first that the route would never go. It was too steep and unfeatured. But sure enough, it'll be a classic one day. We're calling it the 'Lithe Church.'"

"What's the title all about?" Joy asked.

"I'm not supposed to tell."

"What do you mean?"

"Oh—just remember the name." Enhanced by the darkness of his skin, Aiden flashed his brilliant smile at Joy as he stood tall and stretched his muscles.

The entire group prepared themselves, studying the various cracks and lines up the wall. Above them, Cathedral loomed ominously like an enormous poltergeist, glowing in the inky blackness. Alluring, yet harboring the unforeseen and perilous, the tower of granite stretched upward over 1300 feet. A study in contradiction, it terrified yet it beckoned, calling out now the way it did to Muir—*Climb me.*

"Last one to the top"—Aiden smiled before finishing his sentence—"is one of Leo's rotten climbing shoes." And just like that, inhibitions vanished.

Woody couldn't help himself. He laughed out loud at the absurdity of it all. Joy seemed to relax, too.

"Over there," Woody directed Joy. "I'll follow you."

They rushed across the sloppy base of the giant peak to the crack system farthest to the left.

"This actually feels really good," Joy said. She was moving hand over hand, cautious but confident, up a left-facing corner. "This low angle is really comforting and the granite has all of these little crystallized nubs. It's so—so easy."

"Just keep doing what you're doing. Yeah, um, this corner ends in that ledge by the little pine tree up there. Yeah, you're doing great." Woody stayed three moves behind Joy, coaching and directing her.

To their right, the vast sparkling-white expanse of Cathedral sprawled around a massive shoulder and into the night. Bodies of other climbers could be seen moving up the various cracks and flakes shooting out in weird intersecting lines like the roots of an upturned redwood. Occasionally, one climber could be seen silhouetted against the night sky, her brightly clothing glowing in the moonlight. Woody then realized he had probably chosen the wrong outfit for the evening and would have been better off with his blue-and-gold tracksuit. His pants were a well-loved pair of dark-khaki Pranas; his shirt was a long-sleeve gray synthetic blend of fleece and polypropylene. With his brown hair and tan skin, he was practically invisible on the wall.

"Whew! That's not too bad," said Joy as she grabbed onto the tree at the first ledge.

"Yeah, it's pretty much like this the whole way up," responded Woody.

"So, are those other guys actually racing?"

"Um, looks like it." Woody leaned out and peered up the wall. "Yeah, I can see Leo, then there's Stuart and Aiden above him."

"You want to go—you know, on ahead, don't you?"

"What? No, I'm fine."

"Why don't you go ahead? I'm feeling really comfortable with this climb right now. And, well—you don't need to stay back and babysit me any longer." Joy looked down at her feet.

"It's all right, Joy. I, um, *like* babysitting you." Woody laughed.

Joy gave Woody a swift punch in the gut. "Ah--" In the next motion, she reached out and grabbed onto Woody, pulling him into the wall toward her.

Woody fell toward Joy. His body sandwiched her into the wall. Joy's face compressed against his chest. Neither spoke for a moment. This was the first time they'd ever been close to each other like this. Woody could smell a citrus hint in Joy's hair. They lingered, not speaking, just listening to the sound of each other's breath and the wind caressing the valley below.

Finally, Joy spoke up. "Go and hang with the big boys. It's okay—really it is. My sister and Rebecca are coming up behind us."

"Are you sure?" Woody pulled away with some hesitation.

"Yeah."

"Well, remember"—Woody sensed Joy's confusion and shifted gears, "at some point, about eighty percent of the way up the climb, you'll need to be slightly farther to the right on this big ledge, and then you'll squeeze through a chimney."

"Okay, now get out of here." Joy leaned out from the tree, her cheeks slightly flushed, and gave Woody a small kiss on the side of his face.

"Um...what was *that* for?"

"That was for waiting and climbing with me."

"So—do I get another if I wait even more?"

"No..." Joy hesitated. "But you get another if you finish with the boys on top."

Woody smiled back at Joy, not sure what to say.

"Go on then."

With that, Woody practically leapt off of the ledge and started motoring up the wall. This was the third time he had climbed Cathedral, and he had the peak pretty much dialed in. He knew where one crack terminated and where each ledge ended in a good series of easy face moves to the next ledge; this was going to be fun. Maybe free-soloing wasn't that bad.

The brisk night air was perfect, his perspiration was at bay and his fingers seemed to stick to everything they touched. He hadn't dipped his hands in his chalk bag since he started. The crystallized granite seemed to fly underneath his feet. His breathing was controlled; his foot placements were solid.

Right.

Left.

Reach.

Whump.

Push.

Mantle.

Left.

It was like he was plugged into his trance music, thundering down an alpine trail. Confident. Strong. Fast. His speed was almost startling. Woody reached four feet, then five feet above him, making huge moves, all the while continually forecasting two or three moves ahead. His grip on the bumpy surface was solid but light. His legs contracted and expanded, their elastic power propelling him upward. The cool night air was invigorating.

Suddenly, the urge swept over Woody to actually dyno up to a large flake in front of him; he crouched ready to spring, and—

In that instant, he was airborne, sailing vertically up the granite wall.

He brought his hands out in front of him and easily snagged the next move, bringing his feet back into the wall and continuing onward. *Yeah, going all points off is probably not the best idea. No more dynos,* he considered.

He could see Aiden and Stuart up ahead of him, but where were Leo and Paul? *That's funny.* He had seen them all together when he had looked up from the nook with Joy.

Woody heard something just to his right.

"Whew. I'm exhausted," said Leo, looking whipped and sweaty, sitting in an alcove talking to Paul, who had just come up the crack terminating at his feet.

"Tell me about it. I'm not used to this whole multi-pitch thing. Twenty feet and I'm *done*," said Paul.

"Come to think of it, Stuart and Aiden are the only real serious big-wall climbers here. No one else has any endurance. We're all freaking boulderers or single-pitch sport climbers," Leo shot back.

"*Well, almost everyone,*" Woody thought as he rocketed silently up the wall undetected just fourteen feet to Paul's left. Not only was Woody a strong climber who just happened to have a lot of experience on this wall, but, considering his running prowess, he had cardiovascular capacity as well.

This whole free-soloing thing—maybe I was wrong. Woody scampered across another ledge and plugged right into the next series of liebacks.

Move after move, *reach, pull, step,* Woody was practically running up the side of Cathedral. The wind caught his hair, and Woody paused for a moment, taking a deep inhalation—"*Yeah.*"

Right there in front of him now was Aiden, laughing as usual. He called something up to Stuart, who glanced backward and gave Aiden a taunting smile. It was clear that Stuart wanted to beat Aiden up the climb. Aiden was one of the best in the world, and to beat him at anything related to rock climbing would be a major achievement.

They still didn't see him. "*That's amazing,*" Woody thought. *My grayish outfit might have its advantages after all.* In the next few minutes, Stuart and Aiden would be at the chimney, the great funnel and an inevitable traffic jam for climbing parties on Cathedral.

Woody remembered the first time he had climbed Cathedral with his father, just a few years ago. They had arrived at the ledge before the chimney and were startled to find no fewer than four other climbing parties queued up and waiting for someone who claimed to be *stuck* in the chimney. "That's kind of the idea." Woody's father laughed as he belayed Woody up to their fifth position in line. What would be an annoyance for most was just another source of humor for Woody's dad. "You see, son, I just ain't got the time to be bitter."

Then, Woody's dad had an idea. "You know, the chimney is really neat, but there is another way around." The climbing to the left and just around a corner from the chimney ledge was certainly a good bit more difficult and exposed, but it sure beat waiting in line.

"You want to lead it, son?" Looking up at the moves, Woody could clearly see the left-facing corner with amazing crystal knobs sloping gradually up to the next ledge. That section would be fairly straightforward, but getting to it was not so clear-cut. He would have to work up a tight finger crack that was definitely more vertical than the other sections of the climb and then make one, maybe two, friction moves across the face of the rock to the corner. He remembered taking a while to evaluate the pitch and then turning to his dad and saying, "Sure, I'll do it."

Now, Woody thought, *I'll use that same corner to sneak up on Aiden and Stuart.*

He shifted to the left, leaving the obvious crack system that ended in the chimney directly above Aiden. Reaching the small finger crack, Woody deliberately reduced his tempo and stood silently on the ledge looking up at the moves, just as he had years before. He chalked up his hands and reached outward, slotting his fingers in the crack to the first knuckle. Carefully, he pulled up, twisting his right toe into the crack and smearing his left foot out on the wall, feeling for any inconsistency that he could use to apply friction.

One move.

The next move.

A third.

He was at the traverse to the left. Keeping one hand locked into the crack, he reached out for something positive to grab onto. His arm span was longer now than it had been last time, and sure enough, he landed on a sloper just positive enough for him to trust and literally half a move away from the corner. Slowly and precisely he found a foot chip and transferred his weight out of the crack and onto the friction-face moves. Bringing his right hand across, he found a tiny ledge on which he could crimp the tips of his fingers.

"Here we go. Just a little move now," Woody said to himself. Pulling down on the crimp, Woody carefully released his grip on the sloper with his left hand and reached out the final bit to the corner and to the safety of a jug.

Then, it all went wrong.

Woody's left foot had been toeing into the wall on what he thought was a solid foot chip. Suddenly that foot placement cut loose as the chip broke free from the wall. Without warning, Woody found himself suspended in between moves with only the smallest right hand crimp and—

Yes.

Woody's left hand had just barely crossed over the left-facing corner. As his body cut loose from the wall, he slammed his left hand down over anything he could find. Searing heat shot up his arm as one of the granite crystals tore into Woody's ring finger under the full dynamic weight of his swinging body. Clawing back at the wall, Woody reached up with his other hand and grabbed another section of the corner. Next he brought his feet over to the edge and felt all four points in solid contact with the wall.

It was only then that Woody, slowly and painfully, pulled up on his left hand. The granite stalagmite of rock gradually worked its way out of Woody's wounded hand. It was deep. It was red. It hurt.

Woody knew he needed to stop the bleeding as soon as possible, so despite the added pain, he dipped his left hand squarely into his chalk bag. The open wound sucked in the alkaline from the white powder and stung more than Woody had expected. He kept his hand in the chalk bag for as long as he could stand it and then removed it, checking the damage. It could hold until he got up to the next ledge.

Ah, such an idiot.

Why hadn't he just followed Stuart and Aiden up the chimney? He knew this was the harder way to go, and it depended on seeing tiny little holds in less than favorable light.

He was through it now, and he just wanted to get up to the next ledge so he could properly wrap his finger. Woody sighed and moved upward. He gingerly grasped any left handholds and moved quickly back to his right hand.

Coming to the top of the ledge, Woody looked to his right. There was Stuart standing astride the top of the chimney and looking down, jeering at Aiden who was most certainly squeezing his way up the vertical granite shaft. Woody was surprised that even with his slip, he had still managed to catch up with them.

To make room for Aiden, Stuart backed up away from the flaring top of the constriction, but didn't turn back toward the wall to continue on. *Maybe he's waiting for Aiden,* Woody thought.

Then Aiden appeared—first his hands, then his head, then his signature smile. Next, his broad shoulders twisted sideways and came into view. The top of the chimney flared outward in many granite cracks; the most room to exit the body-sized constriction onto the ledge above was at the outermost part of the chimney, right at the edge. It was onto this precipice that Aiden now pulled himself.

"Man, I hate chimneys," Aiden said with a laugh as he stood and looked to Stuart for a response. "Give me a face climb any day."

"Aiden," said Stuart.

"Yup?" responded Aiden, who was shaking his head and looking back down the hole out of which he had just pulled himself.

Stuart spoke his next words with precision, as if he had been rehearsing them in his head for some time.

"What you have been working for—it will be achieved."

The next second seemed to happen in slow motion for Woody. There was Aiden on the edge of the wall, dusting himself off from the chimney. There was Stuart to the inside of the same ledge. In that instant, Stuart sprang out from the wall directly at Aiden. Aiden must have sensed the sudden movement and looked up. Right as their eyes made contact, Stuart took the full weight of his motion and thrust his fists into Aiden's chest and stomach. Aiden doubled over, as if the air had just been sucked from his body, and catapulted backward off of the ledge and the cliff face. He flew out from the wall and into the empty space beyond.

Woody gasped, then caught himself, throwing his hand over his mouth, which made a small but audible clapping sound.

Stuart's head snapped around in Woody's direction, his eyes probing the silhouetted cliff.

PRESS SECRETARY

Sunday, 8:01 P.M.

"I t's going to be a long night—ay, Chief?" Jeffrey hopped up into the passenger side of the Park Service GMC Yukon.

"In all likelihood, Jeffrey," Rick said and started driving as Jeffrey closed the door.

"Antsy?" asked Jeffrey.

"Yeah, I suppose I'm taking this, you know, personally. Climbers can be nuts, but as a rule they're not mean-spirited." Rick breathed heavily. "I'm just afraid that whatever the outcome of this fiasco, it'll have a negative impact on access to climbing here in the Park."

The light-green Yukon exited the valley and barreled up the canyon road, winding past waterfalls and around granite edifices. In the early 1900s, visitors to Yosemite had to have their horses lowered by rope onto the valley floor because the paths were too steep and inaccessible. Now, two tunnels chiseled into the rock eased the passage in and out of the valley on the north side.

"So Jeffrey, tell me about Abigail. What did you find out?"

Rick knew that even with the campfire phone call and probably a number of other interruptions, Jeffrey still would have managed to complete some of the research Rick had requested.

Jeffrey opened his laptop and pulled up some files. "Well, she works for the Sierra Club, some kind of director. She also writes articles and lobbies the state and federal—uh, I guess I should say *lobbied* the legislature. I was listening to her speak not more than ten hours ago—"

"It's all right, Bud, go on."

"It seems like she's been with—*was*—with the Sierra Club for a while, maybe five years. Most of her writing was about the conflict between industry and environment, you know, like the BP oil spill in the Gulf of Mexico, or the impact of water usage on native fish populations in the Bay Area. Oh yeah, she was actually a pretty well-known climber, too. She's been featured in a few advertisements for some climbing shoe company—Evolve, or something."

"But why kill her? And why reference Muir?"

"I'm not sure, Chief."

Jeffrey closed one file and opened another, bracing himself against the door and center console as Rick zipped the Yukon around another steep corner and into one of the tunnels.

"There's all sorts of bizarre stuff happening on the blogs right now. That picture I showed you made the rounds. I mean—it's already on CNN."

"Hmm."

"Yeah, anyhoo—I saved the blog conversations that might be useful. There are some outraged people, environmentalists mostly, but then—"

"What is it?" Rick asked.

"Well, there are these oddball postings, like, um, coded language, messages or something."

"What do you mean?"

Jeffrey scratched his head as he scrolled down on his saved

documents, looking for a good example. "Here's one; it's from 'Adams Ansel,' and it just reads 'Yosemite.'"

"Don't you mean, Ansel Adams?"

"No, it actually has his name inverted."

"Really?" Rick whipped the SUV around the gas station at Porcupine Flat. Knowing that most bear fatalities in the Park resulted from speeding vehicles and remembering this area around the gas station is a popular bear spot, he flipped on the lights and sirens.

"I'm not sure what that posting is all about, and what any of it has to do with Abigail. I saved some of the articles she wrote— the ones with the highest amount of online views. Some of them have to do with Western Power & Gas. Looks like she had a pretty dim view of them."

"Who doesn't?" Rick chuckled. "But what else?"

"Well, do you remember the whole 'west coast real estate tycoon' thing?"

"Eh, vaguely. He was that guy who was using false names and shady paperwork to acquire more and more property."

"Yeah, Jim McConville. He was finally sent to jail not too long ago on fraud and money laundering charges. Abigail was one of the ones who helped shed light on his scheme."

"But would he be behind this?"

"Well, he did use a million of his illegal dollars to bankroll that horror movie...*Red Velvet*, or something.* So the whole gruesome message thing wouldn't be that much of a stretch. You know, some of the reviews of the film were actually pretty good."

"*Focus*, Jeffrey—"

"Oh, uh—"

"Who else?"

"There are lots of people she upset, Rick. Abigail took on... well, most anybody. Fearless, you know? Some of the big lobbying firms in Sac, the ones bankrolled by big corporate interests. Some of her most popular work shows the direct connection between corporate money, lobbyist salaries, political influence, and legislation. She's got a way of spelling it out that makes the collusion obvious."

"Hmm," Rick grunted.

"Remember that whole right-to-vote initiative Californians struck down in 2009?"*

"Sorry."

"Well, it was a total *bunk* ploy to consolidate power generation in California. Yeah, and despite forty-four million dollars in misleading television and radio commercials—you know, calling it on the ballot as '*the right to vote*' and all—Abigail helped educate people enough to defeat it."*

"Okay," Rick said. "But were any of Abigail's projects so controversial that someone would want to kill her?"

Jeffery paused and stared out the window at Douglas firs, ponderosa pines, and sequoias whipping past him in a haze of moonlight. He turned excitedly to Rick.

"Abigail was speaking in part about the Hetch Hetchy Reservoir at the symposium this weekend—

"That's not controversial."

"Hold on—this was that big thing I was going to tell you about, and how it's finally time to reconsider whether or not the dam was even necessary. She even quoted that dude Hodel, you know, Reagan's Interior Secretary or whatever, saying that restoration 'would not be a major problem,' but..." Jeffery paused.* "It was weird; she was very careful about her words. I listened to a few interview excerpts online and she has this great style, like... familiar banter. You know she made her living choosing the right language, and she was so good at it, but it was different this time. Sort of like the President's press secretary is sometimes, like he knows things he can't tell us and he's trying to measure his words and decide just how much he can or cannot say."

"Why would she do that?"

"Yeah, I was thinking that, too. And I noticed the symposium had some strange guests, not just the professors, activists, students, and such, but some *suits* in the back of the room, not saying much but, well...making their presence felt."

"Really? Who were they?" Rick said.

"Wish I had asked."

17

WHAT ABOUT THAT KID?

Sunday, 8:45 P.M.

Aiden's screams reverberated up the wall.

Stuart wasn't listening. He scanned the rock, his eyes penetrating the night for the source of that distinct clapping sound. *No one could be up here but Aiden and me. Everyone else is too slow. Leo and Paul are bouldering specialists, and the girls—well, they're girls,* Stuart thought. *Many were still putting on their shoes when we started to climb. But what about that kid?* Stuart's mind was racing now. *That kid—who is he? What's his name? Will? Warren? Woody. It's Woody.*

Shrieks from the other climbers interrupted his train of thought. Stuart scowled and turned back from the brink. *No one is up here—relax,* he told himself. *Aiden probably just kicked a loose rock into the wall behind me.* It was important to him that no one try to downclimb—it was dangerous—and Stuart needed to reinforce a lie that Aiden had just slipped. He must also ensure their silence with fears of being implicated themselves as accessories.

Stuart slinked back through the chimney and out onto the ledge below. He stared down, looking for someone.

"Stuart, what happened?" It was Leo.

"I'm not sure, man . . . Aiden was ahead of me and then––"

"Jesus. I can't believe it. Not Aiden!"

"He's gone, man––fucking gone. Look, Leo, I don't think anyone should try to downclimb. It's far too dangerous. Let's all just finish this and then decide what to do."

"Yeah, you're right," Leo called up.

"Tell anyone you can reach that Aiden must have slipped, to keep their shit together and finish the climb, and that down-climbing is not worth the risk."

"Okay, got it."

Stuart sat on the ledge and listened as Leo communicated to Paul, and Paul communicated down to Jesse, Doc and the others.

THE EVENING AIR had chilled the granite and penetrated Woody's shirt, making his perspiration freeze onto his bare skin.

He saw me.

No, if he saw me—I'd be dead, too.

Slowly, Woody peeled himself from the wall. He had seen Stuart slide back into the chimney. *What to do?* Woody had just witnessed murder, though everyone would assume that Aiden had slipped. After all, Woody himself had almost slipped off the rock a few minutes ago.

I need to make it back down to that ledge, he thought.

Gradually, Woody started to move toward the arête he had ascended just minutes before. As he lowered himself off the ledge and began downclimbing, it dawned on him that he would have to cross the same perilous section on which he had nearly fallen earlier. As the realization swept over him, Woody decided he would take a moment to collect himself. It would be awhile before everyone reached the chimney; they would be scared; they would be moving slower now.

If only they knew how scared they really should be.

He pulled himself to a seat on the ledge and dangled his feet over the side. Though it seemed like the most unnatural thing to do at the moment, Woody reached into the small pack and pulled out a granola bar and some water. This would raise his blood sugar and help him think and move better. He stared out into the night. The starry horizon flickered beyond the black silhouettes of Yosemite's high alpine peaks like the edge of a great, all-consuming fire.

What had Stuart told Aiden? Woody wondered. Stuart's phrase was just loud enough for Woody to hear and seemed so strange. *Something about an achievement? Something about what Aiden was working on?*

No, not working on, like establishing a route or setting a boulder problem. Stuart had said working for. *He had not said* on.

'What you are working for...' that's what Stuart told Aiden a split second before he pushed him off. What you are working for—then something about achievement.

Woody sat on the edge, unwrapping his granola bar, sipping his water, and trying to remember.

It wasn't achievement.

'What you are working for—it will be achieved.'

'It will be achieved.' Now, what the hell could Stuart possibly mean by that? And what could Aiden be working on, or more precisely for, that was worth killing him over?

Woody was just relieved that he remembered it. Sitting on the edge, Woody shut his eyes and quietly repeated the phrase to himself over and over:

"'What you have been working for—it will be achieved.'"

"'What you have been working for—it will be achieved.'"

Woody's eyes flashed open, his breath stopped short in the back of his throat.

What was that noise?

He peered back toward the opening at the top of the chimney. An unmistakable shaggy mop of blond hair followed by a bright white goatee emerged, as Stuart climbed onto the ledge and, to Woody's sudden horror, slowly headed in his direction. frantically searching the area. Woody was frozen stiff and more visible than before, no longer leaning back against the granite wall, but exposed and out on the edge.

Woody touched something at his left side, moist and thick. Not daring to look anywhere but toward Stuart to gauge his next move, he realized the chalk that had absorbed into his wound was no longer sufficient to stem the flow. He was bleeding again, down his hand, and onto the rock.

Then, Stuart moved. He sprang toward the wall and began to climb towards Woody's position.

For a brief instant, Stuart was concealed by the rock. Woody knew he had to act fast. Simultaneously shoving his wrapper into his pant's pocket and easing his bag over his shoulder, Woody dove off the cliff edge and onto the arête. The holds were good and jug-like, so he allowed his body to descend at near falling speed as he worked the rock from one hand to the other. Then, fully-conscious that out on the arête he would be wide open and easily seen, Woody took a leap of faith and swung himself around the arête to the inner corner, where the spine of granite reconnected with the wall. As his momentum shifted his body into the shadows, Woody's leg reached out for something, any foothold at all. Just when it seemed like he was going to swing like a barn door back out onto the outer corner of the arête, his toe caught on a small ledge which he used to stabilize himself.

Woody took a deep breath. He knew he couldn't stay where he was. His hands would still be visible on the arête and his body was under so much tension that he could probably only hold this position for a minute before having to release. Digging in with his toe, Woody shifted his weight into the shadowy V-shaped corner and reached in with one hand, feeling around in the darkness for something to grasp. Finally, he found a handhold large enough to trust and pulled himself into the corner—prepared to wait for as long as it took.

LESS THAN FIFTEEN feet above Woody's hiding spot, Stuart leapt onto the barren ledge where he thought he had seen something. His immediate surroundings were empty, just shadows of granite. He walked all the way around the area, peered over the edge, stared at any possible direction of ascent, and found silence, stillness, nothing.

Stuart hadn't felt this way after Abigail's murder. There, he was sure his act had been observed, though no one would be able to tell what was happening and no one would know it involved him. Here on Cathedral Peak, nearing the midnight hour, how could anyone, anyone at all, have seen him? It was just in his head.

Taking a moment to clear his thoughts and calm his nerves, Stuart sat down in the obvious spot, right where the distinct knobby arête terminated into the ledge. He lowered his feet over the side and stared off at the distant peaks.

I'm fine, he told himself and set his hands down on the granite next to his seat.

Instantly, he pulled his left hand up. It was wet—wet and slimy.

He brought his hand up to his face and examined it. Some sort of thick liquid on his palm and little finger glistened in the moonlight. Stuart knew its consistency from earlier today—*blood.*

What is blood doing up here? Did another climbing party leave it earlier in the day? If so, why hadn't it dried up in the sun, over time? Maybe some animal?

Stuart was no longer as confident of his perceived isolation. Again, he looked around; he looked up the wall, he looked around the side of the ledge; down the knobby arête; back toward the direction from which he had approached. *Nothing.*

"Stuart, where are you man?"

It was Paul. He was at the top of the chimney calling for him.

"Over here," responded Stuart.

"The girls seem pretty freaked out. I'm not sure what to tell them," said Paul.

Stuart shifted gears. He had to make sure everyone had the story straight. "Tell them to make it the last bit to the top, and then we'll all talk about it."

"All right. You might want to help point out the easiest way up the rest of this wall," Paul said.

"You're right. I'll be right there." Stuart scanned the ledge one more time—still nothing. Reluctantly, he moved off toward the ledge at the top of the chimney where Paul was waiting.

WOODY HAD HEARD THE CONVERSATION. Then, he didn't hear anything. He waited. *Maybe I should just stay here*, Woody thought. *Maybe that's the safest thing to do.*

"No," Woody whispered in the dark corner. *I need to go through the chimney like everyone else.*

Slowly, Woody worked up the nerve to reach back out of his safe corner and grasp the knobs on the corner. Not knowing whether or not Stuart would be there peering down at him, Woody took a deep breath and swung himself back out into the moonlight and around the edge. He looked up immediately to the place where he had been sitting.

Nothing—okay. So far so good.

Woody started the rest of the way down the arête and to the place where he had slipped before. The stalagmite of a rock no longer glistened with his blood but had turned a dull shade of red. This time, Woody wasn't taking any chances. He lowered his body down and felt around with his feet for a good thirty seconds, testing foot chips and small bumps in the wall for a placement that he could trust. Finally when he decided on one that seemed to support his weight, even when he bounced on it, Woody brought his hands out to the friction-face moves. Everything felt better now. He moved with assurance off the face and into the safety of the crack, following it down to the ledge where the chimney began. Rounding the corner, Woody saw Jasmine and Rebecca looking up at the chimney, and there, pulling herself onto the ledge beside her sister, was Joy.

"Hey," said Woody.

Joy looked up at Woody and moved toward the inside of the ledge.

"I can't... I just don't want to believe Aiden's gone," she said while wrapping the fingers on her left hand into a fist and cracking her knuckles.

"Me too."

Joy leaned in, put her head on Woody's shoulder, and looked down.

"Hey—what happened to your hand?"

18

BLOWING AGAINST THE WIND

Sunday, 9:31 P.M.

Mojo had been wasting more time on Facebook, or *Mombook,* as Woody liked to call it. She started using the online social network in order to keep tabs on her son, but now even she had to admit that it had become an obsession. Her husband, John, a tech Luddite, would often say things like, "give *real*-book a try" while chucking a paperback with deadly accuracy at any friends or family who happened to be bent over their phones in his presence.

John Jackson had met Monet Huntington in the autumn of 1981 at Simon & Garfunkel's famous Central Park concert in New York City. They dated, got engaged, and were married within two years. Some West Coast friends had given them the couple's name of 'Mojo,' for Monet and John, and Monet had adopted the name as her own. When John was diagnosed with adult acute myeloid leukemia, was denied coverage by their insurance company, and faced the false choice of fighting the insurance company or bankrupting his family, John had chosen instead to head to Yosemite to spend time with Woody, and when asked why he wasn't fighting, he referenced a lyric from the little known Paul Simon song, "I Know What I Know," in the *Graceland* album, replying, "Who am I to blow against the wind?"*

Mojo would often lapse into daydreams about her late husband. Even though it had been two long years since his death, tidbits of songs, smells from the kitchen, and oil stains on the driveway would bring John crashing back into her conscious ramblings. Her name, adopted in jest as way to distance herself from her privileged East Coast upbringing, now served as a constant reminder of John's absence. Her friends encouraged her to start dating again, but despite the offers, she didn't want to do that to Woody.

That evening, Mojo was working on a new piece until someone texted telling her to go to the Sierra Club's URL. Once there, she immediately saw the disturbing image of her former confidant Abigail. Studying the picture, she gawked at the gruesome and bizarre nature of it. *Why would someone defile a tragedy like this? Why include a message? Why Abigail Edwards?*

Already, online comments and speculation were circulating. Clearly, foul play had transpired, and fingers were pointed at those large enough to be a target: the CIA, the fishing industry, oil and power companies, and certain powerful state lawmakers. It was clear that Abigail Edwards had enemies, and those enemies were often influential people. One blogger on the *Earth First!* website claimed that her death had to do with the federal government and Abigail's vocal opposition to the recent expansion of fracking. Other anonymous postings advocated for violent retribution. And there were weird coded posts.

Mojo had crossed paths with Abigail Edwards on a number of occasions. She was even researching a specific piece on her— something that would highlight the risks inherent in Abigail's life and draw a metaphor between the dangers of climbing and the dangers of being an outspoken and articulate voice of modern environmentalism.

On a whim, Mojo logged onto the *Earth First!* website and clicked on a newly created topic in its open blog: "Here lies Muir's mountain temple." She froze, her right index finger holding the mouse starting to twitch as adrenaline coursed through her. Mojo's eyes scanned back and forth across the page. *This is most unlike them.*

Violent rants erupted from various sources. One blogger, calling himself—or herself—"Monkey Wrench," stated, "We must respond with bloody and sudden retaliation! We must release the power of our Mother without regard for the consequences!"

Mojo scrolled down, and there was that same cryptic posting she had seen on the *Sierra Club* website: "Lithe churches empty helm;" posted by someone who referred to himself or herself as "Adams Ansel." Mojo didn't think much of it the first time she read the four-word statement; but now here it was again in conjunction with the fiery rhetoric of environmental extremism. She paused and squinted at the screen, remembering back to the *Sierra Club* site. *Yeah,* lithe *was the adjective... I'd remember that,* she thought.

As she was reading, the browser refreshed and there popped up another posting— "Action is necessary. Dormant cells must be activated." *This confrontation could get uglier than a porcupine versus a python.*

Mojo knew that since Operation Backfire and the indictments handed down in 2006, militant environmental advocacy had essentially ceased. Even Earth Liberation Front (ELF) now advocated for nonviolent collective action as innocuous as education and political petitioning. Gone were the days of covert teams of Earth First! activists sneaking into nuclear test sites in the Nevada desert to block further contamination of groundwater.

Operation Backfire brought together seven FBI investigations and prosecuted the suspected activists for domestic terrorism. With some creative deciphering of the coded language referencing environmental pioneers, eleven people were arrested on charges ranging from arson and conspiracy to use of destructive devices and destruction of an energy facility. The conspirators referred to themselves as "The Family" and, despite the oath they had taken to protect each other, were eventually found guilty of many of the initial charges, including the firebombing of Vail Ski Resort in Colorado.*

Since the trial and sentencing, two things had happened to radical environmental activism in the United States. Mojo had published a piece on this evolution in *SFGate* and other West Coast newspapers. In it, she had analyzed the change in rhetoric and the mainstreaming of much of Earth Liberation Front's agenda, stating that, "while ELF still advocates direct action, those actions have become noticeably more within the confines of society's social and legal norms. Think Muhammad Ali with his gloves tied to his shoe laces."

The other force at work that discouraged ELF and other advocacy groups from doing anything too militant or overt was a powerful new tool of business interests and media groups—the term *ecoterrorism*—a dangerous moniker that, in Mojo's oft-quoted words, "lumped tree-huggers and weekend activists in the same category as bin Ladens and militant sadists."

Mojo had argued persuasively that the prevalence of the term *ecoterrorism* was a radical shift away from the politics of protest and civil disobedience emerging from the unrest of the sixties, and the tactics of founding environmentalists for the past three generations. With the abundant use of *ecoterrorism* in courtrooms, magazines, and the nightly news, environmental activism had nearly vanished overnight.

Now, reading the increasingly inflammatory blogs, it seemed

like activists had come to accept and even embrace the ecoterrorist label, regardless of consequences.

Damn. Abigail would have been proud of y'all, Mojo thought. *At least she died in Yosemite.*

As soon as she considered the word *Yosemite*...

Woody!

19

WHAT DID I MISS?

SUNDAY, 9:32 P.M.

The evening serenity here in Tuolumne Meadows is worth preserving, Rick thought. He cut the Yukon's flashing lights as he rounded the bend at Olmsted Point. Tenaya Peak presided over the lake of the same name, and powerful moon rays made the glassy surface of Yosemite's Stately Pleasure Dome luminesce like a glowing fog of white light cascading to the lakeshore.

"Who's going to be there tonight?" asked Jeffrey.

"Well, it'll be David and Jason, but probably some others," Rick answered.

"You think, um, that hot new girl, Alexandra, will be there?"

"Easy there, flyboy," Rick chuckled. "She's a bit old for you, isn't she?"

Jeffrey cleared his throat to hide his embarrassment. "Never mind."

"Sorry, partner. I'm not sure who else will be at the trailhead."

"I guess we'll find out soon enough."

They pulled up a small incline and into the vast expanse of Tuolumne's central meadow. As the road opened up next to the low-angle Pothole Dome, Rick stepped on the gas and sped into the valley toward the John Muir Trailhead.

As usual, the road was lined with cars stretching out alongside the shoulder in both directions. Rick saw there were already three Park Service vehicles at the trailhead's designated parking area for emergency and official use. He still wasn't completely sure that his present course of action was the most advisable. If they were actually going after a killer, shouldn't regional law enforcement be involved? But the timing wouldn't work; they were too remote. And there was no guarantee this wasn't just a wild-goose chase.

Rick drove the Yukon diagonally onto the gravel shoulder, spraying rock and small asphalt chunks as the tires dug in.

Hopping out, Rick grabbed a topographical map and a flashlight and headed toward a Park Service Crown Victoria. Other rangers emerged from their cars and converged on him.

"Coming in a little hot there, weren't you Rick?" asked Ranger David Chapman, recently reassigned to Yosemite.

"Well, I knew you guys would be snoozing." Rick was unfolding the map on the hood of the car as he spoke.

"So, what's the deal?" Jason Wilcox, another Park Service ranger, rubbed his dark eyes and tucked in his shirt.

"We have a dead female climber out by the base of Half Dome, possible homicide," Rick said. "We know there's a message about 'Muir's Church' next to the dead body."

"And we know there's a sizeable campfire out by Budd Lake," Jeffrey chimed in, "which means that its probably climbers and—"

"They're going to Muir's Church?" Jason chimed in.

"We don't know." Rick took control. "But we need to gather as much information as possible, and we are going to haul every one of those *dirtbaggers* in for questioning to find out whatever we can."

"Threat level?" David asked.

"Real." Rick considered his next words carefully. He didn't want any more deaths in the Park today. "Use caution. Stay in groups of two or more. In terms of the level of danger and your use of force, everyone is to assume that you are potentially dealing with a killer and be prepared to exercise the appropriate measures." Rick paused and let the cadre of rangers evaluate his words. "Chances are we'll just be rousing some sleepy climbers, but given the earlier death, I need... everyone to be ready."

"Dumb climbers," David commented. "I wish the Park Service would get serious about them."

Rick took a very audible breath. Those who knew him well understood this was a sore subject for Rick. "Look, David, we're in a rush here, but I can take thirty seconds to educate you as our newest transfer." Rick paused, conveying the full weight of his annoyance. "Who can tell me what the first major killer of people in the Park is?* Here's a hint: it's not rock climbing."

Jason rolled his eyes. He'd heard this lecture before. "It's driving, Rick. There are many more driving fatalities and injuries in cars than we ever see from rock climbing. That's the most reckless activity people engage in here."

"Next?" Rick prodded.

"Followed by hiking," Jason continued. "The next most dangerous activity is hiking."

"So rock climbing is next on the list, right?" Rick asked.

Jeffrey jumped in this time. "No, it's actually water-related deaths, like slipping into waterfalls and drowning in the Merced or freezing in the water. Yeah, rock climbing certainly kills some people here in Yosemite, but so do horses, pack mules, and... you know... other people, and... well... getting lost; lots of other stuff."

"All right, all right, I get it," David said, looking down at his new hiking boots.

Rick smiled at him. "Sorry for the lecture, but our job is to apprehend. That's it." Rick paused again.

David nodded deferentially.

"Now, let's talk about the logistics of getting there." Rick flipped on his Maglite and twirled it up onto his shoulder, cocking his head to the side to shine the light down onto the topo map. The eight rangers present gathered closer.

"Here's the Muir Trailhead, where we are now, and here's Budd Lake. There's basically only one path up to the lake, and it runs along Budd Creek, right here. At this point in the trail, when Cathedral Peak becomes obvious, I want us to—"

Suddenly, everyone looked up. Flashing lights and wailing siren ripped into the meadow as another Park Service Yukon whipped past Pothole Dome. The vehicle cut the siren and lights just before coming to a halt. The door was open before the SUV had fully stopped. Jogging up to the group was a slender female figure, tall with dark hair and strong symmetrical features.

Jeffrey smiled.

"Gentlemen, what did I miss?" Alexandra said before anyone could greet her.

"Not much, Alex. I, um, didn't know you were working tonight," Jason said.

"I heard something exciting was going on and figured you could use the extra... *man*power."

"All right, all right everyone." Rick spoke more loudly than before. "Alex, Jeffrey can fill you in as we head up to Budd Lake, but right now we're losing time. I was saying that I want us to split up at this point on the trail." Rick swung his flashlight back around to the map. "Those slower in the group will make for Budd Lake, and the faster half of us will make for Cathedral Peak. We're looking for any signs of activity, and we're to take into custody anyone we find out there in this general vicinity. The rendezvous point will be back here," Rick said, pointing at the map, "in the meadow directly between Cathedral and Budd Lake."

Glancing around the circle, Rick checked the group to make sure people understood. "Everyone have headlamps? Warm clothes? Handcuffs? Pepper spray? Firearms? Good hiking shoes? Water containers?"

"Yeah, Mom, we're all packed," Jason chided.

"All right, let's go," Rick grunted.

Walking back by the SUV, Rick grabbed a small pack and checked to make sure Jeffrey had everything he needed. He hesitated for a moment, watching the members of his crew assemble their belongings.

"Remember," Rick spoke loudly. "Assume they are dangerous. Approach in groups of at least two." He spun around and started up the John Muir Trail into the darkness.

20

THE TRUTH?

Sunday, 9:39 P.M.

"Yeah Joy, um, I had to catch myself," Woody said to explain the blood on his hand.

"Oh God, Woody. That could have been *you*."

"No. What happened was..."

"Was *what*?" Joy demanded.

Woody hesitated. "I'm not sure how it happened."

"Could you see anything? You were closer to Aiden."

"No, um, not really."

"*Woody, what did you see?*" Joy whispered.

"Uh, look..." His eyes pleaded.

"Woody..."

He paused, glanced at the chimney above them, then pulled Joy close and whispered back, "I'll tell you once we're off of this mountain, when we're all somewhere safe. Not now."

"What? Why?"

"Joy, *please* trust me."

They pulled back from one another on the moonlit ledge. Joy scowled at Woody and cracked her knuckles before turning away.

"Joy, I'm really sorry, I just need to think..."

"About *what?*"

Stuart yelled down from the top of the chimney, "Who's still down there?"

"It's just us—Joy and Woody," said Joy.

"I think we're the last ones," Woody added.

"Okay. Just come on up the chimney and follow everyone. We're going to stick together from this point on." Stuart stared a moment longer at Woody and then turned away from the ledge to begin leading the group up the last couple of pitches to the summit.

Joy and Woody entered the chimney and fell in line behind everyone else, methodically working their way up the easiest crack system and then around the final bulge before the summit of Cathedral.

The absolute peak of Cathedral is barely more than a five-foot-by-six-foot rough rectangle with an adjoining flake of rock protruding like the spine of a giant knife.

As Woody and Joy rounded the adjoining subpeak before the rock bridge, they saw the rest of their group gathered around the summit plateau and adjoining flake. It was a small space for even five or six people; with sixteen of them there, it would be dangerous.

Woody pulled himself onto the subpeak, "Are you sure we should all meet here?" he asked. "It's kind of a small summit."

"It'll be fast," Stuart shot back. "Come on up."

The group scrunched up, clinging to the small obelisk, standing along the rock bridge, or perching on the flake. Shaking his head, Woody reached up and inserted his hand into the crack he knew was there and pulled himself to the top.

"Look's like you've been here before," said Paul.

"But, man, what the hell happened to your hand?" asked Leo.

As Woody extricated his hand from the crack, it was clear that the blood was starting to seep through the tape he had wound around his finger. He could almost feel Stuart's eyes scrutinizing him.

"Nothing, it's nothing," Woody said. "I just slipped." His taped finger wasn't concealing his wound as well as he had hoped, and thanks to Leo's inquiry, Stuart was now keenly aware of it.

Joy pulled herself onto the summit as well, and there was some last-second jockeying for position. Jasmine and Rebecca were seated next to Doc on the flake, and Leo was crouching out by the edge of the crack. Stuart had been right in the center of the plateau and, when Joy pulled herself onto the top, decidedly took a position in the ring of people between Woody and Joy, next to the downclimb and the thousand-foot drop to the valley floor. Space on the summit dictated that each person was in direct contact with the persons to his or her immediate right and left.

"Okay, so we need to all be in agreement as to what happened," Stuart began. "If anyone is questioned about Aiden, we all need to say that we didn't even know where he was or what he was doing or what happened to him."

"You mean like he was the only one out here tonight?" asked Jesse.

"Exactly," replied Stuart.

"Right." Paul said. "No one has to know that we all climbed this or even, you know—camped at Budd Lake."

"I think I'm going to make for the valley along the Muir trail," Stuart continued. "I'd advise many of you to just vacate the area. You can head back to wherever. There's no reason you have to be associated with this tragic incident."

As Stuart spoke, Woody couldn't help but try to inch away from him. With a well-timed push, Stuart could easily send him backward off the precipitous summit. *No,* Woody thought to himself, *he wouldn't do that... not with all these witnesses.*

"So we should just pack up and leave?" asked Paul.

"I think that makes the most sense. Unless anyone has a better idea?" Stuart asked.

"Why not just tell the truth?" Rebecca chimed in.

"Well..." Stuart measured his words carefully before saying them. Woody could feel Stuart's lungs expand and contract as he prepared to continue his deception. "See, if we're all brought into this, well, then the authorities will want to know all sorts of things—like why were we camping illegally; why were we climbing in the middle of the night; why were we free soloing; was something going on with Aiden that would account for this?"

The impulse to shout out "I saw you! You pushed Aiden!" was overwhelming. He could just scream it out right now and be rid of the horrible truth, put it out in the open, but Woody knew this would only lead to chaos and, in the present dangerous position, possibly more death.

"If we're all questioned," Stuart went on, "then there's a chance we'll be held partially responsible for what happened. And as much as we all may feel bad for Aiden—"

Here it comes, Woody thought.

"Aiden wouldn't want his death to mean that climbing would become more restricted or more difficult for any of us."

With that, there was no more argument. "Agreed then?" asked Stuart.

Around the small circle of bodies clinging to the pillar of rock, people looked at each other, shrugged their shoulders, and nodded.

Slowly, one by one, each climber negotiated the small down-climb to the ledge that led to the hike down. Before exiting the summit, Woody noticed Stuart checking his phone and reading a text message. Not wanting to seem too interested or too anxious to climb down first, Woody saw a brief look of concern sweep over Stuart's face. When his turn came, Woody was glad to get off the pinnacle and even more relieved when he was able to finally remove his climbing shoes and put on the cross-country sneakers he had been carrying.

Once everyone was safely off the wall, Paul pointed out the obvious trail back down to Budd Lake.

"Don't wait for everyone when you get there. Just grab your gear and head whichever way you see fit," Stuart added.

As Woody began hiking back down the trail to Budd Lake, he could sense Joy right behind him, and he knew she was anxious. He just wasn't sure how to explain the horror of it.

21

RANGER RICK

Sunday, 10:02 P.M.

Rick was fast on foot. He was out almost every day hiking with his sketchbook and charcoal and didn't have the same social and family distractions as did many of his colleagues. "Hmm," he grunted as he glanced over his shoulder. *No one; I should wait. Groups of two or more.*

He was already past the first two-mile section of trail that ran alongside Budd Creek and into the open expanse of glaciated granite. Taking a seat on a rock, Rick dropped his pack and drank some water. The air temperature had plummeted since the meeting alongside the highway in Tuolumne Meadows. A breeze agitated the trees and brought goose bumps to Rick's exposed forearms.

What will we find? Rick wondered. *Probably just some scrubby climbers hanging out and enjoying the backcountry. They won't have a permit, of course, and we'll have to bring them all in.*

Rick scowled and closed his eyes. He didn't like disrupting campers and climbers this deep into the backcountry, as long as they exercised good judgment, following the major backcountry rules—no fires in unofficial rings, no trash, no defecation near running water. He usually gave these sorts of infractions a pass, it was a small karmic adjustment that he felt he might owe to the climbing community. Rick guessed that the campers would have cleaned up and followed the leave-no-trace ethic, just like he always did ever since that summer in the late seventies when he first entered Yosemite as a reckless teenager named Heyoka.

Heyoka. In many ways by his choice of the name Rick, he had come full circle. Originally, it was a way to upset his family, to distance himself. Now it seemed as if every tourist he encountered had something funny to say about a ranger named *Rick.* He had even contemplated changing his nameplate to *Richard,* but he had grown used to the jovial heckling and tentative slaps on the shoulder. *Ranger Rick* was a catchy alliteration that seemed to put people at ease, which ultimately made his job easier. And for that fact alone, he could put up with the constant reminder that he had left his culture for that of another.

"Rick," Jeffrey called out.

"Over here, Jeffrey." Rick shook his head as Jeffrey came panting up the trail toward him. He was working hard, hiking fast for someone hired mostly for his computer savvy. *You can count on Jeffrey.* Rick smiled as his thoroughly bushed colleague approached. Jeffrey always dove into any task with unbridled enthusiasm, even if he wasn't quite cut out for it.

Then Rick saw another reason why Jeffrey might be working up the trail with such gusto. Alexandra pranced alongside him as if this were just another pleasant day-hike instructing tourists on the flora and fauna of the region.

"I thought we were supposed to stick together," Alexandra chided Rick as she approached.

"That's why I'm waiting."

"Great. Then you won't mind if we wait a little longer," exclaimed Jeffrey as he collapsed on the granite next to Rick.

"Sure thing." Rick laughed and clapped Jeffrey on the back.

"You just catch your breath there."

Jeffrey stared up at Rick but stopped suddenly and squinted, looking past Rick's backlit silhouette toward Cathedral Peak.

"What is it?" Alexandra asked.

"I thought I saw—"

Rick and Alexandra turned to look in the direction Jeffrey was staring.

"There!" exclaimed Jeffrey. "Did you see that?"

"Yup." Rick breathed a deep sigh. "That's the hike climbers use to get down from Cathedral Peak."

"I thought it was the other side," said Alexandra.

"Well, you can head west to John Muir Trail, but it's longer and more dangerous, especially at night. What we're looking at there is the official mountaineers' hike down," Rick said.

"And those look like headlamps to me," added Jeffrey.

"Do you think—?" asked Alexandra.

"It's got to be." Rick gathered his thoughts and turned toward his companions. "One of you needs to wait here and explain that the group of climbers we are apprehending is coming down from Cathedral right now. Send at least one pair of rangers toward the Budd Lake site and one pair around to the Muir Trail to catch anyone who may have exited on another side of the mountain. Everyone else should make directly for the Cathedral base. It looks like we have quite a few suspects heading down the trail."

"I'll stay and direct people," offered Alexandra. "You can leave some of the excess supplies with me if you want to move faster."

"Done," Rick said. "Jeffrey, take your sidearm, some water, your radio, and a flare, and leave the other contents of your pack here."

"Got it."

"Alexandra, will you be all right?" Rick asked.

"No sweat, Chief."

With that, Rick nodded at Jeffrey, and shot off toward Cathedral Peak with Jeffrey racing behind.

22

PERCENTAGES

Sunday, 10:21 P.M.

There he lay.

Cold. Crushed. Lifeless. Gone.

Aiden's once powerful physique reflected no sense of serenity in death. His arms twisted out at acute angles with bone and blood visible not only at the separated joints but in other places where his forearms had made contact with a rock and halved open like an apple. His body had bounced after initial impact, glancing off the lower apron of the wall and smearing blood in long calligraphic lines toward the base of Cathedral. Aiden's ankles, neck, hips—everything—was in disarray, except his face, which was turned up, his eyes pulled back as if blinded by the oncoming finality of his descent. His mouth was open, like there was something else he wanted to communicate before he died.

Woody had only seen human death once—his father in a hospital bed. Aiden's passing was nothing like his father's. Woody remembered talking with his dad a year before his death during one of their Yosemite backpacking trips. They spoke specifically about dying, about his beliefs, about his spirituality. John had characteristically been lighthearted and playful during their discussion. It still bothered Woody even now, how nonchalant his father had been about his own mortality.

"What do you mean you don't particularly like the idea of heaven?" Woody demanded. "Don't you care what happens to you when you die? What about salvation?"

John just smiled. "You've been talking with your Catholic buddy Oscar again, haven't you?"

"So?"

"Look, Son," John began, "I'm not comfortable with *salvation*, you know—the idea that I need somehow to be *saved*. There are too many strings attached," he said with a laugh.

"It's not funny, Dad. You could be dead next year, next month, next week for all we know—and you think this is some kind of joke?"

"Sorry, Woody, I know; let's sit down up here."

John led Woody to a spot overlooking a small stretch of Rafferty Creek on the way to Vogelsang High Sierra Camp. He set down his pack and filled up his water bottle, pondering his next words. Woody stood with his pack on his shoulders, impatiently glaring.

"Take a load off, Son."

Woody tossed his pack onto the ground and leaned against a tree.

"Have it your way." John took a long pull from his water bottle and stared into the cascading stream. "So when I die, what will happen? Truthfully, I don't know. There are things I can control in my life and things I can't control. What happens when a person dies is something that, in my humble opinion, any human shouldn't presume to be able to control." John looked up at Woody. "You with me?"

Woody sat down on a rock facing his father and nodded.

"But for the sake of discussion, let's just say I devoted my remaining days here on Earth to becoming a devout follower of Jesus. Let's say that rather than doing what we are doing now, I spent my time in prayer and asking forgiveness for my sins, and all that." John picked up a granite pebble and ran his fingers over its texture. "So then when I die, I'd have a reasonable expectation of what's to come, you know, a bright, warm light drawing me nearer, surrounded by people whom I have known in the past who are welcoming me through some *pearlescent* entrance into a golden city where time stands still."

"Dad, save the sarcasm."

"Right, in all seriousness, those people meeting me and ushering me into heaven, they are supposed to be people who have since passed and who have meant something to me in my life, right?"

Woody nodded.

"Well, if that's the case, then what happens with my Jewish friend who died a few years ago? He didn't accept Jesus as a savior. He's a Jew. Will he be there? What happens with Muslims, you know, that family we stayed with in Brooklyn? Where do they go?"

John turned to look at Woody. "I don't like division. I don't like the exclusionary philosophy that says if there is a heaven then there is also a hell, that you're saved or you're damned. I cannot accept that one religion is right, because then I'd be saying the opposite about the others. For myself, yeah, I'm dying, not as quickly as the doctors told me, but we both know I'm getting weaker. What happens to me when I die? Yeah, I care about all that too, but all I feel—all I know—all I can do, right here and right now, is live my life as best as I can, be kind, be compassionate, be honest, be thoughtful and caring, and trust that I've lived a good and moral life."

John grabbed his pack and stood up. Turning to his son still seated by the creek, he flashed a playful smile. "Besides, being surrounded by intense light, in a golden palace, listening to angels singing for eternity would definitely get on my nerves after, like the first ten minutes."

Woody reluctantly smiled and rose to his feet.

WOODY LOOKED down at Aiden's distorted corpse and wondered if Aiden ever had a chance to process life and death. He wondered what Aiden believed. As he studied the disfigured remains of one of rock climbing's most inspirational figures, a resolve welled up inside him—a resolve to do right by Aiden, to bring Stuart to justice.

He had not yet said anything to Joy. He wanted to be confident no one was around, that regardless of Joy's reaction, no one could suspect anything.

People were gathering around Aiden's body now. Rebecca was crying on Jasmine's shoulder. Leo squatted next to the body and seemed to be having one last communication with his friend and mentor.

Woody felt a tugging at his elbow. It was Joy. She dropped her hand down his sleeve and interlaced her fingers with his, then gave a slight pull, which Woody understood; looking at Joy, he nodded, and they headed off, away from the group and back toward Budd Lake.

Rather than plunging directly into the meadow, Woody led Joy out and around the base of Cathedral Peak, slightly west of where the others would be traveling. There, he found some large stones, debris from Cathedral, and brought Joy around behind one of them. He looked backward over his shoulder to make sure no one had followed.

"Woody, this is some length you're going to," Joy began. "This better be—"

"Look, Joy, what I'm going to tell you is dangerous and confusing, and I'm not exactly sure yet what to do with it," said Woody.

"Okay."

"Here goes. Remember how you told me to go ahead of you to the summit?"

Joy nodded.

"And how I said I had climbed this peak a couple times before?"

"Yes."

"Well, at first I caught up to Paul and Leo, but, um, very quickly I was up even with Aiden and Stuart. They were across from me actually laughing and talking..." Woody paused, deciding how to tell Joy the rest.

"I wanted to... I guess surprise them. So below that chimney we all squeezed through, I knew another way around. That's where I cut myself when I slipped. Well, I... I took this other way up there, and Stuart and Aiden didn't see me. It was looking like I would be able to run into them on the ledge above the chimney, but—"

Woody paused again. Joy didn't say a word. The wind had been moving across Cathedral Lakes below them in sporadic gusts, but now it too paused as if Yosemite itself was holding its breath.

"Joy, I saw Stuart push Aiden off."

Joy's eyes widened. She didn't speak. She didn't blink. Her eyes searched Woody for verification.

"I was perched above them on a small ledge where my route finished...and watched as Stuart, well, flung himself at Aiden right at the top of the chimney where it flares at the edge. And right before he did it, he said something curious to Aiden. He said, 'What you have been working for, it will be achieved.'"

Woody kept talking, faster now, relieved to finally be able to tell someone. "You see, when we were up there, on the side of the mountain, I didn't want to freak everyone out, you know... or even tell one person, because I wasn't sure how Stuart would react. He looked in my direction after pushing Aiden, but I don't think that he saw me because of the dark color of my clothes. I'm not one-hundred-percent sure, though. I mean, there's a chance—"

"Well, *I'm* one-hundred-percent sure, *now*." Stuart's shadowy figure appeared above them on the rock; the black silhouette of a gun pointed in their direction.

Joy screamed.

23

COURTESY

Sunday, 10:44 P.M.

Terrain streamed beneath Rick's feet like clear rushing water under an outstretched hand. He knew he was leaving Jeffrey behind, but he cast aside his normal prudence to be able to intercept the climbing party before they had a chance to scatter or were alerted to the oncoming contingent of rangers stomping heavily through the woods.

Here and now, with his heart thundering in his chest and his every cell pulsing with adrenaline; with a clear and urgent purpose propelling him onward, Rick felt more like himself than he had in years. As the silhouette of trees shifted, and the moon illuminated his path toward Cathedral Peak, Rick connected deep within himself to something larger, something powerful.

Ahead, Rick could see flashing headlamps. He slowed down to evaluate. They seemed to be huddled in a group at the base of Cathedral, right where most of the climbs started. Gradually, a few climbers peeled away from the group; most were heading in the direction of Budd Lake, but not all of them. Rick was glad he left Alexandra with instructions on how to split up the rangers. It was clear that all the climbers were not going to conveniently congregate in one place.

Rick decided he needed to seize the opportunity. If he waited for Jeffrey, the group could become even more scattered, and Jeffrey's noisy clamor through the underbrush would cause a panicked dispersal of the climbers that would further complicate things.

He would approach them himself—and he would do it now.

Looking up the climbers' trail to see if anyone else was coming, Rick slid out of the cover of the forest and onto the trail above the small group, the same trail the climbers had used to approach their current location. Carefully and quietly, he walked at a normal gait toward the group, hoping they wouldn't realize he wasn't one of them until he was right there. He could hear voices as he got closer. The group seemed to be in a loose circle, only about ten of them. They were looking down at something. Their body language was odd, not what he expected to see in the middle of the night in the Tuolumne high country. They were hunched over, mournful. Two girls hugged each other, and one guy squatting near the center of the circle slowly got up and backed away.

Ten more paces and he would be there. Rick's eyes alternated between the ground and the climbers, making sure his feet landed on areas that would make the least noise. Aiming for an opening in the group, Rick floated, barely noticeable, into the space left between two of them. Now he could easily see what they were all gathered around. Taking only a fraction of a second to evaluate the scene, Rick looked over the mangled body of Aiden Watson and quickly evaluated that the death most likely occurred from a fall. He then drew his breath and calmly stated, "Would someone do me the courtesy of explaining precisely what happened here tonight?"

24

WHERE DID YOU COME FROM?

Sunday, 10:49 P.M.

J asmine spoke first. "What the—where'd you come from?"

"Ma'am, I beg your pardon, but I—" Rick paused. "I will be asking the questions. So again, someone please explain what the hell happened here."

Silence. Rick knew he had made the right choice. He had managed to corner what looked to be the majority of the group. As for those who had slipped away earlier, they would be apprehended soon enough.

"It was all a terrible accident!" exclaimed Jasmine.

"We were all free-soloing," Leo said. "You know, climbing without ropes and gear, up Cathedral. Aiden here," Leo gestured. "He was out in front, along with somebody else—"

"Who?" asked Rick.

"Stuart," said Paul.

"Yeah, Stuart," Leo confirmed. "Then somewhere near the chimney up there, Aiden fell."

"Is Stuart here?" Rick asked.

Everyone glanced around the loose circle of climbers. "No," Paul said.

"How many people in your group, how many are not here, and where do you think they are right now?" Rick followed up.

Paul checked around, "Let's see, we were seventeen at first. I see eleven, counting um... Aiden. We're missing that kid Woody, I think, and your little sister, Jasmine. What's her name again?"

"Joy."

"Right—then there's Stuart, Doc isn't here, and maybe two others; looks like John and Gabe. They're all probably on their way to Budd Lake. We left some camping gear there—" He hesitated. "But didn't Stuart say he was going in a different direction?"

"Yeah," Jesse spoke up. "Stuart was heading for the main valley."

Suddenly, Jeffrey appeared in his slightly tattered Park Service uniform, crashing through the underbrush and breathing heavily.

"I'm here, Chief," said Jeffrey as he came to a halt between Rebecca and Jesse, who parted to make room for the new uniform.

Jeffrey immediately looked down at Aiden and said, "What the hell? Another one?"

Curious looks were exchanged around the group as the climbers mouthed to one another the words they had just heard.

"Jeffrey," Rick started. "I need you to radio down to Alex and tell her we've got ten climbers here directly at the base and there are approximately six more out there. It sounds like most should be on their way to Budd—"

Rick never had the chance to finish his sentence. A shrill scream pierced the evening air.

"What was that?" Jeffrey, Paul, and Jesse all said in unison.

"It sounded like—like—" Jasmine began.

"I know," said Rebecca. "It sounded like Joy."

"Jeffrey, you stay here. No one goes anywhere." Rick's eyes

flashed around the circle to ensure compliance. "I'll radio instructions."

"Fuck no. That's my sister." Jasmine blurted out. "I'm coming."

"Ma'am, I have the gun. You are staying here." With that, Rick took off in the direction from which the gut-wrenching cry originated.

25
___

WILL DO

Sunday, 10:51 P.M.

W*ell, that will do... most certainly.*
       The Professor downloaded the image of Aiden's
       corpse. It was impressive that Stuart had managed
to get this image with all of the climbers standing around. The
array of headlamps encircling the contorted form even made it
possible to identify the body as Aiden Watson, though barely so.
From the angle of the photograph, Stuart must have held the
phone at his side and snapped the image without looking.

This will do.

Unlike with Abigail's final photographic tribute, this time The
Professor only titled the image with Aiden's name before posting
it to the same sites that Abigail's shot had been sent. There would
be more to come and now was not the time to muse over the
exact phrasing of environmentalist vitriol. But another thought
made it's way into the mind of The Professor and a short phrase
was inserted along with the photograph: "a secreting twirl norm."

This will do for now.

Yes. There were other things to attend to. Stuart had already been alerted to the search party of Yosemite Rangers fast approaching his location. Now he needed to keep moving, and it would be best if no one knew which way he was headed.

26

BUZZ

Sunday, 10:52 P.M.

Stuart pounced from his rock top perch to the side of Woody and Joy.

Brandishing a small but obvious pistol, Stuart wrapped his hand quickly around Joy's mouth and shoved the weapon into the small of her back. Joy winced as the barrel bumped against the knobs of her spine.

"Not another word." Stuart breathed out the command, barely audible through his clenched teeth. Taking the gun and pointing it at Woody, Stuart motioned for him to start walking westward through the forest and added, "No headlamps."

Instantly, the three figures were crossing the loose rock and small trees at the base of Cathedral Peak, heading west toward Cathedral Lakes and the John Muir Trail.

Woody's mind raced. *Why didn't I wait longer to tell Joy? How did Stuart sneak up on us? What can we do now?*

We still have one advantage, Woody thought to himself, which no doubt was the reason for their rapid movement. *Everyone must have heard Joy's scream, and surely people are coming to investigate.*

Then Woody heard something. It was a quiet, but distinct *buzz*, like the kind from a vibrating cell phone. Woody glanced backward over his shoulder, and sure enough, Stuart was staring purposefully down at his phone as he followed them. Woody's head snapped back around, just as Stuart began to glance up.

Clearly, Stuart was in contact with someone else. Aiden's death had to do with more than just Stuart. *What Stuart had said to Aiden, something about what Aiden had been working for—*

Then Woody had an idea.

Casually, he unwrapped his bandage from around his finger, leaving it in a long strip mixed with blood from his wound. He ripped the tape quietly into two lengths. He would only have one chance to do this right. He looked over his shoulder again. Stuart was obviously typing something into his cell phone. He glanced at the moonlit path ahead for the right canvas. It was now or never.

Coming over a small crest, the trio walked into a loose field of decomposed granite. Woody glanced over his shoulder one last time, and then went for it. Being as discreet as possible, he dragged one foot as he walked forward to make a two-foot long indentation. Then, he rapidly placed his other foot and the first foot outside of that indentation and swished his feet together at intersecting angles to form a distinct arrow. At the point of this arrow, and at the same time as his feet were coming together, he dropped some of the bloody tape on the ground. The entire motion had taken only seconds and would look like Woody had just stumbled. They kept moving. With each passing moment he felt more and more confident that Stuart hadn't noticed. Now anyone attempting to follow them could see an arrow in the dirt with a bloody bandage at its head next to three distinct tread marks.

Hopefully.

27

ONE DB

Sunday, 11:13 p.m.

"**A**lex, are you there?" Jeffrey's voice crackled over the radio. Alexandra had been waiting for the other rangers at the open granite slab where Rick had instructed her to stay.

"Yeah, Jeffrey," she responded.

"I've got ten climbers here at the base of the climb and one male DB. Rick took off in the direction of a female scream we heard farther west. Have any more rangers made it up to you yet?"

"No, not yet... wait a second. Ah, yeah, now I see a few of them. Hold on, Jeffrey." Alexandra paused. "You said one male DB, and a scream?"

"Yeah. It looks like a climber fell while free soloing up Cathedral. At least, that's what we think. You said some of the others were almost to you?"

"Affirmative."

"Look, I know Rick told me to stay here," Jeffrey said, " but I don't want him out there tracking what could be a killer by himself. How many are in the group approaching you right now?"

"One, two, three. Looks like three," Alexandra responded.

"Leave one ranger with most of the gear there to wait for the rest of the team. Tell him to make for Budd Lake when more people arrive. Take the other two rangers and meet me at the base of Cathedral as fast as possible."

"Got it." Alexandra signed off and began waving at the three rangers approaching to hurry up.

28

TREAD MARKS

Sunday, 11:13 P.M.

A short distance from Aiden's body, Rick studied evidence of the disturbance he had just heard. There were tread marks in the decomposed granite surface. Two led to one area behind a boulder while all three led away from the area.

They can't be that far.

Rick followed the shoe prints west toward the main Yosemite Valley.

Homicide. He couldn't believe it. Yosemite claimed lives from time to time, but usually those of careless adventurers and inexperienced hikers. Homicide in the Park was infrequent if not outright rare. There was that husband who shoved his wife, Dolores Gray, off a cliff near the Wawona Tunnel in order to collect on numerous life insurance policies, but that was back in 1987.*

Why kill climbers? It was unnerving and way outside of the realm of his normal procedures: the reference to Muir, the collection of climbers, and the scream. *What is happening?*

Rick closed his eyes and brought himself back into the moment.

Tracking. Tracking was something Rick knew. It was logical, it was sequential, and he was good at it. He had learned the basics from his grandfather and then perfected the art in the endless wilderness of the Rocky Mountains in Wyoming. As he moved forward, occasional talus would obscure the trail, but on the other side, he would always find it again. *They can't be far ahead now.*

Just then, Rick came upon a sign that confirmed everything for him. It was an arrow in the decomposed granite soil with an unmistakable piece of athletic tape at its point—the type of tape climbers use to bandage their fingers and hands. *This is definitely the trail; definitely three people on this trail, one of them was smart enough to leave a sign.*

Rick picked up his radio. Before connecting to Jeffrey, he scanned the horizon.

"Damn." *Where the hell are they?*

"Jeffrey, are you there?"

"Yeah, Rick."

"I'm following tread marks due west of your location. What's your status? I'll need some backup here."

"One step ahead of you, Chief. Alex and I are on our way. Jason and Nate are back with the climbers at the DB."

"Great. Head directly for Cathedral Lakes. I'll wait where I am now. It's a large opening before the woods. Make it quick."

"Got it."

29

TIPPING POINT

Sunday, 11:21 P.M.

S tuart put his phone away. "Okay, now *jog.*"
They dug their toes into the dusty soil of Tuolumne
Meadow, moving forward, faster now, through the night.

"Why?" Joy spoke up. "Why kill Aiden, you asshole?"

Stuart snapped back, "This is bigger than just Aiden—or any of us. Now where the hell is that damned Muir Trail?"

"We should be just about to it," Woody responded.

"We'd better not miss it, young man."

Woody cringed at the remark. He didn't know if being helpful to Stuart was advantageous for Joy's and his situation or not, but he figured they would have more of a chance of running into people and possible avenues of escape on the trail rather than off of it.

"Why is it bigger?" Joy asked, cracking her knuckles. "What the fuck could possibly be gained by killing Aiden Watson?"

Woody looked over his shoulder at Joy. Rivulets of tears streaked through the granite dust that had settled on her cheeks.

Stuart didn't answer for a long time.

"Well... let's just say Aiden is—*a tipping point.*" Stuart measured his words as he jogged. These two youngsters weren't going to see the sunrise today, but he didn't feel like vocalizing the plan as he knew it. Doing so would somehow betray the trust of The Professor. Stuart did not want to violate his code even in this remote location and with these two disposables. *Although,* he thought, *The Professor has not exactly been forthright with me—why the fucking message?* Under the picture Stuart had just seen online, there was a cryptic posting saying something about Muir's Temple. Stuart pondered. *I thought Abigail's death was to appear accidental.*

Joy interrupted Stuart's thoughts. "Tipping point for *what?*"

Stuart put his doubts aside. "His death, well, his death will set certain things in motion. Those things, those—let's call them *justifications*—" Their hurried pace slowed as Stuart found his words. The crunch of granite pebbles punctuated the stillness of the evening.

"Once they have been established, then these justifications—established and reinforced—they will alter the course of—" Stuart paused again. "Yes, alter the full course of history. The entire ethic of conservation—it will never again be of value."

"So, you're implying the environment and—" Joy began.

Stuart snapped back, "That's enough!"

PICASSO

Sunday, 11:48 P.M.

Mojo Jackson checked the clock on her desktop computer—just before midnight. She had been wide-eyed, piecing together as much of the mystery around Abigail Edwards as she could for the past two hours. Her motivations were two-fold. First, she needed to make sure that her son couldn't be anywhere near what just happened and, judging from the timing of Woody's departure and when Abigail had her fall, she felt better. Second, she wanted to figure out what Abigail had been working on and where she had been prior to her death.

The blogs continued to fume over Abigail and that bizarre message coupled with her photograph. Of particular concern was the posting of some inflammatory calls to arms. Mojo had begun to notice a pattern. At intervals that seemed choreographed, posts would appear that demanded action. *To what end?* Mojo wondered. *The FBI must be salivating over all of this chatter.*

Mojo closed her eyes and stretched her arms and back, pressing her fingers down on her desk.

Since Operation Backfire, the FBI had not produced any noticeable ecoterrorist convictions for over five years. Quite the opposite Mojo thought, they had been bumbling one operation after another; after spending millions trying to frame one of the founders of Earth First! the operation yielded little more than a conviction for minor property damage.* There was also the bomb planted years before in an activist's car, which cost the agency over four million dollars in restitution after a court case showed it had framed and mistakenly crippled the activist.* And then there was the eighteen-year-old female contracted by the FBI to spy on a few radical activists; she ended up coercing them to commit some act of ecoterrorism in order to sleep with her. *Yeah, the FBI needs an unambiguous win.*

There's something strange going on with these posts. It couldn't be the FBI themselves, could it? Since September 11, 2001, the FBI had nearly quadrupled in manpower in order to identify and track down homegrown terrorism. Unfortunately, as Mojo wrote about in a few of her investigative pieces, that manpower did not necessarily draw a distinction between radical Islamic terror and radical environmental activism.

Mojo's head was swimming as she got up from her midnight electronic vigil. On her way to the hallway, she reached above her head and grabbed the old wooden Glulam beam that supported the opening between her study and the rest of the house. At only six feet nine inches off the floor, it was barely code-compliant and startled many visitors when they entered her little workspace. Mojo stretched upward and pressed her palms against the manufactured wood, relieving the pressure on her neck, arms, and shoulders.

Reaching down to scratch her Chesapeake Bay retriever's belly, Mojo completed her informal yoga and headed into the kitchen. Chessie, of course, got up to follow Mojo.

"What do you want, old girl?" Mojo chided her late-night

canine companion. "Do you miss Woody, too? Are you also going to *ground* him when he gets home, for like—*eternity*?"

The big old hunting dog cocked her head and looked up at Mojo.

"I know, I know, I shouldn't be that hard on him. He's just a kid."

Chessie's tail wagged expectantly.

"I know what you're looking for." Mojo laughed to herself. She knew she really shouldn't spoil the dog like this, but at this point, at almost fourteen years old, Chessie was a creature of habit.

"Oh, all right, here you go." After switching off her coffee pot, she reached above the refrigerator and grabbed a small Milk-Bone dog treat. Chessie bounced around on the kitchen floor, her nails scraping against the hardwood, until she responded to Mojo's raised palm and sat dutifully.

Mojo tossed the bone in the air, and Chessie grabbed it with a small spring to her right.

"Good girl," Mojo said, patting Chessie on top of her head.

After walking down the hallway to her room, Mojo couldn't resist checking the Internet one more time. The Apple tower whizzed out of sleep mode and the black screen flashed on. Mojo clicked on an Internet browser and pulled up the Earth First! blog, which she remembered had a number of particularly angry participants.

Let's see what's flying from the cuckoo's nest.

Immediately she saw a photo, and her brain registered it as another reference to Abigail and the ubiquitous photograph that had appeared earlier this afternoon, but when she looked at the photo's caption, the words she read did not match up: "Aiden Watson dead at the foot of Cathedral Peak. Aiden was a tireless supporter of environmental . . ."

Aiden... that's not Abigail.

Mojo scrolled back up the screen to the image she had glossed over. There, lit by numerous headlamps and surrounded by a forest of legs and shoes, was the dead body of another climber. This one had not fared as well as Abigail Edwards. Bones were broken, and blood was smeared all around in odd arcs and disconnected pools. The figure, while obviously human, was distorted and abstract as if Pablo Picasso himself had arranged the body.

Why are all these people gathered around? There's no message this time, just an inexplicable congregation of... mourners?... murderers?

Climbers. Yes, they all look like climbers, with—what did Woody call them?—approach shoes, and some of the pants have black smudges, just like Woody's pants often get from contact with climbing-shoe rubber. And then there's—

Mojo froze. Her heart cinched tight.

Those shoes, Mojo thought as she zoomed in on the photograph. They were bright and clean, incongruous with the other climbers' dusty attire, with thin red stripes and bright yellow laces on a backdrop of perforated white nylon. Mojo knew those ASICS shoes; they weren't hiking shoes, or approach shoes. These were running shoes.

Her pulse quickened as Mojo looked at the skinny, tan legs in the photograph extending out of rolled-up dark-khaki Prana pants, with long adolescent brown and blond hairs sticking out of them. Then the socks. They weren't hiking socks; they had the low-cut style associated with running. Mojo knew she had purchased those shoes less than two weeks ago at Famous Footwear. She absolutely knew...

Oh God... Woody!

31

MANURE

Sunday, 11:49 P.M.

They hiked in silence across moonlit fields of high alpine lupines and over fallen pine trees absorbing into the forest floor. The earth seemed in motion under Joy's feet, not the other way around; it spun and shifted keeping pace with her thoughts. Occasionally, she stumbled forward, tripping over the ground as they jogged ever onward. What Stuart had said was the ramblings of a madman. And if he was insane, if he believed that his cold-blooded crimes had some grand purpose, then she and Woody stood no chance of release.

Joy didn't feel sorry for herself. She didn't even think about herself. Instead, she thought about her sister, Jasmine. As much as she quarreled with her about the inane and the irrelevant, she cared about her eccentric older sibling. Their grandmother was getting older now and couldn't really be there to help either of them.

Even though she was younger, Joy always had her sister's back. Joy had ensured that her sister would graduate from high school, rather than flunk out just days before she was to receive her diploma. It was a senior project, the capstone that all California students in their final year of high school had to complete. Jasmine, already interested in medical marijuana, had somehow persuaded her advisor to allow her to do her senior project on setting up and running a successful dispensary. She had done a fair amount of research and had actually completed all of the required interviews and even gave an admirable defense of the practice at her critique. The problem was the paper. The principal, at the time, had a particular vendetta against Jasmine Cooper and had specifically requested to read the culminating work of Jasmine's high school experience in hopes of using its poor grammar, lack of evidence, and questionable legal claims as reason to hold Jasmine back from graduation. Unbeknownst to her sister, Joy had typed a second paper that gave a more complex and balanced consideration of the legality of marijuana for medical purposes. She quoted from professors and advocates of both positions, ultimately creating a twenty-eight page paper worthy of not just high school but easily acceptable at the collegiate level. She managed to exchange the papers in a folder marked "Senior Projects" that Jasmine's advisor had left on her desk.

"The trail is right there," Woody suddenly announced.

"Good," Stuart responded.

Joy looked up. Sure enough—there was the John Muir Trail, an unmistakable highway in the otherwise infinitely wild landscape. Every time she saw the trail, she couldn't help but be reminded of what Jasmine had called it: "the John *Manure* Trail," because so many horses and pack mules used it. Any hikers following its graded and maintained path were undoubtedly going to find the bottom of their shoes imbedded with the unavoidable excrement of these animals. "They want us to pack out our feces in little Ziploc bags, but they, like, let the horses shit all over the place," Jasmine would say. A sad smile turned the corners of Joy's mouth.

"Turn left, follow it, and pick up the pace," Stuart demanded. Woody and Joy did as instructed.

32

ASICS RUNNING SHOES

Sunday, 11:51 p.m.

Alexandra and Jeffrey ran. *Not the safest thing to do over questionable terrain, miles from any main road, and in the middle of the night,* Jeffrey thought to himself. At least the full moon was high enough now, enabling him to distinguish the contours of the land without his glasses.

Jeffrey managed to vocalize in between his labored exhalations. "He said... he'd be... in a clearing."

"There's one," Alexandra responded, charging ahead.

Over the next rise was a large field of loose dirt and pebbly granite remains. Alexandra and Jeffrey bounded over a few rocks and started into the field.

Jeffrey was secretly glad he ended up with Alexandra on this middle-of-the-night adventure. As horrific and bizarre as it all was, he now had the chance to spend more time with her and hopefully prove he could handle the drama and physical exertion. Jeffrey never considered himself a ladies' man. He was always the friend that girls relied on for camaraderie and lightening the mood. He had a couple of relationships in college, one with a photography professor, but he generally had slipped into the role of boy*friend* rather than *boy*friend when it came to relations with members of the opposite sex.

"There," said Alexandra. She veered off to the right in the direction of a solitary figure who was crouching and studying the ground.

Rick stood up and turned to greet his companions. "Thanks for hurrying," Rick said. "Let's keep moving." Rick spun on his toes and sped off at a faster pace toward the woods on the western side of the field. Jeffrey, hoping for a break, struggled to keep up.

"What were you examining?" Alexandra managed to ask.

Rick slowed his pace as they neared the woods, realizing that they all would need to have some energy when they encountered the owners of the three sets of footprints. "There was a signal, left by one of the three," Rick began. "Whichever one is wearing ASICS running shoes—left the signal. At first I thought, '*Great*, it's an arrow with some climber's tape.'" Rick paused. "Then, I studied it more closely. There was blood on the tape—maybe from a climbing accident."

"What do you think it means?" Alexandra asked as Jeffrey caught up with them.

"I'm not sure, Alex. But if one of the hostages is injured and being forced to run, well—" Rick raised his eyebrows and looked at Alexandra.

"Yeah, not good," Alexandra said.

33

HOLDING GROUND

Sunday, 11:55 P.M.

Woody was now desperate. Ever since hitting the John Muir Trail, Stuart demanded that they accelerate. Joy was tired. Woody knew he could carry on at a jog for many miles, even with his pack, but he could sense Joy wasn't going to be able keep this pace much longer. If she asked to stop, Stuart might be tempted to finish them off.

Fortunately, Joy kept moving.

Woody scanned the woods for something to use as a weapon, a distraction, or a means of escape. He continued to leave scraps of athletic tape, hoping someone would be tailing them. Woody figured they were moving at roughly a fourteen-minute-mile pace and whoever was following them—well, if anyone was following them at all—probably wasn't running.

There won't be a rescue.

The fact they were still alive probably had more to do with putting some distance between his last homicide, which he clearly wanted people to see, and where he would dispose of Woody and Joy.

No one is supposed to find our bodies.

It could happen, too. People slipped into rivers only to be smashed into indistinguishable fragments in the rapids or at the base of a waterfall.

They rounded a bend just before reaching Long Meadow. Soon they would be at Sunrise High Sierra Camp. Stuart might decide to make his move before the camp in order to avoid a potential run-in with another hiker or even a ranger.

Woody's thoughts looped in frantic circles. *What to do?* His eyes darted around, searching for ideas. He kept checking the woods, the meadow—*the trail!*

There, in the dirt, in successive and undulating steps, were the tracks of a large bear moving in the same direction they were heading. A chill shot through him as an idea—perhaps a crazy one—took shape; this could, just maybe, be the way to alter the equation with Stuart.

Woody had to catch himself from tripping as he studied the ground. The tracks looked fresh. They were on top of other hiking footprints. He knew that bears often used the same well-graded hiking paths intended for human use, especially when —*Is it possible? Yes.* Right alongside the large indentations left by the bear, there were other smaller prints—*two cubs.*

Last year Woody had done an exhaustive project on bear encounters, interviewing members of local law enforcement who had bear experience and members of the local Bear League who rounded up or scared off bears from residential neighborhoods.

Seven years ago, at eight years old, Woody had been charged by a black bear. He knew about their bluff charges to provoke a reaction and to answer a simple question: *predator or prey?* Rather than scream or run, Woody froze in abject and ineffable terror. Instead of averting his eyes and slowly backing away, as he later learned would have been the correct course of action, his gaze remained unshakably locked on the bear. Within two seconds, the bear had charged. The world shrank into an imaginary

alleyway inextricably connecting Woody with this creature as it
bounded toward him.

Woody stood still. The bear crashed to a stop about five feet
from him. He could feel the dirt and air pushed forward by the
beast as the mass and momentum of the animal came to a
screeching halt. The bear didn't rear up. It didn't roar. It just
sniffed the air, rolling its massive head up and down and side to
side. Then, as if the weight of his skull were the ultimate arbiter
of its decisions, the bear's body seemed to follow its head off and
to the right. It ambled with nonchalance away from the horrified
child.

He knew that bears have become almost desensitized to guns.
Since the restriction in bear hunting throughout most of the
western United States, bears no longer have a healthy fear of
humans, nor do they have an understanding that the loud bang
made by a gun is something that could kill them. They are used
to bear spray that rarely reaches them and also to annoyed RV
campers banging pots and pans together in a futile cacophony.
Bears generally are not shot at and don't appreciate the gravity of
what a man with a gun could mean.

Woody also understood a key piece of Yosemite trivia he had
researched during his science report. Despite the vast paranoia
surrounding bear encounters, despite the cottage industry
around bear sprays, bear repellents, and bear bells, and despite
all of the anxiety about the size and predatory nature of these
creatures, fear of bears in Yosemite National Park is largely, if not
wholly, unwarranted. The fear is unfounded because no one—
not one single tourist, ranger, climber, camper, rafter, or other
human visitor—has ever, in the recorded history of Yosemite
National Park, been killed by a bear. When Woody had first read
this fact, he refused to believe it. He searched numerous sources
and even inquired with Park Service employees directly, but
could find no evidence that any human life had ever been
brought to a close by a bear in Yosemite. This little known fact

gave him some confidence, but he didn't really want to be the one person to alter that statistic.*

As the trio moved further down the trail, Woody gradually began to separate himself from Joy and Stuart. He slowed and controlled his breathing as much as possible so that he could listen for the thick huff of a bear or the snapping of branches.

Long Meadow appeared to his right, clear and open, shining brightly in the moonlight. The trail continued. Woody was careful not to get too far ahead and checked over his shoulder to gauge the distance. Despite her fatigue, Joy persevered; she was strong. She was obviously exhausted, but her gaze was fixed and she was determined not to show weakness. Stuart, jogging along behind her, seemed preoccupied with his thoughts. His scraggly blond hair bounced in a measured rhythm as he moved.

At first Woody didn't see anything, he only sensed an ursine presence. He jogged a few steps farther and heard a crackling sound and a quick hearty rush of breath.

Woody's heart rate soared. All of his childhood feelings from his encounter years ago coursed through his veins until his entire body tingled with primal fear and anticipation. He had to calm his nerves; he had to think clearly—*animals sense fear.*

Then Woody saw her.

34

GAINING GROUND

Sunday, 11:56 P.M.

"There it is," Rick said.

Up ahead of them the John Muir Trail appeared awash in moonlight. In the forest Alexandra, Jeffrey, and Rick had to slow their pace so as not to lose the three tread marks and occasional strips of athletic tape. Rick was hopeful the people they were following would take the Muir Trail, which would mean the tracking could go faster.

Rick reached the trail first. "Looks like they paused here," he began, "but not for too long. Then, they started heading south-west on the trail this way; the ASICS shoes are still in front and the Vibram soles are still in the rear. And look at this." Rick moved a couple paces forward and knelt down, turning on his headlamp.

"What is it?" Alexandra asked.

"See how deep these prints become right here, and the spacing suddenly changes over there—and then there?"

"Yeah," exclaimed Jeffrey, out of breath and leaning over his knees.

"Well, Jeffrey... hmm, this is bad news for you, my young friend," Rick continued.

"Why's that?"

"Looks like they picked up the pace quite a bit, which means—"

"We need to do the same," said Alexandra.

"Marvelous," Jeffery said as he took a knee in the dirt.

Rick mussed Jeffrey's scraggly hair before crouching next to him to further examine the trail. He shifted his weight from one boot to the other and let out a slow exhalation. "I need you two to stick together. I'm faster than you, so I'll go ahead and try to figure out where they are and how best to approach them. I'll wait for you before confronting anyone. Remember, stay together." With that, Rick stood up, pulled the straps down tighter on his pack, and took off at a full run down the trail.

Alexandra and Jeffrey watched as the forest gradually enveloped their supervisor.

"Has he always been like this?" Alexandra asked as she started to hike.

"Funny you should ask," Jeffrey said. He swung his pack around in front of him and pulled out a small Ziploc bag with assorted peanut M&M'S, granola, dried fruit, and nuts. "I've worked with Rick for three years now and it seems odd to say it, but he—" Jeffrey caught his breath—"he actually has never been like this. He seems more—" he paused and took a small handful of his gorp and tossed it into his mouth midstride—"more, I don't know, just happy or something, right now. No, maybe not happy." Jeffrey handed the bag to Alexandra, who picked out three M&M'S, a couple of raisins, and a walnut before returning the trail mix to Jeffrey.

"Just *clearer*; know what I mean?" Jeffrey asked with his mouthful of goodies. He was thoroughly enjoying this opportunity to spend time with her.

"I think so," answered Alexandra. They hurried along in quiet contemplation for a moment, chewing on Jeffrey's homemade recipe. Alexandra seemed to ponder the assessment of Rick, her dark eyes growing distant. She pulled herself out of the daydream and ran her finger across an eyebrow. "We better pick up the pace. Thanks for the gorp, Jeffrey."

"Yeah." Jeffrey tossed the bag into his pack and started jogging down the trail. "You know the joke about gorp on the PCT?"

"No," Alexandra said, "just that the Pacific Crest Trail cuts through Yosemite and overlaps our John Muir Trail, for about twenty miles right here in Tuolumne."

"Well, the day hikers, like us you know," Jeffrey began, "bring some gorp on the trail."

"Or night hikers." Alexandra smiled.

"Right, sorry, or night hikers. They, you know, make up some gorp, just like I've got here and while they're hiking, they—" he caught his breath—"will be snacking on their mixture and will from time to time drop some gorp on the trail. Then they'll say something like, 'Damn, I dropped my gorp.'"

Jeffrey took a second to suck in more oxygen while catching back up to Alexandra. "The section hikers," he continued, "you know—the kind of guys doing a hundred-mile or so chunk of the PCT at a stretch—they wouldn't bring gorp with them, because it's just too heavy and impractical. They'll come plodding along and see the discarded gorp laying on the trail and say, 'Man, I wish I had some gorp.'"

"I can see where this is going," Alexandra said, looking over her shoulder.

"Yeah, then the through hikers on the PCT, the guys and gals doing the whole 2,650 miles, they'll come strolling along the trail at a good clip and zero right in on the gorp lying there in the dirt like some sort of, you know, predator drone. They'll pick it up and say, 'Oh sweet, some gorp!' Then they'll pop it in their mouths."

Alexandra chuckled, mostly to humor Jeffrey. "Yeah, that's in keeping with the character of through hikers I've seen. Tell you what, Jeffrey, you set the pace."

"Is that a challenge?"

"No, but if it will help you go faster, you can consider it as such."

Jeffrey blushed and accelerated, hoping to impress her.

35

ENCOUNTER

Midnight

There she is.

    Woody took a deep breath. *This is going to happen fast, very fast.*

He looked backward over his shoulder at Joy. Her eyes studied the trail. Woody wondered how he could possibly signal her. *Should I even?*

Joy looked up.

Woody nodded his head and winked, then turned to see that the bear had noticed them and was heading downhill off the trail. Beside her, barely perceptible in the moon shadows of trees and manzanita, were her two cubs. They dutifully followed her toward the cover of the meadow's undergrowth.

Good thing I do lots of sprint training, Woody considered. Like pistons firing into a drag-racer's cylinder, Woody's well-trained cross-country legs broke instantly into a sprint.

One.

Right.

Two.

Three.

His toes stabbed the ground and his knees fired upward with each split second.

Stuart looked up and managed to utter, "What the—?"

Woody veered to the right, off of the trail. He careened toward where he thought he could intersect the path of the bear as she descended with her cubs toward Long Meadow.

Grabbing Joy viciously by the arm, Stuart forced her into a run while reaching into his pocket to remove his handgun.

"Woody, watch out!" Joy screamed.

Woody was already ten rapid paces off the trail now and heading towards the bear. Hearing Joy's warning, he landed his left foot directly on the tree in front of him and sprang sideways, executing a snowboarder's rodeo flip. Barely touching his hand to the earth for balance, Woody continued barreling downhill.

He felt it before hearing anything—a searing pain in his left shoulder. Then, the explosion of the gunshot rang in his ear.

Despite the realization that he had just been shot, a toothy grin spread across Woody's face. He smiled not because Stuart had only grazed him, but because he knew that the bear upon which they all were rapidly descending now felt threatened. He hoped the bear would have to do something about it.

Five more strides. No second shot. Woody jockeyed to the left in the shadow of another massive tree. Three more strides. *Where is that b—*

Then, in this battle of species, the balance shifted. The scales of power tipped decidedly away from humans in favor of something else.

Woody dug his heels into the soil and came to a screeching halt, skidding in the dusty forest undergrowth. The mother bear appeared, erupting like some prehistoric force from out of a manzanita grove. She lurched forward at Woody and then raised herself to full height, shifting her gargantuan bulk onto her hind legs and expanding to a height of seven feet.

She was mad. Her jaws gaped and out came a resounding roar that trivialized any other conflict happening in Long Meadow that evening.

Woody refused to become immobilized like during his previous encounter. He dug his toes into the soft ground, pivoted to the right—away from the bear, the cubs, and Stuart—and sped down the hill toward the safety of Long Meadow, charging head-long into the tall grasses, then keeping his body low to the ground as he moved forward.

More shots rang through the evening stillness.

Focus on the bear, Stuart. Woody didn't know a lot about guns, but he knew from his science report that bears generally don't go down with a few shots from a handgun. He also guessed that Stuart would run out of bullets if he kept firing like he was. Woody stopped heading toward the meadow and doubled back on his previous path, keeping well below the trail. He moved silently on his hands and feet. It didn't look like the bullet had hit anything besides skin and surface tissue, but the wound stung and was bleeding down his arm.

The mother bear had come down onto all fours and her voice had again filled the night with loud growls of anger. Woody paused behind a fallen fir tree to see what would happen next. He hoped that Stuart would become so preoccupied with the bear that Joy would have a chance to escape as well. He hoped that the bear would finish this. Would finish Stuart. He hoped that he could find a way to connect again with Joy.

Woody felt around and grabbed a small, pointed stone at his feet. *What good will a damn rock be against either Stuart and his gun or an enraged mother bear?* he mused.

Suddenly above him, the mama bear charged, likely toward Stuart—and Joy. *Jesus, she's fast*, thought Woody as he cautiously made his way back up the hill toward them.

Stuart held Joy with his left hand and the gun with his right. He took aim again and fired repeatedly. The bear kept moving, accelerating even, unaffected by the barrage of bullets. The ground beneath her exploded in a cloud of pine needles, dry earth, and decaying bark as the mother bear tore through the distance.

Stuart let go of Joy and put both hands on the gun.

Please, Joy, run. Now! Run!

For a moment, Joy seemed frozen in shock and fear. Woody was about to yell at her to move when he saw the flash of her hair tossing and, just like that, Joy was dashing directly up the hillside above the trail, away from Stuart and the charging bear.

Stuart only had moments to decide. He turned and aimed toward Joy. Woody panicked. Leaping to his feet, he desperately hurled the rock at Stuart. The small chunk of granite arched through the air and past Stuart as he took aim.

Please, no! Joy was only ten yards away, an easy shot. Woody waited in agony, but nothing happened. No gunshot. The rock had missed.

He must be out of ammo, Woody thought.

Stuart looked distractedly at his gun, and then, his face contorted in rage, turned toward Woody, who was now fully visible. The bear was nearly on Stuart now; he spun and bolted away from the bear, running as fast as he could in the direction from which they had come.

Crossing the trail, Woody dropped his pack as he tore off up the hill, slashing through branches and scrambling over boulders, heading in the direction that he saw Joy run. He found her huddled behind a fallen tree.

"Is she following us?" Woody asked. "The bear?!"

"No. She's got ahold of a bag or something in the trail and—"

"Let's keep moving," Woody said. "I'm faster. Give me your pack."

Joy turned and threw her pack at Woody, who caught it midstride and slung it over his shoulder. They raced up the hill, through manzanita bushes and around logs, crashing upward.

At one point, Woody turned back to glance down in the direction from which they had come.

Darkness, quiet.

Still they ran—the farther, the better. After many non-stop minutes of running uphill, of heart-pounding scrambling through the forest, they paused. Woody turned and motioned for Joy to close ranks. They made their way to a spot near a ridge top under the cover and darkness of an overhanging granite boulder.

Woody pulled Joy down and they waited for their breathing and heart rate to lessen, scrutinizing the forest for any sign of movement. Woody's heart felt like it would punch a hole through his rib cage. The adrenaline coursing through his body was unlike anything he had ever experienced.

After a period of silence, Joy started to crack her knuckles. The sound of her popping cartilage and bone was like a lightning clap compared to the quiet vigil they had been keeping, so she clamped her other hand down over her fingers. "I feel bad for that bear," she whispered.

"I know," Woody replied.

They leaned into each other.

"Do you think she'll be all right?"

"I think so but, um, it's hard to say."

"Stuart probably landed quite a few of those shots."

"Yeah."

They sat in silence for a while longer. The moon had reached a place of prominence in the evening sky, and from their hillside vantage point, Long Meadow seemed to pulse with cool and airy colors as the shifting grasses twinkled in and out of the moonlight.

Breathing deeply, Woody tried to relax so he could hear the evening sounds with greater accuracy. Their sweat had cooled and was chilling their bodies. Woody put his arm around Joy's shoulders, and they huddled closer for warmth, listening to the impenetrable stillness of the night.

"So now what?" Joy whispered, "Stuart has to be looking for us."

"I haven't heard anything. Have you?"

"No."

They remained silent for another minute, their eyes scanning the hillside below, their ears tuning in to the slightest groan and motion in the forest as occasional gusts of wind stirred the trees.

At last Woody spoke. "We need to avoid him, get back to civilization, and tell the authorities what we saw and what happened."

"We could head toward the main valley, but Stuart was going that way. Also, being on a trail might not be the best idea right now," Joy offered. "I could tell you which direction north is, but getting out of here, well—"

"I think I know where we are. But it might make more sense to, you know, stay hidden—at least until daylight." Woody brushed his hair out of his face and looked at Joy. "Are you all right?"

"Yeah, I'm better now. What about you?"

"I'm fine."

"You're bleeding, aren't you?"

Woody felt the tear in his shirt at his shoulder. "It seems to have stopped."

Their foreheads were touching now. Woody and Joy were exhausted, physically, mentally, and emotionally. The warmth between their bodies felt good. They leaned in closer.

Joy looked up at Woody. His brow was tight in concentration. His eyes scanned the high alpine landscape. Joy reached up and put her hand on Woody's cheek and tilted his chin toward her, preparing to kiss him. In doing so, she saw something. "Hey! What's that?" Joy practically shouted into Woody's mouth. "Down there. Look in the valley. See that? Stuart wasn't using a flashlight with a powerful beam like that."

Woody hesitated.

"No. Woody, look over there." Joy turned Woody's head.

"Yeah, um, I see. There are three of them. That can't be—no —there's no way that is Stuart," Woody acknowledged.

Far below them on the Muir Trail, or at least what they presumed was the Muir Trail, were three lights moving and circling, pointing at each other and then circling around again on the ground.

"It has to be three people at least," Joy said.

"What should we do?" Woody asked.

"Let's get back down there."

"But Joy, hold on. What if it's Stuart trying to trick us? Or what if it's friends or like, um, partners of Stuart?"

"That's not logical. If he had accomplices, they'd have been with him earlier."

"Yeah, I agree, but let's not go screaming and running down the hill."

"Yeah... you're right."

They got up and slowly started making their way down the hillside, stopping and crouching behind trees and downed logs to check their surroundings.

As they got closer, they could hear voices. One of the voices definitely belonged to a woman and the other two were men. Not one of them resembled Stuart in the slightest.

Woody pulled Joy down next to him near a growth of manzanita bushes where they studied the three figures.

There was a newfound physical closeness between them. Joy rubbed her knuckles in Woody's upturned palm. They crouched hip to hip and used each other's weight to remain steady as they inspected the three people walking around below them. These people had a similarity. They weren't climbers though. Was it a uniform that they were all wearing? Or was it the way that they conducted themselves? They definitely seemed to be studying the ground, looking at tracks. Then, Woody saw it.

"Hey, check that out," Woody said, getting excited. "The larger one—he had it in his hand, and then when he stood up, he put it on his head. Do you see it...the hat?"

"That's not just any hat, is it?" Joy was getting excited, too. "That's a ranger's hat."

"Do you think?"

"We're here! Over here!" Joy sprang up and began running down the hillside toward the voices, waving her arms over her head.

Woody stood up, shrugged his shoulders and jogged after her.

36

DAMN

Monday, 12:20 A.M.

"**D**amn!" Stuart said aloud.

The earth sped by under his feet even faster than before. At least now he didn't need to deal with depositing bodies upstream of Nevada Falls. Just the thought of hiking that far with the kids was too tiresome to bear. If he could have left the bodies elsewhere, that would have been preferable, but they weren't part of the plan and needed to vanish.

Damn! It's not like they could have stopped the forces in motion anyway, Stuart thought. *And now, they won't slow me down.*

That, and there was the matter of his identity—Stuart, the climber with the bleached goatee. Soon, he wouldn't have to worry about that anymore either, and identifying him would be almost impossible.

Stuart had been hiking just off the trail and bushwhacked his way further out of sight and skirted Sunrise High Sierra Camp.

It was not the time to run into anyone else. A smile spread across Stuart's face as he realized the rest of his actions—the terror-provoking objectives that remained—none of them required more than superficial interaction with others.

He looked over at the backcountry camp. A few headlamps roamed around in the darkness surrounding the white army tents. Probably, people had heard the gunshots and were debating what it might have been. Stuart did not want anyone seeing him or the direction he was heading. He switched off his headlamp and slowed his pace through the forest, relying completely on the light of the moon. He hiked like this for another twenty minutes, in and out of moonlit patches beneath the forest canopy, weaving his way through the night.

Regaining the trail, Stuart checked his phone—still no reception.

"Damn."

He would have to report directly to The Professor soon. No problem. They had a plan for this. He was on his way now.

Stuart's long, shaggy hair seemed one beat behind him as he started again to jog toward Little Yosemite Valley.

Where had that bear come from?

That kid—Woody or something, that was some nerve. Stuart couldn't help himself; angry as he was, he had to hand it to the kid. That stunt was something he might have tried in similar circumstances. *Creative.* That's what his commanding officer had said about Stuart's tactics in Iraq. Stuart and a few others would go out at night in Baghdad, dressed in full head-to-toe robes that concealed their weaponry. They would hot-wire vehicles and complete missions, apprehend members on the Al-Qaeda deck of cards, and conduct reconnaissance in secret. Stuart was famous. He was a machine. He had been on a different plane than his fellow soldiers back then, back before he was let go—discharged.

Thirsty, Stuart loosened the straps on his pack as he slowed his pace and swung the bag around in front of him. Being careful not to trip on a log or rock, Stuart opened the bag and reached in for his topo map of the area. He still had about four or five miles to go, and his last real stream crossing looked to be about one mile ahead. *Perfect,* Stuart thought.

He tossed the bag back around, cinched it, and picked up the pace.

WE'LL FIND HIM

Monday, 12:30 a.m.

Mojo pulled her late husband's trusty 1979 Jeep CJ-7, named Rusty, into the driveway of her best friend, Rosa Martinez. Before driving over to her friend's house, Mojo had called down to the Yosemite ranger's office, but wasn't quite sure what to say.

Did they know about the dead climbers?

They weren't at liberty to say, but there was an ongoing investigation and search and rescue resources had been mobilized.

"Look, I'm worried about my son. Based on what I saw from a photo online, I think he might be mixed up in some of this. He's just fifteen, and he's been hanging out with a bunch of—"

"Ma'am," the voice on the other line interrupted. "What is your son's name?"

"Woody Jackson."

"Do you know where he was going in Yosemite?"

"No, just that he was climbing—at least—I think he was climbing."

"What does your son look like?"

Mojo gave the rangers information about Woody's appearance and then described the girls that she suspected Woody was traveling with as best as she could. She asked if they had any information about the deaths in the Park, but the person she was speaking with couldn't volunteer anything further than she already knew. Frustrated, Mojo had decided to take matters into her own hands and drive down to Yosemite herself. Rosa agreed to come with her, despite the crazy hour of night and peculiar conditions.

Mojo was about to turn off the motor and go to the front door when the house-to-garage door creaked open and out walked Rosa. She was overly dressed and heavily-equipped. Sporting a slim-fitting down jacket and stylish backcountry hat, Rosa toted a large hiking pack filled to capacity with much more than their little trip would warrant. Additionally, she had a cooler and another bag. Mojo shook her head as she pulled the emergency brake and left the old Jeep idling.

"*Solamente una noche,*" Mojo quipped in her friend's native language.

"*Sí, sí,*" Rosa responded, smiling at her friend. "You know me."

"*Está bien.*" Mojo opened the rear window of the Jeep and shifted a few things around to make room for Rosa's supplies. "How did you get this packed so quickly?"

"I usually keep my camping things together, you know, just in case."

"Just in case of what?" Mojo shoved the huge duffle more securely in place and smiled at Rosa.

"*Siempre estoy lista para cualquiera—*at the drop of a hat."

"Good. I'm glad one of us is prepared."

They got in, and Mojo backed out of the driveway.

The two friends had gotten to know each other through the

bilingual education program run by the school district. Trained as a school psychologist, Rosa was the elementary school's counselor, and Mojo had done a great deal of volunteering while Woody was young.

"Thanks for coming with me on this nutty mission, by the way," Mojo said as she pulled onto the main road.

"*No hay problema*, but why Yosemite?"

"Well, Woody lied to me." Mojo let the simple answer sit in the car for a moment.

Rosa knew Mojo well enough not to take the bait and just stared at her, as if to say, "go on."

"And there are freaky things going on in Yosemite involving climbers right now—" Mojo paused. "I know that two climbers were killed during the last ten hours and I—"

"*¿Es verdad?* Two dead climbers? *¡Oh, Dios mío!*"

"I'm worried about Woody."

"We'll find him."

Mojo's jeep, Rusty, which had been her husband's favorite mode of transport, rolled along the empty streets and eventually onto the desolate Highway 395 heading south. The Jeep could only go so fast, and these quiet expanses of highway seemed all-consuming.

Rosa watched as Mojo dug her fingernails in the steering wheel and ground her teeth. Woody was all she had left and it was clear that her friend could think of little else.

"So... *mi amiga*," Rosa tried to break the tension. "Tell me about *la controversia de Yosemite*."

"Oh, right." Mojo blinked her eyes and shook her head. "There's some bad stuff going on right now that defies logic...."

"*¿Qué?*"

"Well, the only similarity as far as I can tell between the two climbers who died was their connection to Hetch Hetchy."

"*¿Qué es Hetch Hetchy?*" Rosa asked.

"It's a valley, named like Yosemite by the native people, the

Ahwahnechees, who lived in the Park before it was a national park."

"¿*Los Mexicanos no estaban allí primero?*" Rosa joked.

"Sorry, *mi amiga*, the Native Americans were first."

They both laughed.

"Anyway," Mojo continued, "Hetch Hetchy means 'tall grasses,' or something having to do with grass, not pot, but actual grass —like in your yard."

"Okay, Mojo. I got it."

"Apparently, it was so beautiful in its time that John Muir used to say if you took all the people who came to see Yosemite Valley to Hetch Hetchy instead, only a small fraction, like five percent, would know the difference. He said something like they'd see graceful waterfalls and massive stone edifices set in a beautiful high alpine meadow and think they'd seen Yosemite Valley, when in fact they were in the next canyon north."

"What do you mean it *was* so beautiful? Can't we still go there now?"

"That's exactly the problem, Rosa," Mojo said. "You see, Hetch Hetchy is no longer the place of tall grasses; it's a lake."

"¿*Es un lago?*"

"*Sí.* Back in, I think 1913, right before Muir's death, Congress passed a law, the Raker—or other garden tool act—I'm not sure. But basically, it gave the city of San Francisco the right to put a dam in Yosemite, to actually dam a national park."*

"No!"

"*Sí, es verdad.*"

"No wonder Muir died."

"Yeah, that would break my heart, too."

"But isn't that illegal?" Rosa asked.

"The way I remember it, Yosemite hadn't become a national park, or more precisely, the National Parks Act wasn't passed until a few years after that Rake and Shovel Act. So the dam was already, you know, in the works."

"Why would people want to do that?"

"Hmm... well, as I understand it, the dam had a lot to do with water needs in the Bay Area and specifically in San Francisco; as well as that big earthquake in 1906 that you always hear about, which caused an even bigger citywide fire for which the fire department lacked adequate water and water pressure to battle."

"Oh, necesitaban más agua."

"Actually no. That was a total B.S. scam to fool voters. The fires had more to do with broken gas mains and broken distribution pipes for water." [*]

"So they had enough water?"

"Affirmative. They just didn't have a way to get to it."

"Damn."

"Exactly... a *damn dam*. So the dam was justified to prevent further loss of life and property in the event of a future quake in San Francisco.[*] Then, like two years after the dam was finished, the City of San Francisco did some shady deal with WP&G, muddling the ownership of the dam, its water, and its power, all of which were supposed to be public property as per the shoveling shit and plowing cow dung Act."

"No way," Rosa said.

"Yeah. The Supreme Court even jumped in and tried to put the smackdown on all the monkey business going on. They ruled that what WP&G and the city were doing was straight-up illegal."

"Wow, the Supreme Court?" Rosa smiled egging Mojo on to one of her usual *rant and rolls* as she had once described them.

"*Sí.* Yosemite has quite the checkered history, lots of big names, you know. Abe Lincoln set the original land aside. John Muir and the Sierra Club got their start fighting for Yosemite. It's basically the reason we even have environmentalism.[*] And yes, even the big boys in black robes, the Supreme Court of the United States ruled—I think it was in 1939—that WP&G couldn't profit from public power, from public water, in a public park, for the public's sake.[*]

"But even then, it was a freaking decade before the water and power from Yosemite National Park stopped making the rich richer, but—" * Mojo hesitated, which was not normal for her in these circumstances.

"¿Qué es?"

"Well, something might be coming to light about the compliance with the Supreme Court decision. I don't actually know for sure, but there have been a flurry of investigations and closed-door discussions in Sacramento lately, between the governor's office, some power company executives, and some federal judges. Everyone is really tight-lipped. I've been trying to figure out what is happening, but no one will talk."

They sat in silence for a while. The old Jeep was noisy and a little bit cold. Rosa zipped her coat up and leaned forward, stretching her back. "But what does any of that have to do with dead climbers?" Rosa asked.

"Ay, there's the rub," Mojo said. "And truthfully, I'm not sure yet. I think it's not so much that Abigail and Aiden were climbers."

"Then, what?"

"They were also activists."

38

CLEARING

Monday, 12:33 A.M.

Despite Woody's insistence that the blood congealed on his hand and shoulder was no big deal, Rick had Alex clean and bandage his wounds. He then prompted Joy to recount the evening's events. Reluctantly, she divulged that they had free soloed, everything she knew about Aiden's death, how they were captured, and the encounter with the bear.

"Damn, girlfriend," Alex commented while stowing the first aid gear.

"So, where do you think he was heading?" Rick asked when Joy was finished.

Woody spoke up. "I think he was taking us toward the main valley, at least, um, we were going down the JMT toward the valley. But it felt like he had something else in mind, you know, before getting there."

"What do you mean?" Alexandra asked.

"I'm not sure. He... read a text message and then sent one, I think. And then read another one, and then, I'm pretty sure he wrote this long text message while we were hiking; at least... he was working at it for a while, but I don't think he was able to send it."

"He could probably send it from the valley," said Rick.

"Or another high point between here and there," added Jeffrey.

"Or back in Tuolumne Meadows," Alexandra said.

"Do you suppose he's texting, you know, someone who wanted Aiden dead?" Woody asked.

"That would make sense," Alexandra responded.

They pondered Woody's question as filtered moonlight streaked through the canopy, laying a patchwork of illumination on the pine needles and red-brown earth.

"Oh... Woody, this must be your pack," Jeffrey said, handing over a soggy-looking daypack. "Feeding the wildlife, huh?"

"Yeah, um, sorry about that. *Eww...* looks like my gear is okay, but that's, uh, pretty gross." Woody inspected the pack he had dropped for the bears. Surprisingly, it was not ripped but pulled open at the zipper and covered in bear saliva. Woody rubbed it in the dirt and pine needles to clean it off and inspected his cordelette and other clothing and gear for damage.

"I'm going to try to locate his tread marks farther down the Muir trail. It looks like you were Mr. ASICS," Rick said, pointing at Woody. "And you had that funny foreign tread." Rick pointed at Joy. "So what's left are the Vibram soles."

"It's too bad so many hikers in the backcountry have Vibram soles," Jeffrey said.

Rick spoke again. "It's still closer to Tuolumne Meadows from where we are now. Alex, take Woody and Joy back to the meadows. Jeffrey, you're coming with me."

"Wait a minute, Rick," Alexandra said. "What if you're wrong? What if this Stuart guy is behind us on the trail? Shouldn't we stay together?"

"I think she's right, Chief," Jeffrey added. "And, just for the record—" Jeffrey paused to make sure he had everyone's attention. "It's not that I don't want to be the *only* one to have to keep up with you; I'm just saying, you know, staying together makes more sense."

Rick laughed and shook his head at Jeffrey.

"One other thought," Joy added. "How are you guys going to identify Stuart when you find him? Woody and I know what he looks like. You... um, don't."

"Shit. That's a good point," Jeffery said.

Rick clenched his fists and grunted. Turning to Woody and Joy, he said, "I know you've had a rough night, but—"

"We're okay," Joy interrupted him and glanced at Woody, who nodded agreement.

"All right then," Rick said. "We ought to keep moving. Are we all ready?"

"Almost," Joy said. "I'd... I'd really like to contact my sister, just to let her know I'm all right. She's with the other climbers."

"Of course." Rick picked up his radio from his pack, put the device on speaker, and made a call. "David, are you there?"

There was a pause of several seconds and then, "Yeah, Rick, we've got everyone out by Budd Lake. I think it's the lot of them."

"Nice work, David. We've got two kids, Woody and Joy. We're trailing the perp, a guy by the name of Stuart, toward Sunrise Camp. Pass this up the chain of command. Send some other personnel after us."

"Roger that."

"Send available rangers in from all trailheads: Tenaya Lake, Glacier Point, and the Valley. We need to find this guy."

"Got it."

"And David, one of the kids with us, Joy, would like to speak with her sister. Is—" Rick paused and covered the speaker grill with his hand. "Joy, what's your sister's name?"

"Jasmine."

"Joy would like to speak with Jasmine. Is she there?"

"Let me go look for her."

After another minute of waiting and overhearing bits of David's questions, the speaker on Rick's phone came to life: "Someone named Joy wants to talk to you."

"Joy! Oh my fucking God! Are you all right?" Jasmine blurted out.

"Yes." Joy and everyone else on the trail laughed. Jasmine was definitely nothing like her sister. "I'm fine now."

"Oh, thank sweet baby Jesus. I was, like, totally insane with worry—and Woody?"

"He's okay—mostly. We're with the rangers. Stuart is still out there, but we're safe."

"That son of a bitch! Him and his little lily-white sissy-ass goatee. He's the one who tried to hurt you?"

"Listen, Jasmine. Yes, he's responsible for Aiden too. We'll tell you all about it late—"

"Where are you? I'm coming there, like, right freak'n now."

"Hold on. We actually have to keep moving, uh, with the rangers. You can probably meet us in the main valley in the morning."

"No Joy. It's seems super dangerous. We should be together."

"Jasmine, we're safe. The rangers are here, and we'll stick with them. We're fine." Joy's voice seemed to have a calming effect on her sister. "Besides, Jaz, we're like miles from you now and we'll be okay." There was a long pause in the conversation.

"All right, I'm just glad you're safe."

"Thanks. Me too. I'll see you soon," Joy responded.

Rick turned the phone away from Joy, "David, are you still there?"

"Yeah, boss."

"Go ahead and take everyone back to the station in Tuolumne. Make sure you get all of Jasmine's information, and then have Dave follow her down to the valley in the Yukon I left at the Muir Trailhead. Everyone else stays."

Jasmine interrupted just as David was going to respond. "What about Rebecca? She's with me, yo."

"Fine, Rebecca too, but that's it. Everyone else stays."

"Got it, boss."

Rick shook his head and put the radio away. "That's some sister you've got there," he said to Joy.

"Uh... thanks." Joy's cheeks flushed.

Rick shouldered his backpack. "All right crew, let's hit the road."

The forest seemed to grow dense as the five hikers started westward on the trail. The excitement of the past few hours had morphed into a quiet exhaustion for Rick and his followers. Sweat began to turn cold, and despite how hard they hiked, a chill incrementally worked its way over their bodies. Compounding this feeling was the increasing wind gusting in eastward bursts, striking them on their chests and faces.

When they reached Sunrise High Sierra Camp, they were thrilled to see a small but obvious campfire crackling in one of the designated fire pits. Without asking permission or debating the idea, all five of them headed straight toward the fire and promptly began rotating their bodies like shish kebabs on vertical skewers.

"Rick, that you?" A man in a Park Service uniform with a noticeable country gait approached.

"Hey, Hayduke. It's good to see you," Rick responded.

"What were them gunshots all about?" Hayduke had joined the fire-lit circle. A questioning look swept over his stern features as he inspected Woody and Joy.

"We're tracking someone, a homicide suspect. This is Woody and Joy, I believe you know Jeffrey here, and this is Alexandra."

"Good to meet y'all." Hayduke tipped his hat to people as Rick introduced them, but gave a particularly indulgent nod to Alexandra.

"Have you seen anyone come through camp since the gunshots?" Rick asked.

"Nope, definitely not. And I've been looking, too," Hayduke added. "Right after them shots, quite a few people were out of their tents and all worked up. I got everyone into the mess hall here." He gestured over his shoulder at the tent about twenty yards away. "They're all packed in there like sardines. I lit this fire here and have been keeping watch on the trail and, well, there ain't much to tell. No hikers, no nothing." Hayduke shrugged his shoulders, then added, "Hey, do y'all want some hot cocoa? We made this huge pot and—"

"Yes," Joy, Alexandra, Jeffrey and Woody all said.

"All right then. Can I get a hand?"

Joy jumped up and followed Hayduke toward the mess hall.

"Well thanks, little lady," he said while unconsciously tipping his hat. Joy just smiled.

Rick stared into the fire, watching it dance in and out around the logs and dead wood. The warmth felt good, and he was glad for the kids to have a chance to rest and relax, but wished he felt more confident about their present course.

"What do you think, Chief?" Jeffrey asked.

"It's not good, Jeffrey. We should have seen those tracks by now. I guess he could've left the trail, but that's not exactly an easy thing to do, especially at night, unless, well, unless you are really familiar with the area."

"Do you think we should head back the other way?" Jeffrey asked.

"I'm not sure," Rick responded.

Joy and Hayduke arrived back at the fire with a bunch of cups, a sizable ladle, and a large industrial-size cooking pot filled halfway with steaming hot liquid. Joy filled cups and handed them to Hayduke, who distributed the chocolate around the fire with a touch of southern hospitality.

"What's that for?" Hayduke asked Alexandra, who was unfolding a little red straw from the breast pocket of her uniform.

"The drink. I don't like to let sugar sit on my teeth," she said as she inserted the small coffee stirrer into the hot liquid.

There was an awkward pause until Jeffrey spoke up. "Hey, Woody. You said Stuart was communicating something while you were hiking, right?"

"Yeah."

"Do you think he might have been communicating about where he was going?"

"Could be."

Jeffrey took a sip of his hot chocolate. "Well, I know we can't see what Stuart communicated specifically, but we figured out he was going to be at Cathedral Peak by deciphering a message online, so it's worth a shot to try again."

"But how are we going to get online?" Woody asked.

Jeffrey smiled. "Alex, you wouldn't mind if we used that fancy satellite phone of yours, would you?"

"Of course not." Alexandra opened up her backpack and pulled out a small device. Before handing it to Jeffrey, she said, "Just let me clean up something I was working on."

Jeffrey took the phone from Alexandra and quickly navigated to the same blog site he was on previously. As he did so, Woody and Joy gathered around behind him to examine the small screen. "Here's the image of Abigail Edwards and the message we saw earlier about Muir's temple," Jeffrey began.

"'Here lies Muir's mountain temple?'" Woody asked, reading the odd phrase from the text below the image of Abigail.

"That's right. When we heard about an illegal campfire by Budd Lake and after having read this message, we put two and two together. Budd Lake is near Cathedral Peak, which could be considered, 'Muir's temple,'" Jeffrey added. "You see, we headed up to Cathedral and, sure enough, we found you, but that's not all. On the way to the Tuolumne Meadows, I researched a bit more and found these weird cryptic messages that kept appearing on the blog sites. They seemed to come from different sources, but they were all nonsensical, like this one, posted by someone calling himself Adams Ansel; it just says 'Yosemite.' And then this other one about 'lithe churches' posted by someone just calling themselves 'Mad,' and then a bunch of stuff about some sort of 'holy temple.'"

"What is most recent?" Joy interrupted.

"Right." Jeffrey refreshed the blog and, to everyone's surprise, there was Aiden, or rather what was left of Aiden, surrounded by a group of spectators, visible only by their legs and shoes.

"Joy, that's you over there. Look. Those are your pants," Woody said.

"Huh." Joy cocked her head to the side. "The person who took this had to have been directly across the circle from us. Who was that?" Joy asked.

"Stuart," Woody said. "He must have taken it while our head-lamps were shining down on Aiden.

"So Stuart took this picture and then posted it online around the time he was holding you captive?" Rick had joined the group now.

"It certainly looks that way," Alexandra said.

"Did he post anything in writing, like last time?" Rick asked.

Jeffrey scrolled down on the screen and there, sure enough, was another cryptic message. The poster's name was "Adams Ansel," and the post read: "a secreting twirl norm."

"Now that doesn't make any sense," Jeffrey immediately said. "I mean, there's no reference to any feature or landmark in Yosemite at all there."

"Hmm, no Muir, no religious talk," Rick said.

"Is that what we're supposed to be looking for?" Alexandra asked.

No one answered. They sat for a moment staring at the text.

Joy stretched her hair back into a tighter ponytail, pursing her lips and systematically cracking each one of the knuckles on her left hand. Suddenly, she exclaimed, "It's an anagram! Of course it is. It's too weird not to be an anagram. Who was the poster? Adams Ansel? Well, that tells you that it's an anagram right there; he's reversed the name. 'A secreting twirl norm,' has to do with Ansel Adams."

"You're right." Jeffrey was excited now, too. "You think it's an Ansel Adams photograph?"

Joy tilted her head back and mouthed the words to herself. *A secreting twirl norm.*

Joy stood up and walked toward the fire. "Twirl norm—secreting—twirl—norm." She smiled and turned to the group. "Oh yeah, it's a photograph. Just think about the word 'norm.' Listen to it, *norm*. What does it sound like?"

"Norm?" Woody repeated.

Rick chuckled. This would be the first time his art interests would ever help him professionally. "I get it—storm. *Norm* sounds like *storm.*"

"Of course." Jeffrey was already navigating away from the page to Google images. "And what's Ansel's most famous photograph? *Clearing Winter Storm*," he said.

Nods of recognition circled the group as one by one each person understood the anagram could be transcribed as Ansel Adams's *Clearing Winter Storm*, that is, each person except Hayduke.

"What's, uh, *Clearing Winter Storm*?" Hayduke bashfully inquired.

"Here, check this out." Jeffrey turned the small screen toward Hayduke, who had gotten up to have a look.

"*Clearing Winter Storm* was arguably Ansel Adams's most famous work. It certainly was his most influential." Rick said. "It's, you know, the quintessential Yosemite view from the Wawona Tunnel, looking out toward Yosemite Valley. But different; it's not taken in early spring with waterfalls all going, it's a more subtle, elemental capturing of the simultaneously permanent and fleeting nature of the valley."

Everyone looked at Rick.

"Way to *geek out* on us, boss," Jeffery said.

"Yeah...the image was the cover photo on his best-selling photography book," Rick continued. "It was gifted as an enlarged print to President Ford, and it was instrumental in getting financial support for environmental conservation, specifically protecting Yosemite and supporting the Sierra Club."

"Yeah, I've seen that one before," said Hayduke. "It's real nice. But how's that gonna help you find this guy y'all are looking for?"

No one answered.

"That can't be it," Jeffrey said.

Joy gathered around behind Jeffrey along with Alex. The three of them stared into the little screen, hoping to glean some other message from the photograph. They looked at Bridal Veil Fall, at the mist surrounding El Capitan, and the massive trees in the foreground, but saw nothing else that would clue them in to where they were supposed to be heading.

The forest surrounding the camp seemed unwelcoming and oppressively dark when juxtaposed with the campfire. Rick kept running the images and messages through his mind, trying to establish some other connection or explanation.

Alexandra stretched her arms above her head and yawned saying, "It's getting late."

"You know, there's plenty of room in—" Hayduke began.

"Wait a minute," Joy interrupted.

"No, really, it's plenty cozy in—"

"Sorry, Hayduke, I think I figured it out."

"Really?" Jeffrey said.

"Yeah, Jeffrey, you said a few minutes ago that one of the other weird posts you read was from someone calling themselves Adams Ansel, right?"

"Yeah."

"And what did that post say?"

"Just one word: Yosemite," Jeffrey answered.

"Right." Joy paced next to the fire. She had the second knuckle of her right forefinger at her chin and occasionally bit down into it as she thought. "So, 'Yosemite,' right? Now, if we apply or assume that same anagrammatic rule that we just used to figure out *Clearing Winter Storm*, if we use that same rule on the earlier posting of 'Yosemite,' I think we can get the word 'omit' or 'omits,' and I think the rest of the letters will give us 'eyes' or 'eye.' So, the word 'Yosemite' can mean something else entirely: *eyes omit*."

The group sat watching Joy as she moved in and out of the firelight. Rick smiled again. Jeffrey's eyebrows furrowed in confusion.

"Do you see?" Joy continued. "Now think about what your eyes have been omitting from that Adams photograph. Think about what should be there but is obviously omitted. What thing, what landmark, what obvious symbol of Yosemite is not in *Clearing Winter Storm* and has been omitted by your eyes?"

"Half Dome!" Jeffrey exclaimed.

"It seems like a stretch." Alexandra said.

"That's how we got Cathedral Peak," Rick shrugged.

39

ASSASSIN

Monday, 12:40 A.M.

"Are you sure its okay if I use the computer?" Rebecca asked, pulling up to the only desk in the Tuolumne Ranger Station. "There's not like confidential Yosemite Park stuff on here, is there?"

Jason laughed. "Yeah, like how many speeding tickets we issued this summer? Don't worry. I try to use that thing as little as possible."

"All right—so, well—let's just try Google."

"You've got to be kidding, with a last name like White?," Doc said.

"Okay what if I use other keywords like 'climbing.'" Rebecca typed in a few different versions of 'Stuart White,' 'climber,' 'killer,' and anything else she could imagine. Jason sat behind them, looking over Rebecca's shoulder while she worked. One of the other rangers had lit a fire in the cabin's wood stove. All around the floor, their friends and other climbers from Budd Lake were stretching out on sleeping pads, cots, and sleeping bags.

"Hella crazy slumber party, huh?" Jasmine said, coming to join Rebecca.

Jason smiled at Jasmine. "Are you sure you guys don't want to wait until tomorrow to drive down to the valley to meet your sister?"

"Oh, that's so *temptalicious*." Jasmine laughed, looking around at the multicolored collection of down sleeping bags. "But I think I gotta pass on the sardine tin."

"Suit yourself," Jason said.

Doc leaned in between Jason and Jasmine and couldn't resist adding, "But you gotta admit, it is a nice collection of fart sacks."

Rebecca rolled her eyes. Jasmine giggled.

"Wait a minute," Jasmine said. "If this guy, Stuart, if he really is a bad applesauce, which I guess we've got that shit dialed by now, maybe 'White' is fake. Maybe it isn't his name."

"What do you mean?" Rebecca asked.

"Well, White is pretty common, so maybe Stuart just used White as a way to remain, you know, *incognito*." Jasmine did her "Thriller" headshake.

Jason looked impressed at both the idea and the head movement.

"Incognito?" Rebecca chuckled. "Nice, Jaz. That's actually a word—this time."

"Yeah, you know, *hidden*," Jasmine responded.

"So what do I search for? Just 'Stuart?'"

Jason perked up. "How about 'Stuart' and 'murder'?"

"Why not?" Rebecca typed the words and hit search.

The page reloaded and a new series of website links appeared on the screen. The first link was a *New York Times* article about Capwater operations in Iraq. The second link also had to do with Capwater and was from a website called "Dark Government."

"Hello, what's this?" Rebecca got excited.

Everyone leaned in as Rebecca opened up the *New York Times* article. There was an image of the Capwater insignia, and the heading read: "Military Contractors Scrutinized After Assassination." * Scanning through the text, Rebecca eventually found what she was looking for—the name "Stuart."

"There!" she exclaimed, pointing at the screen.

Jasmine, Jason, and Doc looked closer.

"Yeah, Stuart White. That doesn't sound like him," Jason said.

"But maybe—" Rebecca began.

"He used to be in the military," Jasmine said.

"Really?" said Jason. "The military is often a feeder for private security contractors like Capwater. It could be that he worked for the military first."

"Is there an image?" Jasmine asked.

"Let's see." Rebecca scrolled around on the page but couldn't find anything.

"Do a Google image search for his name," Doc said.

Rebecca did as Doc suggested. "These don't look like him," Rebecca said. "I'm going back to the Capwater thing."

They checked some of the other links. It seemed like a "Stuart" had been involved in something controversial in Iraq and was extradited from the country. But they couldn't be sure this Stuart was the same as their Stuart.

Jason grew impatient and went over to talk with David and some of the other rangers.

Eventually, Rebecca found something slightly more promising. Checking into old military photographs using the name Stuart White, Rebecca looked for someone who seemed to correspond to the approximate age of Stuart. What she found was a group shot from fifteen years ago of a cadre of marine recruits with a "Stuart White" listed as one of the twenty or so faces in the image. After studying the photograph for a few minutes, Rebecca thought she saw someone who looked like the Stuart who had been so amped to free solo Cathedral this past night. As Jasmine looked over her shoulder silently, Rebecca zoomed in and cropped the image. Then, she adjusted the highlights and shadows until the image of the young man was about as clear as it could be. Rebecca and Jasmine had to admit that one of the faces did look an awful lot like the Stuart White they had met— no goatee and certainly much shorter hair, but still similar in appearance.

They waved at Jason to come back over and then explained to him what Rebecca had uncovered.

"It may be nothing," Doc said.

"But you guys have, you know, crazy access to other information and intelligence agencies and all. So you could, like, check into this," Jasmine said.

"Something like that," Jason smiled. "I'll save your search history and make sure the right people get it."

"We should really get going," Rebecca said.

"The fart-sack slumber party offer still stands," Jason said, giving Doc a nod.

"Thanks, but I really want to be there when Joy gets out of the backcountry."

"I understand. Thanks again for your help, and drive carefully. David already went out and he's waiting at the JMT trailhead in the Yukon. He'll escort you down to the valley."

Rebecca and Jasmine tiptoed out through the maze of sleeping bags and back into the Yosemite evening. The air was cold and crisp; a slight wind tousled the trees in sporadic and playful gusts. There was something warm despite the frigid temperature of the High Sierra at night. Maybe it was the openness of the place or the fact there was almost no light pollution or maybe, for Jasmine and Rebecca, it was just that they were on their way see Joy and Woody again.

"I'm still worried about them," Rebecca said.

"Yeah, me too." Jasmine responded.

Rebecca and Jasmine opened the doors to their Subaru and took their seats, staring out the windshield into the night. The old car groaned stubbornly to life in the cold air, and Jasmine nudged it out onto the road connecting Tioga Pass with the central valley through Tuolumne Meadows.

"How do you think Woody is holding up?" Jasmine asked.

"He's a hard kid to read," Rebecca responded. "Fine, I guess."

"You mean besides the major crush on Joy."

"Well, besides that, he doesn't really open up to us that much," Rebecca lamented. "It would be nice to know a bit more about his dad and what happened."

"Joy was telling me that Woody said his dad's terminal illness was totally treatable, but they were denied coverage by the insurance company."

"Get out! Really?"

"Yup," Jasmine continued. "Woody's dad didn't want to, like, spend his last days fighting it out with some faceless insurance company, and just accepted it—you know, like a death sentence."

"Wow. That has to have been rough on Woody," Rebecca said.

"Maybe. Joy told me his dad's decision was, like, really one of the best things that happened to them."

"What do you mean?"

"Well, they spent all this *rad* time together—you know hiking, camping, backcountry skiing, climbing, and hanging out as a family all around the Sierra Nevada. Yeah, the doctors told him that he'd only live another six months, or something like that, and he ended up living for, like, two more years."

"Wow," Rebecca said.

After meeting David at the JMT trailhead, the small caravan headed down toward the valley. Jasmine and Rebecca drove in silence for a while. The Subaru wound its way around the narrow mountain highway, heading to Porcupine Flat. Jasmine was driving on autopilot. She had traveled this road hundreds of times and knew its dips, curves, and sketchy sections like the creaks in the old staircase of the house where she grew up.

"It'd be nice to see Woody and Joy score," Jasmine broke the silence.

"Really?" Rebecca was surprised.

"Yeah. It'd be good, you know, for Woody."

"Oh, so like, a *pity hookup?*"

"No, no. I mean, I know Joy is older and they're going to be in very different places, but—"

"But Woody doesn't need someone else he really cares about to leave him. And Joy, she knows all this. And your sister is way too pragmatic to just, you know, spontaneously go too far with Woody."

"Nah. Spontaneity is good, you know? I don't care how logical my punk-ass little sister thinks she is." Jasmine considered her next words. "They care about each other and—"

"And that's why they aren't trying to be any more than they are right now," Rebecca said.

40

BROWNIES

Monday, 12:45 A.M.

"You sure y'all want to keep going along with them kids?" Hayduke asked.

"It's a fair point," Alexandra said.

"We've got rangers coming in both directions, right?" Jeffrey asked.

"True. Hayduke, update dispatch for us." Rick said.

"Not a problem."

Rick glanced over at Joy and Woody who were chatting while chewing on some trail bars. There was no indication they wanted to stay here or would have trouble keeping up on their middle-of-the-night hike.

"This sort of thing ain't in the manual, is it, Chief?"

"No, Hayduke, it sure as hell isn't." Rick took a deep breath. "All right, time is wasting. Hayduke, give instructions to the rangers to meet up in Little Yosemite Valley at the intersection with the Half Dome approach trail. Instruct those rangers following us from Tuolumne to pick up the pace. The kids are coming with us. Let's keep moving."

Everyone thanked Hayduke for the hot chocolate and started briskly walking down the trail toward Little Yosemite Valley. The night didn't seem so overpowering anymore, and they talked casually as the terrain passed by. The group strategized about Half Dome as a destination and what Stuart's motives could possibly be.

After about fifteen minutes, Jeffrey couldn't stand it any longer. "Woody, so what exactly were you thinking running at that bear?"

The group bunched together as they hiked to hear how Woody would explain his Promethean act.

"Well, um, it's not that big of a deal."

"No, come on, man. We've got the time. How did you do it?" Jeffrey insisted.

"I don't know—I just—"

"Thought, *what the hell?*" Jeffrey badgered him. "Really, what went through your mind?"

"Okay, so most people, they, um, have an irrational fear of bears. I don't think they're harmless or anything, but—" Woody thought about his next words. "I guess I just hoped Stuart was one of those people who didn't know much about bears."

"What about you?" Alexandra followed up. "Why weren't *you* scared?"

"Yeah, I suppose—" Woody wasn't sure how to answer. "Joy, do you remember that story your sister told about the bear that broke into her house last year?"

"Why?" Joy responded.

"Well, you see, um, bears aren't really interested in us. They're only interested in our food," Woody began. "So, well, to fill you all in, Joy's older sister, Jasmine, the one you all heard on the radio—"

"Definitely remember her," Jeffrey said.

"Well, she, um, she runs a marijuana dispensary and some-times she makes some of the products her dispensary sells. You know, she doesn't grow them, but she'll make pot brownies, cookies, or Rice Krispies treats."

"Which I'm sure you sample from time to time?" Jeffrey suggested.

"No, not me. I don't, and I don't think Joy does either."

"That's right," Joy quickly confirmed.

"But your grandmother, on the other hand—" Woody paused. "She's the unofficial pot-product taste tester."

The humor elevated everyone's spirits.

Woody continued, "Well, so one night Jasmine had created this particularly large batch of pot brownies, the kind with walnuts and M&M'S. It was early fall and she had her windows open, um, because the oven had made the house pretty warm. So Jasmine and her girlfriend, Rebecca, they, well, tried some of these potent brownies, watched a bit of TV, and then went to bed."

Getting into the story, Woody stumbled on one of the many rock drainages carved into the trail to prevent erosion. He quickly caught himself before landing in the dirt.

"You all right?" asked Jeffrey.

"Yeah, sorry." Woody continued, "So, uh, like I was saying, there were these sweet-smelling pot brownies cooling on top of Jasmine's stove, and the window was open right beside them. Well, at some point in the night, a bear catches a whiff and comes, you know, crawling through their window. Jasmine and Rebecca didn't catch any of this. They were... apparently sound asleep due to the potency of the brownies I guess."

"Right into the house, huh?" Alexandra asked.

"Yeah, well, this bear devours all—I think it was—three sheets of these brownies, licking the pans completely clean. Then, before the bear can get to more food in the kitchen or crawl back out the open window, he like—just passes out on the floor."

"No way," Jeffrey said.

"It's the truth—all night long. So in the morning, Rebecca I think it was, she gets up to make some coffee and rounds the corner into the kitchen. There, asleep on the floor, is this big old bear. As you can imagine, Rebecca screams. The bear wakes up. And then they both run in opposite directions—Rebecca into her bedroom, and the bear right back out the window."

"Damn," said Jeffrey.

"So, when I was trying to build up the courage to charge that bear, I just thought of Jasmine's story—you know, of a bear in her kitchen, passed out on the floor from pot brownies—and, well, that gave me enough confidence."

"That's a riot," Jeffrey exclaimed. "A stoned bear, just hanging out in the kitchen."

"Pretty much," Woody responded.

"Can you vouch for any of this, Joy?" Rick asked.

Joy quietly responded, "I'm afraid so."

At least for a while, the group plodded along the Muir trail distracted by thoughts of a bear high on pot and not of the killer they were tracking.

PART III

BRINGING THE STORM

It is all very beautiful and magical here—a quality which cannot be described. You have to live it and breathe it, let the sun bake it into you.

—Ansel Adams, *Letter to Alfred Stieglitz*

41

TRUST THE RUBBER

Monday, 1:30 A.M.

Based on information gleaned from the Ansel Adams photograph, Rick, Alexandra, Jeffrey, Woody and Joy continued to head west on the John Muir Trail. A confirmation of their decision appeared a quarter mile past Sunrise High Sierra Camp in the form of fresh Vibram sole footprints Rick guessed belonged to Stuart. The same tread marks stopped by Sunrise Creek about a mile later, presumably to resupply a water bottle.

They hiked briskly and in close proximity to each other; the combined illumination of their headlamps made progress steady and safer than it might otherwise be. Woody noticed Joy keeping her distance from him and wondered why, considering how affectionate they had been toward each other earlier on the hillside. Then, it struck him—*Of course, the bear story. How could I be so stupid?* He hung back for a second, pretending to adjust his backpack, and slid in line behind Joy.

"Hey," Woody said.

"Yeah?," Joy responded.

Woody took a deep breath. "Listen, um, I didn't really think about it when I was telling that story about the brownies, but I'm... really sorry."

Joy waited a moment to respond. She stood to the side of the trail and grabbed Woody's hand, pulling him toward her. Alexandra and Jeffrey, who were behind them, began to stop, too, but Joy said, "Go ahead."

"Sorry," Jeffrey responded. "We're not going to let you out of our sight again."

"It's alright. We're right behind you," Joy said.

When they had passed, Joy started to follow.

"Thanks," Joy began. "Thanks for saying that."

"Everyone wanted to know why I did what I did with the bear and when I started telling the story—I just—"

"It's okay." Joy said, "I need to be less, well, concerned about my sister. Jasmine is who she is; she always has been. People can insinuate whatever they want about me. I guess—"

"I shouldn't have said anything in front of the rangers. I mean they are—"

"Woody, it's alright. Really it is." Joy squeezed Woody's hand for emphasis. "I'm fine. No hard feelings. I may not like everything about my sister, but... I ought to at least start accepting her."

They hiked quietly alongside each other in the darkness, the light from their headlamps bouncing along at Jeffrey's heels. Eventually, when the trail narrowed, Joy gave Woody's palm another squeeze and stepped in front of him.

Woody watched Joy hiking in front of him. Her clothing was tucked neatly back into place, giving almost no indication of the odyssey they had experienced. Joy's ponytail swung like a metronome, perfectly in sync with the rhythm of her athletic stride. Woody became captivated by the seductive sinuous flow of her body and imagined himself running his hands through her hair while kissing her full on the lips. *What is it about her?* he pondered. *There's something wild within Joy, and it's subtle, not blatant like with Jasmine.*

Woody smiled. *Joy and Jasmine.* At first blush, they appeared to be polar opposites—but that was just a veneer. Watching Joy climb was antithetical to her polished physical appearance. She dove headlong into a climb, as if every move had been choreographed three moves ahead. She never fumbled through her gear; in fact, she hardly even looked at it. She would just reach down to her harness, feel the carabiner, grab the piece, and plug it in. Occasionally, if a piece didn't quite fit, she would hold it between her teeth and make two or three moves until she was at a section of the climb where the gear would slot. If anyone else were to climb like this, Woody would see it as reckless, but with Joy, it seemed instinctive.

And then there was her computer expertise, like getting access to syllabi and coursework for a college course in which she had yet to enroll. He had heard rumors about her grades throughout high school; there was no denying she was brilliant. Her scores on exams and assignments were nearly always perfect, as well as her SAT scores. But her GPA, which should have placed her at the top of her class, didn't do so. Joy wasn't shy. She didn't lack confidence. But she hated attention. The idea of being a valedictorian or receiving other honors was more of a disincentive. Joy often lamented that academic recognition was superficial and irrelevant. If somehow she modified her grades in a negative direction, then wasn't that just as reckless as Jasmine's more overt behaviors?

Woody looked down and shook his head. *I hope my dumb-ass story didn't toss out any chance I had with her.*

When the group hit the soft soil of Little Yosemite Valley, Rick turned to face the others.

"Rick, are you sure those are Stuart's tracks heading north?" asked Alexandra. "It could be another hiker. Vibrams are ubiquitous."

"There you go with the big words again," Jeffrey said.

"Sorry—the most common tread out here." Alexandra rolled her eyes. "I'd guess just about every other tread mark we see is a Vibram sole."

"Hmm." Rick cleared his throat. "Look at the depth of these indentations. They're consistent with what we've seen and seem to indicate this guy is moving quickly."

"Should we wait for the other rangers?" Joy asked.

Alexandra nodded her head to echo Joy's concern. "We've got him cornered now, right?"

"Yeah, now it's pretty much up the trail, up the cables, and then you have to come back down this same way," Jeffrey replied.

"Maybe it's the phone reception thing again?" Woody offered.

"It would be good to get a hold of that phone and see what our perpetrator has been communicating about and with whom," Rick said. "How's everyone feeling?"

"I'm good to keep going," Woody volunteered.

"What about you, Joy?"

Joy hesitated and put her hands on her hips.

Alexandra spoke up, "Rick, I'm pretty exhausted myself, and I need to use the, uh… 'forest facilities' here somewhere. Why don't you guys head on and Joy and I will hike off the trail for a while. When you come back, we'll be all rested up."

"Hmm. We should stick together," Rick replied.

"I have a gun," Alexandra said, looking to Joy. "We'll be out of sight and quiet."

"Okay then," Rick responded. "Just head south here, back toward the creek; I want you to walk completely off the trail and close to the water. We'll rendezvous later."

Joy looked up fondly at Alexandra, who smiled back at her.

"Okay then." Rick stood up, took a deep breath, and regarded Jeffrey and Woody. "Gentlemen?"

Under Rick's direction, they took off up the trail toward Half Dome.

"How many times have you been up the cables, Jeff?" Woody asked.

"Man...good question—a bunch, for sure. You know it used to be considered 'perfectly inaccessible.'" Jeffrey made quote signs with his hands.

"Oh, I know. My dad and I used to talk about the history of the Park, good ole Josiah Whitney, the 'tallest peak in the lower forty-eight' guy, said that Half Dome..." Woody lowered his voice for emphasis, "'never has been and never will be trodden by human foot.'" *

"Pretty funny, huh?" Jeffery laughed.

The trio crested the small granite shoulder and gazed out across the saddle at the glistening steel cables stretching for over five hundred feet in a vertical corridor and disappearing into the night sky.

Moving down to the start of the cables, they stopped for a moment. Woody removed his backpack and got out his climbing shoes. Jeffrey chose a pair of mismatched gloves from the abandoned collection spread around. Rick stared up at the dome while running his thumb and forefinger along his rigid jawbone until they converged at his chin.

"We have to assume he's up there," Rick began, almost whispering. "We have to assume he's armed. There's also a good chance he'll be able to hear us climbing the cables."

"We could just wait here," Jeffrey quietly added.

They all considered Jeffrey's suggestion for a moment.

"But then we'll have no chance of hearing whatever phone conversation he might be having," Jeffrey added.

"Exactly," Rick said.

"I, um... can make it up there without making any noise, Rick," Woody offered. "Really, I'll smear with my climbing shoes and just use the cables when I have to."

"There's not a chance in hell that's going to happen, Woody. You've already been in harm's way once tonight, and I'm not even sure it was wise of me to bring you along."

"Well... look, I'm not exactly excited about this either, but we all know those posts jostle back and forth in their holes, the cables grind on the rock, and those wooden planks practically clap down on the wall each time you step on them."

They sat in silence, surrounded by the multicolor mosaic of discarded gloves, staring intently at the foreboding cables. The wind had been slowly building momentum and here in the saddle below Half Dome the three of them felt particularly vulnerable.

"Hey Woody, I was just noticing something," Rick began. "You've got some pretty large feet. What are those buffalo hooves, anyway––size twelve?"

Woody chuckled. His cross-country teammates would frequently give him a hard time about covering extra territory by virtue of shoe size. "Yeah, I'm actually twelve and a half in street shoes; these climbing shoes are eleven and a half though."

"Woody, you may not believe me, but I actually used to do quite a bit of climbing here in the late seventies and early eighties, and while I'm not going to let you smear your way up the cables to confront Stuart, I'll borrow your shoes and do it myself."

"Really?" Woody said. "I mean, of course you can borrow my shoes, but are you sure you're, um, comfortable with smearing up that whole way?"

"What the hell?" Rick chuckled quietly as a thought crossed his mind. "What's that old and... you know, vulgar expression dirty climbers tell girls when they're taking them climbing for the first time––about the bottom of their climbing shoes?"

Woody smiled. He knew what was coming—and it affirmed for him Rick had most certainly spent some time on Yosemite granite.

"Spread your legs and—" Rick began.

"Trust the rubber," Woody and Rick said, almost in unison.

"I'll wear my headlamp and, periodically, I'll turn my head

and flash once to signal I'm okay and to stay where you are. If I flash twice or more, that means it's okay for you to come up."

"I'll climb up that shoulder behind us there so I can still see your signals even when you're at the top," Jeffrey added. "But Chief, what about the, you know, 'I'm in trouble' signal?"

"Let's just say if you don't see a signal from me for five minutes, you need to hightail it out of here, back to Alex and Joy and then back to the main valley," Rick said as he strapped on Woody's shoes. "See you guys in a minute."

With that, Rick turned and headed skyward alongside the narrow alleyway of granite framed by steel cables he would try to avoid. Woody and Jeffrey watched until Rick was about a third of the way to the top.

"I didn't realize he used to climb," Woody stated.

"Yeah, he doesn't really talk about his past much," Jeffrey responded, "but he dropped some names like John Bachar and Royal Robbins in passing; I'd say he knows his way around more than just the *horizontal* landscape of Yosemite."

"Cool."

"What's that?" asked Jeffrey as Woody fastened some webbing from his pack around his waist and through a carabiner, tying a quick bowline by his navel and then a water knot by the carabiner.

"Well, let's just say it's always good practice to have a backup plan. Most hikers who go up the cables just hope for the best and don't have a contingency of any sort in case they pass out from the heat or someone knocks into them. The webbing and carabiner are just a way to tie in to the cables or the posts, if I have to."

"Makes sense," Jeffrey said. "I'm going to go on up that ridge behind us to keep a better eye on our fearless leader up there."

"Got it."

42

HELLO GORGEOUS

Monday, 2:11 A.M.

Rick was making surprising progress. He had yet to use the cables or the poles, but a steep section with a fairly sizable step was coming up soon. This step was the source of much trepidation and delay on the cables during the busy summer months and perhaps one of the reasons the Park Service eventually established a quota and permit system to restrict the number of hikers going up the cables each day. At each crack or horizontal shelf Rick would pause and signal with his headlamp down to Woody and Jeffrey, letting them know he was okay.

Glancing up and ahead of him, Rick saw the large granite shelf, only about sixteen inches tall, but jutting at an overhang directly out from the wall. He reached up and put his hand on it. "Hello, gorgeous," he whispered to the rock.

Standing upright, he looked over the top of the shelf and around the dome's surface for anything to hold on to. Nothing. All Rick had was friction and the knowledge that on either side of him were the cables waiting to save him. Rick removed his gloves, wiped the sweat off of his hands and placed his right hand on top of the shelf, palming it down hard on the smooth granite surface. He placed his left hand under the shelf as a counterbalance to steady the small friction move he was about to make. Then, ever so carefully, he shifted his weight off of his left foot and onto his right. He felt his toes dig into the climbing shoe rubber, and the rubber press down hard on the rock. Like a tightrope walker, Rick then brought his left leg up as high as his waist. Being careful not to lean too far forward and threaten the tangential placement of his weight over his right foot, he inched his left leg out over the shelf, pressing down hard on his right hand. When he felt good about his left foot's placement on the steep and polished rock, he took a deep breath, and a rebellious smile spread across his face, the type of expression that hadn't creased his cheeks in years. Then––he shifted his weight.

Rick half expected to fly backward and catapult down between the cables, desperate to grab at anything. But he stuck. And before he knew it, he was on two feet again and moving up higher and higher. Soon, Half Dome gradually began to tilt backward toward the flat surface at its apex.

Rick turned again and gave Jeffrey and Woody one more flash of his headlamp before smearing the rest of the cable length to the top.

Now, where the hell is Stuart?

Rick slowed down as he finished the last ten smears to the top of the cables. Rather than exiting the top, Rick slipped under the cable to his left and traversed the side of the dome. He scanned the stark top for anything, any sign.

Nothing.

The summit of Half Dome stretched out into the darkness like an alien landscape. Its massive granite zenith plummeted thousands of feet in three directions and could well have been another planet, devoid of life, monolithic in color and texture, otherworldly, especially in the glow of late summer's moonlight.

Perhaps, Rick thought, it was the heat captured during the day by this immense rock slowly escaping into the cold night, but something seemed to make the expansive summit radiate, as if a thin veil of fog hovered one foot thick across its surface.

Rick steadied himself and his nerves. *Chasing a killer to the top of Half Dome is not in the typical duties of a park ranger*, he thought.

Now on firm footing, Rick removed his handgun from his hip belt and kept searching the summit.

Still nothing.

Then a thought began to dawn on Rick. He found a comfortable fracture in the rock where he could sit and be calm. He lowered himself, rotated onto his hip and tried to slow his pounding heart. The wind intensified, stirring the entire scene around him into a frenzy of granite dust, unflinching moonlight, and anticipation.

He closed his eyes and took several deep breaths. The wind briefly abated and then—Rick heard it, or rather *him*. Just a muffled voice somewhere off to his right and back a little ways toward the center of Half Dome's broad summit. *It's Stuart.*

Rick's eyes flashed open and he started to crawl toward some outlying rocks that would afford shelter and a better vantage point. There, Stuart White stood, talking on the phone and sorting through some items in his backpack. Rick could just barely make out some of Stuart's words, seemingly a response to instructions of some sort as he nodded his head in agreement from time to time.

What now? Rick pondered.

43

IMMENSE HALL

Monday, 2:21 A.M.

"This park, this thing that we're about to do, it will all come full circle," The Professor said. "Environmentalism started here in Yosemite over a century and a half ago, and today, with the dawn fast approaching, it will end." The voice, as usual, sounded mechanical, altered.

"Alright then, I'll get to it," Stuart responded.

"And the instructions... are they clear?"

"Yes, but should we be concerned with the rangers coming after me?"

"Have you heard the cables yet?"

"No." Stuart stood and walked over toward the cables. There was no movement, no jostling, no sound. "No one's coming up the cables," he confirmed. Stuart couldn't see the base of the cables due to the grand arc of Half Dome, but felt confident he was alone on its summit.

"Are there any further questions before reaching the Rover?"

Stuart hesitated.

"Stuart?"

"Yes, Professor?"

"What is it?"

"The message you wrote with the picture of Abigail. I saw it online, on my phone. Wasn't Abigail's death to look accidental? Why did I go through the trouble if you just wanted an assassination?"

"Hmm... Stuart, we're at the point now where you deserve a little more... shall we say... historical context. What we are doing here is not a simple matter of eliminating some targets. The deaths of Aiden and Abigail and the manner of their departure were meant to provoke a certain element of the population and it has been successful in this endeavor. There is an online firestorm raging as we speak. When the dust and depths settle to the new norm for Yosemite, the question of who's to blame will seal the fate of more than just this park; is that enough context for you?"

"Okay, Professor, alright."

A breathy chuckle vibrated across the phone, "Stuart, Muir once said the harmony of Yosemite when, and I quote, 'comprehensively seen, looks like an immense hall or temple lighted from above.' Well... you are about to alter that lighting arrangement."

The Professor abruptly hung up the phone. Stuart listened until he was sure no one was on the line and depressed the end-call button.

"Fucking wacko. Jesus."

The Professor's garbled voice always reinforced just how secret this whole operation was. It was clear some sort of voice-modifying software was being used. And the number from which he received his notifications from The Professor was always blocked.

Reaching again into the backpack he had been carrying, Stuart removed his climbing harness and methodically stepped into the two leg loops and then wrapped the waist strap around his stomach, securing it well above his hip bones as was the standard. After rifling around inside his bag, he removed a loop of webbing, girth-hitched it to his belay loop, and attached a self-locking carabiner to the other end. Finally, he reached back into the bag and started pulling out a long, thin rope.

WHAT'S HE DOING? Rick thought. *Who's this Professor? Why all the climbing apparatus?*

Then, Rick realized why Stuart had seemed nonchalant about his pursuers during his conversation on the phone. He wasn't going to exit the summit of Half Dome via the cables; Stuart had other plans.

Rick didn't know how best to handle this. The open expanse at the summit of Half Dome provided no cover and no easy way to approach Stuart without being noticed.

Woody had said Stuart had a military background. If Rick drew his weapon from this range, no doubt Stuart would feel more confident about drawing his as well, and getting into a gun battle on the summit of Half Dome did not seem like a particularly good idea. Even if he managed to disarm Stuart without killing him, chances are Stuart would be wounded, and getting a wounded body down from this place would not be easy. If Rick shot him dead, then whatever grand scheme he had just been discussing would go unresolved.

I need him alive and unimpaired, Rick told himself.

Rick waited until Stuart was occupied with his gear. Then, he slinked backward on the rock to a point just beyond the convex bend of the dome where Stuart wouldn't be able to see his flashing headlamp signaling Woody and Jeffrey to come up. He hoped the sound of the cables would be enough to distract Stuart so he could sneak up on him. Rick lowered his head to the ground, covered the upward angle of the headlamp with his palm, and flashed the small device two distinct times.

Almost instantaneously, the cables and posts started jostling around. Woody and Jeffrey must be sprinting up them.

Rick looked toward Stuart and froze.

Stuart had heard the cables, but rather than moving away from them and beginning his escape, he was actually moving toward them and toward Rick. *Why isn't Stuart running away?*

It soon became evident what Stuart had in mind. He was going to use his advantage with devastating consequences.

Pulling his handgun from the backpack, Stuart swaggered toward the cables.

Rick flattened himself against the rock as Stuart strode toward him.

What have I done?

When Stuart reached the end of the cables, he set his pack to the side and peered down the rattling steel. Woody and Jeffrey were rushing up the cables directly toward a loaded gun.

Stuart continued to wait while the cables scraped and rasped against the granite slope.

What the fuck have I done? Rick questioned himself as he lay there flattened and immobile, knowing he had little time left to confront this killer. *I have to act*, Rick thought. Jeffrey and Woody would not be added to the list of fatalities in the past twenty-four hours.

Then, without warning, Stuart did something unanticipated. Apparently sensing he was missing some vital piece of gear, Stuart suddenly crouched down by his pack, facing away from Rick. As he did so, he set down his gun on the slab by his side so he could hold the backpack open with one hand and rummage though it with the other.

Without thinking or second-guessing, without a moment's contemplation, Rick rose and leapt forward, simultaneously removing his handgun from its waist strap.

Feeling there was something amiss, Stuart jerked his head toward Rick and extended his arm back down for his gun.

Rick skidded to a halt directly behind him, shouting, "Freeze!" Stuart turned his head.

"Easy there, compadre," Rick declared. "Hands in the air! That gun wouldn't even make it off the ground."

44

JUMP

Monday, 2:35 A.M.

"**S**tuart, is it?" Rick began.

There was no response. Stuart, solemn and conde-scending, glared at Rick.

"Let's put those hands of yours behind your back, shall we?"

Stuart silently acquiesced and brought his clenched fists together while Rick administered handcuffs, noticing how readily Stuart brought his wrists into exactly the right position for him to attach them, like he's done this before.

Woody burst onto the summit, panting and wide-eyed, scanning the rock in all directions. When he saw Stuart handcuffed, he eased up and relief spread across his face.

"Nice! Hey there, Stuart!" Woody was jubilant. "So good to see you again. How does it feel for *you* to be the captive?"

Stuart glared back without responding.

Rick smiled at Woody's excitement while he picked up and unloaded Stuart's gun. "Quite the goose chase he led us on here." Turning to face Stuart, Rick read his miranda rights. "Stuart, you've been accused of murder. You have the right to remain silent, which you are clearly exercising. Anything you say can and will be used against you in a court of law. You have the right to speak to an attorney. If you cannot afford an attorney, one will be appointed to you. Do you understand these rights as they have been explained to you?"

Stuart still didn't reply.

"Well, I'll just have to assume your silence implies consent," Rick said. "What do you think, Woody?"

"Oh, I think he knows what's happening."

Jeffrey stumbled up the last few steps to the top of the cables. "What'd I miss? You got him, right?"

"Yeah, Jeffrey, he's over here," Woody replied.

Jeffrey caught his breath and looked over toward Woody. "How was he expecting to get out of here, anyway?"

"Looks like he was going to rappel off somewhere," Woody responded. "He's wearing his harness, and check out this long rope."

"Hmm, that'd be one hell of a rap, man," Rick declared.

Stuart remained silent. He lowered his head so his dusty blond hair hid his face and drooped down to his bleached goatee. He seemed to be somewhere else, totally disengaged from his captors.

"There's something else," Rick said.

"What's that, Rick?" Jeffrey responded.

"He knew we were coming for him."

"What do you mean?"

"I heard him on the phone with someone—someone he referred to as *The Professor*—and he knew we were tracking him, coming up the cables."

"Really?" Jeffrey said, poking Stuart tauntingly in the ribs. "How could your 'Professor' know all that?"

Stuart didn't flinch or acknowledge he had been spoken to. Woody thought under the mess of hair encircling Stuart's down-turned face he could make out the slight glint of teeth.

Now it was Woody's turn to be agitated. "So Stuart, what did you say to Aiden before pushing him off?"

Stuart tilted his head back enough to glare at Woody.

"Something about, 'What you have been working for will be achieved.' What did you mean? What had Aiden been working for?"

Still nothing.

"And while we're asking questions, who is this Professor guy anyway?" Jeffrey demanded.

Stuart remained silent.

"Why kill climbers? Why Aiden and why Abigail?" Rick asked.

Stuart looked up with a quizzical expression.

"That's right, Stewie, we know about Abigail, too," Jeffrey added.

Stuart lowered his head again and stared blankly at the rock surface.

Frustrated by Stuart's refusal to acknowledge any of their questions, Woody, Jeffrey, and Rick ceased badgering him and went about readying for their descent. Rick located Stuart's phone, which luckily hadn't been turned off. Checking through some of the text messages, it was clear Stuart had taken a few photographs of Aiden's flayed corpse and he had been transmitting information, but the recipient wasn't identifiable. Mostly, the information and images were posted online, not sent to one number.

"Hey Jeffrey, can you take this phone and get these numbers down to headquarters somehow?"

"Sure." Jeffrey grabbed the phone and took a seat, busily copying and pasting into an email.

A huge weight had been lifted off Woody's shoulders. He began exploring around the top of Half Dome, remembering his father and their plans to make it to the summit together at night.

Woody shook his head and smiled down at the starlit valley below. The wind tousled his hair, like his father used to do.

I finally made it here in the moonlight, Dad. You're right. It's pretty special, he mused. He breathed a deep and contented inhalation; his father would have been proud of him tonight, and Woody was glad it was all coming to a fitting conclusion.

"All right, team—time to move out," Rick announced.

Rick gathered up Stuart's bag, put the rope inside and placed it over one shoulder. He checked around the area to make sure he hadn't missed anything. Satisfied, he began marching Stuart back toward the cables.

When they reached the first uprights, Stuart finally spoke up. "Do you really expect me to try and walk down this treacherous thing with handcuffs?"

"Oh, you can indeed talk! Glad to hear that. And no, I guess that wouldn't work too well, would it?" Rick responded. "Let's see. Jeffrey and Woody, I'm going to send you down first. Stuart here, he'll be right in front of me, and— " Rick weighed his options —"Stuart, why don't you put this pack back on while we're at it?"

"I can carry it," Woody offered. "I didn't bring a pack up here."

"It's all right, Woody. It might serve to slow old Stewie here down a bit, too."

Once Rick had Stuart confined in between the steel cables, he removed the handcuffs and handed Stuart his backpack. Stuart put the pack around his shoulders and cinched it tight, and then turned and solemnly started making his way down the cables.

Jeffrey and Woody were in front, followed by Stuart and Rick, who stayed right on top of him, literally breathing down Stuart's neck and keeping his right hand close to his sidearm. They worked their way down past a number of the upper sets of upright posts. Gradually, the rock got steeper, and the cables groaned under the combined pressure of the bodies holding on against the near vertical surface.

"I wonder how many people have died on these cables?" Jeffrey asked.

"Not, um, the best time to ask that question," Woody responded.

"Just wondering. There were those two people back in 2006, but what about before that?" Jeffrey took a hard step down onto one of the wooden boards and wedged his leg in behind the steel post to take the pressure off of his hands for a moment.

"Yeah, I'm surprised, um, it doesn't happen to more people," Woody said. "You know, average hikers are used to standing and walking on flat ground; this is basically vertical and totally out of their element."

"And besides, they are doing it after a long and grueling hike up from the valley. It's a good thing, the quota—" Jeffrey never had the opportunity to finish his thought.

Stuart jumped.

Turning swiftly backward, Stuart thrust his arm through the backpack shoulder straps running vertically down Rick's chest, pulling Rick off balance and toward him. As he did so, he clipped a carabiner girth-hitched to his harness belay loop onto one of the runs of cable and then quickly leapt backward into the air away from the dome, arching his spine as if attempting a backflip. Rick, who had been keeping one hand near his gun, didn't have time to react and grasp firmly onto the cable; Stuart had managed to yank him right off of it.

Woody looked up. "Jeffrey, duck!" he shouted as he clipped himself into the steel cable, using his webbing and the self-locking carabiner.

At that moment, out of the four bodies on the cables, two were tied in—Woody and Stuart—and the other two were not.

Jeffrey collapsed onto the rock near a steel post as Stuart and Rick came flying down toward him. Below the post, Woody checked his carabiner, harness, and girth hitch, and braced himself.

Suddenly, Stuart's carabiner caught on the post opposite where Jeffrey was crouched. His body jerked, swung across, and slammed against Jeffrey, who barely held on as Stuart's legs and torso whacked down onto Jeffrey's head and upper body, smashing his face into the granite.

Rick had tried to hold onto Stuart as they plunged downward, but was unable to do any more than tear Stuart's shirt and leave several gashes in Stuart's abdomen with his fingernails. Rick was rapidly falling toward Woody.

Woody saw what was coming and knew it was going to hurt. Rick's desperate grasp at Stuart had rotated his body to a vertical position, aiming him feet-first and directly at Woody's midsection. Rick, still airborne, dropped almost parallel with the cables.

Bracing for impact, Woody raised his arms up. Just as Rick's feet were about to collide with his chest, Woody, still tied in to the cables, threw his body beyond Rick's and deflected him down onto the surface of the steep arc of Half Dome. In doing so, Woody had absorbed some of Rick's momentum and was able to grate him against the rock, creating enough friction to slow their descent before encountering the next set of steel posts.

The entire series of impacts, from Stuart's initial leap to his collision with Jeffrey, and Rick's subsequent collision with Woody, had taken just a few seconds.

With his back now against the rock, Rick reached out and tried to grasp anything to slow his descent. One foot pushed desperately against the underside of a cable, and the heels of his hands scraped against the rock as he plummeted toward the next set of posts. Woody forced Rick to the left, directly under one of the cables. This motion pushed Woody's weight to the right under the other cable. This would be Rick's only chance to stop his fall.

The impact came fast. Rick struck the post directly with his stomach, collapsing like a wet noodle around both sides of the steel pipe, his knee crashing into a step board, splitting the wood with a resounding crack. The crushing blow had evacuated all of the oxygen from Rick's lungs, and he lost consciousness.

Woody, who knew his harness and carabiner would catch him, focused on avoiding direct contact with the steel post on his side. He pushed against the wall with his hands and feet, and managed to barely graze the outside of the rigid metal. His carabiner connected with the top of the post and swung Woody back around underneath, spinning him wildly across the inside of the cables to a spot just above Rick.

In horror, Woody saw Rick's languid body slowly slipping off of the post he had smashed into. Committing to his awkward position, he desperately reached out and grasped one of Rick's wrists with both hands; the limp body of his friend now pendulumed below him as they swung back to the other side. Woody hung inverted from his harness, connected to the steel post by his carabiner and webbing.

The dead weight and swaying motion was almost too much for Woody's strength. His fingers squeezed into Rick's flesh, and his muscles, from his hands all the way through his arms to his shoulders and back, tensed and constricted; his spine stretched to its limit.

"Aggh!" Woody yelled. "Rick! Riiiick!"

The swaying ceased and Rick flopped down, coming to rest below Woody against the step boards, still dangling by one arm, still unconscious.

"Rick! Please!" Woody yelled at him. "Rick!"

Still, there was no response. Woody could feel the fatigue gradually overtaking him.

"Rick," Woody said, no longer shouting it. He began to sweat and feel his arms twinge.

Rick's face was upturned and his eyes were closed. Desperate and not knowing what else to do, Woody worked up the biggest ball of saliva he could muster. Once he had collected enough phlegm on his tongue, he half spat-half drooled it down on Rick.

Woody's aim was good enough. The massive cold, wet loogie landed squarely on Rick's left eye and pooled up.

Momentarily, Rick grimaced, slowly shook his head, and instinctively went to wipe his face, but found he couldn't because his right arm was suspending him.

"Grab onto the fucking cables!" Woody yelled with renewed vigor.

Suddenly realizing where he was, Rick quickly grasped a cable with his free left hand.

"Feet on the wall, Rick!" Woody commanded.

"Okay, okay," he said as he started to pull himself up. "Jesus, my spine!" Rick moaned. "The impact with the post must have tweaked or broken something. . ."

"Can you support yourself?"

"Not sure yet." Slowly, Rick twisted around and then stood upright, taking numerous deep breaths. Finally, Rick scrambled up a couple of steps to where Woody was still hanging and said, "I think you can let go now."

"Okay, Chief," Woody gasped.

Rick looked confused for a moment, and then..."Shit! Where's Stuart?"

45

SNAKE DIKE

Monday, 3:01 A.M.

Jeffrey felt the weight of Stuart's body smash down on him. His face compressed against the rock and he registered a distinct snapping sound on the ridge of his nose as a gush of blood spurted across his lips.

Barely managing to wrap his arm around one of the steel posts supporting the cables, Jeffrey clung to the side of Half Dome. Already, Stuart was moving. *He must have planned this whole thing*, Jeffrey realized.

Stuart yanked himself up by the cables and glanced down at Jeffrey. Before he took off toward the top of Half Dome, he slammed his foot down on Jeffrey's right forearm, smashing it against the two-inch steel pipe.

Again, Jeffrey heard a snap. He thrust his left hand up and grasped the post just as his right arm gave way and fell useless at his side. The pain was intense, but Jeffrey managed to pull himself upright, using his left hand and the friction of his body on the wall.

Stuart was way above him now, past the point where he had

jumped only seconds before. Jeffrey shook his head and braced himself between the cables, then looked back down toward the saddle.

Below him, Woody held Rick and was yelling at him to wake up. Jeffrey stared aghast at the two suspended bodies. Hearing the scrape of metal above him, he turned and saw Stuart exiting the top of the cables onto the summit of Half Dome. Looking back down, he saw that Rick was conscious.

An unprecedented wave of rage swept over Jeffrey. His eyes narrowed, and the pain radiating in pulses from his right arm seemed to channel like an electric current shooting through his neck, up the back of his head, and over his scalp, consolidating to a point at his forehead. He resolved to get Stuart, even if he had to shoot left-handed.

Seeing Stuart exit the cables and deciding not to shout down to his companions and alert Stuart of his pursuit, Jeffrey spun his body skyward and launched himself up the cables in desperate thrusts with one hand. Reaching the top, he sprinted forward onto the dome's massive summit. As he did so, he swung his backpack around and reached inside for his gun. Stuart, in the distance, was running down the low-angle western slope of the dome. Infuriated, Jeffrey raised his gun, released the safety, and fired a shot in Stuart's direction.

Stuart turned his head and looked back, but kept running.

Jeffrey took off after him.

He was not a man of action; Jeffrey was a researcher, a strategist. He could tackle long, complex assignments, sifting through tomes of data and synthesizing viewpoints to arrive at a logical and prudent course of action. Whenever his superiors had doubts about the application of a particular policy—how best to instill a fear of tourists in the bear population, how many hiking permits per day should be issued for Half Dome—Jeffrey was the go-to guy. Running with reckless abandon after a murdering psychopath across the dangerous confines of a summit thousands of feet in the sky was about as far from Jeffrey's norm as he had ever been. However this was different. Stuart had broken Jeffrey's arm, killed visitors to his park, and nearly killed his friend and mentor. Stuart had violated the sanctity of this place—of *his* place. He had to pay.

Wiping away the blood pouring out of his nose, Jeffrey focused intently on the figure disappearing over the massive arc of Half Dome's west-facing flank and charged after him. His right arm dangled at his side like a recess tetherball.

In his obsession, he was nearly oblivious to the increasing angle of his descent. Like a voyager sailing across the ocean when the world was believed to be flat, Jeffrey hurtled toward the edge of an unknown terrain where the sea could abruptly give way—to nothing.

He caught a glimpse of Stuart, who had slowed and seemed to be searching for something. Abruptly, Stuart caught himself and cautiously descended into what looked to be a crevice.

Jeffrey charged on, making a beeline for the same point where he had seen Stuart disappear. He got his gun ready and felt confident that at close range, he would be effective using his left hand. Jeffrey didn't think about the axis on which the world around him was turning—horizontal slanting toward vertical.

Approaching the spot where Stuart vanished, Jeffrey tried to slow himself. He quickly lined his trajectory up with a horizontal part of the rock surface and prepared to use this small bulge to halt his momentum.

He realized where Stuart had gone—a narrow stone corridor, layered slabs on each side, about seven feet deep and barely wide enough to stand three bodies across. He dug in his heels and leaned back against the rock, skidding on his hip, like cheese across a grater. The small rock hallway was nearly at Jeffrey's feet and he slid rapidly off one side, colliding into the other.

Everything went momentarily black.

He blinked his eyes and braced himself on the granite wall.

Despite the jarring impact, Jeffrey had managed to hold onto his gun.

Gaining his feet, Jeffrey saw his prey; in fact, Stuart was not more than six feet from him, perched just above him on the forty-five-degree-angled surface. *What the hell is he doing?* he wondered.

Stuart had a rope out and was finishing tying a knot at its end. He smiled at his pursuer, his white goatee seeming to stretch the crazed expression on his face.

"How's the arm, ranger?"

"Fuck you! Hands in the air, asshole!"

Stuart continued to deliberately work with his rope while he talked. "Okay... but, I don't think this is going to go the way you want." Stuart clicked two carabiners into an anchor he had built on the side of the rock. "So you want me... to come... with you, right?"

"That's right," Jeffrey said as he watched Stuart click his rope through the two carabiners. "This insanity ends now!"

"Well, Jeffrey—that is your name I think? I will indeed go with you—"

Stuart rose to his feet. Jeffrey noticed more carabiners dangling from Stuart's harness. "Let's go together."

Sensing something going horribly wrong, Jeffrey leveled the gun at Stuart's midsection and tried to pull the trigger.

Stuart crouched and leapt directly at Jeffrey, knocking him off balance.

The shot went high as they flew backwards out of the stone hallway.

Landing on the sheer diagonal surface, they immediately began to slide downward. Stuart grabbed at Jeffrey's left hand as it scraped across the rock, lifted it up off the sliding surface, and then smashed it down, forcing the gun out of Jeffrey's grasp.

The two bodies now accelerated while the world of Half Dome whizzed by beneath them. The rock tore at their skin and clothes as they skidded. Stuart rotated to a seated position and then abruptly stood up as he fell forward. Jeffrey, not sure of what to do, spun over to his butt and fumbled forward, clasping onto Stuart's harness as Stuart began to take long strides down the rock, as if he was a bird preparing to take flight.

Ten feet with one step.

Fifteen feet with the next step.

Then twenty-five.

Then even farther.

They were nearly in free fall now, and Jeffrey grasped at Stuart as Half Dome sped by impossibly fast. Stuart looked to be concentrating on landing square and even foot placements.

In the next moment, the rope made a zipping sound as it momentarily adjusted to its center point and, in one sudden and jarring moment, caught on the carabiners, now well over one hundred feet above. The climbing rope had just enough spring and dynamic action not to snap Stuart's body in half, but it was entirely too fast for Jeffrey, who had barely managed to wrap his good hand around one of Stuart's gear loops. The force of the rope catching rotated Stuart instantly to a position facing upward and simultaneously spun Jeffrey like a forefinger flicking a quarter on a smooth table.

Jeffrey catapulted into the air in a wild, revolving arc.

Stuart was abruptly whisked upward by the elasticity of the rope, turning his head to watch Jeffrey, his would-be captor, hover momentarily in space before beginning to plummet, and then cascade down the side of Half Dome in long, bounding tangential curves, like shooters from a waterfall, until he all but gracefully faded from view.

REGAINING THEIR CENTER OF GRAVITY, Woody and Rick had managed to stand and secure themselves on the escarpment. There was no sign of either Jeffrey or Stuart.

"Up?" Woody asked. "Jeffrey is up there I hope."

"Yeah." Rick was shaky and sore in places, but able to push on.

They headed back up the cables. Rick moved slowly, assessing and testing his injuries. When they reached the final steel upright, the gunshot rang out.

"That can't be Stuart; I've got his gun," Rick said.

"Maybe Jeffrey shot at him?"

They scrambled to the apex of Half Dome, braced themselves against the wind, and scanned the area in every direction.

"There's Jeffrey." Rick pointed west down the convexity.

They took off after him. "Watch yourself. The angle will get steep before you know it," Rick said as they ran down the vast shoulder.

"Snake Dike is down here, right?" Woody yelled.

"Yeah, that's probably... where he's going to rappel off." Rick breathed heavily, still in some pain. "There're bolts basically the whole way... Take it easy now, Woody. Stay behind me."

"Okay, Chief." With growing respect for Rick, Woody had settled upon this honorific title.

They slowed to a near crawl, occasionally relying on their hands as they reached the corridor that Jeffrey had careened into only a few minutes before. Slipping down and into the chasm, they looked around.

"Where the hell are they?" Rick pulled out his gun.

"That's Snake Dike," Woody said, pointing further down Half Dome at the serpentine prominence of rock about two feet wide, one foot thick, and hundreds of feet long working its way up to them from the void below.

They stood for a moment surrounded by the uncompromising elements of night and rock, wondering how Stuart and Jeffrey could have so rapidly disappeared.

Then came an unmistakable noise—a high-pitched whizzing of nylon on steel.

"The rope!" they both exclaimed.

Behind them and a few feet to their right, they saw an anchor from which two locking carabiners hung, with a rope rapidly zipping through them.

Rick, who was closer to the line, lunged forward and reached for the nylon sheath and core. His hand wrapped around the rope just as the end whizzed up and into view. Desperately squeezing as tight as he could, Rick screamed in agony as the rope burned deep into his skin and inexorably continued to race by, until at last the loose tail passed out of his grip, through the anchors, down the vast side of Half Dome, and into the night.

46

CONTROVERSY

Monday, 3:30 A.M.

Highway 395 was desolate in the middle of the night and Mojo and Rosa hadn't seen headlights for the past twenty miles. Small towns came and went in the blink of an eye.

"*No comprendo.* I mean, what do climbers have to do with the whole Hetch Hetchy thing?" Rosa was frustrated with Mojo's explanations. "You said Woody is with a bunch of these climbers and two of them were killed?"

"Well, it's not their climbing that made them targets. It's the other things they were involved in," Mojo responded.

"So? *¿Cuál es la importancia?*" Rosa asked.

Mojo didn't answer at first. She had been wondering the same thing. What was so important? Why kill climbers? "You know what? That's a damn good question," Mojo said as she put on the brakes and pulled Rusty off the road and onto the gravel shoulder. "Switch driving?"

"*Sí.*"

The women changed spots, and Mojo pulled a tote bag from

the back seat and onto her lap and switched on the map light.
"Before leaving I printed out these blogs and emails about
Abigail 's death, and then Aiden's," Mojo said as she sifted
through papers in her folder. "Not every single one, but some."

"How did you choose?" Rosa asked as she pulled the Jeep
back onto the highway.

"Well, certain posts were more 'cuckoo for Cocoa Puffs.' You
know—*inflammatory*." Mojo yanked out a specific sheet. "Like
this one: 'Abigail Edward's death must be a catalyst for active
revolt. The time has come. We must hasten the dawn.' Not exactly
the language you'd expect from the hippie community."

Mojo pulled out another piece of paper. "But then I also
looked for these weird coded messages. Check it out. This
blogger keeps appearing. He or she just goes by the name 'Adams
Ansel.'"

"Like the photographer?" Rosa asked.

"Sort of, but backward."

"*¿Por qué?*"

"I'm not sure."

Mojo selected another group of pages and rifled through
them. "Listen to this one: 'Vengeance is now. Lithe churches
empty helm.' Or this one: 'Beware the power of the holy temple.'"

"It doesn't make sense."

"You know what I think?"

"*¿Qué?*"

"Well, most of this rhetoric is mournful, a little ticked off, but
generally reasonable—not in the crazy bird nest—but the other
stuff, these weird messages, that's an entirely different side of the
tracks, you know? Whoever is posting these things, they actually
want us to figure them out," Mojo said.

"*¿De verdad?*"

"Makes sense to me."

The old Jeep drifted onto the rumble strip separating the road
from its shoulder and a twenty-foot drop into the West Walker

River. Rosa brought the vehicle back between the lines and exhaled. "Who the hell is writing all of this?"

"It's coming from all of these different sources, like some giant sociopathic round table with all these wack jobs spewing crazy at each other." Mojo dug back into her bag. "Here, check it out. 'Monkey Wrench,' that guy that appears a lot and definitely has a head seat at the crazy conference, but the name is fairly generic. I mean *The Monkey Wrench Gang* is like the most famous environmentalist manifesto out there."

Mojo put the papers down for a minute and stared at the empty highway. The whistles and rumblings of Rusty seemed to grow louder in defiance of any contemplation.

"Alright," Mojo's voice cut through the Jeep's noise. "Let's try a couple conspiracies on for size."

"Okay."

"Well, let's say there is some radical environmental plot that Abigail and Aiden were a part of. It sounds like they knew each other, but let's go one step further and just say for the sake of argument that they were co-conspirators in some, you know, super secret group."

"They climbed together, too, right?"

"Exactly. Who knows what they could have been up to. Then, someone who is being targeted by their group finds out about this nefarious hippie environmental plot and decides to kill them to prevent whatever it was that they were planning on doing."

"*Sí.*"

Mojo tapped her index finger on the dashboard as she was thinking. "Then, you know, logically, the rest of the group is provoked into action. So, they announce their action in this weird *hippie speak* on the Internet, referencing Muir and using all these odd phrases, which I guess makes sense—so no one can trace them."

"*No lo sé*" Rosa said.

"Exactly," Mojo responded. "To me, it doesn't feel right. It's not... authentic or something, but to the trigger-happy FBI...well, I doubt they'd think twice."

The Jeep crested a pass before plunging into the wide-open valley of Bridgeport.

"Yeah," Mojo continued. "I guess, I'm afraid that when the dust settles on whatever is motivating these killings and all the cuckoos fly home, there will be some unintended consequences. I just want to get Woody from whatever the hell is going on down there."

47

HE REALLY WAS

Monday, 3:35 A.M.

J*effrey's gone.*

As soon as the rope disappeared over the edge of Half Dome, Rick understood. Jeffrey didn't have a harness; he wouldn't have been tied to the rope, and he was nowhere to be seen.

Rick's face contorted in anger and pain. Jeffrey had been his partner for the past three years. They had shared so much together—so many good times, so many adventures.

Why Jeffrey? Why did I let Jeffrey come on this hunt? Rick felt a toxic mixture of emotions descending on him at once. Earlier tonight, he felt enrapt by the hunt, as if some forgotten part of him had been reawakened by the challenge of rescuing the kids and tracking a killer. Now, swirling into his psyche was a strange concoction of grief and guilt, commingling with the adrenaline from earlier. His emotions spilled together into a blood-red river of primal anger. He felt like transforming himself into some other creature, painting his face, shouting into the air, and chasing down this monster that had killed Jeffrey, not to apprehend him, but to bludgeon him slowly to death. Squeezing his eyes tight, Rick yelled and slammed his bloody palm against the rock.

His scream startled Woody, who backed up against the rock corridor, giving Rick some space.

Why Jeffrey?

Rick put his forehead against the rock and breathed into the cold granite.

Do something. Fucking do something.

A valve seemed to close inside Rick; the physiochemical change was immediate. If Jeffrey was gone, they were going to get the son of a bitch who was responsible. Rick threw down his backpack and pulled out his radio.

"Come on, Paula. I know you'll be able to hear me," Rick said as he switched on the device and brought it to his mouth. "Curry Village Ranger Station, this is Rick. Is anyone there?"

Silence. Rick stared at the small screen.

"Will the signal reach from where we are?" Woody asked.

Suddenly the radio came faintly to life. "Rick, this is Paula. Where the hell have you been?"

"Paula, we're on the western shoulder of Half Dome tracking the murder suspect from earlier this evening. Did you get all that?"

"Yeah, I think so. I'm walking to the middle of the parking lot. That usually helps with reception. It sounds windy up there."

"I'll try to speak slowly." Rick paused. "Now Paula, this is very important. I need you to send another team up, whoever you have available, to intercept this guy. He'll be on the Mist Trail heading back to the valley. He's Caucasian, about six foot, with long blond hair and a bleached-white goatee."

"Got it."

"He's wearing gray pants and a black shirt with white letters. His name is Stuart White. Tell them to exercise extreme caution. White is very dangerous. It looks like he killed Jeffrey."

"Killed Jeffrey?!"

"We don't know for sure, but it's not looking good."

There was a long pause on the line as the weight of Rick's announcement settled over both of them.

Rick continued. "Make sure they are equipped to handle this guy, and block off the Happy Isles Trail to prevent anyone else from getting up here."

"Copy that."

Rick put away the radio and threw his bag back over his shoulder. "Let's move," he said to Woody. Quickly and silently, the two marched up the fourth and third-class slabs toward the summit.

Once they reached the top, Woody turned to Rick and said, "I'm sorry about Jeffrey, Chief. He was a really great guy."

The statement startled Rick. He took a deep breath and responded, "Yeah, he was, Woody. He really was."

48

LITERALLY EXPLODES

Monday, 3:36 A.M.

S tuart looked down the length of his rope at the moonlit base of Snake Dike. On any other day, in a matter of a couple hours, the small clearing that began one of the world's most famous climbs would be crowded with parties queuing up to follow the long geological anomaly, like some monstrous rock python out of the Jurassic Age, twisting up the side of Half Dome.

Not today.

He clicked into the last set of bolts and strung his rappel rope though the final two carabiners. Stuart checked his equipment, unhooked himself from the anchors, and lowered the last eighty feet to the ground.

Ahhh... Stuart felt invincible—all of his military training and work were paying dividends. He could deceive. He could plan. And he could kill.

Looking around Snake Dike's base area, Stuart didn't immediately see any evidence of his most recent trophy. Given the distance Jeffrey fell, there may not be much left to see anyway.

Unlike Abigail Edwards, who fell less than four hundred feet, or Aiden, who slid and careened off the lower concave base of Cathedral, Jeffrey's total plummet was over a thousand vertical feet. He pictured when a human body falls that distance and finally connects with the ground, especially if that ground was hard and uneven, the body quite literally explodes; appendages and body segments burst apart, like a medieval drawn and quartered execution.

No matter, a photograph isn't really necessary—this time.

Besides, time was of the essence. Soon, the Park Service would be out in force looking for him.

Stuart left his rope hanging from the last set of bolts and left his harness on the ground. From there he ran about a hundred feet from the base area to where he left something of importance. It was common for climbers to hide a pack and some gear at the base of a climb, and he felt sure his pack would be where he left it a few days ago.

Sure enough. There it was behind a log and under the dense cover of some saplings. Stuart smiled as he reached down and lifted the pack onto his shoulders.

Quickly now.

49

PSYCHOLOGY

Monday, 3:37 A.M.

"Hey, sorry that took so long," Alexandra said as she strode back toward Joy.

"What? Where'd you go?" Joy shook herself awake and looked up at Alexandra.

"I got a little disoriented and had to backtrack. It sure is confusing hiking around at night. Oh, I'm sorry, were you sleeping?"

"It's all right. I'd rather have the company," Joy responded as she sat up and dusted herself off. "Thanks for this emergency blanket and the jacket. I guess I must be pretty tired."

"Those things work surprisingly well, don't they?"

"Yeah." Joy held up the reflective material and examined it. She thought of Woody.

Alexandra took a seat next to Joy. The temperature seemed to drop in the hour or two before sunrise as the moisture from the Merced River finally absorbed into the otherwise dry alpine air. Joy didn't know how long she had been sleeping but guessed it had to have been at least fifteen minutes.

"So I wonder how they're doing up there," Alexandra mused.

"Stuart seems like one dangerous guy," Joy answered.

"Oh, I'm sure it will all work out. Rick's knows what he's doing."

"Do you like him... like that.?" Joy asked.

Alexandra appeared startled by the question.

"What? You mean romantically, sexually? Me? No. Certainly not." Alexandra laughed. "I don't really get involved with anyone at work; kind of a rule of mine."

Joy looked questioningly at Alexandra. She was drop-dead gorgeous, a little too polished and refined for Park Service work, but she wore the uniform well. Joy had certain outfits that fit predetermined formulas depending on the image she was trying to convey. Alexandra would look good no matter what she wore, and Joy couldn't help but feel self-conscious around her. "But the guys, like Jeffrey, it seems they would all, you know, fall all over themselves to date you."

Alexandra burst out laughing.

"What's so funny?"

"Oh, I don't really approach it—dating and all—that way." Alexandra stood back up and took a step away from Joy toward the Merced. Her dark profile glowed, thin and distinct against the moonlit river. She reminded Joy of a fashion designer sketch, with charcoal edges and rigid angles on heavy linen paper.

Alexandra turned back toward Joy. "I'll clue you in on something. The guys on the Park Service staff, they don't really want *me*. They want"—she tilted her head, a smile barely creasing her cheeks—*the pursuit of me.*"

"What do you mean?" Joy asked, unconsciously preparing to crack knuckles on her right hand.

"You're in college, right?"

"Not yet. I'm off to Berkeley in just a couple weeks."

"Berkeley—really? I received two of my advanced degrees there. That's great. Congratulations."

"Thanks. I'm excited."

"As you should be. It's a life-changing experience." Alexandra looked up for a moment toward Half Dome. "Anyway, like I was saying, have you ever heard of the study of behaviorism?"

"That's psychology, right?"

"Yes, it is psychology. That's good, Joy."

Joy leaned in closer. "And psychologists like B. F. Skinner tested the effect of certain positive and negative reinforcement on human behavior."

"You mean like Pavlov and his dogs?"

"Exactly!" Alexandra smirked. "The dogs salivated whenever Pavlov rang a bell, even when the food stopped being offered."

"Right, I remember that."

"Well, guys or men, they operate in much the same way when it comes to women; they are enticed by the idea more so than the actual thing."

"I'm not sure I follow," Joy said. "So guys are like dogs?"

"You could look at it that way, but not necessarily just like the dogs. According to the behaviorist school of thought, people don't necessarily want the reward at the end of the journey, as is the case of my coworkers, like Jeffrey. The reward actually is not a date or to get me in bed."

Joy was taken aback. Alexandra was so clinical about the male gender.

"You see, they are just as enticed and happy by the pursuit, by the bell, not the food. They salivate regardless. I can pretty much get whatever I want here because I keep myself just out of reach."

"That's manipulative though, isn't it?"

Alexandra paused. The stars behind her had begun to grow dim in anticipation of the coming sun. "Maybe it's manipulative, but if the guys are happy, then what's the harm? I'm actually more of a positive force than negative; I ring the bell, they drool. It's classic conditioning. If I were to suddenly date just one person, then I'd ruin that positive environmental stimuli for all of them––

even... the guy I was sleeping with. By keeping everyone at a comfortable distance, everyone gets the positive stimulation."

"I see." Joy nodded but still felt a little uneasy.

"What about you and Woody?"

Joy drew a sudden breath. The question, though she should have expected it, caught her off guard. She had feelings for Woody, but they were so contradictory. "Oh," she stammered. "We're, um, not really a thing."

"You act like you are."

"No, really, we're just good friends."

"Just friends?"

"Yes, Alex," Joy sighed. "I'm going off to college and Woody, he's just a junior in high school. It's not really fair to either of us, you know, to get in a relationship."

"But it sounds like you guys spend a lot of time together."

"Yeah, I guess we do."

"Isn't that manipulative on your part?"

Joy smiled up at Alexandra. "Touché."

She didn't feel like she was toying with Woody's emotions, but realized she was stringing him along; sort of like Alexandra did with her colleagues in Yosemite. Then again, *there are my emotions to consider, too.* That was an uncomfortable notion for Joy. She had made it a rule to not let entanglement hamper her goals. Unlike her emotionally volatile older sister, who had no patience for things that didn't bring happiness, Joy was forbearing to a fault. She would work an equation or rearrange a thesis hundreds of times until she settled on the right direction.

Despite her personal rules, she couldn't deny what was developing between her and Woody. She couldn't deny how she felt, huddled next to him on the ridge above the John Muir Trail. And she couldn't deny that for a brief instance there she had lost control and allowed her emotions to overrule her judgment.

"You see, Joy," Alexandra began as she stared up at the final stars of the early morning sky, "you're making him happy just by holding the hope out there."

"I'm not sure I'm comfortable with that," Joy said.

"Well, then don't whine about it."

"*What?*"

At that moment Alexandra's radio buzzed at her side. "Alex, this is Rick. Can you meet us back on the trail?"

Alexandra picked up her radio and depressed the call button. "Okay, we're on our way. Do you have Stuart?"

There was a long pause. "Alex, it's not good. Jeffrey's likely gone. I'll explain when we're all together."

50

IGNITION

Monday, 3:51 A.M.

Stuart took off down the Snake Dike approach trail, charging through the bushes and talus.

Speed is essential. This must happen before daybreak.

Stuart sprinted down the slab portion of the approach and then cut immediately to his right toward the main Yosemite Valley. He knew this summer approach trail intimately, including the brief third and fourth-class mountaineering sections, as it made its way down to the north of the majestic dome of Liberty Cap and onward to the left of Nevada Falls.

Once below Liberty Cap, Stuart connected back with the Mist Trail. The adrenaline still pumping, he figured his heart rate was hovering around one hundred beats per minute, just where he liked it. Through his training and research, he knew many stressful situations would skyrocket a soldier's resting heart rate of sixty to eighty beats per minute up to one hundred and thirty and beyond, which automatically decreased their fine motor control and cognitive processing of complex tasks. He had even seen grown men defecate in their uniforms, a sign of full loss of motor skills, which usually happened around one hundred and seventy beats per minute. In contrast, Stuart liked a somewhat elevated heart rate; he wanted just enough adrenaline to sharpen his mind and push out distraction, but not so much that he couldn't think clearly. That's why he didn't engage the rangers in conversation at the top of Half Dome. He was planning and keeping his heart rate right where he needed it to be.

After a few more minutes of fast hiking, Stuart hopped into the woods off of the established Mist Trail and headed down along the north side of the Upper Merced River, before it plunged over Vernal Falls.

This is the spot.

The trail Stuart had just abandoned would cross the Merced at a bridge above Emerald Pool before it led up to the brink of Vernal Falls, and then over the steep cliff along a narrow ledge of rock.

Approaching the north shore of Emerald Pool, Stuart set down his pack. The normally clover-green iridescence of the water was hidden in the predawn darkness. Next, he took off his shoes, socks, pants, shirt, and finally his underwear, leaving himself stark naked in the woods of Yosemite. Stuart left his clothing in a careful pile and reached into his backpack, removing a battery-powered hair clipper. The Oster Classic 76 brought back memories and anger as he held it in his hand. Though lighter in weight than the one he brandished for three long and humiliating years in the US Marines, he knew every ridge, rumble, feature, and capability of this device.

Naked, Stewart walked forward to the edge of the water. There, he set the clipper down on a rock bordering the pool and waded in. Despite the frigid temperature, the water felt incredible, restorative even. It penetrated his sore muscles, numbing and soothing them, and reawakened his senses. He took a deep breath and submerged himself totally in the icy embrace of Emerald Pool.

Gaining firm footing, Stuart strode over to the shore and grabbed the clipper. He used to be able to do this in thirty-seven seconds, but this evening he was not going for any records, just for credibility. He flicked the switch on. First, the goatee he had dyed white was removed. Then, without looking at the settings, Stuart switched the depth of the blade and made three clean cuts across the top of his head. He knew he had the gauge set correctly by how the thick stubble felt to his thumb as it followed the clipper's efficient path. Next, he brought the depth of the blade up and finished the remainder of his head. Finally, he shaved his face and the back of his neck, then set the clipper down. He ran his fingers over his scalp to inspect the finished product; flawless —a perfectly executed military-style crew cut.

Stuart took the device with him this time as he waded back into deeper water. Once he was immersed to his waist, Stuart hurled the device toward the end of Emerald Pool where he knew the current would pick it up and carry it over Vernal Falls to be dashed into pieces on the rocks below.

Stuart dipped his full body and head back into the cool and cleansing water, running his hands across his submerged skull and face to remove any errant hairs left by his recent modifications. He then waded out of the pool.

Arriving at his pack, Stuart reached inside and removed a smaller bright green North Face camelback daypack that had never been used. He also removed two new Asolo hiking boots, fresh from their packaging. The rest of the contents of the pack remained, including two large, long, and clear bottles that contained a liquid anyone would have guessed to be water. Stuart threw the pack over his shoulder, grabbed his clothing, and headed into the woods.

Arriving at the first pile of wood that he had gathered two days before, Stuart, still naked, took his old black long-sleeved shirt and doused it with a healthy portion of clear liquid from one of the bottles. He then shoved the shirt into the center of the pile of dead wood, tree limbs, and bark. He splashed a little more of the liquid on the pile, so that he had used exactly half of one of the bottles. Pulling the end of his shirt, he left a sleeve hanging partially out of the wood and bramble. Next, Stuart opened a Ziploc pouch, also in the backpack, and removed a lighter. Casually and without a second thought, Stuart lit his first bonfire.

The flames spread efficiently on the kerosene-laced shirt and into the dead wood, erupting into a massive pyre within a minute. Not that Stuart watched any of this. He was onto his second heap of dead wood; this pile was lit with his old gray pants. He then moved onto his next pile, which he lit with his underwear and socks. Then to his fourth and final pile, which he lit with his backpack that contained his old shoes.

Once the final pile had ignited, Stuart stepped back to admire his work. The flames leapt and danced skyward into the stoic trees; motionless and quiet, the trees observed the tiny infernos nipping at their heels until one by one they began to ignite.

Stuart remained, watching his creation build upon itself. The instantaneous warmth felt good on his bare flesh, and he reveled in its power for a moment, closing his eyes and raising his arms high above his head as if to worship this thing called fire that he had created and bestowed upon the forest.

Suddenly the wind gusted a flame at Stuart and he stumbled backward to avoid becoming part of the conflagration. He laughed as he did so.

Yes, I know. I need to keep moving.

Stuart jogged back to his daypack and new hiking boots by Emerald Pool. He quickly scrubbed the slight odor of kerosene from his hands and changed into the clothing he had kept pressed and neatly folded inside the small trendy-looking daypack. He put on a brand new pair of khaki Patagonia hiking pants and a new bright red Columbia button-down backcountry nylon shirt. To top off the outfit, Stuart placed a mesh and nylon hiking hat with a wide tan brim on his head, a fancy camera around his neck and shoulder, and an expandable hiking pole from the pack in his hand. After lacing up his shiny Asolo boots, Stuart stood up and strode back up to the Mist Trail, hiking briskly over the bridge above Emerald Pool.

Stuart now looked like the typical summer tourist out hiking in Yosemite. When he reached the edge of Vernal Falls, he looked down and saw five sets of headlamps working their way up the slippery stone steps, which received nearly constant watering from Vernal's powerful spray, giving the Mist Trail its name.

The headlamps probably belonged to the rangers on their way to apprehend him. Stuart looked over his shoulder as he began walking to greet the rangers. He could see the flames engulfing tree after tree. He smiled.

Strolling down the steep cliff ledge with its protective metal guardrail, Stuart flipped on his new Petzl headlamp, which was placed neatly below his hat. When he reached the corner of the rock, he waited for the rangers. The first one appeared, laboriously plodding up the steps, and nearly ran into Stuart before noticing him.

"Oh, hello."

"Yes then, hello there." Stuart had changed his tone to be decidedly foreign, Eastern European maybe.

The ranger hesitated and looked Stuart up and down. "Have you seen a climber with long blond hair and a white goatee?"

Stuart paused and leaned in as if he hadn't quite understood the question.

"He was wearing gray pants and a black shirt with white lettering," the ranger said.

"Yes, actually, he's, eh..." Stuart paused as if looking for the correct words. "He's one reasons I am not sitting at the Nevada Fall waiting sunrise."

"What do you mean, sir?" the ranger inquired.

"He is—how you say—fire lighting?"

"*Lighting a fire?*" The ranger seemed alarmed.

"Yes. Just eh... the Vernal Fall, above..." Stuart used his hands to supplement his labored speech. "I saw man fire lighting. I not get good look, but... description, it sounds... he's one you... looking for."

"Where exactly did you see him?"

"Well, you know, eh, bridge?"

"Above the pool?"

"Eh—"

At this point other rangers were joining Stuart and listening along.

"The small lake? The pond?" the first ranger continued.

"Ah, yes. Bridge above pond. There he is."

"Thank you, sir. Billy you stay here and get this guy's information before following. Sir, do you have and ID?"

"Yes," Stuart responded.

"Everyone else. Let's move."

Immediately, the rest of the rangers took off up the trail.

Stuart dug out his fake passport and handed it to Billy who quickly copied down the false information about the Czech Republic before turning to follow the other rangers. Stuart sat in his little corner and watched them go up the steep ledge. While he was still within earshot, he yelled up, "Take care now—with fire lighting."

SMALL TOWN GOSSIP

Monday, 4:03 a.m.

"Fill up at 'Whoa Nelli' there." Mojo gestured ahead to Rosa who was still at the wheel.

"*Si.*"

Rosa pulled Rusty into the Tioga Gas Mart in Lee Vining, the last place to gas up before entering Yosemite National Park and famous for its summer concerts, outdoor trapeze, wine tasting and gourmet fare.

Mojo got out of the Jeep, stretching and yawning in the chilly air while she walked around to fill up the tank and switch positions. Rosa headed into the store. Having exhausted just about every theory she could imagine to explain the targeted killing of climbers, Mojo could only point to the connection between Hetch Hetchy and the idea that some new revelation was impending—*maybe even dam removal?* An Army Corps study exhaustively looked at the feasibility of the dam removal proposition.* A litany of research compared water reuse and conservation to providing new water, and lambasted the city of San Francisco for not doing more to conserve and recycle.* But everything was public knowledge well-disseminated by local and national newspapers. *What was so freak'n novel and controversial? What was worth killing over?*

Mojo replaced the nozzle and screwed tight the gas cap. She was tired of thinking about it. Rosa emerged from the Tioga Gas Mart with two coffees, humming a tune and staring out at Mono Lake.

"You're in awfully good spirits for this outrageous hour," Mojo commented as she took her seat behind the steering wheel.

"Oh, yeah, I guess. I was just thinking about those girls Woody is with."

"You've got to be kidding. You mean the predatory cougar patrol?"

"*Cálmate.* They're good girls, and you should feel better knowing Woody is with the Cooper sisters."

"How so?" Mojo pulled the Jeep out of the station and took a left onto Highway 120 heading over Tioga Pass.

"I knew Jasmine and Joy in elementary school." Rosa leaned back in her seat. "Jasmine, she was often labeled as a troublemaker by the school and community, but was not in any way cruel or destructive. I mean, well, I'm not so sure how much I should share with you—legally, you know."

"Oh, come on. We live in a small town. How much do you *really* think I don't already know?" Mojo huffed. She lowered her voice to mimic a radio announcer. "'The Coopers moved to town, like a lot of locals, drawn by the activities and the allure of the Tahoe lifestyle. They didn't have a plan; they just had a dream. When they landed decent paying jobs at Harvey's Casino, they decided to start a family.' Stop me if I'm wrong on any of this."

Rosa just laughed. The Tahoe local storyline was commonplace and its basic narrative could be recycled for family after family.

Mojo switched back into character. "'So, like a lot of folks that depended on good old Harvey Gross, they did well for a time, but when Harvey's sold out to Harrah's—well, you know the sad story folks—the lifestyle the Coopers had become accustomed to went down like a bad poker hand. Then, let's see...'" Mojo dropped the artificial accent. "There was something about serious drug use with the parents, and then while the kids were in elementary school there was a divorce, and the dad ran off to some other part of the country and—wait, don't tell me—they spent some time being looked after by an uncle, but that ended with the uncle being arrested, and ever since then a grandmother has basically raised Jasmine and her sister. That's pretty much it, right?"

Rosa smiled at her friend. "*Sí, señora*, that's pretty close to accurate. But what your gossip circle doesn't get is that the Cooper sisters did just fine. Joy is brilliant with a near 4.0 GPA. And Jasmine, as wild and unhinged as she appears to be, is one of the most resourceful kids that I've ever run across."

"Her business seems to be doing really well."

"Exactly. That's the sort of thing that would get her in trouble before. Now, somehow it's condoned. Strange times, huh?"

"I guess so."

"They're doing fine, and all while being raised by their grandmother on a fixed retirement income." Rosa stared off into the deep volcanic canyon of Tioga Pass. The moon had nearly vanished behind the distant peaks as the Jeep made its way between the canyon walls.

"My point is, Mojo—Woody is in good hands. That's all."

52

A LITTLE MODESTY

Monday, 4:35 A.M.

J oy watched as the moon sank lower in the sky and lost itself behind a wall of evergreen trees flanking the predawn horizon. The chill wind came in aggressive sporadic pulses, making her yearn for the sun to appear.

"There they are!" Alexandra said as Rick and Woody emerged from the trees.

"Any sign of the other rangers?" Rick asked as he approached.

"No."

"Let's head down the trail toward the valley. We have to cross paths with them soon."

"Rick..." Alexandra grabbed his arm, "what happened up there?"

"Jeffrey—he went after Stuart alone. I'm not sure if he could have survived the..." With that, Rick turned and kept moving westward.

Alexandra, Woody, and Joy fell in line behind Rick.

"How are you holding up?" Joy quietly asked Woody.

"Yeah, I'm not sure." Woody slowed down. "It was all going so well. I mean we *had* him; it was *over*. But... it happened so fast. Stuart—he was so damn quick."

Not sure of what else to say, Joy took Woody's hand as they rejoined the main trail. Up ahead, the Merced River wound its way to Nevada Falls and to a wooden bridge made of massive timbers.

"Hey, what's that glow?" Woody asked. "Over there, by Liberty Cap."

"It's not the sunrise. We're looking west," Joy said.

At that moment, a flicker became visible within the trees. Then, a few more tongues of flame leapt out of the small basin below Nevada Falls and ignited the forest alongside the shoulder of Half Dome.

"No," said Alexandra. "It can't be!"

Without conferring, they started to run.

"Let's make for the Muir Trail. The Mist will be too dangerous," Rick said.

He's right, Joy thought. *The Mist Trail drops alongside the drainage of Liberty Cap. Too close to the flames.*

"Alex, get on your phone. Call Valley Fire. We have a situation."

As they ran, Liberty Cap began to glow as the fire swirled around its base, catching tree after tree, raging in sudden gusts up the backside of the rock.

"There hasn't been any lightning," Woody said.

"It has to be man-made," said Rick.

"Do you think—?" Joy began.

No one said his name, but everyone had to be thinking it: *Stuart.*

"This is the perfect tinderbox," Rick said. "No rain in over a month, these crazy Mono winds, and all this dense undergrowth—"

Rick's right, Joy thought. For years, the US Forest Service and the National Park Service had a policy of putting out forest fires, even those caused by lightning strikes. Smokey the Bear, whom Joy grew up with, had done a good job. She remembered reading about the Ahwahnechee people, who inhabited Yosemite Valley before white settlers; they would burn the valley floor on an annual basis. When one of the last surviving members of the Ahwahnechee tribe was brought back to the Park in the 1940s and asked what she thought of her former home, she described the environment as "bushy," meaning overgrown and improperly cared for. Joy watched as the nighttime silhouette of Liberty Cap became engulfed in flames. *There's so much fire.*

"Wait a minute!" Alexandra shouted. "We can't stay on the Muir trail. We'll get too close to Liberty Cap!"

"You're right. We have to find another way." Rick was already heading south off the trail and toward the Merced River. "We should be able to ford the river somewhere."

They turned and followed Rick toward the river, charging into the sandy forest.

"What about the waterfall?" Woody asked.

"Let's hope the current is weak," Rick yelled over his shoulder.

The wild and gluttonous fire surged into the woods, reaching further into Little Yosemite Valley and challenging the backside of Half Dome. The blaze was almost at their backs as they approached the banks of the Merced.

"Damn, the water is faster than I thought," Rick said.

They scanned up and down the river, looking for something to ease their crossing. Peering into the inky blackness, Joy's eyes could hardly adjust from the intense light of the forest fire to the nocturnal darkness of the powerful river.

"There!" Alex said, and took off downstream toward a downed tree wedged against some rocks just above the current. The skinny tree angled steeply downward from the higher riverbank and terminated on a massive boulder. From there it appeared they could push their way through shallow water, holding onto the rocks as needed.

"That doesn't exactly look safe," Rick said to Alexandra as they jogged toward the log.

"Any better ideas?" Alexandra asked.

"No. We need to be upwind of this fire as soon as possible."

Joy could feel heat from the conflagration raging closer to them.

"I'll go first." Rick put a foot out on the log and transferred his weight. The log appeared to sag, but it held. Joy watched as he took two steps out. Below him, the Merced plunged down a small drop.

"Okay, I'm safe," Rick yelled back once he was on the large boulder in the middle of the current.

"I'll go next," said Alexandra. She hopped on the log as Rick held the end of it tightly against the boulder while she crossed.

"How deep is it from the middle on?" Joy asked Woody.

"Less than here, I hope."

Alexandra reached the center boulder, then turned and waved toward Woody and Joy to hurry up while Rick took on the rest of the crossing.

"It's too bad I never practiced jumping on Jasmine's slackline." Joy forced out a nervous laugh.

"You go first," Woody said to Joy.

"Are you sure?" Joy asked.

Behind them, a loud crack was heard as fire surged toward the river, toppling one massive fir tree into a grove of smaller ones.

"No time like the present," Joy said, stepping onto the narrow wet log. She moved cautiously, step by step, fixing her sight on the end of the log, just like Jasmine had advised her on the slackline. *Pick a point on the tree that you're heading toward and just move towards it. You're feet will know where to go.*

Another step.

I'm almost there.

Then it all went wrong. Joy's foot hit a small branch stub jutting out of the log, and she tripped.

Desperately, Joy tried to regain her footing as she stumbled and landed on her chest on top of the slim wood surface.

She wrapped her arms and legs around the log as she rotated to its side and slid toward the water.

Woody sprang forward.

"Joy, hold on! I'll be right there," Woody yelled while he scampered down the tree's wet bark.

Joy was beginning to slip. The freezing Merced water splashed against her pack and the small of her exposed back with terrifying force. In desperation, she locked her ankles around the log and clasped her wrists.

Now above her, Woody reached into the top of his backpack, grabbed a cordelette and quickly undid the figure-eight knot at the end.

"I'm here," Woody said as he crouched down. "This is what you're going to do, Joy."

Joy grimaced as her muscles throbbed.

Woody slipped the cordelette through both of Joy's backpack shoulder loops and across her chest as he spoke. "When I tell you to, let go of the log and grab as hard as you can onto this cordelette."

Joy felt the river surging like the rhythm of a heartbeat, pulling the backpack down as Woody girth-hitched the small cord.

"I'll guide you to the small eddy just downstream of the rock." Woody spoke the directions loud enough for Alexandra to hear as well. "Okay?" Woody asked.

"Okay." Joy nodded.

"You'll be all right. I've got you." With that, Woody maneuvered toward Alexandra and the boulder. He couldn't quite get the cordelette to reach all the way to the rock, but he was able to lock himself on the log with the back of his knee and get one hand into a crack on the boulder's granite surface.

"Grab my backpack and hold onto me," Woody yelled at Alexandra.

"Okay," Alexandra said.

They braced themselves on the rock and dug in their heels, readying for the imminent thrust. The cordelette stretched out above Joy's face and her eyes followed it backward along the underside of the sopping log to Woody and Alexandra. Rick watched from the far bank.

"All right, Joy," Woody began. "On the count of three. One—"

Woody was cut off by a loud crashing sound—a burning tree just upstream of their location fell into the Merced, sending a wave of water down the river, slamming into Joy and knocking her loose.

With a mouthful of water, Joy flew upside down as the cordelette cinched tight. Joy rotated onto her back in mid air, frantically grasping for the rest of the rope. Woody heaved forward, but locked his leg tightly around the tree and grasped the rock as Alexandra hung on.

With a resounding splash, Joy fell into the current. Woody grunted loudly as he strained to pull back on the cordelette with both arms and pushed into the rock with his feet.

"Pull her up!" Woody yelled to Alexandra.

Alexandra moved from where she had been behind Woody to the downstream edge of the rock and lay flat on her stomach, reaching out toward the water, but the boulder was too tall.

"Climb to my hands, Joy!" Alexandra yelled.

Joy could feel the slick granite surface as her legs and arms churned in a futile attempt to climb higher. Woody's cordelette was the only thing holding her from plunging back into the main surge of the current. Joy inched up and in the next moment her feet would give way and send her back, sometimes deeper into the frigid water.

"I can't get traction." Joy's teeth started to chatter.

Rick, who was too far away to assist with Joy's initial redirection, had made it back to the rock and reached down for Joy.

"Damn, she's too deep," Rick said. "Woody, we need your rope to pull her up. Joy, you may slip deeper in when we bring the rope over. Just hold on, okay?"

Joy nodded and tried as best she could to wrap her numb fingers around the slim cord.

Rick put his hands on the cordelette and started to pull toward the center of the rock.

Joy looked desperately toward Woody. *I can't be in this water much longer.*

"Alright, I've got her weight," Rick cried out. "Go help, Alex. I'll pull now."

Woody dislodged himself from the tree and scampered up the boulder to Alexandra's side.

Joy had slipped down deeper into the water. Between the weight of her frozen clothing and the backpack, she could barely keep her chin above the roiling surface.

Rick tugged hand-over-hand on the line, but could only get Joy about chest high out of the water.

"This isn't working," said Woody.

"Let's move toward the other side of the river." Rick strained to walk the rope to the far side of the boulder, dragging Joy along.

Joy looked up the length of the cordelette as it pulled her around the far side of the massive boulder. She could no longer feel her feet or legs as they knocked helplessly against the submerged rocks. Her fingers too were numb, and though they looked to be wrapped around the slim rope, she couldn't feel whether they were helping at all. Above her, Woody jumped to a lower flat rock and reached out for Rick to hand him the cordelette.

"Okay, I think we can get her up on this rock." Woody urged.

Rick leapt down and took the rope back. "Woody, you and Alex yank her up out of the water with your hands, I'll bring her as far out of the river as I can."

Rick wrapped his wrist and forearm in the rope and leaned backward off the upstream edge of the boulder. Woody pulled with one hand on the rope and groped for Joy with the other. Alexandra was barely able to snatch a shoulder strap of Joy's backpack by her fingertips, when Woody reached farther down the rock, grabbing onto Joy's armpit. Rick worked himself back onto the center of the rock by pulling up on the cord. Joy kicked with her numb legs in the swirling dark water and flopped onto her rib cage and then belly up onto the rock's edge. Woody tugged and rotated backward, pulling Joy up on top of him.

"Everyone okay there?" Rick asked.

Alexandra separated herself and eyed Rick. "Everyone's all right."

Rick stood up and looked down at Woody and Joy lying exhausted on the rock. "Now Joy, your body temperature—"

Joy sat upright, her clothes dripping the cold water into puddles all around her. Her teeth chattered uncontrollably. She glanced down at herself and promptly began removing her backpack and clothing.

Rick reached inside his pack. "Here's my emergency space blanket."

"Let's ss... see." Joy was shaking all over. "It's only ba... been a few minutes—ff... five at the most; I can't feel mum... my fingers or legs. Ca... core temperature should be stable... no risk of ... of afterdrop from vuv... vasodilation if I wa...warm my extremities ta... too quickly." She already had her pastel-colored fleece pullover on the rock, her Patagonia shirt off, and was struggling to remove her shoes and socks. "Woody... wa... would you...?"

"We're only two easy boulder hops away from the opposite bank, Joy," Alexandra said.

Rick had already jumped to the next rock. He turned and added, "Once you feel your body temperature is up, we really need to keep moving."

"Ag... agreed," Joy responded.

Woody had removed his soaked pants and one shoe and sock. Joy knew he was painfully shy about his body. He glanced self-consciously back up at Joy for some direction on how far to undress.

"See you on the far side there," Alexandra said as she slid cautiously off their boulder and hopped toward the next. Joy thought she could barely make out a little knowing wink from Alexandra as she exited the rock.

"Let's see," Joy began. "Lay some of your cul... clothes out on the rock here along with your pup... pack, for padding."

"I have more clothing. Do you want me to get it now?" Woody asked.

"Nun... no, not yet."

"Okay."

"Shirt too." Joy forced a smile. "Ka... keep your boxers though."

Woody did as instructed, laying his pants next to the other articles of clothing in a line down the center of the boulder.

"Nun... now, a little ma... modesty. Hold this up," Joy said, handing Woody the unfolded emergency blanket.

Woody held up the silvery reflective metallic sheet so that it was even with Joy's shoulders.

"Yeah, even my panties... are frr... freezing wet." Joy slid her sports bra over her head and then pulled her underwear down.

Woody stood like a statue, eyes wide and knees locked tight, waiting for Joy to give him his next set of directions. Joy reached up and grabbed the corner of the emergency blanket out of Woody's right hand and curled it over her shoulder as she rotated around inside the blanket, turning to face Woody and then tossing the other end of the blanket around his neck, enveloping them together inside. "Okay, lul... let's lie down now."

Awkwardly, Joy took a seat while Woody went down first to one knee and then rotated onto his side. In the confusion and attempts to keep the reflective sheet wrapped around both of them, Joy bumped her head into Woody's chin. "Sss—sorry."

"That's, um, okay," Woody responded.

"Nun... now, this only works if our... bodies are ta... touching."

"Um... all right then."

As Woody inched closer, Joy reached over and put her arm around Woody's waist, pulling her body toward him until they made full contact.

Woody shivered all over as he felt Joy's cold wet skin press against his.

He must feel like he's lying down bare-chested on a frozen lake, Joy thought.

Joy closed her eyes and hugged Woody against her, allowing his warmth to interact with the chilliness of her body.

Woody's mind was spinning as he fussed to adjust the reflective blanket, tucking it under his feet and pulling it tight over his head so that it cocooned them completely before he could begin to gradually relax. After an awkward silence, he brought his arm over Joy's shoulder and around to the center of her back where he ran the warmth of his hand back and forth across Joy's frozen shoulders and then up and down her spine.

Joy took a deep a breath. "Mmmm, that feels sooo good, Woody." She could feel warmth slowly returning to her body. She poked him lightly in his ribs with her elbow. "Hey, I thought you said you had bub... bad circulation."

"Well—" Woody bit his lip—"right now, my heart's definitely racing."

Joy smiled and snuggled closer.

"Are you getting warmer?" he asked.

"Yeah... thanks."

"Hey, you know, anytime you need me to do this—"

Joy and Woody both laughed out loud inside their cozy silver shell. Joy felt an overwhelming urge to kiss Woody. She pulled herself even closer.

"It's funny," Woody said. "All that fire and heat just on the other side of the river and here we are—"

Joy suddenly remembered her compelling conversation with Alexandra. *Is this that Pavlovian classic conditioning? Am I just using Woody?* She was going to college. He was staying behind. She didn't really care at the moment, because she knew she cared about Woody. Her mind was a jumble of conflicting thoughts and feelings. What did she feel?–– like finally allowing herself to trust and give in to her emotions. What did she think?––about how emotion and feelings had betrayed her in the past and that being deliberate was the only—

Before Joy could finish her train of thought, Woody brought it to a screeching halt. He brought his hand up to cradle Joy's neck, tilted his head down, and kissed her full on the lips. In this moment, their personal doubts and fears and the chaotic scene around them simply vanished. It no longer mattered that they were two young people with big plans for the future lying naked in the middle of an icy torrent on a cold granite boulder wrapped in a thin blanket and surrounded by darkness and a raging forest fire. For this moment they could have been anywhere––in the back seat of a car, on a tropical island beach, in a bridal suite...

"Joy! Woody!" Rick shouted from the far bank. "We need to keep moving, you two!"

Woody pulled away. "God, do we have to, Joy?"

"Afraid so,"

"Hey, you could fall in again and––"

"Shut up!" Joy playfully poked Woody and gave him a parting kiss on his cheek."

They emerged from their silver cocoon and quickly got

dressed. Woody handed Joy a soft fleece pullover from his pack, and in it they stowed the blanket, clothing, and gear. Then, hand in hand, Woody and Joy cautiously made their way to the far bank, each of them imagining what reactions to expect from their curious companions.

53

CLOCKWORK

Monday, 5:11 a.m.

J asmine and Rebecca were catching some much-needed shut-eye in their car in the Curry Village parking lot. Rebecca knew the Park Service generally frowned on sleeping in vehicles and routinely fined "car baggers." Under the current circumstances, she figured just collapsing from exhaustion would be tolerated as an excuse if questioned.

Rebecca had managed to get about two hours of sleep, despite the awkward conditions. Snug in their sleeping bags, she and Jasmine rested, until sunrise when the valley seemed to detonate with activity.

At first, it was just one or two sirens rushing by, echoing off the canyon walls. Annoyed, Rebecca shifted in her seat, adjusted her prized purple sleeping bag, and rolled over to look at Jasmine in the misty early morning glow of Camp Curry's streetlights. She was still asleep, as expected. Rebecca woke up at the slightest disturbance while Jasmine could sleep though just about anything.

But even Jasmine awoke at the next set of sirens. It seemed

every Park Service vehicle in the valley was rushing to or from somewhere. Sirens, speeding cars, and loud conversations combined in a cacophony of activity that roused Jasmine from her cozy position between the steering wheel and the upturned armrest. "What the—?"

Rebecca was already sitting up and looking around. "I don't know, Jaz. I'm not sure what the hell is going on."

"Let's move," Jasmine snapped.

"I doubt they're all coming after us for spending the night in our car," Rebecca responded.

"I... I'm just not comfortable here. I mean, look at that." Jasmine pointed over her shoulder. "Check out that whole mess of rangers around that building."

"That must be some kind of station," Rebecca said. "Hey, let's go find out what's going on."

Jasmine leaned forward and pulled the plastic lever to bring her seat back to an upright position. "I just want to, like, drive."

Wriggling out of her sleeping bag, Jasmine started the car, rubbed the sleep from her eyes, and exited the Curry Village parking lot. She headed down the two-lane road toward Stoneman Meadow and pulled onto the side of the road.

"I wonder... I've never seen it like this," Jasmine declared. "You think all this is about Stuart?"

Another fire engine zipped past them heading toward the Happy Isles Trailhead, so nearby that the little Subaru rocked side to side on its drivetrain.

"Jesus, that was close!" Jasmine said.

Rebecca didn't answer.

"I mean, this is so weird, right?" Jasmine continued. "Rebecca, I asked what the hell you thought all of this was about... " Jasmine turned in her seat to look at her girlfriend. Rebecca wasn't paying attention to Jasmine; transfixed, she stared directly ahead of her out the windshield. "What the hell are you looking —?" Jasmine glanced across the meadow and into the valley.

Both doors on the Subaru flew open at once, as they exited the vehicle, walked forward, and gazed up, aghast, at the early morning skyline.

"Oh God," was all Rebecca could say.

An ominous orange glow surrounded the northwest side of Half Dome. Rebecca suddenly understood why the valley was electrified with sirens, rushing Park Service vehicles, fire engines, and exiting tourists.

Flames, barely distinguishable, nipped at the base of Half Dome and were spreading in all directions. The face of Tis-se'-yak was aglow as gusty winds blew red and yellow balls of fire from treetop to treetop.

"Where the hell is Joy?" Jasmine cried out, captivated by the scene in front of her. "I just hope she's not back there."

"Have you checked your phone?" Rebecca responded as she stepped backward and took a seat on the hood of the Subaru.

"Yeah, right." Jasmine jumped around to the back of the Subaru, opened the hatch, and dug around for her phone. "Damn, you're right. I've got three new texts."

"What does she say?"

"Well, let's see. No, okay, it looks like they're heading up to Glacier Point on the Panorama Trail."

"Should we go pick them up?"

"Wait, uh, she says someone from the Park Service is going to pick them up and bring them down to the valley floor."

"Oh... sweet," Rebecca responded absently.

The luminous growth on the face of Half Dome crept wider; it resembled a giant electric bulb of granite, like a textbook image of the Earth's molten core. Jasmine joined Rebecca on the hood of their car. They couldn't quite draw their eyes away.

"So... we just wait here?" Rebecca asked, heaving a sigh.

54

PANORAMA

Monday, 5:12 A.M.

"I know we all want a break, but we need to make it out of
here before the fire jumps the river," Rick advised.

The group followed Rick, moving quickly along the
dark southern banks of the Merced toward the thundering sound
of the waterfall. All along the northern side of the river, the fire
seemed to taunt them, shooting red streaks sizzling into the
water. As they came up to the falls, another frightening sight
confronted them.

"Oh my God!" exclaimed Joy.

Twenty feet from the brink of Nevada Falls, the massive
timber bridge spanning the Merced was in flames. Before their
eyes, the imposing structure gradually crumbled into the water
with resounding booms that sent vertical log shafts skyward
before succumbing to the tremendous force of the current.

Joy and Woody ran up to the precipice just in time to see the
flaming bridge being consumed by the churning white cascade.

"Stuart, what the hell have you done?" Joy yelled out, looking
downriver into the valley.

"Okay—" Rick closed his eyes to compose himself. "The Merced is keeping the fire mostly on the north side, but you can see a few places where it has crossed. The route the JMT follows so far appears to be open, but it's hard to say for how long. Our safest bet is to take the Panorama Trail to Glacier Point. If we take the JMT, there's a chance that—"

As Rick spoke, there was a dramatic explosion of fire south of the Merced.

"I'll call to see if someone can collect us at Glacier Point," Alexandra said.

"It's a crown fire," Joy spoke up, "jumping from treetop to treetop, like the one we had in South Lake Tahoe, the Angora Fire that took out over two hundred homes. They're so crazy and unpredictable."

"Let's just do Panorama," said Woody.

"Alex... that call?" said Rick.

"I'm on it."

They started jogging southward from Nevada Falls toward the start of the Panorama Trail. Swinging a wide arc around the southern rim of the Merced River canyon, the Panorama crosses over the seldom-visited Illilouette Falls and gives hikers a bird's-eye view of the upper Nevada and lower Vernal waterfalls. As they moved out of the center of the canyon and onto its lower flank, the sun exploded into the landscape, throwing magnificent shafts of light that cut with microscopic precision through the thickening haze of black and brown smoke billowing into the sky.

55

AHWAHNEE

Monday, 5:59 a.m.

Stuart encountered a couple of early morning hikers and advised them to turn around, that there was a wildfire in the canyon and it was moving fast.

The solitary ranger standing vigil at the Happy Isles Trailhead stood little chance of identifying Stuart. Given the fire outbreak, he was tasked concurrently with answering a multitude of questions about evacuations and closures from wide-eyed vacationers awoken early by the flashing lights and sirens engulfing the valley. The ranger was told to look for a single male climber with long blond hair, gray pants, a black shirt, and a bright white goatee. Stuart, of course, matched none of these.

Employing his adopted accent, Stuart inquired congenially about where they were from, for how long they were on vacation, where they might go now instead of Yosemite, and suggesting Amador County's wine country. The couple thanked him for his kind thoughts and they left Stuart just past the trailhead where the lone ranger was besieged by other tourists.

Ahhh... the valley at last, Stuart sighed. The tall grasses and towering trees seemed to soften the embrace of the massive granite cliffs defining the narrow Y-shaped gorge. *I am nearly there, Professor.*

At Curry Village, Stuart hopped aboard one of the hybrid buses circumnavigating the valley floor. All around him, the sounds of sirens, panicked tourists and the diesel roar of fire engines echoed off the walls. Stuart smiled with satisfaction.

Somewhere near Yosemite Village, the message on the intercom switched from tourist-friendly Yosemite history to a compulsory evacuation order. "Due to the forest fire currently in the Merced River canyon, it is mandatory for all visitors to evacuate the main Yosemite Valley. Please gather your belongings and exit the Park immediately."

The other shuttle passengers clutched each other and talked in hushed tones, strategizing about how and how soon they would be able to leave.

He got off the shuttle at the Ahwahnee Hotel and walked down the red-carpeted entrance to the world-famous resort. Stuart cherished the opulence of the Ahwahnee, named for the first known inhabitants of the valley, who dubbed their magnificent tribal home *Ahwahnee,* or "land of the gaping mouth."

On this day the normally tranquil environs of the hotel were anything but relaxing. People rushed around in a frenetic jumble of activity, frantic porters ushering hastily packed luggage in hotel carts, families yelling in foreign languages looking for each other and shouting directions amid the confusion. The stately dining hall, normally serene and contemplative as it basked in the glow of its three-story high windows framed by massive granite buttresses, was now empty; no one seemed to be bothering with breakfast on this chaotic morning.

How ironic, Stuart thought. He knew that the Ahwahnee,

conceived by Gilbert Stanley Underwood in 1925, was built mostly out of massive granite stone and concrete—at an impressive cost of construction—explicitly to withstand a forest fire. *These tourists running around like decapitated chickens ought to consider just chilling out.*

Stuart reveled in chaos, especially when it was his doing. That was something the military never quite understood about him.

After walking up two flights of stairs, Stuart found the hotel's halls in a similar state of hysteria as visitors grabbed their luggage and marshaled their children this way and that. He strolled to the end of one hall, politely sidestepping open suitcases and screaming toddlers. There he waited until he was confident one of the rooms had been emptied entirely of guests, belongings, and hotel staff. He then casually walked over to the door, which had been propped open by the deadbolt latch, and entered the room, retracting the deadbolt to allow the door to fully lock.

The amenities of the Ahwahnee were not something to be passed over. *Very nice. Very nice indeed. I'll take my time.*

He removed his shoes and clothing and showered, using the complimentary soaps and shampoos. After watching a little TV and some breaking news on the Yosemite fire, he set the alarm clock for two hours, lay down on the luxurious bedding, and closed his eyes. The crisp linen, heavy from a thorough starching and bleaching, triggered something in Stuart that gave him pause before his slumber. While climbing, he always seemed to sleep soundly in a grubby sleeping bag with the sounds of the forest singing to him. It was different here. The sterility of a hotel room brought back loneliness.

In a rush of recollection, overtaking him like the pull of quicksand, it all came back. These crisp sheets felt the same on his flesh as they had when he was eight years old, the year he had suddenly become an orphan.

Stuart grew up a military brat, shuffled from base to base as his parents took up new positions and traveled to hot spots around the world. Stuart always stayed behind in the States—in Georgia, Missouri, or Nevada. He would live with various military families, sharing meals with other parents' children. Every year, he would be in another state, living in the spare bedroom of another family while his parents were redeployed. Under normal circumstances, the military would not allow both parents to be deployed simultaneously, but by design, his parents did not get married and each continued to seek deployment whenever possible.

Stuart felt like a stranger in the homes of these other families. And when his parents were with him, he knew they would rather be somewhere else. They preferred combat to childcare.

The summer he turned eight, the Army Chaplain told Stuart his parents had both been in a Blackhawk helicopter crash in Bosnia. They were casualties of war. They would not be coming home. He was now an orphan. He was alone.

Stuart already knew this way of life. He had been alone for many years.

Stuart lived with an Army Chaplain's family at the time. The sheets were always crisp in that house—military style, tucked so tight you had to fight to get into them each night. The Chaplain brought Stuart to church after school to teach him about Jesus and sacrifice, that he was never alone.

One day that summer, walking home from school, some older kids were picking on Stuart, taunting him and throwing soggy clumps of red mud at him. That day Stuart decided that Jesus didn't care, that none of it mattered, that if he was alone, he had nothing to lose. He ran ahead to escape the cruel bullying of the bigger boys, and concealed himself in the bushes. The older kids split up, as Stuart knew they would, and Stuart followed one of them, the ringleader, who went alone toward his house on the other side of the Park.

Stuart approached the boy quietly, with confidence. Taking his time and aiming carefully, Stuart flung mud at the older boy, landing his shot squarely on the back of the kid's head. Instantly, the older boy turned around to face his attacker, and laughed when he saw it was only Stuart. The big boy smiled, slowly reached down, and picked up a particularly large clump of muddy red earth and then ran at Stuart.

Stuart had anticipated this and was ready. He had sharpened a tall, stout branch, which he kept concealed behind him, wedged into the soft earth. When the boy went to tackle Stuart, he simply allowed it to happen. It was so simple, so easy. Stuart just fell backward and slightly to the side. The sharpened implement had grazed Stuart's mid-section, tearing his shirt, but it easily slid through the skin and into the stomach of Stuart's attacker, impaling the boy in one fluid and efficient motion.

Stuart heard the boy gasp as he collapsed on top of him. He felt the rush of breath escaping from the lungs of his victim. He wriggled out from under the boy's sizeable bulk and brushed himself off.

Kneeling beside the kid, who lay prostrate with a branch jutting out of his belly, Stuart grabbed his muddy backpack and calmly walked back to the Chaplain's house. He felt good. He felt, for once in his life, *powerful*. He was in control. Stuart cleaned himself up and changed his clothes, then sat in the living room, waiting for the Chaplain.

The Chaplain didn't come. He had been called to the hospital. Stuart just sat there on the couch thinking and reveling in the overwhelming glow of freedom that seemed to exalt him. He thought about the movements, the angle, and the forces at work. He also thought about how defensible his actions were. His attacker literally did this to himself. Stuart was just defending himself; he was younger, smaller, and had been provoked.

The boy would be all right. Surgery was required, followed by a long period of recovery; someone had found him early enough and the medics had managed to stabilize him in time.

Stuart was relocated the next week. He was sent to live with a family with whom he had stayed the previous summer.

And so it went. Stuart kept to himself. He was smart, and a little too methodical and calculating for a boy his age. He was not the highest achiever in school, but school wasn't difficult. Every year Stuart would act again, never unprovoked, but always decisively. He lanced a jock in Hawaii during nighttime spearfishing, who had nearly been eaten by sharks. Then there were those three meatheads Stuart ran off the road in Alabama. He never acted in haste, but he never failed to act.

By the time Stuart graduated from high school, he had a reputation, and despite all of the trouble that seemed to follow him as he was bounced from base to base, the military was, strangely, home.

At eighteen, Stuart enlisted in the Marine Corps. This was what he wanted. And he was good—almost too good. His commanding officers quickly promoted Stuart and gave him new challenging jobs. Stuart didn't have family to visit on holidays, so he became immersed in his training.

But his violent tendencies followed him. After one live-fire incident where Stuart's role in the unfortunate fatality of one of his squad was contested, he was given the humiliating assignment of cutting hair. Day after day with his military-issued Oster Classic 76, Stuart performed the same repetitive motions, crew cut after crew cut. This was a small hell for Stuart. There was no challenge. There was no conflict.

Finally, when Operation Iraqi Freedom began, Stuart made sure he was on one of the first platoons to ship out. Killing was at last sanctioned, encouraged.

Everything was going well for Stuart in Iraq. He had learned some Farsi and was relied upon by his superiors to gather intel and conduct clandestine operations. But eventually, he crossed another line. Stuart disobeyed a direct order and led a raid into a compound that, though it yielded numerous high-value kills and captives, cost the lives of two service men—a cost one of his superior officers argued could have been avoided.

Stuart was quietly let go; not dishonorably discharged—his contributions had been too great—but discharged nonetheless.

Without missing a beat, Stuart was picked up by Capwater, the independent defense contractor hired by the Pentagon, and was back in Iraq with a different uniform and a newfound license to kill. He felt liberated, untouchable. On paper, Stuart was to provide security for certain traveling businessmen and dignitaries. In practice, Stuart took his security assignments too seriously. He would map out and run routes by himself ahead of time, looking for trouble spots and identifying threats. He would eliminate people at random, if necessary. His success rate was unparalleled, and clients began to ask for Stuart. His reputation within the company was invulnerable.

However all good things for Stuart seemed destined to fail. In his eagerness to protect his current assignment, he ended up brutally and silently assassinating, with a concealed knife, one of the heads of the Baath regime who had strayed too close. Capwater hurriedly whisked Stuart out of the country and deposited him on US soil, without a job, without a direction, without a plan for the rest of his life.

Stuart couldn't assimilate into a nine-to-five hair cut style job or regimen. He had some money saved, but it would not last forever. Debating his life, he answered a phone call one afternoon.

"Stuart, good to speak with you again," It was one of his old bosses at Capwater.

"Likewise."

"So what have you been doing?"

"Well, I don't exactly have a game plan yet."

"That's why I'm calling, Stuart. In the coming week, someone identified as 'The Professor' will contact you at this number. There will be a job."

Stuart asked some follow-up questions of his former employer, but no more information was volunteered. He was told that this Professor would explain everything.

The Professor did call. There was a job. It did involve killing, and something else–– something much bigger. Some of the deaths would need to look like accidents. There was a handsome payment associated with it, of course. And there was a curious training assignment that Stuart would have to undertake. The Professor told Stuart he would receive a package that would both explain and fund the training. A box arrived the next day. In it was a cashier's check for $120,000, a typed note saying that he would be contacted once he had completed his training, and three books—*Rock Climbing: Mastering Basic Skills* by Craig Luebben, *Big Wall Climbing: Elite Technique* by Jared Ogden, and Chris McNamara's famous siren's song, *The Road to The Nose*.

56

MEDITATION

Monday, 6:03 A.M.

T he trail had become a setting for meditation.

No one spoke. The panorama to their right, for which the famous hike was named, was too gut-wrenching to discuss. They occasionally glanced furtively down the canyon walls to the furnace cannibalizing itself like a vision out of Dante's nightmares.

Woody wondered what his dad would say about all of this. Would the pain and senseless loss of life and beauty be enough to alter his father's unshakable adherence to a Taoist worldview? Even before his terminal diagnosis, John Jackson had been an ardent believer in Taoism, the spirituality most commonly known by the symbol of the yin and yang gracefully arcing in on each other. When they went hiking or adventuring, his dad would carry a pocket version of Stephen Mitchell's *Tao Te Ching* translation. Invariably at some opportune and scenic respite, John would whip out the little book and read short passages of unmetered verse. Overlooking a waterfall deep in the Sierra Nevada Woody would hear:

STOP THINKING, and end your problems.
What difference between yes and no?
What difference between success and failure?

I DRIFT like a wave on the ocean,
I blow as aimless as the wind.

AT FIRST THIS was an enjoyable routine, but with the onset of cancer and realization that his father was going to accept his fate, the words took on a new and infuriating meaning for Woody. How could his father really be content and *rejoice in the way things are,* as one saying proselytized? Woody loved his dad, but he could barely contain his anger over his father's refusal to fight; fight against the insurance company that told him because he had omitted certain information on his enrollment form and they could not cover his treatment; fight the cancer that was eating him away; fight in the hospital, even if that meant selling their home and worldly possessions; fight for his life. *Why wouldn't Dad fight?*

His dad answered him only once. They had just climbed the Royal Arches above the Ahwahnee Hotel, with Woody leading some of the stout sections. They were in the middle of the massive one-thousand-plus-foot rappel off of the face, John rappelling first to locate the next set of anchors, and Woody following. On a particularly inhospitable ledge, no more than six inches wide and curving up sharply, Woody left John hanging—literally—from his harness, intentionally stranding him on a small shelf tied to two bolts. Woody came down the rope and sat still in his harness alongside his father, just barely out of reach. Woody had intentionally stranded John.

"Dad, I've asked you before and you've never given me an answer that I can accept, so now that I've got you here tied to a rock and me as the only means of escape, you're going to give me a decent answer." Woody grinned at his father who, rather than being upset, was beaming back at him.

"So that's how it's going to be now?" John said.

Woody tied a stopper knot on a bite in the rope and went hands-free, dangling against the shear vertical wall.

"Yup, Dad, I've got all day. Now tell me why you aren't in a hospital right now fighting this thing?"

"Well, Son..." His dad could sound like Jimmy Stewart in *It's a Wonderful Life* whenever he started a sentence with "Well, Son," and this was one of those times. "You see, I've told you about how I feel about hospitals and drugs, how I want to live my life without being kept alive artificially. I've told you how I feel about the cost; I won't throw away your life and your mother's so that I can have a fifty percent chance of living an extra couple years. I've told you about Galen Clark and the restorative power of this place. I mean, take a look!"

John turned and made a sweeping gesture across the vast canyon of Yosemite, behind him the late afternoon sun and dropping air temperature seemed to mingle in a strange glow that softened the sweeping vista of the fifteen-hundred-foot Yosemite Falls, past the shoulder of El Capitan and over to Sentinel Rock.

"Where would I rather be? Bald, penniless, and broken in a hospital bed? Or here, drinking in the majesty and beauty of this place with my son? But you've heard all that before."

Woody swung back and forth on the rope. "Yeah, but it'll take something more this time, Dad."

"Fair enough," his dad said, laughing. "So, let's see if I can remember this." John took a deep breath. Below him the Merced River drifted lazily through the peaceful valley, reposing in the waning sunlight. "Thousands of years ago, deep in the countryside of ancient China, there was a village in which lived a farmer."

"Oh boy." Woody rolled his eyes and pushed off the rock with his legs. "Come on Dad, not Taoism again."

"Just hear the story. So, as I was saying, there lived a farmer. He was not a wealthy man, but he was happy and he grew enough for his small family. One day, the farmer's horse ran away in the mountains and everyone in the village said, 'Oh no! This is terrible. Now, how will you cultivate your crops without your horse?' The farmer simply replied, 'Well, it could be bad—but it could be good.'"

Woody just stared at his father, attempting to look as patronizing as possible.

John continued. "Now the horse, while it was out in the mountains, befriended a few wild horses, and when autumn came and the temperature began to change, the farmer's horse returned to the farmer and brought three other wild horses with him into the stable that the farmer had built. Everyone in the village looked at the four fine horses that the farmer now had in his possession and said, 'Wow, you are so fortunate. Now you have four horses, whereas before you just had one.' The farmer simply replied, 'It could be good, but it could be bad.'"

John paused and began to nod his head ever so slightly as he recalled the full story. "The farmer's only son was out training the new horses to pull a plow and the other routines of a domesticated animal, when one of the wild horses tossed the boy off of its back and onto the ground. The fall broke the boy's leg, and everyone in the village—"

"Let me guess," Woody interrupted. "They all thought it was awful that the kid had a broken leg, but the old farmer didn't care."

"'Could be good, could be bad,' the farmer told the village. The next month the Huns invaded China and the ruling monarch called for all able-bodied young men to be enlisted to fight against the invaders from the north. The farmer's son could not go and fight because his leg was still too badly broken, and the old farmer sat and thought to himself, 'Could be good, could be bad.'"

"So when you die it could be a good thing?"

"No, it will be a bad thing. But knowing I am going to die and having the opportunity to live out my life— here and now, in whatever form I choose—that is a wonderful thing. And as for you, well, just imagine I didn't have this knowledge, this power, and I just died sometime next year, without us having the opportunity to go on adventures and debate the merits of ancient Chinese philosophy while tied into the side of a rock a thousand feet off the deck." John had a mischievous twinkle in his eyes. "Now, that would really be tragic. So I could look at my prognosis in a lot of ways. I could see it as a death sentence, a noose hanging over me, but I don't see it that way. I see it as a life sentence, a demand that I make the most of what time I have left."

They sat there for a while. Woody swayed back and forth on the rope. His father chuckled to himself and took in their surroundings.

"Hey, tell you what, Son. I'm getting pretty hungry, and I've always wanted to test the Ahwahnee's dinner dress code. What do you say we waltz in there with climbing gear hanging from our harnesses?"

"I thought you didn't want to bankrupt the family?"

"One nice dinner at the Ahwahnee isn't going to do that much damage."

"Okay. I'll buy your story."

"Finally," said Rick as they crested the last hill to Glacier Point. Woody blinked his eyes, bringing himself back into the moment. There waiting for them by the trailhead was a Park

Service Yukon. Even at seven in the morning, there were a few blurry-eyed tourists out for an early photo opportunity. This morning these camera-toting visitors got more than they bargained for. Glacier Point, once the location of a famous hotel, was still an oft-visited viewpoint. Today that view was not the idyllic mountain vista expected, but something else entirely.

Rick pulled open the passenger side door. "Thanks for coming to retrieve us," he said.

"No probl—" The neophyte ranger in the driver's seat cut himself off, startled by the blackened and trail-weary appearance of the Chief Ranger. He began counting the number of bedraggled bodies entering his car and couldn't help but ask, "Hey, where's Jeffrey?"

No one answered at first. Finally, Alexandra spoke up. "It's Cliff, right?"

"Yeah, that's me."

"Stuart, the guy we were chasing, it looks like he killed Jeffrey."

"No! Jesus."

The doors on the Yukon closed in unison. No one spoke. Cliff started the SUV and pulled out of the parking lot. They drove in silence for a time, most of them haunted by thoughts and images of Jeffrey.

Woody felt exhaustion settling over his body and closed his eyes. The comfortable leather interior and forced-air heat lulled him irresistibly out of consciousness, his head coming to rest against the end corner of the backrest. As Joy also succumbed to sleep, she drifted diagonally onto Woody's shoulder.

Cliff maneuvered the Yukon adeptly along the winding road from Glacier Point across the high plateau and back to Yosemite Valley. He glanced back at his passengers and said, "Boy, those two didn't last long."

"They've had a rough night," Rick said. "So Cliff, tell me what resources have been mobilized. How are we handling the fire situation?"

"When I left to come get you, they had issued an evacuation order in the valley."

"Good," said Rick.

"And pretty much every Park Service employee was either helping with the evacuation or with fighting the fire."

"What about outside resources?" Alexandra asked.

"I'm not real sure. I know they are calling up people from other parts of the Park, and I think I overheard mention of CAL FIRE being deployed. And I'm not sure why, but as I was leaving, all these FBI blue coats were pulling up."

"Okay," Rick said. "I'm going to use your radio now."

"Go right ahead," Cliff responded.

"Rick to base, who's on right now?"

"Rick, it's Paula. Are you back?"

"Yeah, Cliff has us now. We're on our way."

"Good to hear."

"Cliff says that CAL FIRE is coming?"

"That's right, Rick. We've got four helicopters with drop buckets. They'll try to pull water from the river."

"Might be kind of tight."

"Yeah, we'll see how it goes. Oh, Rick, the director wants to see you when you get in. He's in with the Bureau guys right now."

"Fine, fine. Have we communicated with High Sierra Camps yet?"

"Just Little Yosemite Valley. The ranger is marching everyone up to Sunrise Camp right now."

"What's that about Sunrise Camp?"

"We've sent a few of your Tuolumne Meadows team out to Sunrise. They'll get everyone together and assist with the hike out, as well as locate any of the backcountry campers that we've got permits for."

"Well done. How about Stuart White?"

57

WALTER

Monday, 6:31 A.M.

Walter Ashgood woke up happy. Things were looking up for the young scientist. He had a great apartment in San Francisco's Mission district. From there, he could ride his bike to the job he scored three months ago at WP&G. And this past weekend, he hooked up with the woman of his dreams. When she accidentally tripped into him at his favorite bar on Friday night, spilling just a little of her martini on his shirt, Walter thought all he'd get was a snooty apology. The tall and gorgeous black-haired babe dressed to kill was clearly above his pay grade. But he and Lisa had ended up spending the whole night together, and then part of the day after.

He shut his medicine cabinet, stared at his smiling reflection, and flashed on the great sex with the passionate and sophisticated Lisa.

Not bad for a poor kid from Fresno.

Walter sat on his bed and reached down to tuck the right pant leg of his khaki trousers into his sock to keep it away from the chain grease of his new single-speed Cannondale road bike.

He couldn't help but smile. *Maybe today I'll pop in for a pricey coffee—and a biscotti. Why not? I'm making big bucks now.*

With a degree in environmental science focused on soil and biodiversity, Walter was surprised when he had been approached at a job fair by recruiters from the WP&G table. He wasn't even planning on talking to that company and was a little alarmed when they requested his contact information. Environmental science did not generally go hand in hand with high-paying corporate positions, and what would WP&G want with him anyway?

As it turned out, WP&G had miles of old gas pipeline that occasionally leaked, negatively impacting the soil, as well as the plant and animal life that depended on that soil. Walter's job thus far had been to methodically sift through reams of field data and test reports and then prepare executive summaries with recommended actions. Walter loved his new work and loved the fact that, unlike his older brother, he was actually making an impact. Walter's sibling chained himself to trees and stood for hours with picket signs outside of power facilities, only to watch in agony as that which he sought to protect was destroyed. By contrast, Walter was working from the inside. He was quite literally fixing the system and, despite his sibling's condemnation that Walter was selling out, there were real changes taking place as a result of the work he was doing.

Walter checked his personal computer before leaving. It seemed to be running slower, much slower, than it had just the week before.

Funny, the damn thing is brand new. He logged onto his personal email, ignored lately because of his whirlwind affair with Lisa. Just the usual nonsense: his mom was making Thanksgiving plans already, and some friends from college were bragging about their latest exploits on *World of Warcraft.*

He glanced at the computer's clock. *Time to go.*

Grabbing his bike, Walter had his hand on the front door-knob when there was a firm knock.

Who the hell could that be at quarter after seven in the morning?

Walter opened the door to a flurry of blue jackets, guns and badges; he was abruptly pushed down over his bike and onto the floor, then turned onto his stomach, his face pressed into the wood.

"Who are—?"

"Walter Ashgood?" declared the voice behind the heavy knee pushing squarely on Walter's backbone.

"Yeah," Walter barely managed to utter, despite the weight compressing his lung cavities.

The man repeated his name, followed by his Miranda rights, and then identified his team as F.B.I. agents. Walter strained his neck to see legs in black slacks and shoes dashing through his small apartment.

"Got the hard drive?"

"Yes."

"Any other intel?"

"We're checking."

His clothes, books, food, music, and all of his worldly possessions were rifled through with startling efficiency.

"What did I do? What's going on?"

Before he could ask anything more, he was yanked to his feet by the handcuffs now around his wrists and forced out his apartment door, down the front stairs, and into the back of a black Suburban double-parked in front of his building.

58

PLOWSHARES

Monday, 7:46 A.M.

"Woody? Is that you?" Mojo's panicked voice came over the phone.

"Yeah, Mom, you got me." After waving goodbye to Cliff and the other rangers, Woody had powered on his cell, which had been out of range and turned off in his backpack most of the night. The instant he turned it on, the phone rang as if his mother had been calling him every thirty seconds for who knows how long.

"Oh, Woody, thank God you're all right! I mean with holy hell breaking loose and... just tell me where in Christ's name have you been?"

"That's a lot of religion there, Mom."

"Save the sarcasm, kiddo. I know what happened to some climber named Aiden, and I think I saw your legs in a picture by a dead body. So, spare me the usual 'Don't worry, Mom' nonsense and tell me exactly what is happening."

A wide grin spread across Woody's face as he stood in Yosemite Village.

"Okay, Mom, you're right, nice deduction. Some bad stuff has gone down, but I'm fine. I'm with the rangers here in the main valley."

"The main valley! Christ, Woody there's a fire! They're not letting anyone in at all, and you're telling me that you're there —*right now*?"

"It's alright, Mom. We're nowhere near the fire—it would have to like, hop roads, rivers, and meadows to—wait a minute. How do you know they're not letting anyone in? Where are you?"

"I'm up on Porcupine Flat. That's the closest they'll let me come."

"Why... are you there?"

"Rosa and I drove down last night to find you."

"Wow, Mom, thanks for coming down. I'm, uh, sorry to have put you through all this."

"I'm just glad you're safe."

"Thanks." Woody lowered his gaze from the smoky sky and looked at the ground. He kicked some loose rocks with his running shoes. After the ordeal he had been through, it was comforting to hear his mother's voice and concern for his safety. He glanced over at Joy, who appeared to be having a similar conversation with her sister, as evidenced by her periodic eye rolls and head shakes.

"Umm... how did you find out about Aiden?" Woody asked.

"Oh, I was communing with the midnight computer gods again, but that doesn't matter. How do we get you out of there?"

"I'm sure I can get a ride. Did you find out, you know, a motive?"

"Not exactly, but the one thing they had in... wait; you know, Woody, I'd much rather discuss this in hypothetical terms with Yosemite in our rear view mirror."

"I know, just let me ask a couple things... please."

"Okay, so what did Aiden and Abigail have in common, besides climbing. That's what you want to know?"

"Yeah?" Woody responded.

"Hetch Hetchy,"

"Really? What did Abigail have to do with it?"

"Oh, she's famous... great journalist, works for the Sierra Club. She was speaking at some important symposium there in Yosemite right by where—wait a minute—aren't there shuttles leaving the valley?"

"Don't worry. We'll figure something out, Mom. I'm in good hands now. I'll be able to come up to you soon."

Woody was glad he had waited to switch on his phone until the Park Service Yukon came to a rest beside the Yosemite Village Ranger Station. He somehow expected that a conversation with his mother was imminent and didn't particularly want to treat everyone else in the vehicle to overhearing his attempts at calming her down. What he hadn't considered was that his mom could be helpful in figuring out just what Stuart was up to.

"Mom, I need to tell you something, but I don't want you to freak out, okay?"

"Now how do you think I am going to react to that?"

"Look, I think you'll be able to help figure out what is going on here and why these two climbers ended up dead, but I need to tell you what I know, and, um, you're not going to like hearing it, so don't get too excited."

"Okay. I'll try."

"Really?"

"Jeez, kiddo—go ahead."

"So last night, I was there when Aiden died."

Mojo gasped, but tried not to interrupt Woody.

Woody pressed on, "More precisely, I was there and—witnessed Aiden's murder."

"What? Woody! How did you end up mixed up with—"

"Mom."

"—with these sorts of freaks, vagrants, and—"

"Mom!"

"—criminals? I can't—"

"Mom, just listen. This is why I wasn't going to tell you."

"Okay... sorry. I'll try to keep my mouth shut."

"Just give me fifteen seconds. Please."

"Alright—Mama Grizzly under control, fifteen seconds and counting—"

"Thanks. I just happened to be watching when this other guy, Stuart, pushed Aiden off a cliff. He said something about what Aiden was working on being achieved." Woody judiciously left out the part about him free soloing. "Then, I found out later, after Joy and I connected with some rangers, that the other death—this, um, Abigail lady—also was caused by Stuart earlier that day in the main valley." Again, Woody decidedly left out the part about being kidnapped and his charging a bear. "So, based on what you just told me about Aiden and Abigail being connected to Hetch Hetchy, maybe even working on something there, why would Stuart want to kill them?"

Mojo took an audible deep breath. "Woody, I just want to get you out of there. I mean, they're evacuating; it's not the safest place to be."

"Mom..." Woody began but had to wait for a passing helicopter before he could finish speaking. "Yeah, you're right. We'll get out of here as soon as possible, I promise, but please answer my question. Why do you think Stuart killed Aiden and Abigail?"

Joy had finished her conversation with Jasmine and walked over to listen. Woody leaned down and angled the cell phone back a bit so they both could hear what his mom might say.

"Well, this dumb-ass wack job... the guy who killed Aiden and Abigail, Stuart or whoever, is obviously not the reason all this is happening. So yeah, he might have been hired, you know, as a contract killer, whatever. In any case, he's just a pawn. There are some pretty big forces at work. The online chatter right now is insane. Blogs are exploding with diatribes and calls to action that I haven't seen since the seventies. I mean, there is real anger out there in the radical environmentalist community. All the hippie flower children are beating their plowshares back into swords, you know? And Aiden and Abigail—they were the spark."

59

MORE SINISTER

Monday, 9:04 A.M.

A h, Hetch Hetchy.

Stuart knew this place well. He spent many days here preparing for what he was about to do. In the vintage VW bus that The Professor acquired for him, Stuart had been coming to the Hetch Hetchy Valley in Yosemite all summer under the auspices of setting new rock climbing routes, but in reality, his purpose was more sinister.

Now in the black Range Rover, left for him in the Ahwahnee Hotel parking lot, Stuart was here to complete the work he'd begun. The Professor would know his location—there was a GPS monitor attached to the vehicle—and considering his close calls the evening before, he was sure his present location would be a relief to his boss.

The ranger at the Hetch Hetchy entrance gate was clearly distracted. It looked like she was alone; a radio played loudly in the background with news about firefighting in the main valley forty minutes South. Her colleagues had been stationed at nearly every bisecting road that connected visitors to Yosemite Valley.

Stuart had passed them in his Range Rover and watched as they turned people around.

He smiled at the ranger in the Hetch Hetchy entry kiosk. "How is it? Fire, yes?" He used his Eastern European accent again.

"Oh, it sounds pretty bad. I'm glad they were able to get the visitors out of there."

"Yes, is good."

"Just a day pass?" the ranger asked.

"Please. Yes."

"Here you go. You need to be out of the Park by five in the afternoon."

"Yes."

In reality, the black vehicle Stuart had been adeptly maneuvering down the curvy road through Camp Mather would be staying longer, but that wouldn't matter, considering the events about to take place. He had brought a large backpacker's multiday pack and would be exiting the park on the other side of the Tuolumne River canyon. There was a falsified backcountry permit and a different car waiting for him in Tuolumne Meadows. It was an idea he'd voiced to The Professor about a month ago. After cutting himself off from his transportation, Stuart would simply hike the two days up the Grand Canyon of the Tuolumne, letting the river thank him for its liberation along the way.

Stuart drove through the granite hillsides toward Hetch Hetchy. It was a broken and extraterrestrial landscape, with odd juxtapositions of rocks—beautiful, but barren. Heading down the shoulder of the canyon wall, Stuart finally spied the great O'Shaughnessy Dam and smiled, knowing that this was the last time he would see it this way.

Moving efficiently, he drove past the designated ranger cabins just above the behemoth of a lake. They were empty; the vehicles normally parked in front were gone. No doubt the rangers had been enlisted to help with the fire, the evacuation, or directing traffic around the main valley.

This is all too easy.

Stuart left the Range Rover in the designated parking area. There were only four other cars in the lot—typical tourist traffic for Hetch Hetchy. If he wanted to, he probably could have driven on the dam itself today. There was no one here to stop him. He removed his large pack from the rear of the vehicle. In addition to the backcountry camping gear for his hike out, the pack also contained some electronics and wiring specifically designed for the task ahead. After wiping down the Ranger Rover to remove his fingerprints, Stuart hoisted the pack onto his back and walked toward the dam.

The top of the O'Shaughnessy Dam was sixteen feet wide, and it arched inward to the lake on its eastern flank. Art-deco style chamfers and massive turret handrail blocks gave the considerable concrete walkway an even heavier feel. To his right, the vast calm expanse of the reservoir reposed, still and reflective, waiting for Stuart to awaken its dormant power. To his left stretched the rest of the graceful green canyon, oblivious of the fiery havoc to the south and the watery destruction about to be unleashed.

Not another soul in sight. This will be relaxing and enjoyable.

Reaching the stone tunnel at the far end of the dam, Stuart didn't hesitate before plunging into its darkness. He had walked this path many times before. He had memorized the puddles and undulations in the muddy double-track road lit only by intermittent electric lights.

At the other end of the tunnel, Stuart checked again to see if anyone else was around. He listened, waiting for his breathing and heart rate to slow down so he could be absolutely sure of his solitude. Still nothing. Quickly, he scampered up a steep embankment over the tunnel area and into the trees—out of sight.

60

PANDEMONIUM

Monday, 9:13 A.M.

J oy listened in as Woody finished talking with his mom. *What exactly was Mojo implying about all the radical talk online? Could there actually be more destruction and death planned?*

Woody interrupted Joy's thoughts. "Let's find Rick."

"I saw him enter the headquarters building over there where all the people are running in and out," she responded.

They tentatively walked up to the entrance to the Yosemite Park Service headquarters.

"Did you see where Alex went?" Joy asked. "We should probably let her know too."

"In here, I guess."

Joy walked up to the large double doors of the headquarters and pulled one back to reveal a riotous scene. Personnel with labels representing various agencies—CAL FIRE, YOSAR, neighboring police department personnel, Yosemite rangers, and some Feds in blue jackets were all crammed into the space.

"Do we go in?" Woody asked.

"Okay." Joy shrugged and entered the room. Someone was writing notes on a whiteboard with a two-way radio up to one ear and a phone propped on his shoulder by his other ear. Another person pushed off his desk on a roller chair and crossed over to a fax machine, spewing an incessant stream of bulletins. If they weren't on the phone talking loudly, they were speaking just as loud to one another. The wood-lined room amplified the conversations, creating an atmosphere of near pandemonium.

Woody and Joy jumped apart to make way for three uniformed firemen who nearly knocked them over as they entered the building.

"*This* is where they are managing the fire?" Joy scanned the room.

"What should we do?" Woody yelled back.

"I'm not sure. We need to tell Rick about Hetch Hetchy. Wait—is that him over there?" Joy pointed to a glass-walled office just outside of the large room. Inside, Rick seemed to be having an animated conversation with someone in a navy-blue windbreaker.

Suddenly, Joy felt a firm hand grasp her shoulder from behind. "So you must be Woody, and you must be Joy."

An imposing stocky man in a sport coat and button-down shirt stood behind them, smiling. "Don't worry, despite the appearance of things, the situation is totally under control." He cocked his head backward and let out a thunderous laugh that made a few people stop midsentence and peer quizzically his direction. "I'm Detective Tandy, and I was hoping we could talk for a bit."

"Detective, we need to speak with Rick, the ranger over there," Joy said, pointing toward the room where they had just seen him.

"Sure thing, guys. I'll take you to him just as soon as we're finished."

With that, Detective Tandy, who still had not released his

earlier grip on their shoulders, pushed Woody and Joy forward through the room, dodging people, desks, phone cords, and scattered papers, until they reached a hall at the other end.

"Let's see, I know they left me a room here somewhere," the detective said.

They walked briskly down the long hallway, passing numerous corridors and other entrances. Joy noted that the farther along they went, the more the rooms seemed to resemble holding cells.

"Wait a minute," the detective said, pausing by the restrooms. "Why don't you two wash up a bit and use the bathroom? You look like a couple of rodeo clowns on the losing end of a bull ride."

"Uh, yes, thanks," Joy said, pushing open the door to the ladies' room and locking it behind her.

Walking to the sink, Joy looked up at her reflection in the mirror. She didn't recognize the person who stared back at her. Every square millimeter of her body and clothing seemed to be covered with a fine gray dust. Her eyes were bloodshot, and her hair protruded from underneath her cap, matted and thick with grime from the forest fire. Normally, she was meticulous about her appearance, choosing clothing the night before and allowing ample time for trace makeup.

I do look like a rodeo clown, Joy laughed at herself.

Joy turned on the faucet and took off the knit cap and Woody's fleece, leaving her half-naked in the mirror. The past twelve hours had turned the world on its head for Joy. Not only did she not look anything like herself, but she felt different, too. It wasn't just the exhaustion. The hour nap on the way back from Glacier Point had helped considerably.

Joy smiled at her disheveled reflection, at her nakedness. With the thoughts that last night, she had kissed Woody, that this morning, she had slept comfortably on his shoulder, a sudden wave of warmth possessed her. Then her body tingled at the recollection of their long naked embrace.

Plunging her hands into the warm water, Joy shook her head. She slid the water up her arms and cleaned her skin up past her elbows. Then she splashed ample handfuls of water on her face and neck, rubbing in the clear and warm liquid under her eyes and behind her ears. The gray dust filled the white porcelain sink and spilled over onto the tile floor. She ran her wet hands repeatedly through her hair until it resembled some semblance of its usual order.

"That's better," Joy said aloud. *That's me.*

Rifling through her backpack, she found a slightly damp rose-colored T-shirt, which she slid over her head. As she did so, there was a knock on the bathroom door.

"Almost finished in there?" The detective sounded annoyed.

Joy pushed the door open. "All set."

She smiled at Woody, who was waiting outside, looking a little more presentable as well. From the long water stain on the back of his T-shirt, it looked like he had stuck his entire head under the faucet.

"All right, then." Detective Tandy motioned for Joy and Woody to continue on down the hallway toward a collection of small rooms near the end.

"Okay, here we go, kids." Detective Tandy reached out and grabbed a steel doorknob on a solid wooden door and swung it open. "Why don't I take these packs of yours, and your phones too, please?"

Woody and Joy surrendered their possessions before they could question the detective, and were abruptly ushered inside.

The room was approximately ten square feet and set up as an impromptu office space. There were two tables, one in the center with some folding chairs and one in a corner with a computer placed next to some disorderly stacks of paper. The room had no windows, pictures, or decorations.

"This was all they had available, considering—you know, all the activity. Go on and take a seat." The detective pulled the door shut and sat down.

"Are we being––interrogated?" Joy demanded.

"Of course not. Just a little chat."

Hesitantly, Woody and Joy took their seats on the opposite side of the table from the detective and scooted themselves forward.

"Look, I know you've had a long night. So I'll try to make this as easy as possible," said Detective Tandy as he reached into his jacket and removed a small tape recorder and a notepad. Joy noticed that the notepad already contained some scribbled ideas and questions. She clearly made out the words "fire," "vicinity," and "professor" on the top sheet of paper before the detective concealed the pad with his hand.

"Let's see, now. . . what can you two tell me about Aiden Watson's death, and someone who goes by the name, *Doc?*"

RENDEZVOUS

Monday, 9:25 A.M.

"Nice flirting." Mojo complemented Rosa as she waved from the car window at the ranger moving the gate aside for them.

"*Muchas gracias. Tú sabes que—los hombres blancos*, you know *—les gustan las señoritas con la complexión morena,*" Rosa responded.

"Yeah, we have an expression for that in English, too—*they like the dark meat.*"

Both ladies burst out laughing as they sped down the highway toward Yosemite Valley. After finally being able to speak with Woody, Mojo felt like she was going to jump out of her skin. Rosa, thankfully, had noticed that one of the officers directing traffic would occasionally glance in her direction, so she casually went over and talked to him after taking off her long-sleeved shirt to reveal a spaghetti strap tank top.

"Really, it wasn't all that scandalous," Rosa implored.

"It certainly looked like it from here."

"No, it's not like that. He noticed we had been waiting since early in the morning, and I just explained why."

Mojo laughed out loud. "Oh really? I'm sure that's why you had to lean *provocatively* forward and bat those long eyelashes of yours."

"Well, *tú sabes—*"

ON OUR WAY 2 U. Jasmine pressed *send,* put her phone away and stood up. "Let's go get them."

"Good, let's get out of this place," Rebecca said as she downed her third cup of coffee at Curry Village Pavilion's buffet.

"Are we a little *caffeinized* this morning?" Jasmine asked. "Or is it the fire?"

"I'd be lying if I told you I wasn't shaky."

"Look around you. There are plenty of people here to fight the blaze. I'm not too concerned." Jasmine gestured at the firefighters, rangers, and police who were grabbing a quick bite to eat.

"Yeah, but there's basically one way in and one way out of this place, and if the fire did spread, I'd hate to be stuck in this narrow valley."

"Aw, you don't want to go down in flames with me?" Jasmine raised her eyebrows.

Rebecca leaned in and gave Jasmine a kiss. "Not today, Thelma."

MOJO AND ROSA drove the abandoned pavement into Yosemite Valley through a haze of smoke and ash. Only once did they have to pull over for a small caravan of fire trucks and emergency vehicles. At Yosemite Village, they parked Rusty in a lot behind a building that looked to be the headquarters.

"This feels so odd," Mojo began. "No tourists are here. I've never seen the place like this. It's always so hectic with vacation-ers, and now all we've seen are those fire engines, some other offi-cials––and thick smoke."

"Where did Woody say he was?" Rosa asked.

"I think he said something about the ranger headquarters." Mojo coughed.

"You think it's right here?" Rosa said as she coughed on some smoke.

"Somewhere here in Yosemite Village. We should start looking."

With that, Mojo and Rosa began walking around Yosemite Village past the general store and the outdoor food court, all strangely quiet. Not even the usual food court residents, the plump chipmunks scavenging for the dropped remnants of tourist lunches, were visible.

As they neared the Yosemite Museum, it became obvious which way they were heading. Streams of firefighters, police offi-cers, and rangers seemed to be coming and going from a building near the Backcountry Office.

"Do you think they're in there?" Mojo asked.

"We can ask," Rosa replied.

Mojo approached the front door to the headquarters. Before she could open the solid wood entrance door, it was flung open from the inside.

"Shit. I mean, what the fucking hell?" It was Jasmine. She looked up and noticed Mojo. "Oh, my bad—aren't you—like, Woody's mom?"

"Mojo Jackson. Yes, nice to see you again—Jasmine, right?" Mojo had only briefly waved hello to the girls whenever they drove off with her son to go climbing over the summer.

"Yeah . . ." Jasmine hesitated. "Sorry about the language, but––they're holding Woody and Joy for questioning."

"What? Those dip-shit jackasses!" Mojo blurted out.

Jasmine smiled. "Yup, you're just as ticked as I am."

"Damn right!" Mojo responded.

Rosa spoke up. "Who do we talk to?"

Jasmine turned back into the building, propping the door open with her hip and motioned over to a corner where a large man in a wrinkly tweed sport coat was on the phone. "That's him."

"I think he's a detective of some sort. I heard someone else refer to him as Tandy," Rebecca interjected.

"Well he's going to get a piece of my mind," Mojo said as she walked purposely from the door toward the detective.

"Uh-oh," said Rosa.

"Sweet," Jasmine said as the three ladies jogged after Mojo through the melee of rangers, firefighters, and other personnel.

Mojo straightened her spine and narrowed her gaze as she strode toward the man in the sport coat. Not waiting for him to put down the phone or pause his conversation, Mojo stuck her hand out for an introduction, right into his protruding belly.

"I'm Mojo Jackson. I hear you have my son, Woody."

Detective Tandy looked up and then said, "Excuse me," while putting his hand up to the mouthpiece of the phone. "Ma'am, I'll be with you in a moment, please wait outside."

"I'll wait right here, thank you," Mojo said as she inched a little closer.

"Look, Ross, I'll have to call you back." Detective Tandy put down the phone and turned to face Mojo, who at this point was flanked by Rosa on one side and Jasmine and Rebecca on the other.

"Okay, ladies." The detective took a deep breath. "Yes, we've got Woody and Joy here, but we're taking good care of them and we'll be finished with them soon. They've seen some things last night that we need to have a better underst—"

"That's all fine and dandy, Mister—is it—*Tandy?* But unless you are charging them with a crime or have some impending reason for keeping them—which you seemingly don't—they need to be released. And"—Mojo raised her voice so that others within a ten-foot radius could hear—"if you are charging them with a crime, I'm sure you realize they are both minors and you have here two adults who can claim legal responsibility for them."

"Well, as I was saying—" Detective Tandy began.

"Which is it? Are they being charged or not?"

Detective Tandy took another deep breath, inhaling through his mouth and out his sizeable nostrils, the hairs inside fluttering with his exhalation. "Look, lady. I'll see what we can do, but you have to realize that a fire in Yosemite and some of the other events of the past twelve hours are extraordinary and we need all the help we can get."

"So if they are just helping you, then it won't matter if we are there with them, will it?" Mojo responded.

"I said... I'll see what I can do." The detective stood up abruptly and left the four ladies standing there as he vacated the room. They waited for a moment and then turned to head back outside.

"Do you think he will do anything?" Rebecca asked.

"Let's give him a few minutes, but I think he got the idea," Mojo replied.

"Has anyone tried calling them?" Rosa suggested.

"Yeah, they aren't answering their phones," said Jasmine.

"Either that, or their phones were taken from them." Mojo folded her arms.

62

ALIBI

Monday, 9:44 A.M.

Sleep.

The drive back to the Bay Area normally required at least three hours, but The Professor needed to stay awake and pushed the limits of the Porsche Boxster on the two-lane foothill and Central Valley roads. The speed of the car kept The Professor alert, and it reduced overall travel time by at least half an hour. As the Swiss-made wheels and high-performance racing tires negotiated the curves, thoughts swirled inside The Professor's mind.

Stuart.

Yes, he had screwed up by not eliminating the kids, but he wouldn't have expected them to be a threat. And despite his error, the fundamentals of the mission were in place—the deaths of the activists as a catalyst to environmental uproar, the igniting of Yosemite Valley as a diversion, and now––based on the information relayed by the GPS tracking on the Range Rover––the final chapter. Overall, Stuart's performance was acceptable and well worth the money.

Walter.

No doubt the FBI will have already picked him up. Walter Ashgood certainly required a lowering of standards for The Professor, but it was necessary for the proper evidence to exist. Besides, the ability to deceive had proven useful time and again.

Around another curve, the road opened up for a half-mile stretch through a vineyard. Almost without any driver initiation, the Boxster leapt forward, devouring the asphalt until the next curve beyond the rows of grapes.

Doc.

Even Doc himself had posted a response to the deaths of Aiden and Abigail. Now the circle was complete. Unbridled environmental activist rage was spewing from numerous online pockets. The coded language of Muir and Adams had by now been recycled and reinterpreted hundreds of times over. Even if the FBI could manage to locate the server, the wireless router, and then the iPad that sent the initial images into cyberspace, there would be no connection back to The Professor. The strongest and most logical connection was from Walter to Doc and from Doc to Aiden and Abigail. The coded language hearkening to Muir and Adams was an eccentric flare that Doc had been using for years— easy to replicate and easy to use to implicate.

Over another rise in the road, the Porsche caught the slightest bit of air as The Professor sailed past an odd juxtaposition of cows grazing in a pasture near some massive wind turbines.

Alibi.

Not that it was necessary, but it would be good to have a place to be when Stuart strikes the final blow. Yes, there were some emails and a live videoconference that would require attention, and The Professor could use the backdrop of the Oakland residence as proof of location and proof of innocence. The Oakland cottage, as colleagues referred to it, was actually not in Oakland at all, but perched atop a nearby East Bay mountain. The little postmodern chalet provided a more convenient staging point for necessary excursions to Yosemite over the past two years.

Public perception.

During the drive back to the East Bay, The Professor scanned news stations hoping to hear a regurgitation of the new blurb sent out earlier. At last the specific words intended to focus attention crackled over the radio: "following the deaths of two well-known environmental activists, reprisal acts of ecoterrorism are attempting to return Yosemite to its original state. A large fire in the main Yosemite Valley has been burning since early Monday morning threatening a multitude of man-made structures...."

Insurance.

The company's insurance contract had been redrawn last year and The Professor had played a key role in its review and editing. Indemnification against any possibility of disruption to their services and assets by ecoterrorist actions was inserted and reiterated. The only concern at the time was whether or not the actions in Yosemite would be construed and broadcast as ecoterrorism. But even national radio was now implicating ecoterrorists.

When the Porsche finally screeched to rest outside the hilltop house, The Professor felt more comfortable and confident in the plans currently taking shape. After the previous evening's close calls and the debacle with the two kids, it felt good to be back on track. The car was red hot, so The Professor parked it outside, rather than pulling into the garage, allowing the mist wafting off the bay to cool the engine.

The Professor.

It had been the longtime associate and contact at Capwater who suggested the use of the pseudonym, "Professor." It would provide yet another layer of anonymity. "And after all," the contact had said, "you should get some credit for all the degrees you've accumulated."

Why not?

63

DOWNTOWN

Monday, 9:49 A.M.

Walter found himself inside a small cold room deep in the bowels of a large nondescript building in downtown. There was a table with two chairs, one on either side. A piece of thick glass ran the full length of one wall. Walter couldn't see through the glass, but guessed that the same could not be said for anyone on the other side. The door that he was shoved through moments before was windowless and heavy.

Bewildered, Walter didn't sit but stood in the corner breathing in sputters, completely aghast at his current predicament. *What's going on? Who are these people? What do they want with me?*

Walter had seen the letters "FBI" imprinted in bold yellow on the back of one of their navy-blue jackets. No one had answered his questions on the ride over to his present location. "Where are you taking me? What's going on?" The agents had sat stone-faced in the front seats as they whisked him downtown and into the unremarkable building where he now found himself.

Walter's khaki pant leg was still stuffed into his sock from his preparation for the morning's bike commute, and his button-down dress shirt was disheveled, the result of being thrown to the floor of his apartment. He looked like he felt—out of place and befuddled.

The door opened.

"Walter Ashgood?"

"Last time I said yes to that, someone slammed me to the floor."

"Well that's not going to happen here. Please have a seat."

Walter took the chair on the far side of the table and cast a quick look toward the glass.

"Walter, I'm Agent Dale Friedman." He took the other seat at the table. As the metal chair scraped across the hard concrete floor, Walter winced at the sound. "Do you know why you are here today?"

"I haven't the foggiest," Walter snapped back. "I was on my way to work, and then your friends rushed in and tore up my place."

"So you *really* don't know why you are here?"

"I *really* don't."

"Well, Walter, we have reason to believe you have been involved in recent crimes committed in Yosemite National Park, including murder."

"*What*? *Murder*?! I haven't been to Yosemite in years. How could I have been involved in––?"

"Walter, we have evidence from your computer at work, and we're gathering evidence from your home computer right now indicating otherwise."

"That can't be true. I don't understand."

"Still don't have anything to say?" the agent inquired.

"You mean, about my computers—?"

Agent Friedman nodded.

"No, I use my work computer for... work. I analyze company

reports and make recommendations. I use my personal computer to Facebook and... um, okay, surf porn sometimes. What exactly are you saying?"

Walter was at a total loss. There was something bizarre going on. That hot chick, Lisa, with the jet-black hair and extravagant clothes who spent the night with him on Friday, maybe she had something to do with this. He had pretty much passed out cold, sleeping harder than he usually would have, assuming it was from all the booze and the great sex that evening.

I couldn't have been drugged, could I?

Agent Friedman reached into a briefcase at his side and pulled out some papers, which he kept hidden. He took his time sifting through them. Walter was reminded of a scene from the movie *Wall Street*. The agent was Michael Douglas deciding how best to maximize his return and fleece the unwitting business owners across the boardroom table. His face was blank as he dispassionately sifted forward and backward through the upturned papers.

Walter anxiously sat and waited.

Finally, the agent landed on the play he would make. He squinted, and slowly turned away as an eight-by-ten black-and-white glossy photograph twirled out of his hand and landed on the table in front of Walter. As Walter stared at it, transfixed, Agent Friedman remained silent.

"Shit!" Walter said through clenched teeth.

64

WHAT DEATH IS LIKE

Monday, 10:05 A.M.

Stuart yearned for the cold water of the Tuolumne River. The numbness and tingling on his face and lips, the only parts of his body not protected by the dry suit, soothed him as the frigid water encompassed his body. There was something Stuart relished about the penetrating force of the cold and the gentle embrace of the water right as the final air bubbles were released and the dry suit vacuumed around his body. Perhaps it was the stimulating marriage of pain and pleasure.

Before slipping into the lake, Stuart looked across the dam at the parking lot, still virtually empty. He also scanned the trail, the dam, and the small collection of ranger cabins nestled on the hillside along the access road to the dam; no movement, no lights, no humans anywhere. Stuart had the place to himself.

Sliding slowly and seductively into the water, Stuart adjusted the straps and weights of his scuba gear. He checked his gauges and tank and tested his breathing apparatus. Scuba diving at high altitude is more dangerous than at sea level. Between the lighter weight of the fresh water and the lack of pressure from the altitude, the entire process is more difficult to gauge. He had to be *on his game.* Stuart had received Basic Underwater Demolition/SEAL (BUD/S) training during his days in the Navy, where he learned the special high-altitude dive tables and how to recalibrate his depth gauges in order to not let the nitrogen loading in his muscle tissue expand too rapidly.

Taking his last breath of fresh air, Stuart inserted the regulator in his mouth and descended into the lake. An insulated charge line spooled out behind him and snaked imperceptibly up the hillside by the tunnel. It was tied to a large black oak tree, next to which rested his pack and his secret stash of gear.

So cold and peaceful—this must be what death is like, Stuart mused as he began his descent. The dam was about forty feet to his right, not visible, but ever-present, like a mythological leviathan, its presence felt without being seen. It waited, invisible in the murky depths. Now twenty-five feet down according to his pressure gauge, Stuart turned and made his way directly toward the dam.

He needed to be at the weakest point in the structure. Based on the information from the blueprints provided by The Professor, the location was about 110 feet down on the opposite bank, a point where the rock sidewalls of the canyon penetrated deep into the concrete structure. It was here, according to the research done by the Army Corps of Engineers, at the request of the federal government, that the composition of volcanic rock, granite, and certain fissures of limestone commingled in such a way as to provide a geological fulcrum. Given the proper motivation, it would break dramatically into the dam, like a medieval catapult, forcing a total failure.

According to the Army Corps, the charges would need to be set in such a way as to first open a small fissure in the dam, acting to eventually weaken it at the critical point. The same phenomenon occurred at the Dale Dike Reservoir in 1864 and the Teton Dam in 1976, when a small leak eventually led to the entire structure being compromised. Stuart had set three charges on earlier trips to Hetch Hetchy. On those trips, he had arranged for a backcountry permit under an alias, and rather than going out to the Muir Gorge and back as his permit indicated, he waited until the sun set and then slipped into the icy waters of Hetch Hetchy. Once submerged and comfortable in his dry suit, he had spent almost four hours in the lake, inspecting and verifying locations on the dam matching the Army Corps' descriptions. When he was confident he had the correct spot, he laboriously hand-drilled holes in the surface of the dam and then marked them with an underwater paint encased in tubes. The charges had to be imbedded in the dam; otherwise the explosions would simply find the path of least resistance and spread throughout the lake itself. Satisfied with the depth of his holes, the markings left on the dam, and some GPS waypoints, Stuart returned to the shore and slept well into the following day.

Stuart spent the next day in hiding, packing and setting the explosive tubes and readying the steel covering plates and under-water epoxy while he waited for enough time to lapse before he could return to the water without getting decompression sick-ness. The following evening, he loaded the designated explosives into a sack, returned to his marked locations, and inserted the charges, covering them with one-inch-thick steel plates and epoxy. The Professor planned on twice the recommended quan-tity of C-4; they would only get one shot at this. Stuart had worked with explosives before, both during his BUD/S training and when he was in Iraq, and he had a rough idea of the destruc-tive force the current amount of material he was attaching to the structure would unleash. *Yeah, this is definitely enough.*

The coldness of the water tickled his cheeks and snapped him back into the moment. Stuart was swimming toward the giant monolith. He kept peering down to his depth gauge so he didn't swim diagonally either farther down or back toward the surface. Nothing was perceptible in the blackness. It was as if Stuart were swimming through a starless night sky, with no landmarks, no ground, no point of reference at all. There was one exception— suddenly the dam would appear with a startling and imposing finality. By the time Stuart saw the massive shear wall of concrete that was the O'Shaughnessy Dam, he was barely five feet from it. Quickly, Stuart reached out his hand and caught himself against the wall. *Hey, good lookin'.*

Stuart turned to the left and began swimming alongside the giant collection of aggregate, steel and concrete—immense, immobile, and seemingly impenetrable. *Seemingly.*

Methodically, Stuart ran cable to the three locations. The cables were color-coded so he wouldn't get confused when the time came. Green was the first charge, yellow was the second, and red was the final charge to trigger the complete internal splintering of the dam.

The final location always bugged Stuart. It was the critical location, and the Army Corps had been exceedingly specific about the composition of rocks and the way they interfaced with the dam's structure. The depth was a little touchy. Being submerged to this extent at altitude was dangerous. If something went wrong, there was no way out. If he tried to return to the surface quickly, his lungs would implode; if a hose snagged or a gauge malfunctioned—Stuart tried not to consider the possibilities. He almost always had a contingency plan or two, but here, there was no margin for error. He had to remain calm, not use excessive oxygen, and focus on the task at hand.

There was something otherworldly about those strange rock formations sticking out like giant granite fingers from under the dam. As Stuart approached them this time, he thought of another analogy, something that eased his apprehension. The giant fingers, Stuart pondered, were like the hand of God. Like the image from Michelangelo's ceiling of the Sistine Chapel in Rome —the one the Army chaplain who taught him about Jesus had shown him. The powerful and omnipotent hand with fingers outstretched in the work of man was frozen—trapped in the concrete and steel of the dam. Stuart would guide the hand and release its dormant power. The divine hand would pound its fist into the dam and forever destroy its watery tomb.

There it is. Stuart saw it, the final charge. He dove slightly deeper and secured the last line to the explosive with the designated clamps. *Done.*

65

DOTS

Monday, 10:12 a.m.

J oy couldn't believe it.

"Well, this sucks," Woody exclaimed, shoving the metal table forward.

"This is the thanks we get. We're treated like suspects, as if we know something we're not telling about the fire and the murders." Joy stood up and started pacing. "I mean this is crazy. We who were kidnapped and almost killed ourselves. What the hell is going on? They lock us in some glorified janitor's closet!"

Woody shrugged his shoulders and slumped back in his chair. Joy continued to pace, running her hands across the gray cinder blocks of their holding room. Above them, an old rectangular fluorescent fixture hummed in the otherwise quiet space. Joy felt abandoned and betrayed—hung out to dry by Rick, Alex, and the Park Service.

"I should have gone to my cross-country training camp," Woody lamented.

"Hell, *I* should have gone to your cross-country training camp." Joy laughed. She knew without Woody being here, the prospect of being stuck in a room and getting grilled as if she were a criminal would be more arduous. At least with Woody, she could make light of their predicament.

Do I trust him though? Joy looked at Woody and then at the computer behind him. Chances are it was locked or password-protected, but that wouldn't be too much of a problem for her––*a simple government standard password lock, seven letters with one numeral string.* Joy had kept her hacking abilities to herself; not even her sister knew. She paused and anxiously began cracking the fingers on her left hand.

Woody cocked his head and looked back at her. "What's up, Joy?"

"Oh, sorry," Joy stammered. "I was just thinking."

"About?"

"Um, well, about why all of this is happening."

"There *is* this computer. Maybe we should––" Woody turned and walked over to the computer and reached for the on switch.

"No, wait!" Joy suddenly announced.

"What do you mean?"

Joy took a deep breath. "You need to turn it on in *safe* mode and then we can locate the login and password through the internal CPU keystroke log."

"Huh?"

"Here, let me." Joy walked over and pulled a chair up beside Woody. Before turning on the computer, she looked at Woody, not sure of what to say.

Woody stared back at her. "Oh, I get it. I'm not supposed to know"––Woody stumbled for the right words––"that you can do, well... whatever it is that you are going to do, right?"

"Yeah––something along those lines." Joy turned her attention to the machine, powering it on while depressing the *F8* key. She then selected the option to restart according to the last known good configuration, while holding down another sequence of keyboard commands at precise intervals in the rebooting process as she listened to the machine's fan increase revolutions, signaling the exact time the internal hard drive became activated. All at once the screen flashed on with a string of numbers and letters. She tabbed through several pages of this code while Woody shook his head in the background. When Joy found a small command option, she selected it, which brought up a new screen, containing lists of words and sentences which didn't seem to correspond to one another.

"Alright," Joy said.

"*Huh?*"

Joy just smiled. "Now, it should be at the start of one of these —no not there—wait. Okay, got it."

"Uhh, okay?"

Joy grabbed a sheet of paper and opened the desk's single drawer, rifling through its contents. She removed a pencil and flipped over the paper while she scribbled down two lines: *jpeterson* and *sakekirintsingtaoi*.

Joy smirked as she wrote the lines.

"What's funny?" Woody asked.

Joy switched off the machine and slid the paper over toward Woody. "Look at the second line. The user likes Asian alcohol."

Woody studied Joy's writing and saw the distinctive names. "Is this—?"

"We'll see in another minute."

Joy let the computer sit for a full thirty seconds before powering it back on. This time, no keys were depressed on the board as the tower whirled to life and the screen flashed from black to an electric blue. When the gray dialogue box appeared requesting a username and password, Joy transcribed the two lines she had copied a minute earlier into the corresponding boxes and hit return. The screen clicked over and the tower's fan began to spin.

"We're in," said Joy.

Woody's eyes lit up. "Nice."

In front of them, a standard Windows desktop flashed onto the screen along with files, an Internet browser, a network connection, and an assortment of folders with labels like *Personnel, Traffic, Financial,* and *Miscellaneous.*

"So let's figure this out, shall we?" Joy said.

"Sure."

Woody and Joy pulled their chairs in closer to each other.

"Where do you want to start?" Woody asked.

"First event and work forward."

"Well, before I saw Stuart push Aiden off of Cathedral... we, um, know there was another murder—the Abigail lady we learned about at the campfire."

"Yeah, Rick and everyone said as much. Do you remember her last name?" Joy asked.

"I think so. My mom said it was Abigail Edwards or something—a falling death, just like Aiden's, but off Half Dome earlier on the same day."

Joy opened up an Internet browser and typed in *Abigail Edwards.* "Really—the same day? Does that mean Stuart was working with someone?"

"Maybe, but Stuart arrived pretty late to the campfire at Budd Lake. He could also have killed Abigail."

"Why do you think Abigail was killed?" Joy clicked around on a few links until she arrived at the image of Abigail's death. "Damn, I had forgotten how grotesque—"

"Ehh... *gross.*"

"'Here lies Muir's mountain temple'—that's how Rick and the rangers found us at Cathedral, right?"

"Yeah, but there could be more to it—you know, with Abigail and then Aiden."

"What do you mean?"

"Well, here's the interesting connection my mom brought up,"

Woody began. "Abigail was writing and working on issues with Hetch Hetchy. Aiden was climbing in Hetch Hetchy and working with Abigail."

Joy wrote "Hetch Hetchy" on the slip of paper in front of her. "Okay, so they both are connected to Hetch Hetchy, but why kill them? What's the motive?"

"Um—"

They sat for a moment. Then, Joy had a thought and looked over at Woody. "Okay, two things: First, the anagram about Ansel Adams we read on Alex's phone helped us figure out the Half Dome meeting point. Well, some of the other things we read on Alex's phone could be deciphered, too. Second, what did you overhear Stuart telling Aiden right before he pushed him off? Something about an achievement?"

"Great. Yeah, um, Stuart told Aiden, 'What you are working for, it will be achieved.' And then when you asked him why he killed Aiden, Stuart said this whole thing was *larger* than just him and Aiden, something about Aiden being a kind of spark to ignite —" Woody froze.

"*A fire*," Joy responded. "Like the fire raging right now."

"Do you think--?"

"That's, you know, pretty literal."

"Yeah," Woody said.

"And the fire is here in the main valley, not Hetch Hetchy."

"Yeah," Woody said. "It doesn't make sense."

"I know."

"What about the online riddles?"

"Well, there's this one by Abigail's body: 'Here lies Muir's mountain temple.'" Joy wrote the words down while she was speaking. "The second was the phrase 'a secreting twirl norm' along with the photo of Aiden where you could see our legs and shoes in the background."

"What do you make of the statements?"

"Since the Half Dome thing was connected, the other statements should mean something, too."

"Here lies Muir's mountain temple—I'm not sure yet, but I seem to remember a famous quote by Muir about a mountain temple," Woody said.

"Okay then..." Joy opened up Google and typed in "mountain + temple + Muir." She immediately landed on text from Muir's *The Yosemite*, but the specific passage was not clear. There were many potential references to mountains. In the opening section, where Muir describes Yosemite Valley, a sentence read: "The walls are made up of rocks, mountains in size, partly separated from each other by side canyons, and they are so sheer in front, and so compactly and harmoniously arranged on a level floor, that the Valley, comprehensively seen, looks like an immense hall or temple lighted from above." *

"That's a description of the valley itself," Woody commented. "Is Stuart comparing Abigail to Yosemite?"

"It doesn't make a whole lot of sense. Unless he killed Abigail first and then set fire to the valley," Joy added.

"Yeah, but that doesn't help explain Aiden and, um, the comment that we overheard. And *mountain*, well, it's such a common word in any description of Yosemite."

"Okay, let's try this then." Joy typed *Muir + temple* and hit *search*. The browser refreshed and Woody and Joy leaned in closer, sensing they would finally arrive at something. Joy put the tip of her index finger to her mouth as her mind raced. The vast majority of the links connected to one passage in particular: "These temple destroyers, devotees of ravaging commercialism, seem to have a perfect contempt for Nature, and instead of lifting their eyes to the God of the mountains, lift them to the Almighty Dollar."

Also, a little further on in the same section, Muir's words read: "Dam Hetch Hetchy! As well dam for water tanks the people's cathedrals and churches, for no holier temple has ever been consecrated by the heart of man.'"

"That's got to be it!" Joy exclaimed. She turned toward Woody. "It connects Abigail and Aiden back to Hetch Hetchy and Muir. And didn't Jeffrey say something about the phrase 'holy temple' showing up? Well, there it is."

"Yeah." Woody read the sentence again and then tilted his head back, staring up at the ceiling. "There's something else, too."

"What?"

"You know what also connects back to Hetch Hetchy? The quote that led us to the Ansel Adams picture."

"*Clearing Winter Storm*—what do you mean?" Joy asked, propping her cheek on her hand.

Woody leaned forward and rested his arm on the back of Joy's chair. "Well, remember what we did to the word 'Yosemite'? We turned it into an anagram as well; it became 'eyes omit,' and in the case of the photograph, what was omitted was clearly Half Dome, right?"

"Sure, it just made sense." Joy nodded her head.

"Well, what else has been hidden in Yosemite? What can't be seen? What else lies, um, omitted or out of sight?" Woody smiled.

"Of course!" Joy exclaimed. "Half Dome, the most famous feature of the Park, is hidden just like the Hetch Hetchy Valley is hidden beneath the lake."

"Exactly! So that clue connects, too. Great. So what is going on with Hetch Hetchy?" Woody asked. "What 'will be achieved?'"

They paused, facing each other, and thought for a moment. "What would be an achievement in Hetch Hetchy?" Woody ran his hand up his forehead and squeezed his hair. Joy bit down on her lower lip and started sequentially going through her knuckles. Suddenly, they both looked up, inches away from each other.

"You don't think--?" Joy cocked her head to the side and tapped her finger to her lips.

"It *is* what Aiden would want, you know, what he's *been*

working for, like Stuart said," Woody responded, lowering his hand and putting it on Joy's knee.

"But that seems almost impossible." Joy put her hand on Woody's. "How would you ever pull something like that off with so much security—you know, all the rangers and the monitoring at the dam?"

Woody said his next words slowly as it dawned on him. "You'd need all of their attention to be focused elsewhere."

"Like now."

"Like on the fire."

"He's going to—" Joy began.

Woody finished her sentence, *"Blow up the O'Shaughnessy Dam."*

Joy searched Woody's face as if the lines on his forehead were verification, or maybe the eyes which stared back at her, unflinching.

Woody pulled back. "But—"

Joy was upset. "That still doesn't explain why he had to kill Aiden and Abigail. Why bother leaving clues? Why not just start the fire and then go blow up the dam? We can't be the only ones who are figuring this out."

"Yeah, right."

Joy went back onto the *Earth Liberation Front* blog site. "So here we go. Let's check some of the messages, the weird stuff." She scrolled though the last twelve hours of activity, scanning and processing as quickly as possible.

"Okay, I think I found something," Joy announced.

Woody looked back at the screen as Joy opened another Internet tab and pulled up an online calculator. She scribbled column headings onto the paper in front of her.

"So..." Joy wrote a list in the upper right-hand corner of the paper. "These are times that a certain type of posting appears. I mean, well, if you just read through the blogs, it looks like a bunch of angry hippies, right?"

"Sure does," Woody agreed.

"But certain posts, the anagrams, the one-word stuff, they are interspersed into the rest of the rants and strangeness, so..." Joy was still scrolling with one hand and writing down times with the other. "If you look at the times these postings appear—not every post, but the weird ones—the coded language—"

"There's a pattern?" Woody asked.

"Not a pattern per se—but I think..." Joy opened up the online calculator and started subtracting the posting times from one another, yielding different numbers which she converted into seconds in her head and wrote in another column farther to the left. "I bet it's—let's just get a few more—"

"What is it?"

Joy scribbled out an equation on the paper.

$$P = \frac{\text{Log}_{10}(n+1) - \text{Log}_{10} n}{\text{Log}_{10} 10 - \text{Log}_{10} 1}$$

"This is Benford's Law. It's basically a way to establish a, well, *fake*, random numerical sequence within a given scale—and just let me check..." Joy started plugging in various numbers into the online calculator.

Woody and Joy suddenly looked up as the doorknob began to turn. Joy only had time to switch the monitor off. They both spun around in their chairs.

Through the door a downtrodden, but familiar face appeared.

"Rick!" Woody and Joy both exclaimed.

"Sorry it took me so long to find you two. I had to check almost every door in the place."

"Rick, we think we know what Stuart is up to right now," Joy began. "He's on his way to—"

"Hetch Hetchy, I know," Rick said.

"How?" Woody asked.

"I'll explain later. Right now we need to get you two away from this building and the Feds. I brought you these." Rick tossed a duffle bag on the table. "Put them on. I'll stand by the door and make sure no one comes in. Knock when you're ready." Rick shut the door and left them.

Woody unzipped the bag to reveal two firefighter jackets, pants, and helmets.

"We're on the fire crew," Joy said as she reached in to grab a jacket.

Once they had pulled on their new clothes, wiped any evidence of their search history from the computer, and powered it down, Woody knocked on the door. Rick pushed it open. "Ready," Rick said. "Let's make like a hockey team."

"What?" Joy asked.

"Get the puck out of here."

They made their way down the hall and toward the rear of the building. A few people passed them; none seemed to notice they weren't wearing proper boots. Everyone was preoccupied with some assignment. At the end of the building was another large room filled with people working on managing the fire response or the evacuation.

Rick held up Woody and Joy at the entrance to the room and scanned the entire scene. He motioned to the door and then powered confidently ahead with Woody and Joy on his heels.

Outside of the building, Rick breathed a sigh of relief and looked at his two young firefighters. "Yeah, that was enough to get you out of the building, but I don't think we would have stood a chance if someone stopped and questioned you."

"Rick, why are we having to sneak around?" Woody asked.

"Let's walk over by my car and I'll explain." Rick reached into his pocket and pulled out the remote keyless entry for another Park Service vehicle. "Let's see. It's one of these." He pressed the unlock button and the lights on a standard Crown Victoria flashed twice. "Over there."

They walked across the parking lot through a brownish haze of morning sunlight filtered by smoke and ash.

Standing by the car, Rick glanced up at the sky and shook his head. "Look guys, normally I have a bit more power around here, but given the current situation and my all-night ordeal, the normal chain of command is—shall we say—disrupted. The big shots from federal agencies and CAL FIRE has imposed martial law on the Park. I've told a couple people who I trust about my crazy idea, but everyone is too strapped to allocate any additional resources to what might well be a wild-goose chase."

"But how did you—" Woody began.

"I pulled up the sites Jeffrey had on his search history in his computer and printed out a bunch of material which led me to the Hetch Hetchy conclusion. Then, I found out that some idiot detective from the local county office had taken it upon himself to detain you both, and after the past twelve hours of BS, I just couldn't let that happen."

"Thanks, but how did you figure out it was Hetch Hetchy?" Joy asked.

"I remembered Jeffrey was all excited about some conference here in the Park where Abigail, the first victim, had spoken specifically about Hetch Hetchy. Then, I looked through the blogs Jeffrey was searching for some other posting by that same person we looked up in the backcountry, you know, Adams Ansel. Well, I found another posting on the *Sierra Club* website. It read 'lithe churches empty helm,' which was... weird, right?"

Joy nodded.

"So I just used the same anagram logic we used before, but this time I used an anagram website to save myself the mental anguish. You'll never guess that 'lithe churches empty helm' converts into—"

"Let me see," Joy interrupted. "There are a bunch of H's in

that phrase, so I'm betting it has some combination of words with Hetch Hetchy in it."

"Exactly. It translates to 'Muir's Temple Hetch Hetchy.'"

"No way," Woody said.

"Yup. Plain as day."

"We came to the same conclusion but—" Woody began. "We basically looked at the first message, 'Here lies—'"

"Guys, sorry to interrupt, but I need to get going."

"Hold on, Rick," Joy demanded. "Why did Stuart and this Professor guy even tell us? Why lay out a riddle with an obvious solution? Why leave a trail for people to follow?"

"Hrmm, that's *the* question, isn't it? I'm hoping to find an answer from Stuart when I catch him in the act," said Rick.

"Great, let's go," Woody responded.

"There's not a snowball's chance in hell you two are coming. I got you out of your detention cell, but I am not taking you with me to Hetch Hetchy."

"You don't expect us to just sit this one out, do you?"

"Sorry, guys––this one's just me."

"What about Alex?" Joy asked.

"She's left the Park, and besides, she's got to be totally exhausted. People know where I'm going, and look... plenty of additional personnel will be dispatched if and when I give the word, so you two need to stay put, let us handle this. Find your families and get some rest."

"But you said this was probably a wild-goose chase, right?" Joy asked. "So what's the big deal? Chances are we won't even run into Stuart and nothing will be happening at Hetch Hetchy right now."

"Yeah, and we can stay with the car or whatever you want," Woody added.

"No." Rick was firm. He opened the driver's side door and got in. "I'm going, and there is no way I'm putting you all in harm's way again. End of story. Sorry. Leave the jacket and pants by the squad car in the lot, walk over to the village and catch the bus that's shuttling people out of the valley by the visitor center. This is not a debate, it's an order. I believe you both have family who are looking for you right now and––" Rick reached into his pocket and pulled out a spare cell phone—"it looks like you have a phone to contact them." He tossed the phone at Woody.

Rick started the engine and shifted into reverse. "Thank you for all of your help. I'll contact you once this is all over."

Before Joy or Woody could protest further, Rick pulled away.

They watched his taillights through the cloud of dust as he sped out of the parking lot and toward the mouth of the valley.

"Now what?" Joy asked.

"Yeah, I don't know," Woody responded.

"I really want to see what happens," Joy said.

"Yeah, and I don't like the idea of Rick going after Stuart by himself."

"Well, we don't even know if Stuart is in Hetch Hetchy."

"True, but––" Woody paused mid-thought and stared over Joy's shoulder. A huge grin slowly worked its way across his face.

Joy turned around and looked in the direction Woody was staring. "What is it?"

Woody turned his smile toward Joy and said one word: "*Rusty.*"

66

DOC

Monday, 10:17 A.M.

"Walter, you'd better start talking," Agent Dale Friedman urged.

Walter took a deep breath. "All right, all right, so I've got a shithead for a brother. That doesn't make me a criminal."

The face in the photo in front of Walter Ashgood was indeed his brother, Nick, also known as "Doc" Ashgood. Though Walter had always been focused on conventional pathways to success in life, his older brother had gotten caught up in some wild environmental activism.

In the early 2000s, Nick and some of his buddies had given themselves false names based on the landmark environmental protest novel *Monkey Wrench Gang,* and decided to take a stand against logging practices in the Bitterroot Valley of southwestern Montana. Leaving signage to alert logging crews to their presence at the base of their chosen trees, they climbed high into the branches of ponderosa pines and camped out.[*] The loggers went to work elsewhere. At night someone would often sneak down and go to the grocery store, returning with supplies, and the group would hang out at the base of one of the massive trees swapping stories and plotting further environmental espionage—until it all went wrong.

The logging companies, fed up with the antics and audacity of Doc and his fellow tree squatters, had enlisted the help of federal agents. During the first day, all the branches were sawed off of the tree in which Doc was camped out. They fell all around him, knocking his portaledge and blanketing him in a thick carpet of sawdust, sap, and pine needles, as he jostled dangerously around. Many of the other tree campers gave up during this first onslaught or later when the federal agents trained high-powered spotlights and announced threats through a bullhorn ensuring that no one could sleep. Doc remained through it all, day after day, night after night, until finally his tree was the lone standing pinnacle on the ravaged landscape, like an Egyptian obelisk in a barren desert. It was then, two weeks into the unrelenting siege, after Doc had spent days without water and nearly a week without food, that the federal agents and logging companies devised a particularly cruel strategy to finally extricate Doc from his solitary tower. Tying guidelines to the trunk of the tree to ensure it would remain vertical and wrapping a single large chain tightly around the bottom, the loggers cut a large chunk directly out of the tree's base, making two level passes with their long chainsaws; then, tying the chain to a piece of heavy equipment meant for clearing access roads, the severed section of tree was brutally yanked out of the base of the trunk.

Dehydrated, emaciated, sleep-deprived, and incoherent, Doc fell straight downward, smashing to a halt as the massive trunk slammed into its stump, but remained upright. Even if Doc wanted to give up now, the loggers and agents were so excited by their new strategy that they quickly tightened the guidelines and repeated the process, carving out another large chunk of the tree and then violently ripping it right out of the tree's base. The procedure was repeated again and again. Each time Doc plummeted another increment of five to eight feet and his weak body collided against the tree he had sought to protect and the portaledge that had been his home. Doc later told his family he wished for death. If he died it would show that the federal government and powerful logging interests had murdered him in the name of clear-cutting forests for profit. He dreamed while being slammed viciously around in a toxic soup of sap, sawdust, and his own excrement that his death would mean a renaissance in environmental protection. But he dreamed in vain.

Doc did not die. When his position was near level with the agents, he was dragged out and onto the ground. Unable to support himself, he was taken to the hospital and given an intravenous injection of fluids, cleaned up, and handcuffed to the hospital bed.

Rather than punishing the logging companies and the FBI for torture and inhuman treatment, Doc was convicted as an ecoterrorist by a jury of Montana civilians sympathetic to the logging industry. In addition to one year of jail time, Doc was banned from setting foot on National Forest land, given three years of supervised federal probation, and billed for many of the expenses incurred by the logging company in its efforts to remove him from the tree.

"Walter, we know this is Nick, or rather 'Doc,' and that he is your brother, and we know you've been sending him and others in affiliate organizations confidential files," Agent Friedman said.

"That's ridiculous. What confidential files? I don't have access to anything remotely considered confidential."

"What about this?" Agent Friedman pushed forward a copy of one of the reports Walter had been examining during the past month.

"So? I look at hundreds of these per month. It's soil science, ecological data—nothing top secret here."

"Really?" The agent reached forward and folded back the first page of the report to reveal the table of contents and the beginning of the executive summary. Written in a clear red marker across the upper right-hand corner of the page were the words *CLASSIFIED: SENSITIVE MATERIAL.*

"It didn't say that before. I swear it. And even if it did, what is so controversial about this data?" Walter reached forward across the table and turned open the booklet. There staring him in the face was a schematic that he didn't expect to see. It had something to do with a power grid, and certain areas of the page were circled in red with the word *VULNERABILITY* listed below them.

"I've never seen this page before in my life."

"Is that accurate?" Another agent entered the room holding a manila folder with additional paperwork. "Then what was this very document doing on your personal computer at your home address?"

"What? I have no idea," Walter stated.

"And there's a whole lot more where that came from. Not just gas lines, but power grids, points of connection––the keys to the entire energy supply of Northern California." The new agent continued. "Mr. Ashgood, we have reason to believe a plot is unfolding right now, and if you cooperate with us, things will go much better for you. Do you understand?"

"Look, guys," Walter responded. "Believe me, I am happy to help you in any way I can. I don't want to be sideways with the federal government. I really don't. I just honestly don't know what to tell you. If you show me what you've got, I can try to decipher it for you, but my job and the info that I have access to are kind of run-of-the-mill, you know? I've literally never seen stuff with *sensitive* and *classified* marked on it before."

The two agents stared back at Walter for a long moment, and then they grabbed their files, turned, and left the room.

None of this made sense to Walter. He knew Nick was working on some new cause in the Sierra Nevada involving rock climbing with a well-known and respected activist named Abigail

Edwards, and that Abigail had written on behalf of Nick and used her connections through the Sierra Club to reduce the charges levied against him.

My brother hasn't even come to visit me since I moved to San Francisco, Walter thought. *So what could Nick possibly have to do with those documents?*

67

AS YOU WERE, BOYS

Monday, 10:21 A.M.

Mojo and Rosa had caught up with Rebecca and Jasmine at a picnic table in front of the ranger head-quarters. There seemed to be a constant stream of rangers, fire fighters, FBI agents, and other personnel coming and going. The wind shifted direction, reducing the density of smoke, and a few hazy beams of sunlight found their way onto the table as the four ladies talked about Woody and Joy.

"What's your theory?" Rosa asked Rebecca. "On why there isn't more, you know... romance."

"Joy's just real practical. She's not going to do anything rash."

"Really?" Rosa said.

"Yup. I got all the heart, and my sister got all the head." Jasmine laughed.

"That's not really fair to either of you," Rebecca said.

"Yeah, well it's accurate."

Although Mojo still wasn't entirely comfortable with the fact that her only son had been spending time around Jasmine, she was slightly reassured by Rebecca's calming presence and her assertion that Joy wasn't taking advantage of her son.

"Sorry to change the topic, ladies, but it's been nearly half an hour." Mojo raised her eyebrows.

At that moment, the wind shifted again and filled their immediate vicinity with smoke from the forest fire.

"What do you say we head back in there?" Jasmine said.

"Fine by me." Mojo got up and straightened her clothing once again, physically and emotionally preparing herself for the inevitable confrontation. "Let's go get them, ladies."

The four women, now more at ease and comfortable with each other after chatting for the past half hour, and bolstered by Mojo's previous browbeating of the detective, marched up to the front entrance of the headquarters.

At the doors, Mojo paused and turned to her companions. "Let's make a little show of this and scare our pudgy friend a bit, shall we?"

The girls seemed to like the idea and nodded in agreement.

"Look saucy, ladies," Mojo instructed. "Ready with the doors? *Now.*"

Jasmine and Rosa, who were on the outside, threw back the double-entrance doors to the ranger headquarters with a dramatic flourish. There, standing in the wide entrance, were four attractive women, none of whom were dressed like a member of the Park Service or a firefighter. In unison, they marched across the threshold and into the room, with a gleaming mist of sunlit smoke ushering them forward.

Following Mojo's lead, they made their way to the center of the floor.

One by one, rangers and officers turned their heads to follow the four. It looked like an advertisement for *Desperate Housewives,* taking place smack dab in the middle of the Park Service Headquarters.

Mojo struck a slight pose and checked around for Detective Tandy. The other ladies mimicked Mojo's general bravado.

As it became apparent that the detective wasn't in the room, Mojo glanced over at Rosa and pursed her lips. Instantly, Rosa knew what she needed to do. Taking a large inhalation, Rosa brought her right hand up to her mouth, inserted her index and middle finger in the manner that her ranch-hand father had instructed her, and let out the clearest shrill whistle imaginable. The impressive note hung in the air for a good ten seconds and essentially eliminated any other conversation in the room.

Right on the heels of Rosa's cattle call, Mojo said in a commanding, yet feminine voice, "Boys,"—and it was mostly men in the room—"we are looking for a pudgy fellow who goes by *Detective* Tandy." Mojo's breathy and innuendo-laced pronouncement of the word *detective* caused a chuckle to circle the room. "He has taken something from us and we need it back. Would one of you gentlemen be so kind as to direct us to him?"

Almost immediately, one eager-looking young ranger jumped up and opened the rear hallway door. "I think I saw him back here—uh, please follow me, ladies."

Not breaking character for even a second, Rosa sauntered forward toward the hallway. Jasmine, Rebecca, and Mojo fell in line. Just before she exited, Mojo turned and said, "As you were, boys. As you were."

Detective Tandy was not where the young ranger had thought he was. In fact, they had to actually exit the rear of the building where they found him nervously smoking a cigarette by the dumpster.

"Detective," Mojo began. "We meet again."

"Lady, I'm not sure how to tell you this, but the kids... they ain't here."

68

GRATITUDE

Monday, 10:35 A.M.

Using a sack and his diving weights, Stuart sent his scuba gear to the bottom of the lake. *All too easy,* he mused.

Pulling out his computer, he began setting up for detonation. The Army Corps of Engineers documents provided by The Professor had explained that the charges needed to go off in a certain order and with ample time between explosions to allow the natural forces of the water to weaken the structure. If all the charges were set off simultaneously, they'd be ineffective.

Since Stuart was on the far side of the dam, he would essentially be cutting himself off from where his car was parked. This was by design. It would also cut off anyone attempting to intercept him.

He brought the wiring together and inserted it into the routing device. All of this had been rehearsed sitting in the comfort of his apartment, plugging in the device to a laptop, starting the software, entering security codes, and activating the charges. Even the timing was rehearsed with precision. The results of the trial were encoded and sent to The Professor for verification. The trial run was to ensure no glitches would result here and now, when he was performing the real task on the real O'Shaughnessy Dam.

Stuart attached the router to the laptop. He checked the connections again and verified the colors running to the right lines. He took a deep breath and powered up the computer.

Easy does it.

The hike out along the Tuolumne River to the high-country meadows where his VW bus lay in wait would be a welcome respite and reward for a job well done. With each footstep beside the gurgling stream, he would listen to the river thanking him for what he was only moments away from initiating.

MOTIVE

Monday, 10:46 A.M.

The cruiser whipped around the curves of Highway 120 from Yosemite Valley through its intersection with Tioga Pass Road and on toward the turnoff to Hetch Hetchy. Rick fixed his attention on the road, laid on the accelerator, hands at ten and two.

Solo. That's how I came to Yosemite, how I define myself, despite Grandfather's "You need your people, they need you."

His cell phone rang. Rick shook his head—a 415 area code—San Francisco. He put the phone on speaker. "Rick here."

The voice on the line sounded authoritative. "Rick Turlock, Park Ranger at Yosemite?"

Rick responded with forced lightheartedness. "You got me."

"Rick, my name is Dale Friedman. I'm an agent with the FBI here in Northern California. It has come to my attention that you—" there was a pause on the line. "That you suspect additional incidents are currently being perpetrated in Yosemite."

"Something like that."

Agent Friedman continued, "Rick, I'd like to share some information with you which may be of use." He paused. "I know some of our guys are in the main valley now, and that they have not exactly been—shall we say, hospitable."

"That's an understatement."

"I want you to know, I believe the current three-ring fiasco going on in Yosemite Valley is a diversion," Friedman said. "Something else has been planned. I guess this is your theory, also."

"I'm listening."

"We have in custody a person we suspect of leaking sensitive information about the California power grid to ecoterrorist organizations. This person you are tracking, Stuart White I believe, he could be working in concert with our suspect."

"What's the target?" Rick asked, wanting to see how much Agent Friedman had pieced together.

"The O'Shaughnessy Dam."

There was silence on the line for a few moments, while Rick weighed the pros and cons of collaborating with the FBI. He was alone, and having support now would be the logical choice. Rick took a deep breath and felt his chest, with its tattoo of a fist, rise and fall against the cruiser's seat belt. "Alright, Agent Friedman. Yes, I also think Stuart is planning to blow up the O'Shaughnessy Dam at Hetch Hetchy."

"Good, we're on the same page. You're headed to Hetch Hetchy for reconnaissance, right?"

"Yes. I'm not too excited about confronting this nutcase again. But if I can prevent him from flooding the valley below and killing more people, well..."

"Rick—I can mobilize forces quickly. There's no need to go this alone."

"10-4. Do you have an idea of the motive?"

"Assuming our hypothetical plays out here?" Friedman responded.

"Yeah, you know, Stuart—he didn't strike me as the overeducated, self-important activist type."

"Well, we don't know much: mid-thirties, 'White' is not his real name, possible military background, maybe an environmental activist component," Friedman responded.

"The climbers I was with seem to think he is some kind of paid killer. He used to be in the armed forces, got mixed up in some controversial stuff in Iraq, and now he's just out killing for hire—at least that's what they think."

"How did they come up with that?"

"Some online research, testing out different theories. It makes more sense to me—Stuart as a hit man, not some radical tree-hugger with a particularly vicious streak," Rick commented.

"Then why all the Muir references? It's consistent with other environmentalist code language that we've monitored. And then there's the angry chatter online: 'Retaliation must be swift,' written by someone with the moniker Monkey Wrench."

"It sure sounds like environmental extremism," Rick said.

"We have another suspect as well that you might be able to help us with."

"Really?"

"He goes by the name of Doc. His real name is Nick Ashgood," Agent Friedman explained. "It's his brother we have in custody here in San Francisco. According to your records from the crime scene last night by Cathedral Peak, Doc was on that climb when Aiden Watson died."

"Great. So, you've got him up at the Tuolumne Ranger Station?"

"Unfortunately, no. Looks like he slipped out sometime before 5:00 a.m."

"Really?"

"Afraid so."

"Damn! Do you suspect he's working with Stuart?"

"He was present at the fatality at the base of Cathedral Peak and could have been involved in the death that took place earlier."

"You mean Abigail Edwards?" Rick asked.

"Yes."

"Hmm." Rick wondered about Stuart's references to a Professor, which would fit with the name Doc, and might explain how Stuart knew he was being tracked. "Who do you have in custody?" Rick inquired.

"All I can divulge is he is related to the person you *had* last night."

Rick drove the cruiser through the winding roads and patchwork of public and private land before Camp Mather and the entrance to the Hetch Hetchy Valley.

"Let's go back to Stuart for a minute though. Who would hire him?" Agent Friedman asked.

"Well, it's all about motive, isn't it?" Rick began. "Who benefits from the restoration of Hetch Hetchy?"

Rick came up to the turn for Hetch Hetchy Reservoir and cut the wheel hard and to the right. The cruiser jostled around on the potholes of the rough side road. Unlike the roads into Yosemite Valley, Hetch Hetchy's asphalt access was less traveled and less maintained. Rick was forced to slow down considerably just to keep off the shoulder.

"Let's see," Agent Friedman continued. "No one really stands to benefit financially from the restoration of Hetch Hetchy. Maybe you could argue that the Park itself would benefit from having another major tourist destination, but that doesn't constitute motive for murder and ecoterrorism on this scale."

"What about looking at it differently—not who is benefited but who is harmed?" Rick suggested.

"There you go."

"So," Rick said, "the City of San Francisco would be hurt the most by the loss of the reservoir. It would alter its income stream, its water use, and its dynamic with the rest of the state."

"San Francisco has some enemies out there, that's for sure."

"And at one time, I think it would have hurt WP&G."

"How so?" Agent Friedman asked.

"If I remember right, WP&G was involved with power distribution from Hetch Hetchy."

"When was that?"

"Back in the early part of this century. But, sometime in the 1950s, the Supreme Court ruled that a private company could not profit from power generated by the O'Shaughnessy Dam." *

Maneuvering past the park entrance, Rick gave a quick wave to the ranger there, and then glanced at his phone to make sure he still had signal strength.

"Agent—Dale—are you there?"

"Yeah, I'm here. So the deepest pockets and likely underwriters of some plot on this scale are WP&G, the City of San Francisco, the National Park Service, or a particularly well-funded ecoterrorist cell."

"That's a wide net to cast," Rick commented.

"I think I know how I can narrow it."

"Good to hear, ranger."

The cruiser rounded a bend, granting Rick a clear view of the Hetch Hetchy Reservoir and the O'Shaughnessy Dam.

"Oh, fucking hell!" Rick cursed. Even though he was still over a mile away, he could see it—on the near side, partway down the massive concrete face, a powerful spout of water was spewing straight out from the front of the dam for hundreds of feet downstream.

"What the hell's going on?" Friedman asked.

"Dale, *send everyone*."

PART IV

UNLEASHING THE HOLY TEMPLE

May your trails be crooked, winding, lonesome, dangerous, leading to the most amazing view... where something strange and more beautiful and more full of wonder than your deepest dreams waits for you.

—Edward Abbey, *Desert Solitaire*

YOUNG MAN

Monday, 10:58 A.M.

"You've been here before, right?" Joy asked.

"Yeah, um, it's this next turn." Woody slowed his father's old Jeep, shifted into third gear, and exited off Highway 120 toward Camp Mather and Hetch Hetchy.

"Hey, shouldn't I be driving?"

"I know this Jeep, and besides, um, the authorities have much more to worry about."

"You're beginning to sound like my sister," Joy said.

Woody glanced at Joy; her expression was deadpan. "Coming from you," he said. "I'm not sure if I should take that as a compliment."

"Me neither."

Woody smiled. He hadn't considered that Joy had something to gain from their intimacy. She seemed less callous than she had been, willing to open herself up to his judgment.

"Hey, I'm starving," Woody said.

"Me too."

"That red bag back there, it's not my mom's. I think it's Rosa's.

Knowing Rosa, she came prepared. Do you mind digging around?"

Joy unbuckled and turned in her seat to rifle through the bags. "Bingo," Joy said as she hoisted a small cooler out from underneath Rosa's duffle bag.

"Sweet. What do we have?"

Joy popped open the lid. "Apples, some water, carrots, other healthy crap and—hello, what's this?" Joy removed an aluminum foil wrapped item and opened it up. "*¿Te gusta el burrito con carne asada?*"

"*Sí, me gusta mucho.*"

Joy handed over the burrito and reached in to grab another. They devoured whatever Joy pulled from the cooler as the Jeep bounced its way through the rough countryside.

"What about your mom?" Joy managed to ask between bites.

"Yeah, guess I should've tried to find her..." Woody took another bite of burrito. "She'll know I'm fine when she looks for the Jeep. I'm in trouble for the next half century, anyway—so what the hell."

Joy playfully punched Woody in the shoulder as Rusty bounded past a few private homes close to the park gate. When they arrived at the entrance kiosk, it was conspicuously silent. No ranger was on duty, and only one car was parked in front of the nearby station.

"Should we just, you know... go on through?" Woody mumbled with his mouthful of apple.

"I guess so."

Rusty coasted through the Hetch Hetchy entrance to Yosemite National Park and forward into the forest.

"Do you think Rick is already there?" Joy asked.

"He was driving pretty fast." Woody checked his rearview mirror to see if anyone had come out of the buildings to flag them down.

"Hey, when we were in the room, you were, you know, about to figure a calculation with some theorem," Woody said.

"Yes—Benford's Law. I still have that paper." Joy pulled it out along with her notes. "The seemingly random coded messages aren't random at all, but part of a computer program."

"Really? You mean they were pretyped and then set up to be… disseminated according to some weird code?"

"That's exactly it."

"But, um, wouldn't they all be coming from the same source?"

"Not necessarily. The person posting could easily change login names and could even be using a single computer and then slaving other hard drives as nodes to a master through access to an ISP's main network."

"Uh, I'll just have to take your word for it." Woody smiled at Joy.

"So this would give the originator total, you know… anonymity and make it seem like lots of people from around the country were involved."

"That's something."

"Is that the lake?" Joy asked.

Rusty had just rounded another bend, which afforded Joy and Woody a view directly over the shoulder of the valley and deep into the Hetch Hetchy canyon.

"It's huge—the reservoir." Joy began. "So that's Hetch Hetchy. I can see why San Francisco would want to hold onto it. That's it, right Woody? That's Hetch… Woody, what are you stopping for?"

"It's started."

Then Joy saw it—the round shaft of water, like a jet stream, powerfully projecting directly out from the concrete face of the dam, straight into the valley beyond.

"Hold on." Woody took off, pushing the old Jeep as hard as he could, speeding around the blind corners of the remaining two miles of winding canyon road to the shore of the lake and the top of the dam.

"Where would Stuart set up?" Joy asked, bracing herself against the door.

"I don't know. I'm not sure how we could tell."

Woody spotted a Crown Victoria cruiser parked above the entrance to the dam. There, at the rear of the car was a lone figure in a Park Service uniform.

"That's got to be Rick, right?" Woody yelled over the increasingly loud sound of rushing water.

The figure popped open the trunk to the cruiser and reached inside, while propping a cell phone up to his ear. He then removed a long black case that seemed to be heavier at one end.

"I hope that's Rick," Joy yelled back.

Woody slowed Rusty down as he got closer. The man pulled out a rifle. When Rusty was about twenty feet away, the figure turned his head toward the approaching Jeep.

"Rick!" Joy exclaimed through her open window.

Rick looked at the Jeep and then shook his head. Woody pulled Rusty up behind the cruiser, cut the engine, and hopped out.

"Dale, I'm going to have to call you back," Rick spoke loudly into the phone. "I know. Dale, look I get it: you don't want me to go any further, but—"

"Hey, did you find him?" Woody asked as Rick scanned the opposite bank.

"Dale, I'll see you when the chopper lands." Rick hung up the phone and turned to Woody and Joy. "I thought I told you two to stay put, to go home, to do anything but follow me here!"

"But here we are—what can we do?" Joy yelled over the roar of rushing water.

"Hrmm." Rick looked through the rifle scope to the other side of the reservoir.

"You're obviously understaffed here. Give us something to do," Joy continued.

"You still have your phone, right?" Rick answered, not looking up.

"Yes."

"Call 9-1-1. Get a hold of any additional authorities you can." Rick stood up and began packing up the rifle. "Tell them there is an attempt to blow up the O'Shaughnessy Dam at Hetch Hetchy, that it is already breached. This will duplicate some of the FBI's efforts, but we need to sound the alarm as rapidly as possible. Tell them evacuations need to take place downstream immediately. Joy, here are the keys to the cruiser. You two stay put in this car, spread the word and if there is any sign of trouble, please— you both know what this guy is capable of—get the hell out of here as fast as possible."

"What about you?" Woody asked.

"I'm going over there."

"The dam is failing! What do you mean you're going over there?" Woody demanded.

"If he was going to blow the entire thing by now, he would have already done it. Obviously, he's in the middle of the process," Rick said as he began walking toward the dam.

Woody followed Rick down the hillside road toward the water and the concrete surface. "But shouldn't we wait? I mean, won't there be, you know––helicopters arriving?"

"It'll be a while. Go back!"

Walking down the final concrete embankment before the top of the dam, a new sound could be discerned. It wasn't coming from the valley beyond, but from the lake itself. To their right, a large funnel swirled and snarled at them, like looking down from space into the eye of a hurricane.

Rick stepped out onto the surface of the dam, and then turned back to Woody. "Go back and stay at the car with Joy. Do it *now!*"

"No way, Rick. I'm not letting you do this alone." Woody stepped out onto the dam as well. It shook like a constant low-level earthquake, causing the laces on Woody's ASICS to bounce along the nylon surface of his shoes. His lightweight climbing pants vibrated against his legs.

"Go back, dammit!" Rick commanded.

"No!" Woody yelled back. "Get off the dam, Rick. Why are you—?"

Rick marched intently toward Woody.

"You don't need to do this alone."

"Woody," Rick said once he was face to face with the teenager. "I'm going over there and you—*you are staying here.*"

As soon as the words left Rick's mouth, Woody did the only thing that came naturally to him—he ran. Ducking around Rick's elbow, Woody took off down the surface of the dam.

"What the—?" Rick turned and pursued Woody, who was racing onto the massive concrete arc of the O'Shaughnessy Dam. Woody gradually slowed his pace and held his arms out like a tightrope walker to maintain balance as he jogged. His concentration was broken by the vibrations, as if the world itself was disintegrating before his eyes. Shooting out of the face of the dam, the horizontal column of water, at least twenty feet in diameter, was eating away larger and larger swaths of concrete. Eventually the fissure would reach the top, where the dam was skinniest—and where Woody and Rick were now headed.

Woody wasn't entirely sure of his reasons for putting himself back in danger like this. There wasn't anything to prove. He cared about Rick, that was part of it, but that couldn't account for this sort of reckless endangerment.

Then, it struck him. *It always comes back to you, Dad.*

At the entrance, Woody paused and examined the ground surface and the sides of the tunnel, then turned and asked Rick as he approached, "Any sign of him?"

At first, Rick didn't answer. He just scowled at Woody.

"Look, going back over the dam might be more dangerous now than staying here," Woody offered.

"You shouldn't be here."

"Neither should you."

Rick headed into the tunnel. Looking over his shoulder, he added, "I imagine he is over where I saw cable lines on the other side."

The two then entered the darkness.

"I remember there being lights here," Woody said.

"There are. The explosion must have affected the power supply," Rick answered tersely.

They picked their way through the half-mile stretch of darkness with their hands along the walls and a trust in their individual vague recollections of this portion of the trail.

At the far end, they stopped and examined the ground.

"The cables I saw went straight uphill above the tunnel," Rick said. "Which means..."

"These must be his tracks going up the hill here," Rick said as he grabbed onto some roots and pulled himself upward, stepping on saplings amid the loose and steep soil.

Woody was about to follow him when a deafening *clap* erupted from somewhere behind him. Spinning around, Woody saw a colossal vertical fountain of water shoot skyward from the reservoir's surface, as wide as a football field at its base and nearly as tall as Hetch Hetchy's Kolona Rock. The explosion was followed by a deep, loud rumbling sound, which Woody guessed were huge chunks of the dam breaking loose. Watching in horror, he heard an ominous groan as the contents of the reservoir heaved forward against its concrete barrier—but not with the results Woody had expected. If Stuart had totally blown the dam, the water would now be rushing constantly in one unbridled torrent, but that wasn't happening. Woody examined the surface of the lake. It was clearly lowering, but it was not disappearing in a sudden rush into the canyon. *That can't have been the final explosion,* he realized.

Then Woody remembered he was following Rick, and tore his

gaze from the reservoir. Shaking his head to refocus on his mission, he followed where he had just seen Rick climb the hillside.

At the top, Woody didn't know which way to look. He stood panting, his heart beating against his rib cage, carefully listening and looking all around him. Then—the sound of two men fighting: frenzied grunts, breaking branches and bushes, and vicious outbursts of anger. Woody quickly made his way through the forest toward the sounds.

As he got closer, he could see Rick and a stranger with short hair and trendy hiking clothing wrestling around on the ground, throwing each other against trees, smashing each other in the face.

Is that—? Yes, it's Stuart—but he looks so different, Woody thought. *He must have done that sometime since the top of Half Dome.*

Scanning the surrounding forest, Woody noticed a large camping backpack propped against a tree to his left. There were three wires running across the ground nearby. On the other side of the tree was a computer connected to a small metal box.

Instantly, Woody knew what he was going to do. Springing forward, he snatched up the computer, closing its lid and the device connected to it with the wiring. He then turned immediately to his left and ran with these items toward where he knew the edge of the cliff above the lake would be. It was only about eight strides for Woody. He reached the edge and readied himself to toss the computer and wiring from the precipice into the water.

"Stop!"

He turned his head back toward where the two men had been struggling. Stuart had Rick at gunpoint and was walking calmly toward Woody.

"I'll need that back," Stuart said.

"Woody, listen to me," Rick urged. "It doesn't matter. You can't let him complete the explosions. There are too many people downstream. Throw it ov—"

"Woody, if it goes, so do you both," Stuart said as he gave Rick another shove forward with the barrel of his gun.

"Stuart, your little charade is up," Rick said. "More rangers will be here any minute, and we all know about your connection with this Professor. We know about how you are making this out to look like an act of ecoterrorist revenge for the deaths of Aiden and Abigail. The whole Park Service and the F.B.I. knows, and it's all over."

Stuart didn't take long to consider Rick's statement. "That's a lie. If you really had all of this figured out, then you wouldn't be here now with just this kid."

"Stay right there!" Woody yelled.

Stuart and Rick had come to within five feet of Woody.

"All right, young man," Stuart replied. "But your friend here is lying to me. You know, he knows, and your girlfriend, she probably knows, and you may have had help from someone else, but that's likely it."

"Woody, *throw the computer*," Rick said.

"Don't do it, young man," Stuart said.

"You're going to kill us anyway, right? So what's the difference?" Woody said. "Unless you want to figure out who else has pieced together your little puzzle game. In which case, you'll just kill us later. So I might as well get rid of this thing and at least keep *some* people alive."

"I—" Stuart began.

"And Stuart," Woody said, "I hate being called *young man*." With that, Woody leaned forward and snapped backward, giving the computer a tremendous hurl into space. The devices and wiring plummeted downward and splashed into the draining reservoir, getting swiftly sucked toward the gaping hole in the dam.

"You just killed your friend, Woody,"

Before Stuart could fire, Rick dove forward to the ground and rolled once toward the edge. Following Rick's movements, Stuart lowered his gun and pulled the trigger, just as Rick disappeared over the edge of the cliff.

"Rick!" Woody shrieked, He was sure Stuart had connected with his shot, and watched in horror as the ranger's body bounced limply off a bluff below, cartwheeled helplessly into the churning depths of the reservoir, and disappeared.

"YOU ARE COMING WITH ME, *young man*." Gun in hand, Stuart grabbed Woody by the arm and brought him back over to the spot where his gear lay in the woods.

"It's over, man," Woody said.

Stuart looked at him and laughed. "Hardly. There's only one more detonation necessary and we have more than one way to trigger it."

Woody's heart sank. Hopefully, Joy had been able to contact the right people to get the lower canyon evacuated.

Stuart forced Woody back toward the path to the tunnel. As they walked passed his gear, Woody noticed that Stuart seemed to shake his head.

Reaching the embankment he had scaled not more than three minutes before, Woody looked back at Stuart.

"Climb down," Stuart commanded.

Once Woody had reached the bottom, Stuart spoke again. "Turn toward the reservoir."

Woody did as he was told.

"Sit down, and tie your shoes together," Stuart yelled.

"What?" Woody said.

Stuart fired a shot into the dirt immediately to Woody's right.

Woody jumped in panic and immediately took a seat facing the lake and tied his shoes together. Stuart then scampered down the embankment and arrived at Woody's side.

"All right, retie your shoes, and stand up."

Woody did so and then felt the barrel of the gun in his back push him toward the left side of the entrance to the tunnel. With his left hand on the wall and his right hand out to catch himself if he fell, Woody began walking into the darkness. Stuart also had his left hand on the wall of the tunnel and his right hand on the gun, which he pressed hard against Woody. The message was clear, *no bright ideas.*

At the other side, they walked out onto the dam. It was vibrating more intensely now, writhing in the last throws before death. With a wide stance, Stuart pressed Woody onward onto the dam's top surface, which shook and convulsed erratically like a human in an epileptic seizure.

Near the center of the dam, Woody saw the chasm that had opened, a gaping mouth through which eight miles of reservoir, hundreds of feet deep surged. Stuart and Woody neared the opening.

Ten feet from the edge, Stuart stopped. They both looked up and down the sheer, crumbling breach. On the opposite side, protruding twisted and torn steel reinforcements dangled downward, some of them bearing huge clinging hunks of concrete. And although it was not visible from their stance, the roaring of the Tuolumne was deafening as it beat and smashed its way through the abyss. At its narrowest, the gap was eight feet; at its widest, close to twenty feet. It was clear to Woody what Stuart had in mind for his final act, but executing it was something that remained to be seen.

"Jump over *there*," Stuart said to Woody, pointing to a spot slightly wider than eight feet, with what looked to be more solid footing.

"You can't be—" Woody began.

"Don't make me shoot you, *young man.*"

Their eyes met. Woody could see Stuart's mind was made up, and so he nodded in agreement. Taking a deep breath, Woody backed up and counted his paces from a spot about two feet from the edge. Like long jumpers he had observed, he wanted to be

sure about his last foot placement before the leap, to maximize
his advantage.

Standing at the ready, Woody tried to clear his head and not
imagine the vibrating dam under his feet, the gushing waters
ripping though it, or the gnarly steel and crumbling concrete
edge he was about to rush toward. *With everything that's happened*
— Woody shook the thought from his head.

No, I can do this. He took three rapid and shallow breaths,
scowled at Stuart, and then took off. Ten explosive paces led to
one solid foot-plant, and—he jumped.

Avoiding looking down and laser-focused on his landing
point, Woody felt the rush of mist billowing out of the gorge
envelope his body as he passed through the open space above the
torrent. He landed within a foot past the edge on the other side
and dove forward onto his stomach. *Safe, sort of,* he considered.

Immediately, he rose up and started running swiftly away
from Stuart and the chasm. He zigzagged back and forth in a
desperate attempt to avoid being shot.

Bang.

Stuart had fired off a bullet, but unlike last time when Stuart's
shot had grazed Woody's shoulder, this one did not make contact.
Between the distance and the vibrations from the dam, Stuart
must have just fired wildly. Woody glanced over his shoulder and
saw that Stuart wasn't bothering with taking aim for a second
shot. He was already lined up to make the jump. Woody put his
head down and sprinted straight ahead, tearing up the distance
from the dam to the cruiser.

Please, Joy, have the car running.

When he saw Joy standing behind the police cruiser, looking
in his direction, he yelled, "Get in! Start the car!"

She jumped in the driver's side door as Woody approached.

As Woody opened the passenger door, two things happened:
the engine started and another shot rang out. The bullet landed
squarely in the center of the windshield, shattering and imbed-

ding itself in the bulletproof glass. Woody threw himself into the car.

"Drive!"

The Crown Victoria was still pointed toward the dam, so Joy threw the car in reverse and slammed on the gas. Stuart had just cleared the dam and was advancing directly in front of them. The car's wheels spun on the asphalt and grass, skidding and screeching as Stuart closed the distance.

The cruiser abruptly gained traction and began to move backward. As it did so, Stuart dove onto the hood of the car.

"Swerve!" Woody yelled.

Joy yanked the steering wheel back and forth as the car began to pick up speed backward.

With great effort, Stuart managed to hold on, lurch forward, and stick the gun through Joy's open window, aimed at her head. Terrified, she stared back at his menacing fractured visage as he screamed, "Stop, bitch!"

Joy slammed on the brakes. Stuart slid off the hood while keeping his gun trained on the driver. He threw open the door and said in a calm and even tone, "Turn off the car and get out."

Woody and Joy did as instructed.

"Give me the keys."

Joy handed Stuart the keys. He carefully went around to the back of the vehicle, opened the trunk and stepped back.

"Hand me that rifle case," he said, motioning with the gun.

Woody reached in and removed the case.

"Get in."

Joy climbed into the trunk of the police cruiser and looked up in desperation at Woody. As Woody crawled over the rear bumper, Stuart took the butt of his pistol and brought it down hard against Woody's head. Woody collapsed into the trunk of the Crown Victoria as Stuart slammed the lid.

71

RELAX

Monday, 11:17 a.m.

The brief rest was sufficient, and the videoconference, just a review of quarterly financials and some budgeting discussions, had been dispatched without too much annoyance. It always seemed so ludicrous that they supported both political candidates, but it was enjoyable watching them spend company money slandering each other. *Yes, someone has to pay for political theater,* thought The Professor.

The notification from the company appearing on the screen was exactly what The Professor had been waiting to see: POWER OUTAGE AT ROBERT C. KIRKWOOD. DETAILS PENDING.

The power generation happened slightly farther downstream at another generator station, but The Professor knew exactly what the message meant.

The company would investigate and then—well, then everything would happen at once. Media, police, evacuations, and the full spectacle would ensue. No doubt Walter Ashgood was already being interrogated and his role would be widely publicized. Walter had allegedly leaked sensitive data about the weaknesses in the O'Shaughnessy Dam, the loopholes in area surveillance, and most important, the Army Corps' blueprint for detonation. The information was primarily fed to his brother, the convicted ecoterrorist Nick Ashgood, the infamous Doc. Not only had Doc made an appearance at the campfire last night and participated in the free soloing adventure up Cathedral Peak that cost Aiden his life, he had also been so stupid and unaware as to actually weigh in online, sharing his own aggravation over the death of his friends Aiden and Abigail.

The plan was coming together; the future was again looking bright.

But something was slightly amiss. That first notification came at a little before eleven o'clock. The detonations should be complete by now, and the reservoir should be emptying into the canyon beyond—but there just wasn't sufficient information. Nor was there sufficient alarm. If the Hetch Hetchy Reservoir were emptying rapidly into the canyon below, there would be devastation in the news.

The Professor checked through all of the normal channels— with the Park Service, the company, and local law enforcement. The reports sent thus far were consistent with only the first two stages of the dam's detonation. *Is Stuart waiting to detonate the final charge?*

There was a back-up plan, a way to detonate charges without being hard-wired.

Relax, The Professor thought.

EVIL EMPIRE

Monday, 11:18 A.M.

"What do you mean they *ain't here?*" Mojo fake-drawled to mimic Detective Tandy's mild rural dialect. "Where the hell are they, then?"

The detective dropped his cigarette and snuffed it out on the asphalt with the toe of his shoe. "Ma'am, pretty soon after we spoke I went to go ask them a couple more questions, and then I was planning on returning them to you—just like we talked. But when I went to the room, the door was still closed—it's, only accessible from the hallway—and, well, inside was nothing, no one."

"Well they didn't vanish into thin air. Who else knew they were in that room?" Mojo demanded.

"No one, really. I just used that empty room as a kind of an office."

"Whose office?"

"Mine." Detective Tandy looked at his shoes.

"How could they have escaped?" Mojo continued.

"Not without help."

"Could they have been taken?"

"I seriously doubt it."

"If anything happens to my sister," Jasmine started, "I swear I'll hold you and that pudgy-ass smile of yours responsible for whatever—"

Mojo stepped in front of Jasmine. "So, Detective Tandy, let's assume they left or escaped on their own free will."

"Well, they weren't too happy about being in there."

"Well then, what are we going to do now?"

"I suppose I could try to figure out who at the station here, if anyone, might have helped spring them, and why."

"That's a start." Jasmine had taken a deep breath.

"Mojo, where do you think they might have gone—assuming they weren't captured?" Rebecca asked.

"For once, I wish they were just making out in the woods somewhere," Mojo quipped. "But Woody was asking me some questions about the murders before, so they probably are out doing something, you know, typical and reckless," Mojo thought out loud. "Detective, can we use a computer somewhere?"

"I can put you in the same room they were in; there's a computer in there."

Jasmine couldn't resist. "Now don't you go *all* locking us in there, too."

"Okay," Mojo said. "After you, Detective."

Detective Tandy led the ladies back inside to his impromptu office space. He apologized for the stark surroundings of the room and logged in to the computer. "Here you go. You just need the Internet, right?"

"That's fine. I won't open up any other files or anything else," Mojo responded, taking a seat at the desk.

"Not much there anyway." Detective Tandy straightened his clothing, and nodded as the ladies took seats at his table. "I'll go see if I can figure out who might have gotten them out of this room. How long will you all be here?"

"It shouldn't take too long, we'll wait here for you," Mojo said.

"All right." Detective Tandy turned and exited the room, making a show of leaving the door ajar.

"So, what's the game plan?" Rebecca asked.

"Woody wanted to know about the connection between Aiden Watson, the death at Cathedral Peak, and Abigail Edwards, the death earlier on Half Dome," Mojo said. "If we can figure that out, then maybe we can figure out where they might be heading."

"Seems fair."

Mojo got online and opened the *Sierra Club* blog. "Abigail worked for the Sierra Club and, well, check out all of the online posts and remembrances."

"Wow, that's a lot of chatter." Rebecca leaned in as Mojo scanned through the numerous postings.

"But *motive,* right—why was she killed and why was the message about Muir a... you know, caption for the image?" Mojo continued.

"What message?" Rebecca asked.

Mojo opened up another window, navigated to the *Earth First!* blog, and located the image of Abigail. "This one. My apologies if you haven't seen it before; it's pretty gruesome."

Mojo, Rebecca, Jasmine, and Rosa studied the photograph.

"'Here lies Muir's mountain temple.' What's so important that you'd write this message?" Jasmine asked.

"As I was explaining on the phone to Woody, it relates back to Hetch Hetchy," Mojo responded. "The project for both Aiden and Abigail —and with their deaths, well—the Hetch Hetchy project dies, too."

"But all the online chatter?" Rebecca said.

"Exactly," Mojo responded. "There has been a massive outcry, rage, over their deaths. If anything, now there is more attention focused on Hetch Hetchy than ever before. Which again loops back to Abigail and Aiden—I think they knew something."

The ladies huddled around the small screen as Mojo pulled

up an image of the reservoir system feeding all of Northern California.*

"So here we are in Yosemite," Mojo said, pointing to the right of the screen. "And here is the Hetch Hetchy Reservoir. Abigail was an investigative journalist by training and she was the real deal, no rewording fake news for her. Abigail spent a lot of time in the past few years on issues in the Sierra Nevada, including water rights, wilderness preservation, and power. When she turned her attention to the Hetch Hetchy Valley, she looked at the entire history anew."

"The whole history?" Rebecca questioned. "I thought most everyone knew everything there was to know. I mean, the earthquake and fire in San Francisco, the Raker Act, or whatever it was, and then the building of the dam, and voilà, San Francisco has abundant clean water." *

"But what about the power?" Rosa suddenly spoke up.

"And that, my friend, is precisely the point." Mojo took over. "You see, not many people realize this, but the power generated at Hetch Hetchy, within the confines of a national park, was designated by Congress to be for use and profit only by the public and specifically public municipalities." * Mojo opened up yet another window and searched for *Raker Act*. The document appeared on the screen. "This is the Raker Act, passed in 1913 by a conservative national legislature over the ardent protests of John Muir; this is the fight that really founded the Sierra Club."

"Founded the club, but Muir lost the battle over the Raker Act, if I remember it right," Rebecca commented.

"Exactly. The Raker Act stipulated—let's see if I can find it—it should be pretty easy." Mojo scrolled through the document. "Here it is: section six." She began to read.

THAT THE GRANTEE is prohibited from ever selling or letting to any corporation or individual, except a municipality or municipal water district or irrigation district, the right to sell or sublet the water or electric energy sold or given to it or him by the said grantee: Provided, That the rights hereby granted shall not be sold, assigned, or transferred to any private person, corporation, or association, and in case of any attempt to so sell, assign, transfer, or convey, this grant shall revert to the Government of the United States.

"So basically," Rebecca began. "They can dam Hetch Hetchy as long as all the water and all the power is used, sold, leased, transferred, and whatever by the public and not by any private companies."

"Not a lot of gray area, is there?" Mojo said. "Yeah, that's how I read it, too. But the City of San Francisco and WP&G had a more, you know, *creative* interpretation of the language."

"How so?" Jasmine asked.

"You see, from about the time the dam was finished and a power station downstream was built—Moccasin Creek or Kirkwood, I think—WP&G purchased power from Hetch Hetchy and sold it elsewhere at a profit." *

"That would be like totally, you know . . . *refutilizing*, this law you just read," Jasmine said.

"*Refuting*, my dear; and that's why in the late 1930s, the Supreme Court ordered WP&G to stop. But even with this federal law and the Supreme Court ruling, it actually took all the way until 1952 for the electricity to finally be rerouted to public municipalities." *

"Who would have thought I'd have another reason to hate WP&G," Rebecca said.

Mojo turned in her chair to face the girls. "It's gets even worse."

"What do you mean?" Jasmine asked.

"Well, here is what I think Abigail was working on." Mojo leaned forward and lowered her voice. "What if they never complied?" She paused and looked around at the three ladies. "What if WP&G *still* sold power generated in Yosemite National Park for profit?" No one answered. "What if, a century later, this federal mandate was *still* being violated?" *

"*¿Es la verdad?*" Rosa asked.

"Really Mojo?" Rebecca followed up. "I mean how would they get away with it?"

"I've been thinking about it since last night on our drive out here. It would be difficult to prove. You know the power grid in Northern California is a complex web of sources fluctuating on demand. Some of those sources are public, paid for by taxpayers and designed by the Army Corps, and some of those sources are private, controlled by for-profit companies, the largest of which is WP&G."

"No way." Rebecca's eyes widened.

"I've written about Abigail and interviewed her several times. I asked about her current research and specifically about information she has been providing to a certain law firm in Sacramento. She was very cagey about her responses and wanted to know exactly how I had obtained the information in my questions to her. It was weird. She was always so confident and casual, but this time—it was different. I almost joked with her about witness protection, but something told me to, you know—be more professional." Mojo paused and glanced furtively around the room. "I haven't written anything about it, but if I had to guess, it looks like Abigail and whoever she was working with were trying to prove the power at Hetch Hetchy is still being sold for profit."

The story felt too big for the confines of a small cinder-block room deep in the bowels of a federally-owned building. The women inched closer to one another, as if trying to physically keep the information private.

"What would the penalty be if that were true?" Rebecca whispered.

"I'm not sure, but it would be considerable," Mojo responded. "It could be paying for valley restoration; the bill for the work would logically go to the company who has been stealing power all these years."

"Unless"—everyone turned toward Jasmine—"someone had already, you know, blown the damn dam up!"

"You mean, like the environmentalists?" Rosa asked.

The office door started to swing open. Immediately the four ladies closed their mouths and looked up.

Detective Tandy came through with a confident smile. "Okay, ladies," he began. "I figured out who let Woody and Joy out of here—Rick Turlock. He was with them last night; he's one of the chief rangers around here." The detective smiled. "Yup, Rick had gone around looking for those two and, as it just so happens, he told them to leave the Park and find their families, which I guess —seeing as you guys are in here—they didn't do."

"Doesn't take much for a degree in criminal science these days, does it?" Rebecca jabbed.

Detective Tandy just stared back at her, still proud of his deduction.

"I don't get it," Jasmine said, just as the detective realized Rebecca had insulted him. "We were right in front of the station. If they had come out looking for us or to catch a bus, we would have seen them for sure."

"They probably went out the back of the building, where you found me."

"Hopefully, they're in the area then," Mojo said. "Let's go drive around and see if we can locate them."

Detective Tandy held the door open, and the four women walked back through the bustling headquarters to the rear of the building.

"We parked right over there, right?" Rosa asked.

"Yeah," Mojo said, walking toward the parking area. "It was

just by the village store and underneath that huge tree, right? Wait a minute."

"What is it?" Rosa asked.

"The Jeep—it's not there. Why would someone—?" Mojo stopped. "No way."

"Do you think?"

Mojo shook her head in disbelief. "No one else knows where I hide the key."

73

WHAT TO DO?

Monday, 11:19 A.M.

Now what?

Stuart leaned on the trunk of the police cruiser and closed his eyes.

Why just the kids and the ranger? Surely other people knew if they were here. They couldn't have just come without communicating to others. There was that other Jeep parked by the cruiser. Who drove that?

Stuart pulled his hand off the trunk and took a deep breath.

What to do? The Professor needs to know what happened. I need to signal that the final explosion has to be triggered remotely and at a time about an hour from now. That's the priority. If I wait here to trigger it, this place will be swarming with cops. I need access to an anonymous network to send the message. Where?

Stuart walked around to the driver's door of the cruiser. *The cruiser.* It would let him leave this area without notice. In fact, the police cruiser would let Stuart go just about anywhere.

Where?

Stuart got in and started the engine.

People would be coming and soon. *I need to get the hell away from Hetch Hetchy.* A grin lifted the corners of Stuart's mouth. *Woody likes the girl. If I threaten to hurt her, he'll tell me whatever I need to know.*

As he drove up the road and out of the Hetch Hetchy Valley, Stuart felt better. Yes, things were not going as seamlessly as designed, but two-thirds of the explosions had been triggered. The collapse was imminent, and now he had a plan. *It is always better to have a plan.*

I just need to get to a place where I can notify The Professor.

74

TO RESPECT IT

Monday, 11:21 A.M.

I t feels like...
  The cold...
    Breathe...
Must...
The force of
It...
Breathe...
Water
Rushing...
It feels like...
Life passing...
Being forced out of me

He was suspended there, floating in and out of lucidity and wondering why he should fight this––why struggle? The numbness was comforting, so easy; it beckoned him to simply consent, to allow the water to take him in, take him back.

No.

Rick's eyes flashed open and he turned his head upward. He

saw half sky and clouds; the other half was a disorienting mass of gray concrete. He was pinned hard against a metal access ladder running up the inside wall of the great O'Shaughnessy Dam by the crushing pressure of the water, one arm wrapped all the way to his armpit around a ladder rung, the other dangling from a painful dislocated shoulder.

Fighting—that's what he knew. Struggle was more a part of his identity than any pseudonym he'd adopted.

That fucking name—Ranger Rick.

Fight, dammit!

Rick reached up with his good arm to grasp a higher rung, locked his knee around the submerged railing. Gathering all his remaining strength, he clutched a still higher rung and pulled his midsection out of the current.

That sun feels so good.

Rick decided to hang there for awhile, catch his breath, and allow the sun's warmth to work its tiny fingers into his frozen back and aching shoulder as the water level continued to lower. He felt himself getting dizzy and managed to stick both arms entirely through the metal rungs.

He had to fight like this before, but he wasn't alone then. His Lakota grandfather once had pulled him out of a frozen torrent, lit a fire, and kept him alive.

"It is good," Rick was told. "It is good to know your place in the order of things." His grandfather smoked rolled tobacco by the fire and looked up at the stars. "Our mother—She is more powerful—it is good for you to see that, to respect it."

Why the hell am I thinking of my grandfather now? Why?

Rick snarled at himself. The water had dropped below his knees, and he risked a maneuver he knew would propel him back into full consciousness. Wrapping his good right arm through the rungs of the ladder, he felt his left shoulder. The cartilage and ligaments were stretched like Silly Putty in the open hole of his socket; the ball joint of his shoulder hung approximately two inches below its proper place.

Okay.

Rick wrapped the fingers of his left hand around a rung of the ladder and held tight, then gradually lowered his body inch-by-inch, providing slow constant pressure on the loose shoulder muscles. Excruciating pain ensued as his ball joint ground against the underside of his shoulder socket.

"Aggh!" Rick yelled as his shoulder snapped back into position. He clung on there in pain for several minutes, while it subsided. Rick rolled his left shoulder around—it had worked.

It's time, he urged himself. With his right hand, he grabbed onto a higher rung, pulled, and then stepped up. When he was clear of the swirling current, he breathed a sigh of relief.

Rung by rung, Rick struggled nearer to the top and looked around. The vast inside of the O'Shaughnessy Dam, curving inwards around him in a massive gaping arc, felt almost as if he were on the eastern face of El Captain, surrounded on all sides by uncompromising vertical granite. To his right, about three hundred yards away, was the breach through which the water was draining. He could barely make out the ravaged interior of the roiling chasm, with water erupting into a torrent of white as it battered its way through the dam.

Rick suddenly remembered Woody and Joy—and Stuart. He immediately started to climb the ladder, hand over hand.

Where would they go?

Pull. Push.

Would Stuart kill Woody?

Rick labored upward.

Scaling the inside of the dam seemed to take an eternity. Between the physical pain associated with his newly relocated shoulder, his body's overall exhaustion, the hypothermia, and the length he had to climb, Rick began to slip into a trance. As his hands and feet made a slow and steady cadence of contact with the rungs of the ladder, he drifted into a half-dream, half-conscious state.

"You do not need to prove anything—"
My grandfather ran his hand over my forehead as he lay next to the fire.
"You merely need to exist."
The hand shut out the crackling and burning wood, the raging waters, the beating of my heart.
"Your place in the order is not always for you to decide. You must trust in the unfolding of things."
The hand circled over my eyes, my scalp, and my ears. It caught the light of the fire, showing its many creases and years of toil. I listened to the hand of my grandfather. I wanted to believe, but I felt doing so would violate something telling me to fight. I wanted to heed the wisdom, but I felt that meant succumbing to some unseen force. I wanted to believe in his family, his blood—but I couldn't.
I am an active force. My choice circles back like a demon, badgering me with second-guesses and self-doubt.
My grandfather tried to teach me—

Rick's good hand grasped the last rung of the ladder, and his head rose above the stone parapet at the top of the dam.
Nothing.
He reached up and mantled his hands on the concrete surface and collapsed over onto the walkway, face down. He looked back toward the tunnel; there was no one. He looked over to where he had parked his car.
Where the hell is the cruiser?

JAYCEE

Monday, 12:13 P.M.

"Well, Son," John Jackson began to speak, but stopped.

Woody leaned in closer to his father. The potent smell of his hospital linens—a combination of cleaning solutions and sickness—made it difficult not to cringe.

"I guess—no more climbing for me." John exhaled deeply to recover from the effort of his last utterance.

Woody smiled weakly at his father.

The night nurse came in. "Are you comfortable?" she said a little too loudly.

Mojo, standing on the other side of John's bed, looked at her husband and then at the nurse. "Maybe a bit more morphine?"

"Okay."

The room was dim. Mojo squeezed her husband's hand while the nurse adjusted the attached drip system. Woody studied his father's hair and the barely perceptible tan line at his temples, from the visor he wore on his hikes in the woods.

As the nurse turned to leave, Mojo cornered her near the

doorway and asked in a hushed voice, "How much time? I mean, how long?"

"Well, what's important is to make sure he's comfortable. As he gets near—" The nurse paused as if she remembered her instruction not to tell patients in these situations. "Well, you know, I shouldn't say—but if you need anything, just press the call button by the bed there, and we'll be here just as soon as we can." She lowered her voice even more. "Just make sure he's comfortable." And then she left the room.

WOODY FELT his body slam against a hard metal surface, then collapse back down into a soft space. He opened his eyes and couldn't make out where he was. A trace amount of light shone on metallic and carpeted surfaces.

"Are you all right?" Joy cradled Woody's head, his hair matted with blood, gingerly in her lap.

It all came back to Woody—the dam, Stuart, the cruiser trunk, and getting pistol-whipped.

"Yeah, how long have I been out?" Woody asked.

"About half an hour. As far as I can tell we are backtracking toward Yosemite Valley. When we got off that bumpy road to Hetch Hetchy, we definitely turned left and we've generally been heading downhill."

The cruiser took a sharp turn and Woody and Joy were thrown against the side of the trunk. Woody winced in pain.

"Why do you think he's going back to the valley?" Joy asked.

"He said something about another way to set off the last charge."

"Why would he need to go to the valley though?"

"Maybe he's communicating with someone else to do it."

Woody wondered if anyone was looking for them. He wondered just how Stuart would kill them. He wondered how Rick died, if it was the bullet, the fall, or the rush of the water as it tore through the jagged opening in the dam. It felt hopeless. What had he managed to accomplish? Is this how it would end? What would his dad think of him? His dad—

"So, I've got this tail light almost knocked out, using this lug nut wrench, or tire iron, or whatever—from the tire tool kit," Joy said.

"You *what?*"

"Well, I figured—if we could, you know, wave at someone through the taillight hole, and maybe even use the tire iron to pop the trunk latch."

Woody shook his head, "How did—?"

"You remember Jaycee Lee Dugard, right?"

"Yeah, that girl kidnapped from South Lake Tahoe a long time ago."

"Not that long ago. All the kids at school had to learn things to do, you know—including how to knock out taillights from the inside of a trunk."

"Will we get the chance?"

"If he has to stop somewhere and communicate with someone––maybe."

DOMESTIC TERROR

Monday, 12:14 P.M.

A gent Dale Friedman's helicopter crested the hillside before the O'Shaughnessy Dam.

"*Shit,*" he exclaimed.

An unmistakable V-shaped opening in the face of the structure jolted him like a missing tooth in a perfect smile.

The pilot's voice broke through Dale's stupor. "Where should I put her down?"

"There is a parking lot adjacent to the dam, southwest side."

"Looks kind of tight there, but"—the pilot circled the area. "But, it should work."

The helicopter descended toward the gradually sloping parking surface. Dale looked back toward the dam.

How did this happen? How did the FBI miss something as big as an ecoterrorist plot to blow up this dam?

Dale had been with the FBI through the attacks on 9/11 and the subsequent intensive reorganization of intelligence gathering. He was credited as part of the team that brought to justice the ecoterrorist cell headed by Eric McDavid. The intel gathered on

McDavid's intentions to build and deploy improvised explosive devices led to a twenty-year conviction. But that was back in 2006.* Since then, the ecoterrorists had become less transparent, less trusting, less willing to be infiltrated.

Is this indeed ecoterrorism? Dale had his reservations. He believed in the law. He believed in absolutes in life; the moral relativism of those he tracked disgusted him. How can people justify murder and violence? But looking out at the dam now, Dale couldn't help but draw a line of distinction. The FBI listed domestic terrorism as acts of violence perpetrated against not only other humans but against property as well.* Dale was always a bit uneasy about this parsing of words. Property was not a person. Property was not a living, breathing human being. But under the definition of domestic terrorism, he was to treat a threat to property with the same gravity as a threat to people.

How many lives does a dam equal? One thousand? One hundred? One?

This was not the World Trade Center. The destruction here, especially since communities downstream of the dam were being evacuated, was something else. Yes, it clearly was wrong. Yes, it was violent. Yes, it was against all sorts of laws--but did the destruction of the O'Shaughnessy Dam belong in the same category as murdering a plane full of passengers?*

The helicopter's landing skids made contact. Agent Dale Friedman took stock of his surroundings. There were five cars in the parking lot—two Subarus, an old Jeep, a Prius, and an oddly new-looking black Range Rover. Dale made a mental note to check the Range Rover more closely. As far as he could tell, there were no people anywhere in sight.

"Should I stay here?" the pilot asked.

"Yes." Dale opened the door of the chopper and, in his dress shoes, stepped onto the parking lot surface. The noise from the blades winding down was replaced by another more frightening sound—the water of the Hetch Hetchy Reservoir cascading through the cavernous fissure in the face of the dam. It was difficult to look at anything else. Pulled as if magnetized, Dale walked toward the dam.

How the hell could this happen?

He wasn't satisfied by the answers given to him by Walter Ashgood, still in his detention cell in San Francisco. Walter was not a terrorist. Hell, Walter wasn't even an activist. None of the characteristic self-righteousness typical of those involved in environmental action was evident in Walter's attitude, mannerisms, dress, or answers. If anything, Walter was just a typical apathetic and self-interested young professional.

It was infuriating. The pieces of the puzzle were all there, and his colleagues were ready to call the case closed—Walter feeds confidential information available from his job at WP&G to his radical brother, Doc, who in turn arranges with his radical environmentalist buddies, one of whom must be this Stuart character, to detonate charges and destroy the O'Shaughnessy Dam.

Dale stepped out onto the edge of the dam's surface as it vibrated and hummed in an internal struggle for survival. The edges of his silk necktie blurred, and Dale strained to focus in order to keep from losing his footing. Looking out toward the chasm, there was something else—a figure at the other side of the dam, desperately waving his arms back and forth and motioning toward a pin on his chest. Dale couldn't be sure, but the clothing looked like a uniform—a Park Service uniform.

Then, it clicked. *It's Rick.*

Agent Friedman waved back and flashed a thumbs-up. Then he turned and raced back to the helicopter.

77

RELIABLE

Monday, 1:21 P.M.

"Stay back from the hatch, all right?" the ranger yelled through the knocked-out taillight. "We're going to cut it open. There'll be some sparks."

"Okay," Woody yelled. "We're shielded."

"Your eyes, too?" The ranger peered down and tried to see through the busted taillight.

Earlier Woody had sensed that rather than parking in the lot at the Yosemite Lodge at the Falls, Stuart had pulled the car off the road near Camp Four, the walk-in-only, first-come, first-served campground near the lodge. Once parked, it sounded like Stuart had dashed over to the lodge, but he couldn't be sure. After thirty seconds, Woody and Joy seized on the opportunity. Joy had poked the taillight completely out in less than a minute and was shouting and thrusting her arm as far as it could reach out the opening. Woody, worked at the trunk latch with the tire iron, taking heavy swings and eventually bending the lid enough to allow some daylight through, in addition to creating even more noise to hopefully get someone's attention.

It worked. One of the few remaining staff at the Yosemite Lodge was within earshot and heard the racket. Within minutes, at least a dozen people were gathered around the car.

"We're covered by a jacket. Get us out of here," Joy said.

Woody and Joy huddled against the back of the trunk as they heard a motor rev to life beyond the confines of the metal container in which they had been stuck for the past hour.

"Here we go!" yelled a voice from the outside.

There was an explosion of sparks inside the vehicle as a metal blade tore through the trunk latch. Keeping their eyes and faces concealed behind Joy's parka, they felt sparks singeing their pants and ankles.

Then there was daylight. The trunk lid flew open. Woody and Joy squinted their eyes at a cadre of rangers peering back at them.

"You alright in there?" one of the rangers asked.

"We are now," Joy responded climbing out.

"How did this happen?"

"The guy who started the forest fire—" Woody stood up. "He locked us inside."

"*What?*" said one ranger.

There was a brief, awkward silence as the rangers glanced at each other.

Joy pounced on the rangers' lull in conversation. "There's more. This guy, Stuart White is his name, and whoever he is working with, someone called The Professor—they planned the murders of Aiden and Abigail, and if you haven't already heard, they're blowing up the dam."

"The O'Shaughnessy Dam at Hetch Hetchy, it's detonating," Woody continued. "Well, mostly. There's still another explosion has to be triggered for it to totally give way. We think that's why Stuart drove back here."

Woody and Joy's roadside testimony overwhelmed the rangers.

"We... Rick—one of your head rangers you've probably been

looking for—and us... we confronted Stuart by the reservoir," Woody continued. "We were able to toss his detonation gear into the water, and it was sucked out of the crack in the dam, but—" Woody paused.

"He killed Rick," Joy added solemnly "Rick fell into the reservoir, and there's no way he could have survived."

"Stuart also killed the other ranger, Jeffrey." Woody, almost breathless, kept talking. "Last night on Half Dome, Rick radioed down to a Paula, I think—and they tried to get Stuart on his way out, but with the fire—"

"And with Stuart having changed his appearance—he shaved and changed clothes. He's got a crew cut and no longer has the white goatee," Joy said, urgently.

"In fact, he's around here... somewhere," Woody added.

"He said he was going to try to send The Professor a message," Joy added. "That's who he's been communicating—"

"You say the remaining charges on the dam needed to be detonated, to finish the explosion?" one ranger asked, incredulously.

"Yeah, and aren't there lots of people downstream from the dam?" Woody asked.

Woody couldn't tell whether or not any of them believed a word they had just said, but it felt good to let this all out.

The rangers looked at each other again, not sure what to make of any of it. Then an older ranger with a grey mustache spoke up. "I'm glad you two are out of that trunk and okay. My name is Dave Chapman. I'm the senior ranger here. So... to cut to the most important part of your somewhat elaborate story, we urgently need to find this Stuart guy."

"Yes!" both Woody and Joy exclaimed.

"Andrea can you verify this information about Hetch Hetchy?" Dave looked toward a younger ranger holding a radio.

"Yeah, let me get on it."

Everyone waited anxiously. Woody unconsciously began tapping the toe of his shoe against the dirt.

"Dispatch, this is Andrea; I need you to check in with Hetch Hetchy for me. Over."

The voice on the other end of the line came through. "I'll do you one better. Let me patch you through to a call I'm on right now." The line went to static for a moment and then a new voice, sounding weary and annoyed––and familiar, came over the radio.

"Look, it's quite simple. We just need a way to stop the final explosion," the voice implored.

Immediately, Woody and Joy faced each other wide-eyed. "It can't be," Joy said under her breath.

"This is Andrea in the main valley. I'm looking for information on the dam at Hetch Hetchy. Who's speaking, please?"

"This is Ranger Rick Turlock––I can give you a firsthand account."

"Rick!" Woody and Joy shouted in unison, rushing to the radio. "You're *alive*," Joy added.

"Hey, who's there?"

"It's Joy––and Woody's here, too."

"Oh, thank God you two are safe!"

Dave took the radio from Andrea. "Rick, I'm glad you're all right, but what the hell is going on? These two youngsters here have told us some outrageous stories and I'm having a hard time––"

"Dave, you believe every damn word those two tell you," Rick fired back. "Yes, there is an attempt in progress to demolish the dam. Yes, we're looking for someone named Stuart White. And yes, Woody and Joy are reliable."

"Got it," Dave responded.

"Good. Now where is Stuart White?" Rick pressed.

Woody spoke up. "We don't know. He... wanted to send some message, and so I think he needed to get to a computer."

"He could have used one in there," Andrea added, pointing toward Yosemite Lodge.

"Hold on," Rick interrupted. "Stuart White is not to be under-estimated. He's a killer, armed and dangerous. Approach with extreme caution."

"Thanks Rick, duly noted. I'll get back to you when we have news of him," Dave answered. He passed the radio to Andrea and looked at Woody and Joy. "You two can identify White, right?"

"Definitely," said Joy. "Early thirties. Blond crew cut."

"Okay then––Charlie, Andrea, Brad, and Chuck, you all go with them to the lodge right now and see if you can find Stuart. Apprehend him, guns visible at all times." Dave then turned his attention back to the radio in his hand. "Rick, what else can you tell me about the status of the dam?"

Physically, Chuck was by far the biggest ranger in the group. "You heard the man. Let's go," Chuck said as he started walking toward the lodge. Woody and Joy fell behind him. "So... Woody, right?"

"Yeah."

"Sure this guy is armed?"

"Most likely, but I'm not sure."

"Everyone, check your Glocks," Chuck said as he unholstered his weapon and verified his ammunition.

"We're going to secure the front lobby. There are only two principal ways in—the main doors and the rear ones toward the amphitheater. Charlie and Brad, in one hundred and twenty seconds, Andrea and I will enter through the front and secure the area. You enter through the rear and push everyone forward. Woody and Joy, you wait out of sight until I signal you through the glass front like this." Chuck raised his hand and rotated his palm forward. "Make sure you can see the palm of my hand; then you come in. Two minutes starts now."

Charlie and Brad moved toward the rear of the building, and Chuck and Andrea continued to walk to the front entrance. They hesitated for about fifteen seconds by some trees where Chuck instructed Woody and Joy to wait for his signal. Chuck pushed open the two large front doors of the lodge, holding his gun out, and spoke in a loud, clear voice. "I am the Park Service. Stop what you are doing and face me."

The entire room fell quiet, and Chuck made a quick scan of the fifteen or so visitors, trying to identify any threats.

"Now everyone, I need you to move over to this location by the reception tour booth," Chuck gestured to his right, and people began to move. As they did, six people coming from the rear of the building, ushered forward by Charlie and Brad, joined them.

"Okay, I need you all to sit here on the floor or on one of these benches."

Everyone sat.

"Brad, check the bathrooms." Chuck then raised his other hand and turned it palm outward toward the front entrance. Woody and Joy entered the lobby and stood beside Chuck.

"He's not here," Joy said almost as soon as she had come to a stop.

Woody scanned the faces, the postures, the clothing, the eyes of everyone assembled. "No, he's not here."

"So now what?" Andrea asked.

"What's going on?" an older man in a dark fleece asked.

"Bathrooms are empty," Brad said.

Chuck flashed a stern look back toward the crowd, "We're looking for the person who is suspected of arson and other crimes. We have every reason to believe he was in this building, most likely using one of these computers here in the lobby." Chuck looked over at Woody and Joy. "What time frame?"

"Probably half an hour or maybe a little less," Joy said.

"He would have been alone and—" Chuck again looked at Woody and Joy. "Describe him again."

"He's about six feet tall. He has a blond crew cut and a

muscular build. I think he, um, would still be wearing khakis and a light blue shirt with a collar," Woody said.

"Do any of you recognize that description?" Chuck asked.

A tentative hand went up among the crowd. Everyone turned to face the small man in the gray housekeeping uniform. "I saw him," he said.

"When and where?" Chuck asked.

The man gestured to one of the hotel's computers on the wall of the lobby. "He was here at this computer. He left maybe fifteen minutes ago."

"Did you see which way he went?"

"Not really."

"Okay, thank you. Does anyone else have anything they can add?"

The remaining guests were silent. Chuck waited a full thirty seconds before dismissing them. He pulled his team together in front of the building.

"I'm hesitant to split us up to start looking for this guy, considering how dangerous he is, but we need to use the time we've got. Andrea, scan the computer to see if you can figure out what he did there. Everyone else, any ideas as to where he might be?" Chuck asked.

At that moment, two men wearing outdoor clothing inscribed with foreign script walked up to the group. "Excuse me, please," one said in a heavy German accent.

Chuck looked over at them, clearly annoyed.

"We have problem," the man continued. "We just return to our tent at Camp Four, and our gear—it gone."

Chuck had heard enough. "Sir, I'm sorry about the theft. You can report it to—"

Woody cut him off. "What was taken?"

The man looked at Woody and then back at Chuck to make sure it was all right for him to continue. Chuck nodded.

"Ya, well, we was just there at Camp Four, you know, getting pack up to leave of dis fire, and when we return to tent, we missing our rope, our portaledge, our aid rack, some other gear—"

"Only one harness, right?" Woody asked.

The man looked at his companion, exchanged a few words in German, then replied, "Ya, *ein...* only one."

Woody looked at Chuck. "I think I know where Stuart is going."

78

NEW PLAN

Monday, 1:28 P.M.

"**F**uck."

Stuart fumed as he headed away from the dramatic scene unfolding at his borrowed police cruiser, which he had wrongly presumed was parked far enough away from the Yosemite Lodge at the Falls to avoid detection.

Fuck. I was supposed to torture them to figure out what they know. Stuart shook his head and tried to control his breathing.

It'll be alright. The Professor had been notified and the plan would be completed. He just needed to escape out of the main valley and make it up to his car parked in Tuolumne Meadows.

Think! Okay, the fastest way there is up Yosemite Falls Trail, which, conveniently is right by the lodge. I'll need some water for the hike, a headlamp, maybe something warmer if I'm going to hike through the night. Too fucking bad all my shit's in the goddamn cruiser. At least I've still got my Glock.

To get to the Yosemite Falls Trail, Stuart had to pass through Camp Four. Some tents and gear had been abandoned during the emergency evacuation. Zeroing in on a daypack with a Camel-back hose protruding from it's top, Stuart picked up the bag, barely examining the contents, and headed for the trail. As he got closer to the Yosemite Falls Trailhead, he could hear talking and the crackle of an occasional radio.

Taking a less direct path, Stuart positioned himself to see without being seen. It was clear that two rangers were stationed at the entrance to Yosemite Falls Trailhead, probably with the express purpose of getting people off the trails, to their vehicles, and out of the Park. As Stuart contemplated whether or not to kill them, he realized that along the narrow and popular hiking trail, there would likely be other rangers asking questions and turning people around. The same would most certainly be true for the Four-Mile Trail, and any other hiking trail out of the valley.

Fuck.

Stuart quietly turned back to Camp Four.

I'm cornered.

He had to find a place to hide. He had to make it up to the North Rim and eventually over to Tuolumne Meadows. He couldn't run into anyone.

Walking back into Camp Four, Stuart threw scornful glances at the few remaining climbers and the abandoned tents still full of haul bags, portaledges, and other climbing gear.

Stuart froze. *That's it. Fuck me. That's so easy.*

Stuart wandered up to one tent with an obvious bulge and unzipped the entry. Reaching in, he removed the haul bag and a long tube holding a portaledge. Digging into the bag, Stuart removed some gear he wouldn't need, the extra harness, a camping stove, and some climbing gear he thought was excessive. A smile crept across Stuart's face. There were a couple of two-litre soda bottles at the base of the bag, filled and ready for a climb.

Stuart hoisted the bag onto his shoulders and started jogging westward out of Camp Four and onto the Valley's loop trail toward El Capitan.

He tilted his head and admired an old oak tree, it's upper branches mingling playfully with light and smoke from the fire.

No one would suspect he would be literally climbing right out of the valley.

SICKLE

Monday, 2:04 p.m.

"Are you sure about this?" Chuck asked Woody.

"No, but I think it's kind of in keeping with this guy's crazy ideas."

"Okay." Chuck collected his thoughts. "Andrea, anything on the computer we can use?"

"The webpage history was wiped."

Chuck took a deep breath. "Andrea, you're coming with me. Brad and Charlie, do a careful perimeter search here at the lodge and then report back to Dave. Woody, which wall would he head toward?"

"With the amount of gear he has, I'd say El Cap."

"Okay then." Chuck shook his head in disbelief.

Woody and Joy hopped into a Park Service Yukon heading for El Capitan Meadow along with Chuck and Andrea.

"We're going to need binoculars, right?" Chuck asked as he pulled the car onto the main road and accelerated.

"Let me look," Andrea responded.

"Now... " Chuck took a deep breath. "What is this guy going to do by himself even if he has a bunch of gear?"

Joy answered this time. "We covered this topic in a class I took. It's the same strategy as, um, leader-rescue situations."

"Leader-rescue?" Chuck asked whipping the Yukon around the next turn.

"Yes. When your leading climber takes a fall and the belayer has to ascend the rope to rescue the leader," Joy answered.

"Okay." Chuck said.

"Right, so in some rare situations," Joy continued, "you might need to rope solo to reach your partner. So Stuart could be using this technique."

"Rope soloing," Chuck repeated pulling onto the shoulder by El Cap Meadow.

"I've got the binoculars," Andrea added.

"Walk and talk." Chuck was already out of the vehicle.

Joy followed him and continued with the explanation. "So basically, climbers will set an anchor, tie in, and then use two locking carabiners with clove hitches at different lengths on the rope, to climb until they become tight to the anchor at the bottom. Then the climber will set some protection and undo the first clove hitch and climb until the next clove hitch and cara- biner are tight to the anchor. When the climber reaches the top of the pitch, he will build another anchor, rap down to the orig- inal anchor, and then jug back up to the higher anchor, pulling the gear along the way." *

They had reached a good observation spot near the center of the meadow, and Andrea was already scanning the rock with binoculars.

"Well," Chuck said. "Basically, even though it's more work and it's more dangerous than partner climbing, this solo thing allows someone to climb without the need for a belay?"

"Precisely," said Joy.

Chuck looked at Woody. "And you think this Stuart guy is up there somewhere solo roping or whatever?"

"Um, if you think about it, he needs to hide. He's in the valley. He's already communicated with whoever he needs to, so all he needs to do is, you know, wait it out." Woody looked at Joy, who nodded her head and gave a slight shrug. "It does make some bizarre sense, right?" Woody continued. "Most people wouldn't think to look up on a wall, would they?"

"I guess not." Chuck turned to Andrea, who was scanning the wall. "Any luck?"

"I'm not sure what I'm looking for... and the smoke from the fire is really obscuring the upper part of the rock."

"He wouldn't be that high yet," Woody interjected. "Can I have a look?"

"Of course." Andrea handed the binoculars over to Woody.

"I know where a few of the routes are, and I have a hunch. He'll, um, be pretty low on the rock, too." Woody started walking deeper into the meadow, checking over his shoulder to gauge how much of El Cap he could see. "So this should work."

Woody brought the binoculars up to his face and looked out at the rock. His father had wanted to climb The Nose with Woody, but they hadn't quite pulled it off. They had made it up to a ledge called Dolt Tower and then had to rappel off from there.

After about two minutes, he found what he was looking for. About one pitch below Sickle Ledge, named for its dramatic crescent shape, Woody saw someone climbing by himself. "Uh, Joy, what color was Stuart's shirt?" Woody asked.

"I think it was blue."

"And he had khaki pants, right?"

"Yeah."

"I got him."

Chuck came over, and Woody instructed him where to look—just down and to the left of the sickle-shaped contour in the rock. Once everyone had taken a peek at the lone climber slowly making his way up The Nose, Chuck said, "Okay, so we know where he is, but what do we do about it?"

Andrea spoke up. "We need to talk to him, right? Figure out who this Professor is and how to stop the explosion?"

"You're right. Let me get Dave on the line." Chuck picked up his radio. "Dave, this is Chuck. Yes, that's right. Yes, we've found Stuart White, but there's... well, a complication—"

80

¡DIOS MÍO!

Monday, 2:47 P.M.

"It still doesn't come together for me." Rebecca had been stewing in the Subaru's rear seat for the past half hour while the ladies drove around Yosemite Village and Camp Curry trying to spot Mojo's Jeep.

"The dam?" asked Jasmine.

"Yeah. So Mojo, you were, you know—hypothesizing that by killing Aiden and Abigail and stirring up some *eco-rage* or something, it would look as if the environmentalists would blow up the O'Shaughnessy Dam?" Rebecca inquired.

"Basically," Mojo responded.

"But then, if it blows and the environmentalists are to blame and all... it wouldn't really free WP&G from the responsibility for restoring the valley."

"Yeah, that's one ginormous bar tab," Jasmine quipped.

"Well, Abigail had all the info, right?" Mojo began. "She's the one who could prove what was going on behind the scenes and which political figures were getting kickbacks and bribes to keep the redistribution of power on the down-low. Now,—no Abigail."

Jasmine pulled the car off the road by the Yosemite Valley Chapel as the four ladies contemplated Mojo's explanation.

"You've got to also imagine WP&G has a... *ginormous* insurance policy," Mojo continued, "which covers things like earthquakes, forest fires and, if they had some foresight, ecoterrorism."

"And if the O'Shaughnessy Dam is all *ka-blewee* by the radical environmentalists," Rebecca continued, "well then, fingers aren't exactly going to be pointing at power companies and politicians anymore, will they? The court of public opinion can be a powerful thing."

"Yeah," Rosa agreed.

"Right, people would be pretty ticked at the environmentalists then, wouldn't they?" Mojo countered. The ladies pondered this question for a minute as smoke from the forest fire drifted across the valley in front of them. "And with the dam gone—well, who's to say if the restoration of Hetch Hetchy would even be considered. You know, what is it that Presidents say, 'We will not negotiate with terrorists,' or something?"

Rebecca gasped, "You mean, if the dam is blown up by ecoterrorists, then no one would want to restore the valley; it would be like—capitulating to demands and all?"

"Especially if there's any loss of life downstream," Mojo added.

"So we'd still lose Muir's Mountain Temple—all over again," Rebecca sighed.

Rosa sat up in her seat. "So if it looks like the environmentalists blew up the O'Shaughnessy Dam and Abigail wasn't around to help connect the dots back to the power connections and bribe money, then chances are the dam might just be rebuilt?"

"Yup." Mojo responded, "And guess who's stuck with that tab this time? You and me, the trustworthy taxpayers."

Jasmine jumped in. "Oh come on, hold the fucking ponies. Blow up the dam? Get real. I don't believe it. I mean the thing is *huge*."

Mojo's phone startled the women.

"Who is it?" Rosa asked.

"I'm not sure." Mojo put the phone to her ear. "Mojo Jackson."

She listened for the next thirty seconds with alternating feelings of relief and panic as the voice on the other end explained that they had located her Jeep.

"Thank you, Detective." Mojo hung up.

"So...?" Jasmine asked.

"Jeep yes. Kids no."

"You're sure it was Rusty?" Rosa asked.

"Yeah, same 1979 Jeep Wrangler with a brownish rust-colored exterior," Mojo responded. "It's got to be."

"Great, so where are they? Where's the Jeep?" Rebecca asked.

"The O'Shaughnessy Dam in Hetch Hetchy."

"Damn," Jasmine said, and they sat silently pondering the implications.

"Detective Tandy said we might not be able to actually get into the Hetch Hetchy area. There might be a roadblock set up by now."

"A roadblock because...?" Rosa offered.

"Yeah—my sentiments exactly."

"So? What's the alternative?" Jasmine asked while fastening her seat belt. "Just wait here? I don't think so."

Pulling onto the main road, Jasmine stepped on the accelerator. "Ain't no cops handing out speeding tickets today, right girlfriends?"

The old Subaru rocked back and forth on its coils as Jasmine negotiated the winding two-lane road into Yosemite Village and then headed west. Rosa, who had not been wearing her seat belt, quickly buckled up and braced herself against the car door as Jasmine used both lanes of asphalt while rounding a corner by the Yosemite Lodge at the Falls.

"The sooner, the better, right?" Mojo said, her eyes widening.

The Subaru exited the forest into the sprawling open space of

El Cap Meadow. Jasmine depressed the accelerator anticipating a flat stretch of road. As she did so, she glanced left, noticing a collection of vehicles and a gathering out in the meadow staring up at El Cap. This was common most of the year—people gawking at climbers. Today was an odd day for it though. Jasmine turned her head to look more closely.

Suddenly, she applied the brakes and tugged on the wheel, swerving the Subaru toward the shoulder.

"¡Dios mío!" Rosa yelled.

"What the hell?" Rebecca exclaimed.

Mojo braced herself by putting one leg up on the dashboard.

Jasmine tried to pull the car in behind a Park Service Yukon but had too much momentum. Just before impact, she yanked the steering wheel even farther to the left, and the Subaru lurched up over the curb and into the meadow, like a wildebeest unceremoniously leaping into a river.

Before anyone could say anything, Jasmine had her door open.

"Joy!"

81

I'LL DO IT

Monday, 3:01 P.M.

Thirty yards into the meadow, Chuck looked up from his phone. "What on God's green Earth?"

Everyone turned to see a Subaru station wagon leaping over the curb toward them. Before it stopped moving, a redheaded figure rushed out of the car.

"That—would be my sister," Joy said, then started running to greet her sibling.

"No way," Woody said.

"Let me guess, you know someone there too?" Chuck asked wryly.

"Yeah, it looks like my mom maybe got over her issues with Jasmine Cooper." Woody took off jogging after Joy.

"Oh shit!" Chuck grabbed the binoculars. "We'll soon be headed your way, Dave," he said, quickly hanging up the phone and scanning El Cap for their fugitive. He had heard enough stories about the amazing acoustics of the walls in Yosemite, especially on El Cap. *Did Stuart hear the car's loud entrance into the meadow? Does he realize now we are watching him?*

"Andrea, we need to get out of plain sight. Drop now!" Chuck fell onto his stomach and crawled through the three-foot-high grass. Andrea followed.

"Let's hope Stuart can't see our cars through the trees from his position."

"Of course," Andrea replied.

Chuck moved as fast as he could on elbows and knees, scrambling after Woody and Joy. When he could risk running forward in a low crouch, he cautiously began to yell instructions, "Everyone out of sight! Now!"

Joy put her leg behind her sister's and knocked her over into the grass. "Sorry, Chuck, I didn't think—can he see us?"

"We're at the tree line now, from the looks of it. Come back toward the road maybe another ten feet, and then let's get out of here before he gets any higher."

"Before *who* gets any higher?" Jasmine asked.

"Stuart. He's on The Nose right now." Joy moved hunched over in line behind Chuck.

As he reached the car, Chuck overheard Woody saying, "Jeez, Mom, I'm glad to see you, too. I'm all right. Really, although, squeezing that hard... I think you're crushing my ribcage."

"Everyone can catch up later," Chuck said. "Does Stuart have any reason to know whose car this is?"

Rebecca answered, "I don't see how he could."

"All right," Chuck said. "The car stays. Everyone in the Yukon, now."

Six bodies piled into the vehicle and Chuck backed up the car, spun it around, and headed the wrong way down the one-way road toward Yosemite Lodge. Once under the cover of the trees, he yanked the vehicle onto the shoulder, parked and looked at Andrea. "Someone needs to keep an eye on our friend up there," Chuck began. "Take the binoculars and––"

Chuck looked up as a Sprinter Van with cameras and antenna

on the roof sped the wrong way past El Cap Meadow and, upon seeing a Park Service vehicle, turned toward the Merced Bridge.

"Damn. How did those media jerks get past the barricades?" Chuck continued. "Andrea, take your binoculars and radio. Find a place out of sight and close to the road. Call someone about those morons in the van and keep us informed on Stuart."

"Got it. I'll cross the bridge and stay near the willows," Andrea said, shutting the door behind her.

Chuck pulled the car back onto the road and sped away. Everyone was silent as Chuck used both lanes tearing up the distance to the Lodge.

"What happened at Hetch Hetchy?" Rebecca finally asked.

"It's draining... the lake... right now," Joy responded.

"Oh my God," Mojo gasped. "Did you see—?"

"Yeah, we were there," Woody answered, bracing himself against the door.

"Jesus, Woody, how did you get mixed up in this?"

Woody rolled his eyes.

"Sorry, I didn't mean to accuse you Wood—I'm just—I'm glad you're all right."

"Yeah, totally—ditto for me. I'm glad this is over and you both are safe," Jasmine added.

"I don't know about that," Joy began. "The fire hasn't been contained, right?"

Chuck grunted and no one seemed to challenge Joy's question.

"And Stuart's still at large," Woody added. "We don't know who he's been working with, and the O'Shaughnessy Dam is in all likelihood going to be totally blown to smithereens at some unknown—"

"Hold on, people!" Chuck yelled. A CAL FIRE engine with siren's blaring came at them from the opposite direction around a blind corner. Chuck dipped the tires of the Yukon off the main road and started to fishtail, but managed to straighten the vehicle back onto the road as the engine blew past.

"That was close," Rebecca said.

The cramped Yukon passengers were silent as Chuck pulled toward the lodge.

Joy finally spoke up, "So Woody was questioning.... are we safe and is this over? Well, *not really.*"

"Look," Mojo said. "At least now you all aren't being targeted, and we're together."

The Yukon screeched to a stop at the front entrance of the lodge. Chuck turned to face the others. "The fire isn't a direct threat to us, but we need to ask you some questions in order to apprehend this Stuart character."

Glances were exchanged as everyone exited the vehicle onto the asphalt. Funneling inside the lodge, Chuck saw Dave and other rangers setting up an impromptu command center in the front lobby. Guns, radios, maps, and climbing gear were being laid on the reception desk.

A news broadcast blared from TVs mounted in the upper corners above the front desk: "The fire in the main Yosemite valley continues to be a threat to vacationers caught by surprise." On screen, a field reporter in a North Face jacket stood at the famous Wawona Tunnel View overlooking Yosemite Valley, now only occasionally visible through shifting clouds of dense smoke. "But NBC News has learned of a new incident in Yosemite; while details are still coming in and we cannot directly verify, it appears that the Hetch Hetchy—"

"Turn that damn thing off, Dave," Chuck demanded. "Any luck with Rick?"

"He's fine," Dave answered, while muting the broadcast. "We have other rangers there to assist him now, but we're no closer to a solution of how to stop additional blasts."

"We need this Stuart White, don't we?" Chuck said.

"I'm afraid so—" Dave paused. "He's really up on El Cap, huh? How high?"

"Probably over five hundred feet by now. Let me check with Andrea." Chuck picked up his radio. "Hey Andrea, copy?"

A voice came over the radio. "Still here."

"How's our soloing fugitive doing?"

"Slow and steady, although it looks like he might be setting something up right now. He's been at one anchor for quite a while."

"Is he any higher than before?"

"Yeah, he's moved across Sickle Ledge and has started up another crack system."

"Keep your eyes on him."

"Ten-four."

"So," Chuck continued. "How do we get to him?"

"We could yell at him with a megaphone from the valley," Dave offered.

"The problem is we need to get information from him, and for that—"

"I agree, someone needs to go up there," Dave cut in.

"Fuck it all," Chuck said. "Do we have any search and rescue people who can tackle The Nose from the ground up?"

"Right now, unfortunately no." Dave shook his head. "There were a couple of parties trapped on Half Dome when the fire surrounded them. We've got almost everyone with technical rope experience pulling climbers out of the smoke on the face."

Chuck looked at his colleagues, not sure of how to proceed. They needed answers. The dam explosion had to be stopped. He could just leave solving the motive puzzle and the murder investigations to the FBI, but—

"I'll do it," said Woody, as he and Joy exchanged furtive glances.

"The *hell* you will," Mojo declared.

No one spoke for a while. There was a visual standoff as

Chuck and Dave exchanged glances with Mojo and Woody. Then another voice spoke up.

"I can, too." This time it was Jasmine.

"No! He's way too dangerous, sis," Joy implored.

"Exactly," Mojo echoed. "Haven't you all done enough to help?"

"I'm just saying," Jasmine responded. "I can get up to—"

Chuck cut in with a hearty laugh. The sound of deep-bellied laughter from the largest man in the room was incongruous amid the tension. Everyone turned to look at Chuck, who was shaking his big head and scratching behind his right ear. "You guys are amazing––after everything you've been through." He laughed again. "Here's the deal. We can take pretty much 100 percent of the danger out of the equation."

"You can *what?*" Mojo's strained expression emphasized her skepticism.

"Listen up, I'll put our best sharpshooter across the meadow fixed on Stuart, and whoever approaches him only needs to come within speaking distance. We just need information from him. And I've been up on some of these walls before, so as long as the follower trails a haul line I can jug up behind them––oh, and I'll be armed."

Woody spoke up. "I've been up to the Dolt Tower on the Nose before, and if I go with Jasmine, we can move fast––and use the second line for Chuck."

"Yeah, and we'll, like, text each other climbing commands and messages," Jasmine added, "so that we don't, you know, act all *cacophonishly.*"

Mojo was too enraged to correct her English. "Look, who gives a crap if the dam blows up? Why are we taking risks to prevent something that everyone in this room probably wants to happen anyway?... Huh?... Well?... *Anyone?* Just evacuate downstream and let the damn thing go!" Mojo raised her voice to its sternest octave. "And do not, according to whatever asinine ratio-

nale you can pull out of your pretty pleated pants, put *my son*—
who's still a *minor* by the way—into further harm's way!"

Chuck decided against humor as a way to break the tension
this time. Mojo did have a point. He knew that if you asked any
one of the rangers and others gathered in the room if they wanted
to have Hetch Hetchy restored, they all likely would say yes.

No one spoke for a time. The vaulted lobby of Yosemite Lodge
—busy just moments before with the sounds of maps rustling,
doors opening and closing, climbing gear and munitions being
sorted—fell silent.

Dave, the oldest ranger in the room, finally spoke up. "You're
absolutely right, ma'am. Our job is to protect visitors to Yosemite,
not endanger them. And yes, having Hetch Hetchy back would be
a great thing. But we need to know who has been killing climbers
and rangers. And we need answers as to who has been orches-
trating all of this madness and violating our National Park. If we
can do it safely, I think we should."

Woody spoke up. "Mom, we can do—"

Mojo cut him off. "Woody, honey, you've been through so
much and this is so unnecessary—and you're all I've got left."

Woody hugged her. "We'll be safe, Mom."

Mojo looked unconvinced. Woody pulled her aside and said
in a hushed tone, "Mom, Dad would want me to do something. I
know he would. And you know he would."

"But Wood, this is insane."

"The rangers will be with us."

"I don't care who will be with you."

"Mom, please. I need to do this. It's not about me it's not
about you. It's—"

"*What?* What could possibly be more important?"

"Making dad proud?"

"Your father wouldn't want you to risk your life."

"He'd want to protect this place, and the people who love it."

Mojo studied her son and then pulled him to her and

wrapped her arms around him. "Oh, screw it," Mojo said. "Time's wasting, and if this stunt will finally expose and topple the death-star evil empire of WP&G, then freaking do it!"

A murmur circulated, "WP&G?"

"Really?" Woody seemed surprised.

"We'll be like, totally safe, Mrs. Jackson." Jasmine flung her arm around Woody's shoulders and winked.

Mojo looked Jasmine in the eyes and said with a wry smile, "You just might be my worst nightmare, girlfriend."

Chuck took command. "What do you need?" he asked, looking at Jasmine and Woody.

"We need a way to communicate with you," Jasmine began.

Dave looked at his colleague. "Charlie—"

"On it. Meet you at the meadow," Charlie shot back, sprinting out of the room.

"Do you have all the gear we need?" Woody asked Jasmine.

"We'll need to charge our phones. And yeah, the gear's all in the Subi Beast in the meadow, and maybe let's snatch a few choice pieces from *all* this sweetness you've got laid out here." Jasmine grabbed some shiny Metolius offset cams from the rangers' table and addressed them, "Oh—*hello sexy*, it's a pleasure to make your acquaintance."

"Then, let's do this," Chuck said, stifling a chuckle. "Two cars only. I don't want a fleet of vehicles parked in the meadow and a nosey crowd staring up at the wall. Brad, find Jorge and tell him to get his sniper rifle and locate by the bridge on the river. Anyone coming," Chuck looked at Mojo, "watch from the other side of the meadow once Jorge is in position. Dave, inform the FBI and make sure they don't blow up this plan, and for Christ's sake, someone," Chuck glanced up at the TV monitor now silenced, "make sure those meddling media idiots are kept in the dark about this until it's over. Woody, Jasmine, are you two ready?"

"Hells yeah," Jasmine said, examining her shiny new gear.

82

YEAH, COWBOY

Monday, 4:31 P.M.

Woody checked his phone message: *OB*. He removed the rope from his belay device.

They had decided on some simple codes for communicating: *OB* was for *off belay*, *BIO* was for *belay is on*, *C* was for *climbing*, and *P1, P2, P3* and so on would describe which *pitch* they were on. Texts would be sent from each belay station, when hands were free. Charlie had preset the group text recipient list so that Woody, Jasmine, and Chuck, who was jugging up the fixed line they trailed, could simply punch and send. Everyone would know where they were and how it was going.

OB, Woody texted back after he had taken the rope out of his ATC.

The nylon rope whizzed up in front of Woody as Jasmine pulled it to where she was standing about a hundred feet above.

BIO, Jasmine texted.

Woody unhooked from the bolts and punched, *C*.

They were past Sickle Ledge already and transitioning into

the The Stovelegs, a crack named for Warren Harding's creative repurposing of items taken from a Berkeley dump.*

Woody was right; they were moving fast. Jasmine volunteering for the job made perfect sense. She was an accomplished and confident aid climber and the climbing on The Nose was clean and comfortable.

Woody reached Jasmine and took the next lead. It was hard but he flew up it to the next set of bolts, where most climbers transition into the main Stovelegs crack. *It feels so good to just climb,* he thought. So much of what had transpired over the past twenty-four hours was senseless. Climbing was the antithesis, and with each move, Woody felt closer to regaining control. He punched, *OB.*

Jasmine received Woody's text. Then another text came through on their phones, from Dave: *Stuart < 100' up & 2 rt. Portaledge.*

Woody belayed Jasmine up to his anchor.

"What do you think?" Jasmine quietly asked.

"I think I see the bottom of his portaledge right there. How's Chuck doing?"

"He had a little trouble with that big tension traverse into the bottom of Stove Legs, but he's a big boy." Jasmine smiled. "He'll be fine."

"What do you want to do?"

"Wait a minute—do you hear that?" Woody listened carefully. "Is that...? No way."

"It's gotta be."

"You think he's—?"

"Yeah."

Woody pulled out the phone and typed: *Stuart snoring.*

They waited for a response and giggled quietly to each other on the side of the rock.

This time it was Chuck who texted as he jugged up a few feet below them. *Let's wake him up then.*

"Wouldn't it be safer above him?" Jasmine suggested after Chuck had pulled himself level with their position. "I mean, Stuart could rappel and pendulum swing over to us, but we're not, you know, rope soloing, so we can climb faster than him."

Chuck looked up at the underside of Stuart's portaledge. "We want this to be as safe as possible. I could take him out from here if I had to. I'd like to be a little bit closer though."

"He's not right on the route, either," Woody added. "We could easily follow that bolt ladder to get above his position. Parties pass one another all the time here."

"Let's call down and discuss this with Dave and the others. I'll do it." Chuck pressed call and held the phone up to his ear.

Dave answered almost instantaneously. "What's going on up there?"

"I think I'm going to get the kids above him before we wake him up," Chuck responded.

"Is that safer?"

"That's the idea." Chuck turned toward the meadow as if to face his colleague about 800 feet below for the conversation.

"Okay Chuck, but if I get a bad feeling about anything I'm going to have my sniper Jorge here shoot him dead."

"I'll take it slow, Dave. I'd like to be closer to our perpetrator."

"Okay. Oh, and Chuck, we're not long on time or daylight, so whatever we do, we need to do it now."

"Got it." Chuck hung up the phone. "Okay, here's the deal. Jasmine you're the next leader?"

"Yup."

"You'll take both lines this time. Fix mine for jugging and belay Woody's like normal."

"10-4, boss," Jasmine said and readied herself to lead.

Woody put Jasmine on belay and she silently ascended the bolt ladder, tensioning into a crack running to the left of Stuart. The climbing went fast, and she passed him with no more sound than the closing of a carabiner gate. At the next set of bolts, Jasmine hooked into the wall and texted, *OB*.

Woody undid the rope from his belay device, relaying *BIO*, then, *C*. Woody began his ascent as Chuck slowly started jugging up the fixed line next to him.

"I'm only going to go up to where I can have an easy shot at Stuart," Chuck whispered as the two began to separate. "You get above him and out of sight."

Woody looked over at Stuart's sleeping bag as he tiptoed vertically past. He couldn't see a gun anywhere among his gear, but knew it had to be somewhere. He climbed the final distance to the belay anchors where Jasmine waited, quietly unhooked gear from the wall and attached it to his harness with as little sound as possible. Stuart was still snoring.

"Okay, Stuart––wakie wakie!" Chuck commanded loudly from his position now level with the slumbering killer.

On the portaledge about forty feet below Woody and Jasmine, they saw the sleeping bag shift.

"We all know you're in there; me, the snipers in the meadow, the team of rangers watching us. I'm armed, and we need to talk––and now!"

There were no movements on the portaledge. Woody and Jasmine peered down the wall. They heard Chuck's previous statement both from Chuck himself and in greater clarity from their phones, which Chuck had on speaker in order to communicate with the other rangers in the valley below as well as those at the O'Shaughnessy Dam.

A few more seconds passed; still no movement. Woody strained outward in his harness from the anchor bolts, looking for any sign at all.

"Stuart. It's time to get up and––"

"You want The Professor, right?" a muffled voice replied from inside the sleeping bag.

"You've got it," Chuck responded.

Stuart slowly sat up in his sleeping bag and looked around. Tilting his head toward Chuck, Stuart smiled. "Nice day for a climb, isn't it?"

"Let's see your hands, Buddy."

As Stuart obliged and raised his hands above his head, he looked up and noticed Woody and Jasmine. "Well... hi, kids." His peculiar smile grew wider.

"Stuart, we need this Professor, and although you are definitely looking at the inside of a prison cell for probably the rest of your life, there are a lot of different prisons out there, and a little cooperation now could go a very long way." Chuck had his gun leveled at Stuart as he sat in his harness.

Stuart didn't respond.

"There really aren't any other options available."

Turning to look at Chuck, Stuart slowly said, "I've never met this...'Professor.'" Stuart made quotation marks in the air with his raised fingers. "I get emails...instructions. I really don't know how to identify this person."

Following another heavy pause, Stuart looked out toward El Cap Meadow. "For all I know, this is just someone's crazy plan to restore the environment. I was only told... well, only what I needed to know, and some nonsense about covering up a 'century-old secret' (more air quotes)––and a bunch of crap about Muir. I don't believe you want me to talk late twentieth century environmentalism now, do you?"

Chuck was not amused. "No, Stuart. We don't want your theories on motive. In fact, there's really only one thing we need. My guess is that you'll know it."

Stuart casually nodded, "I'm listening."

"How is this Professor person going to detonate the final explosion on the dam?"

Stuart inched his raised hands along the taught webbing supporting his portaledge.

"So, if we were in a little room somewhere," Stuart began,

"you'd bring out some agreement... or contract guaranteeing me something for my co-oper—"

"We don't have that luxury, Stuart," Chuck interrupted. "You know damn well we're running out of time here."

Stuart's fingers tapped out a rhythm as they slid up and down the webbing above his head. He seemed to be looking past Chuck at the smoke in the valley in the waning sunlight.

"Tick tock, man," Chuck said.

"I don't like this," Woody whispered to Jasmine.

"Yeah, it's like he's thinking of something else; maybe scheming," Jasmine whispered back.

"Doesn't he know it's *over*?" Woody started looping the climbing rope at his feet.

"What are you doing?" Jasmine asked.

"I'm not sure yet. I've just got a bad feeling about all of this."

"Okay, Mister Ranger." Stuart shifted uncomfortably and brought one hand down to support himself. "The final charge can only be detonated by a shortwave radio signal, so the person would have to be within, say, half a mile to pull the trigger. The receiver is actually on the dam itself." Stuart smiled. "There's a metal post right as you walk onto the dam, to prevent vehicles from driving on the surface. Pull out the post and you'll find the receiver. All you will need to do is remove the three wires connected to the base of the post."

"Rick, did you get all that?" Dave asked.

"On my way there now," Rick said, having listened in on the exchange. They could all hear the rhythmic cadence of hurried footsteps as Rick ran toward the dam.

"All right, I'm at the post, Stuart," Rick said, panting.

"You may need to jiggle it a little as you lift," Stuart offered.

"The post is up and—" There was a pause on the line. "Look at *that*," Rick said. "Okay, I've removed the wires, but how are we going to know when and where The Professor comes to trigger them."

Stuart spoke, "Hello again... Ranger Rick?"

Rick didn't respond.

Chuck interrupted, "Answer the question—how will we know?"

Stuart drew a long slow breath and scanned the walls of El Cap.

THIS SCENARIO FELT strange to Woody. He whispered to Jasmine, "Why is Stuart so damn co-operative? Why all these long pauses? It's too calculated, there's something..."

"What do you mean?" Jasmine whispered back.

Woody tied an eight on a bite to the newly looped rope at his feet and connected it with a locking carabiner to his harness.

Jasmine looked at Woody's new connection point. "Hey, man, don't get any big ideas."

Stuart finally spoke up. "Okay, Ranger Rick. See the lights on the surface of the device? There should be two green and one red."

"Yeah."

"Well, when The Professor activates—"

At that moment, the smoke and clouds drifted into the wall, temporarily capturing the four climbers in a thick water vapor world of grey and white.

A shot rang out, followed immediately by a grunt from Chuck.

"Chuck! Are you—?" Jasmine yelled.

More bullets flew, this time from the meadow. The distinct sound of pings could be heard as they ricocheted off the side of the wall.

"I can't see anything down there," Jasmine said in desperation.

"Stay back, Jasmine," Chuck faintly urged.

"He sounds—" Woody stammered.

"Did they shoot Stuart?" Jasmine asked.

Woody peered over the edge. He could barely make out the contours of Stuart's portaledge. There was frenetic movement upon it and something else—flames appeared.

"On the portaledge... Stuart's bag—it's on fire!"

"From Stuart's gun?" Jasmine asked. "Or bullets from the sniper?"

Before Woody could answer, he saw a blur of motion through the haze, moving from the portaledge toward Chuck's line.

"Arrgh." The grunt came from Chuck.

Woody and Jasmine listened helplessly to the sounds of two men struggling and spinning on the fixed line.

"He's on Chuck's line; I can feel it," Jasmine said.

"He's going to ascend," Woody shot back.

"Maybe the sniper—?"

"Probably can't see well enough."

Woody could just make out the shapes of two people fighting on the rope, and a flash of metal he assumed to be a knife.

"Arrgh," another agonized grunt sounding like Chuck.

Then, in the gloomy haze, a figure was tenaciously ascending the line toward them.

"We have to cut the line," Jasmine said.

"But if Chuck—?"

"May already be dead."

"Chuck! Are you there?" Woody yelled down.

Dave's voice came over the phone, "Cut the damn line!"

Jasmine unclipped a small blade from her chalk bag carabiner and looked beseechingly at Woody.

"Wait. He can't shoot at us now," Woody said. "He's jugging up the line and needs both hands."

"We don't have a choice." Jasmine brought the knife to the rope.

"Wait, Jaz! Stuart's still tied back to his portaledge; cutting the line means we'd only be killing Chuck!"

Woody looked at the rope coiled at his feet and then glanced over the edge. Stuart was ascending as quickly as he could. If he was going to do anything, it had to be now. "If this doesn't work, cut his rope."

Before Jasmine could stop him, Woody unclipped his cordelette from the anchor and, with a "Fuck you, Stuart!," jumped. Facing the wall and falling parallel to the fixed line, he squeezed both feet together.

Stuart looked up. Woody caught a fleeting glimpse of his eyes widening.

It happened fast. The first thing to make contact were the tips of Woody's shoes. They scraped down Stuart's right eye socket and nose cartilage before separating his jawbone. Next, Woody's heels smashed into Stuart's upper torso, forcing the air from his lungs and fracturing his chest bone and ribcage. This contact flipped Woody backwards, his shoulder, then his helmet hitting the wall. There was a loud crack as the helmet split open. He scraped and bounced against the wall as he fell just below Stuart's position, until the dynamic rope caught and bungeed Woody upward, lifting him back alongside the now unconscious Stuart.

Dazed from the impact, Woody fumbled to find the gun clipped to Stuart's harness and dangling next to a rope tied back to Stuart's portaledge. Woody unhooked the gun and pitched it into the void. He removed a knife from Stuart's now weak grip and tossed that as well.

The smoke cloud had lifted, swirling upward beyond the four suspended bodies.

Woody haltingly called up, "Jasmine, I'm okay. Stuart's knocked out, but I think he's still alive. I've tossed Stuart's gun and knife and I'm tying his hands behind his back with cordellette."

As Woody worked, he could hear Jasmine relaying the information to the rangers over the phone. *At least now no one should try to shoot at me,* Woody thought. Woody didn't care if the tightness of his knot injured Stuart any further. He grabbed some of Stuart's extra rope and used that too; he was going to make the best damn cinch knot he could. While he worked, he glanced at Chuck, hanging limp just ten feet below.

"Oww!" Stuart suddenly yelled as Woody tightened a third rope and cinched it off all the way up to his elbows. "You're...separating...my—*Arrgh.*" His speech was strained and slurred.

"Don't expect an apology, *old man.*"

Stuart tried to spin, kick, and bite at Woody, but each movement seemed to bring more pain. Woody decided he was secured enough and swung clear from Stuart.

"Jasmine. I need to get down to check on Chuck. Stuart is alive and not going anywhere. I'm building a little anchor here to take my weight off the rope. Can you feed me about fifteen more feet of slack in my line when I tell you?"

"Um, sure."

Woody finished placing a second piece of gear in the wall and then pulled upward and direct-clipped it and the first piece into his harness. "Okay, ready."

"Here you go: that should be about right."

"Okay. Lowering."

"Oh, so no crazy jumping this time, huh?" Jasmine chided.

"Sorry, Jaz. Think I've had enough of that." Woody used his belay device to rap the distance down to Chuck. There was blood coming from his right arm where it appeared he'd been shot. There was also blood on his shirt, possibly smears from his arm, but maybe from Stuart's knife. Woody put two fingers to Chuck's throat.

"Chuck's alive!" he yelled up to Jasmine.

Woody yelling two feet from his face seemed to revive Chuck. "Ughh... What the hell are you doing here?"

"Should I tie something around your arm? You're bleeding badly from what looks like a bullet wound."

"Yeah. Um... use my shirt. Rip it. I have a little knife on my harness."

Woody cut strips and wrapped them tightly around Chuck's arm, as Chuck used his other hand to put his phone up to his ear and call down to the rangers.

"Situation under control, here," Chuck began.

"The smoke is starting to clear now," Dave responded. "That was one hell of a radio show! Is it you that we're seeing with Woody; and Stuart tied up beside his portaledge?"

"Yeah. Stuart's all tied up, still alive. I'm okay. Shot--and a little beat up--but functioning."

"Good news, my friend," Dave said.

"Do you have all the information needed from Stuart?" Chuck asked.

"Almost. We need to know the proximity necessary for The Professor to make this last light turn green."

Chuck yelled over to Stuart, "Did you catch that?"

"Screw you."

"I could cut him loose," Woody offered.

"Just answer the damn question, Stuart," Chuck said.

There was a long pause as Stuart, bound with hands behind his back and painfully twisting around on the end of his rope, glowered at Woody and Chuck.

"The device can be triggered anywhere within a mile," Stuart grunted.

"Okay," Dave responded.

"Good job," Rick joined in. " I guess that makes sense--short wave radio signal length, yeah, about a mile."

"Now to getting you guys off that rock," Dave began. "Any ideas?"

"Yeah," Chuck laughed. "Getting out of here? Hmmm..."

"It shouldn't be too hard," Woody volunteered.

"Go ahead, Woody," said Dave.

"We're on the Dolt tower rap line. Jasmine and I could just

lower Chuck and Stuart to each new set of bolts. Chuck, do you think you'd be able to clip in at each station?"

"Yeah. No problem. What about Stuart though?"

"We'll just drop him." Woody paused. "Just kidding. We'll dangle him below you, Chuck, on a bite on your rope; he'll just be along for the ride."

"Makes sense to me," Chuck replied. "Although the dropping scenario sounds like a hell of a lot more fun. Dave, your thoughts?"

"*Yes*, on the lowering, if you're sure you can do it safely. *No*, on the dropping."

83

FITTING

Monday, 5:28 P.M.

A WP&G company helicopter whirred up the rolling hills of the western slope of the Sierra Nevada Range toward what remained of the Hetch Hetchy reservoir. The Professor sat in the rear, clutching an open laptop with an antenna attached.

Stuart's posting had been unmistakable. It had confirmed that the job needed to be completed and that he no longer possessed the tools necessary to do so.

Fitting.

The Professor was going to the reservoir ostensibly to survey the damage and make an assessment for the company. At least, that's what it would look like. In reality, once the helicopter was within shortwave radio range, about half a mile at the least, the software and antenna would be able to activate the final explosive charge and, as the sun was setting, The Professor would be treated to a magnificent view of the terminal implosion of the O'Shaughnessy Dam.

Fitting.

The timing was close to perfect. Ever since bribing the court clerk for a look at how the judge was going to rule on the illegal power siphoning by WP&G, The Professor's suspicions had been confirmed—the dam needed to be destroyed. The pompous nature of those words, the sheer egotistical presumption conveyed by what the judge had drafted, made The Professor's blood run cold: "It is as clear as the water of the Tuolumne," he wrote "that the only *fitting* recompense for such a prolonged and heinous violation of the Supreme Court Order, the original Raker Act, and of the sacred trust of the people of this country, is for said corporation to be required to remove the O'Shaughnessy Dam and take full financial responsibility for restoration and revegetation of the Hetch Hetchy Valley."

Fitting. Soon to be fittingly obsolete.

The trip from Oakland was less than two hours. The pilot was on call. Getting everything together had taken no more than half an hour, and the added benefit would be the front-row seat in which The Professor would attempt to enjoy the grand finale to three excruciating years of plotting and executing this glorious, and at the same time monstrous and demeaning accomplishment.

At this point, the helicopter is within range. Now, it all ends.

The Professor initiated the final software sequence.

84

RESILIENCE

Monday, 5:29 P.M.

Jogging back to the small collection of vehicles circled around his colleagues, Rick eyed the receiver in Hayduke's hands.

"Still red," Hayduke said to Rick. "No damn signal yet."

Rick smiled. He was glad Hayduke had joined them at Hetch Hetchy after he had helped clear the Cathedral Lakes and Sunrise backcountry areas last night.

Agent Friedman looked up from his computer propped against a windshield. "Everyone dispatched?"

"Affirmative," Rick said.

"Trails too?"

"The last two rangers are deployed on the lower canyon trail."

Rick and his colleagues figured there were three possible ways someone could access the receiver remotely: by car, by foot, or by some sort of air transport. The main entrance to the reservoir was normally closed by this time of night, but tonight it was purposely left open, and seemingly unguarded. Rangers divided up the trails leading in and out of the valley and set out in teams of two, looking for any hiker who might have a computer. With the fire in the main valley now under control, a second helicopter was requisitioned; it sat idle in the parking lot by the dam.

"All right." Agent Dale Friedman hit *send* on an email and purposefully closed his laptop. "The pilot has his instructions?"

"Yes," Rick replied. "We're in radio contact as well."

"Okay." Agent Dale Friedman took a deep breath. "So, we wait."

"Yup, guess so," Hayduke shrugged, and stood up with the receiver in his hands. "Walk a piece with me, boys?"

"Where to?" Agent Friedman asked.

"Our new valley," Hayduke said, winking back at them.

"Yeah, I suppose this will be a good thing for the Park––in the long run," Rick said. "Take some pressure off it."

"Jeffrey sure would have like it, wouldn't he?" Hayduke replied. "I guess you heard they recovered his body."

Rick nodded, reverently.

The trio walked down to what was left of the dam and looked eastward into the valley. Below them, the reservoir had lost the upper third of its water. The granite sidewalls, robbed of vegetation from decades of submersion in the waters of the Tuolumne, gleamed bright white and orange in the setting sun.

"It won't be easy to restore this place," Agent Friedman said, looking up the eight-mile canyon.

"Hey, Dale." Hayduke slapped the FBI agent on the shoulder. "Let's see if I can remember this: 'We need wilderness whether or not we ever set foot in it... We need the possibility of escape as surely as we need the possibility of hope.'"

"Nice," Rick said. "Muir?"

"Nope. That there's Edward Abbey, the guy who—"

"Hey, we didn't call for another chopper, did we?" Agent Friedman broke in.

"Definitely not," Rick said anxiously. "It could be the media, or—"

Without further discussion, the three men raced to the parking lot and gathered near the waiting CAL FIRE chopper. Listening to the *whoomp whoomp* of the approaching aircraft, Rick focused on the receiver in Hayduke's hands. Just as Hayduke and Dale announced a shape on the horizon, the tiny red light on the receiver switched to green.

Urgently motioning to the sky, Rick yelled into his radio, "Green! That's them; they're in that chopper!"

The CAL FIRE pilot activated his engines. He was up to speed as Rick got close enough to make eye contact.

"Get them on the ground," Rick said.

The pilot pulled up on the stick, lifting the chopper swiftly into the air.

85

AUTHORITY

Monday, 5:30 P.M.

The Professor had expected dramatic results—a violent blast of white spray shooting skyward, a colossal cracking apart of the dam. Instead, there was no enhancement of the existing massive gash in the O'Shaughnessy Dam. The devices had been tested for compatibility not more than a week ago from various distances.

She fumbled desperately with her computer. *This damn software isn't working. Does the computer need rebooting? Is the signal bad? We're definitely in range. This makes no fucking sense!*

Looking up, The Professor noticed an unexpected helicopter lifting up from the paved area near the dam. It pulled directly skyward and spun around as it did so, barely revealing the words "CAL FIRE" on its hull. *Why? The fire is in the main valley; it's not even equipped for a water drop.*

The Professor's pilot motioned to put the headphones on. "They're ordering us to land over there on the parking strip by the side of the dam."

"Don't do it! We're here on company business," The Professor ordered. "Under whose authority are they operating?"

The pilot relayed the question. "He says the Federal Government, and we need to land *now*."

"No way."

The CAL FIRE chopper immediately tilted forward and made for the WP&G chopper's position. Instinctively, The Professor's pilot took their helicopter lower.

"What are you doing?"

"What I'm being told."

"Get this craft the hell out of here!" The Professor yelled into the headset. "Or it's your fucking job."

"I'll get a fucking new one."

86

RUSE

Monday, 5:32 P.M.

Rick watched as the sleek white helicopter with the trademark WP&G lettering on the side lowered to rest on the parking lot. Once the skids touched down on the angled surface, he ducked and ran forward, flanked by Hayduke and Agent Friedman. As Rick approached, gun in hand, he focused in on two people in the machine, a pilot in front concentrating on his instruments, and someone with hands cupped to their face staring out the rear window.

Rick went for the rear door, grasped the handle, and threw it wide.

He stepped back, aghast at who confronted him.

Just as Stuart had described, there was an open computer with an antenna. It sat on the lap of the well-dressed, impeccably manicured young company executive, who glared menacingly back at Rick.

As the throbbing blades were noisily slowing down, Rick leaned in and shouted, *"Hello, Alex*; or rather is it *Professor Alexandra Leach?"*

Alexandra didn't miss a beat. "I'll be needing my lawyer."

"Fine with me, Professor." Rick reached in and deftly snatched Alexandra's computer from her lap. "And we'll be needing this," He handed the computer to a dazed Hayduke, still stunned that Rick knew this person, although she looked somewhat familiar.

Alexandra's gaze burned into Rick from behind the unaccustomed dark mascara. Her bangs, usually pushed up behind her Park Service hat, now fell meticulously in place. She wore a hint of burgundy lipstick that accentuated her raven hair and pale, now furrowed, brow. Her tailored business suit fell precisely on her hips, and its faint silver pinstripes ran cleanly down to her leather pumps.

"Hmm, I always thought you looked a little too fancy for our wardrobe, Alex," Rick said as he grabbed Alexandra by the elbow. "Come along with me."

Rick escorted his former coworker away from the helicopter, placing handcuffs on her wrist before sitting her on a park bench by the lot.

"You know this person?" Agent Dale Friedman asked.

"Oh yeah, Alex and I, we know each other," Rick said. "But less than expected in my case. She's a Park Service worker." He turned to face her. "So that's how Stuart knew we were coming for him on the top of Half Dome."

"You've been volunteering for what—the past three years? I think that's right." Rick sat down next to Alex, who was silent. "You've been building credibility, learning how the Park Service operates, figuring out our weaknesses, and all the while planning."

"Rick, excuse me for a moment, but—Miranda rights?" Agent Friedman prompted.

"Of course. You want the pleasure?"

As Agent Friedman notified Alexandra of her Miranda rights, Hayduke arrived in a Park Service Yukon.

"Agent, may I have a word with you?" Rick asked. "Hayduke, keep an eye on Miss Conspiracy here, okay?"

Agent Friedman nodded, and the two of them walked out of hearing range. Hayduke sat down next to Alex and said, "Oh, now I've got it. You're the pretty one from the campfire last night."

"Dale, I'd like to puzzle through a few things with my former colleague here and maybe collect some more information. How about we all drive together back to headquarters in the valley?"

"I should be taking her directly to headquarters in Sacramento, but... it could be useful."

Alexandra and Agent Friedman sat in the rear of the vehicle. Rick sat in front next to Hayduke, who took the wheel. The pilot was detained for questioning and the helicopter remained secured at Hetch Hetchy.

"Did you inform Chuck we've apprehended the primary suspect, with hands as red as her lips?" Rick asked, glancing at Alexandra in the rearview mirror.

"Not in them words," Hayduke responded. "But yeah, I said we're coming."

The Yukon jostled around the turns on the way back up the canyon. Alexandra, her hands cuffed behind her back, had to prop her legs against the side of the door and the seat in order to keep from sliding around, despite her seatbelt.

"So, ain't none of this makes much sense to me," Hayduke began. "I mean, last time I seen this pretty lady, she was one of us. Now we're arresting her for blowing up the damn dam?"

"And for conspiracy to kill Aiden Watson and Abigail Edwards; and the fire; and the kidnapping—it's quite a rap sheet," Rick said.

"You mean to tell me she done all that?"

Rick turned in his chair to look back at Alexandra, bracing herself uncomfortably in the corner of the bench seat. "Well, Alex, answer the man?"

Alexandra just stared out, unflinching, her cheek against the window.

"You see, Hayduke—" Rick turned back around in his seat and stared ahead as the Yukon whipped through the small collection of buildings at Camp Mather. "Alex there, she's not who we thought. Stuart, the guy we were chasing last night, referred to her as *The Professor*, and she came to Hetch Hetchy, if you'll pardon the expression, *dressed to kill* in that sleek company helicopter." Rick took a deep breath. "There's a whole lot more to Alex than we figured."

"You can say that again. Never was a great judge of character."

"For one, she obviously works for WP&G, right?"

"Or owns the damn company, from the looks of it," Hayduke said.

"Right—so she hires this guy Stuart to kill some people before blowing up the dam—but *why?*"

"Yup, why blow up the dam—or why kill them nice people?" Hayduke asked.

Alexandra now sat upright in back, staring coldly at Rick in the mirror as he spoke.

"Let's start with the easy one—"

"That's what my momma always said," Hayduke winked as he pulled the vehicle out onto the main highway. Alex was able to relax her legs now that the car was off the side road.

"So why does WP&G and Alex here want to blow up the dam?" Rick asked rhetorically. "Well, I for one had been under the impression that San Francisco owned the dam and the rights to the water and power it supplied; but it sounds like WP&G is still somehow involved."

"All right," Hayduke responded. "Gotch'ya so far."

"So if that is the case, they'd be in violation of the law and might be forced to pay damages," Rick added.

"Ya think?" Hayduke took a hand off the wheel and scratched behind his ear.

Rick adjusted the rearview mirror slightly so he could look more directly at Alex. "Yeah, from the looks of it, I doubt Alex here likes to pay damages or part with her money for no good reason."

Alexandra scowled at Rick.

"So let's just say we didn't know WP&G was involved. Who would we think blew up the dam?"

"Them damn hippies, o'course," Hayduke shot back.

"You got it." Rick stifled a laugh. "And if a bunch of damn hippies blew up the dam, what would it mean for WP&G and their damages?"

"They wouldn't have none."

"Yeah, makes sense to me."

Agent Friedman continued to keep a low profile, but listened attentively. He occasionally stole a glance at Alexandra to note her reactions.

"But Rick... how would'ya find out?" Hayduke shrugged. "I mean, about WP&G and all? The dam's been there since the forties—I think—and then that Supreme Court stuff in the fifties. And afterwards, you know, we ain't heard *nothin'* about no issue with how the water and power is used."

"I think that's where our first fatality comes in," Rick responded. "You remember the picture we showed you last night with the dead lady climber and the message, *Here Lies Muir's Mountain Temple*?"

"Yup."

"Well—the deceased was Ms. Abigail Edwards, who was working on an investigation having to do with Hetch Hetchy. Jeffrey thought she knew more than she was telling people in her speech at Yosemite Village."

"So, then—Alex back there had to have her killed?"

"Yeah, and doing so would cause enough of a stir in the environmental activist community that it might trigger some revenge."

"Revenge like blowing up the dam?" Hayduke asked.

"Could be."

"Gettin' rid'a the dam would be somethin' Abigail would want anyway, am I right?"

Hayduke's question hung in air as he guided the Yukon down the curvy canyon road into the main Yosemite Valley. Agent Friedman just stared straight ahead. Rick leaned back in his bucket seat and put his foot up on the dash. He reached up and adjusted the rearview mirror again, flashing a mischievous smile at Alexandra. "What do you think there, Alex? Ecoterrorism sure seems like a good ruse, huh?"

Glaring back at him, Alex couldn't resist. "A *ruse,* huh?" Then she mouthed two emphatic words: "*Prove it.*"

No one spoke for a while. Rick sat up and glanced at Agent Friedman, who blinked his eyes in confirmation and then looked away. Rick turned back toward his view of Half Dome, finally visible through the thinning smoke, and then nodded at Hayduke.

"Hey, Rick?" Hayduke asked.

"Yeah?"

"Ruse ain't a shade of lipstick now, is it?"

87

ELIXIR

Monday, 6:43 P.M.

"It's over," Woody said.

After some logistic wrangling with Chuck and Stuart, they were prepared for a safe descent. Jasmine and Woody created a lowering system directly into the anchor, and using oval carabiners as a reverse pulley, then back to Woody off a Grigri and to an auto-blocker that provided the right coefficient of friction to lower the two heavy men below them. Stuart was repositioned so that he was left dangling about ten feet below Chuck. Woody's improvised rope restraint was replaced with Chuck's handcuffs, because Chuck didn't want Stuart to loose an appendage as a result of what he termed and overzealous tightening. His jaw was so sore by now that he could barely speak.

When they were about halfway through the sequential escape rappel, Woody flashed a massive toothy smile at Jasmine and Jasmine winked back.

He felt something he couldn't express. It was something new to him, a feeling he hadn't experienced since he'd been here with his father years before; it was *good* and *full* and *calm*.

"Okay. Only one more rap after this next one. Should we follow Stuart down?" Jasmine asked, as she finished pulling through the triple fisherman's knot.

"Oh, I don't know. You mean instead of climbing the rest of the Nose tonight?" Woody said with a playful twinkle in his eyes.

"I don't think we've got the necessary, you know, provisions and stuff to handle this beast right now." Jasmine countered, suppressing a laugh.

"Yeah––I suppose you're right."

"Maybe sometime soon though," Jasmine smiled, looking up at the prow of El Capitan, now reflecting the oranges and umbers of the descending sun. "Or better yet... maybe something new in Hetch Hetchy?"

"Now that sounds real nice," Woody said as he set up his ATC for the first rappel. "Quite the sunset tonight; must be the fire."

"Yeah, all that smoky sediment still bobbing and weaving around in the sky." Jasmine exhaled and closed her eyes.

Their bodies had cooled dramatically after the climb and the adrenaline rush of catching Stuart, but El Capitan kept them warm. The Captain's granite facade held the kinetic energy from a full day of sun, a tactile representation of the color of the sunset; like the valley had wrapped them in its arms and was thanking them for all they had done.

Jasmine opened her eyes. "This is sooo nice."

"See you at the next anchors." Woody checked his locking carabiner, rope, and ATC. He then unhooked from the bolts and started to lower. He was exhausted, but somehow invigorated. *This place is restorative—just like Dad always said. It takes from you, but it gives back. It challenges, but redeems.* This had been what his father sought in his last days. He wanted to tap into the power of Yosemite; to let it flow through his veins and warm his heart like the sun, the rock, and the feeling of resolution that now warmed Woody.

Thank you. Woody placed both his palms against the granite wall and breathed into the rock as if he were speaking directly to his dad. *Thank you for this.*

88

PAYMENT

Clinging to a rocky hillside overlooking the exclusive Sausalito neighborhood, the broad expanse of San Francisco Bay, and the skyline beyond, the estate of Doctor Alexandra Leach was a treasure to behold. She sat in the home's third floor study, relishing her view. The Golden Gate Bridge shone in late afternoon sun. Alcatraz Federal Penitentiary, as if formed of alabaster, gleamed like a pearl on its island throne. Alexandra swirled cognac in a crystal snifter as she turned and contemplated the playful dance of flames inside her elegant fireplace.

Because of a glitch as to precisely when her Miranda rights had been administered, her lawyers had fortunately been able to throw out the laptop as evidence in the case against her. Of almost equal import, she had authorized her financial management firm to discreetly dissolve her entire controlling interest in WP&G into a nebulous patchwork of offshore holding companies. Of course, as word of WP&G's scandalous involvement trickled out to the media, the company's stock plummeted, destroying pension funds and 401(k) plans. Unlike those of the

other members of the board, the Leach family fortune had
remained intact.

In court, Woody, Joy, and the rangers were only able to prove
that she volunteered for the Park Service and Stuart White,
dragged out of San Quentin to testify, was laughably useless to
the prosecution. He was a physical wreck, with casts and braces.
His speech was eerily slurred from the permanent damage to his
jaw. He had been unable to either physically identify her, or
recognize her voice, and had recklessly made a snide remark
about her gender, which further discredited his testimony in the
eyes of some jurors. In the harsh cross-examination, her top team
of lawyers painted him as a ruthless mercenary who got exactly
what he deserved.

And then there was Walter Ashgood, brought out of his
obscurity and plopped into the courtroom. But he too was of no
use to the prosecutors. He could not prove it was indeed
Alexandra who had spilled her martini on him in a bar half a
year earlier, then had her way with him and his property.

Alexandra had protected herself well. The case was
dismissed.

She looked out at the Golden Gate Bridge and pondered her
future prospects. There were essentially two questions.

First was the question of wealth. She would need a new
empire to run, a new conduit through which to secure the Leach
legacy. She was comfortable controlling the energy and power
sector. She might even go *green*.

Second, there was the matter of retribution. As a rule,
Alexandra did not subscribe to notions as trivial as revenge, but
somehow the indignity and offense she had suffered at the hands
of two impudent youngsters and a smattering of servile park
rangers demanded a toll. She would be patient. *Accidents can
always happen.*

Doctor Alexandra Leach lifted herself out of the comfortable
recesses of her wing-backed chair and walked the length of the

study, running her finger along the molded edge of a bookcase. Stepping out onto her gracious balcony, she studied the skyline of San Francisco. In the early evening shade, she could still make out the WP&G corporate headquarters near the intersection of Market and Embarcadero. The thought of it taunted her—the empty office, her privileges revoked, her efforts and her family's efforts over generations bankrupted. She took another sip of cognac from her snifter.

This is not over.

PROGRESS

"'Imagine yourself in Hetch Hetchy on a sunny day in June, standing waist-deep in grass and flowers as I have often stood, while the great pines sway dreamily with scarcely perceptible motion.' My friends, it has been over one hundred years since John Muir wrote those words and now, for the first time since, we no longer have to imagine."

The crowd erupted into cheers and applause.

"We are gathered here today to bear witness to a rebirth and to make a solemn vow that this place, nor any other like it, will ever again be submerged and sacrificed in the name of civilization and industry."

Pretty fiery rhetoric. Rick suppressed a chuckle. *Jeffrey would have been proud.*

Rick was seated on a small temporary stage erected in the center of the Hetch Hetchy Meadow, a generous description at this stage of the restoration. The valley was undergoing a slow and arduous process of revegetation and regrowth. After taking the necessary precautions, the irreparably damaged O'Shaughnessy Dam had been dismantled in a more methodical and sequential way than Dr. Alexandra Leach had originally planned. Much of the concrete was repurposed as aggregate for the expansion of the Don Pedro and Calaveras Reservoirs. The buildings were gone and even the road accessing the valley had been rerouted to a less visible location.

Several thousand had gathered for the dedication ceremony and Rick felt awkward sitting on a stage like some sort of dignitary next to the speaker for today's dedication ceremony, Director Fran Mainella of the National Park Service.

"This valley will come to represent what is possible for environmental protection, for restoration, and for low-impact use. Today, I will reveal our plan for the renaissance of Hetch Hetchy, and then I invite you to enjoy and explore, by bicycle, foot, or shuttle, the various locations around the valley."

This is how it should be, Rick mused. Before taking his seat, he had studied the many graphic displays mounted on easels across the stage behind him depicting future plans for the valley. Unlike Yosemite Valley, with its many villages, hotels, and roads, Rick felt the plan for Hetch Hetchy restoration was more logical and respectful. There would be a hotel named for his fallen colleague, Jeffrey, surrounded by the pine trees that also bear his name; this hotel was to be located just beyond the old dam site, and one hundred feet up the canyon wall from the Tuolumne River—inconspicuous to visitors entering the Park.

Rick had thought a great deal about Jeffrey and that fateful night over a year ago on the crest of Half Dome. He had reflected on Jeffrey's courage and the one attribute which epitomized him —his conviction. Jeffrey, like more and more millennials joining the Park Service, was an activist. To him, protecting the Park and supporting the environment meant more than his paycheck; it was his philosophy of life. With his death, Jeffrey had taught Rick something his Lakota grandfather had struggled to instill in him for years—devotion to others and to the earth. For this reason,

Rick had fought for the restoration of Hetch Hetchy in large part to honor his friend. Fran, who now was speaking to the assembled crowd, had agreed with Rick and pushed forward not only the commemorative name for the hotel, but an agenda of restoration based on low-impact use and preserving the natural state of the valley.

"John Muir once described this place as 'one of nature's rarest and most precious mountain temples,'" Director Mainella continued. "This place was special to him, and it is our hope that it will be special to many more people in the future—people like you who have come here today. We hope the Hetch Hetchy Valley—with its graceful Tueeulala Falls, its stately Kolona Rock, its access to the Grand Canyon of the Tuolumne River, and its roaring Tuolumne Falls—will take its rightful place alongside our other treasured natural wonders of the world.

"There have been those who have claimed Muir was a fool; that the destiny of Hetch Hetchy is to be a repository of water and power. These naysayers are wrong.

"From an ethical standpoint, we owe a debt to Abraham Lincoln and the Thirty-Eighth United States Congress, which set aside the Yosemite Grant. They made a promise back in 1864 to the people of the United States of America, and they made a statement to the world, that natural splendor and beauty were worthy of protection. They said this wondrous and special land would retain its unspoiled, unharvested, undrilled, unmined, unexcavated and wild form, to be enjoyed by all citizens as a public right as indelible as life, liberty, and the pursuit of happiness.

"While we may have broken that promise, we are now seizing the opportunity to come full circle—to return to Lincoln; to again say to the world that not only can we protect natural wonder, but we can restore and..."

Sitting in between Rick and Joy on stage, Woody Jackson's

attention drifted from listening to Director Mainella. He was painfully uneasy in the spotlight and had had an especially difficult time as the principal eyewitness to murder at Stuart White's trial last year. He was comforted by the familiar smiling faces of his mom, Rosa, and Hayduke, seated near the front. Woody smiled back and looked over at Joy. The last time they were both in Hetch Hetchy, they had left the valley inside the trunk of a police cruiser. They had grown apart and dated other people over the past year. He felt torn. Joy meant so much to him, and sitting next to her now reminded him of that fact. Joy and Woody each felt the absence of Jasmine, who had decided it was not her thing to be celebrated; instead, she opted for a bouldering competition with Rebecca and their friends.

Gazing out now at the valley walls and waterfalls, his mind wandered further as he felt a sudden connection to his father. They had camped on a picturesque bluff overlooking the reservoir while hiking from Tuolumne Meadows to White Wolf. There, his dad had told him about the history of the valley, about the losing battle fought by Muir and the Sierra Club to preserve it from the powerful lobbyists who wanted to build a dam at its mouth.

Perhaps what Woody appreciated most of all in this new section of the Park was the designated single campground, accessible only by bike, foot, or shuttle—no RVs, no electricity, just clean and simple camping—pack it in, pack it out. The campground was set across the valley from Wapama Falls at the foot of Kolona Rock, the edifice Muir described as "the El Capitan of Hetch Hetchy." The campground sat on a small bluff, allowing for the dual purpose of being hidden from view for hikers and cyclists in the meadow and providing a spectacular vantage for campers and climbers of the entire expanse of the Hetch Hetchy Valley.

Woody had developed a new line up Kolona Rock, using the

same start that the famous alpinist Warren Harding had used years ago, and then veering right onto the very nose of the monolith where the conical-shaped dome falls away in two directions. During the previous spring break and a little after, he and Jasmine had illegally camped out at the top of Kolona Rock. Each morning, while construction crews worked below, they would rap down to the base of the rock along a rappel line they had established to the west of the main wall; they then would rope up and work the route, connecting one crack system with another via face moves. They tried to follow some of the most obvious and aesthetically attractive features of the wall, like the large diagonal roof that terminated in a long bright orange streak of granite. Ultimately, the route they established was eighteen pitches in length, and they tentatively rated it a 5.10 A1, but felt it could go free at 5.13. They resolved to come back that autumn and try it out. Woody asked Jasmine if he could name the route after his father, and Jasmine agreed on the condition that Woody would work with her to establish another line in the valley that she could name later on. It was a fitting remembrance, Woody thought. His father, John, wouldn't want a plaque or bench somewhere, but a climb bearing the name "The Tao of John"—that would be sure to please him.

"From a logistical view, the water once stored in the Hetch Hetchy Reservoir is being easily harnessed farther downstream," Director Mainella continued. "The expanded Don Pedro area and the new substation just beyond the Park are being used to divert water into the mountain and canyon tunnels..." °

Joy smiled, listening to the words of hope and promise. She wished that Jasmine could have been here, but felt glad to be a part of this park, of this history. She reached her hand out and slid her fingers through Woody's upturned palm until they interlaced with his.

As a freshman biology major, Joy had persuaded her department chair to allow her to do some of her coursework as an internship with the UC Berkeley staff involved in studying the habitat restoration of the Hetch Hetchy Valley. Once the dam had been removed, there were the challenges of figuring out the route the river would run and which species of trees, grasses, shrubs, and other vegetation to incorporate. And there was the persistent question of how much human involvement should be employed compared to the alternative—allowing nature to take its course. This is where Joy's research and computer modeling was most helpful.

"From the perspective of energy generation, the O'Shaughnessy Dam had yielded only 0.2 percent of California's energy usage—one-fifth of one percent. In its place, we commend the city of San Francisco for..." *

Joy looked over at Woody. She couldn't help but realize they had an unmistakable closeness, a familiarity and acceptance she could not ascribe to anyone else in her life. Despite this, they had grown distant. Colleges from all over the country with strong cross-country and track programs were recruiting Woody heavily. And as much as the two had promised they would visit each other on weekends and vacations, they hadn't.

"Yes, my friends, this valley symbolizes the full story of environmental protection in this country. It is a testament to what can go right and what can go wrong. That is why visitors to this place will, as they explore the wondrous natural surroundings, also explore the history of this park—from Lincoln to Muir, from the Sierra Club to the Raker Act, from the building of the dam and the manipulation of the public's power supply to what we are a part of here today—the rebirth of this beautiful valley in keeping with the promise made over one hundred and fifty years ago by the Great Emancipator."

Following a round of enthusiastic applause by those in attendance, Director Mainella continued. "At this time, I am proud to recognize a few very special people. As you all know, in the epic story of losing, then reclaiming this wondrous valley, a dramatic and tumultuous chapter has recently been written. Without the heroic efforts of some of those here with us today––and some not here––Hetch Hetchy Valley would not have welcomed us to this celebration of restoration and conservation. Would Rick Turlock, Joy Cooper, and Woody Jackson please stand?"

The joyous crowd rose up as one and applauded—politicians, celebrities, Park Service personnel, conservationists, journalists, outdoor enthusiasts of all stripes, and many others. Joy wasn't accustomed to recognition and accolades. Last year, when everything unfolded, she was merely trying to survive. That hardly seemed worth this attention. The "tumultuous chapter" as Director Mainella described it was now more well-known than Joy would have liked. Thankfully, the writings of Mojo over the past year had helped to set the record straight. As Woody's mother, she had a front row seat to the details and the recounting of those fateful twenty-four hours the year before. Woody, Joy, and Jasmine had been singled out quickly after the crisis, and rather than allowing the press and public opinion to spin whatever conclusions they saw fit, Mojo took it upon herself to tell their story and was in the process of writing a book. She also went on a vendetta against Dr. Alexandra Leach, writing in every publication that would risk printing it, exposing her connection to the explosions and deaths—despite the verdict handed down by the federal court.

As the crowd returned to their seats, Director Mainella resumed. "I'd like to conclude today with some words from Rick Turlock, whom many of you have met over his many years of service here in Yosemite National Park, and know simply as 'Ranger Rick.' Today, Rick will share with us some unexpected background to what we celebrate here today."

Rick, in his best Park Service uniform, stood up and crossed the stage to shake the hand of Director Mainella. Standing at the podium, he looked out at the throng of people. "Thank you,

Director Mainella, for those words of inspiration and strength." Rick paused, caught his breath, and briefly closed his eyes.

"Though many of you know me as Rick, my given name was not Richard. It was Heyoka. I am of the Lakota Nation, and today, standing here in the middle of this spectacular valley, I'd like to share something with you all. I'd like to share a reason. I'd like to share a rationale.

"Why is it that we fight for nature? Why is it that we do battle as John Muir did, to protect that which is natural and beautiful? I say to you now that we fight because..." Rick again closed his eyes and gathered himself.

"We fight because *nature* fights for us. Nature fights to give us everything it has to offer and everything we need. We fight for nature to thank it for our air. We fight for nature to thank it for our water, our food. And ultimately to thank nature for life."

The crowd erupted in applause. The still considerably barren walls of the Hetch Hetch canyon echoed back their enthusiasm— and Rick again closed his eyes.

Raising his hand for people to take their seats, Rick continued. "I am going to conclude with a reading of the *Great Spirit Prayer*, first translated into English in 1887 by the Lakota Sioux Chief Yellow Lark:

Oh Great Spirit, Whose voice I hear in the winds,
    and whose breath gives life to all the world, hear me.
    I am a man before You, one of Your many children—I am small and weak.
    I need Your strength and wisdom.
    Let me walk in beauty and make my eyes ever behold the red and purple sunset.
    Make my hands respect the things You have made, my ears sharp to hear Your voice.

Make me wise, so that I may know the things You have taught my people—the lesson You have hidden in every leaf and rock.

I seek strength not to be superior to my brothers, but to be able to fight my greatest enemy—myself.

Make me ever ready to come to You with clean hands and straight eyes, so when life fades as a fading sunset my spirit may come to You without shame.

THE END

I f you enjoyed this story, please review it on Amazon and sign up for the MC Behm newsletter to get updates and free Tahoe Dad funnies - http://mcbehm.com/newsletter/.

M.C. Behm is a former deep-rural and inner-city schoolteacher, who writes the *Tahoe Dad* column for the Reno Gazette Journal and Tahoe Mountain News. He lives, works, and plays in South Lake Tahoe, California.

WHEN NOT CHASING his children down Heavenly Mountain Ski Resort or pimping window projects for his "real" job, M.C. Behm rock climbs with a zeal bordering on fanatical.

THE PEN-NAME M.C. Behm is an homage to my late grandmother, Marian Coggen Behm, with whom I lived during my first years teaching high school. Despite being diagnosed with polio at age 3 and being told that she would never marry, never have children, and never amount to much, she defied all of those expectations by getting a Doctorate from Columbia University, marrying an

Olympic athlete, becoming the first school psychologist in the state of Delaware, having 4 children and living to the ripe old age of 89. She always wanted to add "novelist" to her list of accolades, so perhaps having her grandson do it for her is the next best thing.

GLOSSARY

aid climbing: Using gear or protection to gain upward progress on a climb. In the circumstances when using only hands and feet is too difficult for all but the most elite climbers, protective gear—such as cams, hooks, and nuts—can be placed into the rock and used to climb.

anchor: A point at the top of a single cliff or crag, or a point at the top of each pitch on a multipitch route, where there are either permanent bolts in the rock or a removable anchor built for climber-carried protection. It is to this point that a climber fixes his or her rope.

ATC: Air Traffic Controller, the brand name of a device used for belaying and rappelling.

barn door: A particular move that necessitates a degree of tenuous balance on a series of in-line holds and could cause the climber to pivot or rotate around the vertically lined-up hold like a large barn door swinging open on its hinges.

beached whale: This maneuver is often clumsy and precarious as it generally involves the climber flopping up onto the next ledge or position using his or her upper torso and stomach, in addition to his or her hands.

belay: The means by which one climbing partner secures the connecting rope to another climbing partner. Belaying is usually done with a belay device, such as an ATC or a Grigri, but in the early days of climbing, it could be done with the rope wrapped around various parts of the partner's body for a hip belay or a body belay.

belay loop: The reinforced nylon loop connecting the leg-strap portions of the harness with the waist section of the harness. The belay loop is generally the loop through which a climber attaches, by means of a locking carabiner, a belay device.

beta: Advice or specific sequential directions given from one climber to another, meant to assist in executing a difficult sequence of moves on a climb. The expression "bad beta" indicates when climbers receive bad advice that they end up disregarding in favor of climbing without any guidance. "Good beta" is the inverse, where a set of instructions is spot on and makes the difference in pulling through a crux problem on a route. Beta can also be used for other advice tangential to actual route climbing, such as finding the start of a climb, escaping a peak, deciding where to bivy for the night, or even giving advice on relationships.

big wall: Any climb up a large rock facade that requires aid climbing and/or multiday hauling and bivying on natural or portable ledges. Yosemite has been a Mecca for big-wall climbing and is where much of the modern technology that makes big-wall ascents possible was developed and tested.

bivy: From the French *bivouac*, to spend the night out either on the wall itself or at the base or summit of a climb. Climbers usually come prepared with sleeping pads, bags, and sometimes a bivy sack, but on occasion get stuck and need to bivy for the night without the proper equipment for comfort and warmth.

bolt: A fixed mechanical anchor in a rock wall. The American Safe Climbing Association (ASCA) has developed guidelines for safe installation of expansion bolts into rock.

bouldering: Climbing closer to the ground. Bouldering takes the difficulty of an entire route and compresses it into a series of moves close enough to the ground that climbers need only rely on a crash pad to guard them against injury in the event of a fall.

cam: An active mechanical device with opposing leaves that, when activated by a trigger, compresses so that the device can be placed into a crack or other feature on a climb. When the trigger is released, the leaves open and hold the device in place. Also known as a "friend" or an SLCD, a spring-loaded camming device.

carabiner: An aluminum oval, or oblong-shaped circle with a snap open/close connection that a climber uses for a multitude of purposes on a climb, generally to connect some element of protection to the rope.

chalk bag: A small pouch that climbers carry, typically behind them, that contains the white powder chalk used to keep the fingers dry and sticky.

chimney: A crack wide enough for a climber to squeeze his or her body inside, that is, a narrow vertical hallway that can be ascended to the ceiling by pressing one's arms and legs on opposing walls.

cordelette: From the French *little rope*, a small cord of dynamic rope used for a variety of purposes by climbers. It can be a method of attachment to an anchor, it can act as a runner from a single piece of protection to minimize drag on the rope during a climb, it can be used as the actual anchor, or it can be used directly on the rope as a Prusik knot or autoblocker.

crimp: A small handhold, usually a ledge or tiny feature that climbers can sometimes only manage to get the ends of their fingers onto. Certain crimps are described as credit-card holds, meaning that they are as skinny as a credit card.

crux: The difficult section or move in a climb.

deck: The ground.

dihedral: An inward-facing corner that a climber ascends by using counteracting pressure or stemming between the two opposing surfaces.

dike: Any bump or ridge seeming to grow out of a rock wall. The most famous dike anywhere is probably Snake Dike along the western flank of Half Dome, which stretches for over one thousand feet and varies in width from two to five feet.

dirtbag: Can refer to a way of sleeping, literally putting one's sleeping bag in the dirt, or can refer to climbers who, after a series of days sleeping in the dirt and climbing, can look and smell like the equivalent.

dynamic move: A move that implies speed and motion, like a layup in basketball (as opposed to a stationary free-throw shot). Generally, climbers spring to the next handhold, accelerating their body and, once they have gained their target grip or stance, decelerating into their new position. This type of move requires more effort than a static move and fatigues a climber at a more rapid rate. A sure indication that someone is new to climbing is the frequency with which he or she uses dynamic moves, especially in situations where a static move would suffice.

dynamic rope: A rope that is elastic and stretches when under pressure from a fall. Think bungee cord but without the massive stretch. Rope manufacturers typically say that after a few good falls, whippers of twenty plus feet, the rope should be retired, but ask any climbing gym proprietor about the how long their ropes have been hanging on their indoor walls and it will be obvious that these skinny cords last quite a bit longer. The key to rope longevity is usually what it has been exposed to: excessive sun and moisture, sitting in the dirt and sand at the base of a climb, or grating over the edge of a rock. Climbing etiquette at popular top-rope and sport climbing crags stipulates that separate parties be very conscious of each other's ropes as they are walking around the base areas so that no human or dog steps on a rope and grinds dirt into the material, reducing its longevity.

dyno: The extreme end of the static-to-dynamic spectrum of climbing moves. Executed, a climber goes "all points off" of the wall, where both his or her hands and feet are no longer touching the rock surface. To continue with the basketball analogy, this is the equivalent of a breakaway slam dunk. Typically, a full dyno is not necessary in the vast majority of climbs and climbing sequences. In fact, many famous climbs that were once completed using a full and glorious dyno, such as Chris Sharma's deep-water solo of an giant arch off the coast of Spain, have since been completed without the need for such a dramatic maneuver. Perhaps the most famous dyno on the planet at the moment is Tommy Caldwell's mandatory sideways dyno on the new ridiculously difficult route he established on El Capitan.

epic: A long day on the wall, often involving at least one unanticipated snafu or issue, such as a stuck rope, running out of water, getting lost, or any number of other occurrences that sometimes befall climbing parties.

figure eight: The basic knot used by a climber to secure a dynamic climbing rope to a harness. The knot is retraced, or followed through, after a climber feeds the tail of the rope through the waist strap and leg straps of the harness.

free climb: To climb a route using protective gear and ropes only to catch a climber in the event of a fall and not to assist physically in making upward progress (like in aid climbing). The expression free climbing is often misconstrued as free soloing, but despite the semantic similarities, they are vastly different; free climbing involves protecting a climber in the event of a fall, and free soloing does not.

free solo: To climb a route that is larger than a boulder problem without any protective equipment at all. Yes, it is as stupid as it sounds.

harness: The nylon straps, padding, and aluminum buckles that make up the basic safety connection that fits around a climber's body.

jug: A large climbing hold that climbers can wrap their whole hand around, similar to a milk jug but usually not a full handlebar.

layback: A technique in which a climber uses counteracting pressure between the hands and feet. While pulling back on an edge with their hands, climbers simultaneously push against another surface with their feet in order to maintain tension and position on the wall. Laybacking is a good example of a time when climbers need to "go skeletal," meaning they hang on their bones and not their muscles.

locking carabiner: A carabiner that can be locked with a screw gate or other means to ensure that it does not open unless the climber wants it to.

mantle: A move in climbing that necessitates that a climber press downward on a ledge and pivot his or her body upward.

multipitch: A rock climb involving more than one rope length.

nut: Passive protection in the form of a triangular-shaped metal wedge that climbers slot into a crack on the wall to catch them in the event of a fall.

off belay: The command called by the lead climber down to a belay partner to indicate that he or she has safely established an anchor, tied in to that anchor, and can be taken off or removed from the belay that he or she was being given by the partner.

off-width crack: A crack that is too narrow to be considered a chimney, that climbers can squeeze their entire body inside, and too wide to be considered a hand or finger crack, that climbers can ascend with a series of moves that involve locking fingers or hands into the crack. An off-width crack mandates that climbers use more ingenuity, sometimes stacking one hand next to another or rotating and using knees, legs, forearms, or other nontraditional climbing techniques.

pendulum: A swinging move whereby a climber fixes his or her rope to an anchor at a higher spot and then swings as would a pendulum to gain a new position or vertical crack up a wall.

Pendulums are different from tension traverses that involve a climber using a high point to lower out and tension walk diagonally to a new hold.

pitch: A single section of a climb, usually anywhere from forty to one hundred eighty feet in length. A climb that is four hundred feet tall usually involves three to four pitches.

portaledge: Literally portable ledge, a rigid hammock or platform of varying proportions made out of reinforced nylon pulled taut over aluminum poles and suspended from an anchor on a cliff. Portaledges break down into a tube that can be carried along with the haul bag up the side of a wall.

pro: Shorthand for protection, as in how a climber would protect a climb. Pro comes in many forms, but essentially is any device, such as a nut or a cam, placed into the wall to protect against the possibility that the lead climber might fall. Climbers often refer to sections of climbs as having good pro or bad pro, meaning that the pitch or section of the climb may or may not be easy to protect. Having good pro generally means that a climber is more confident on lead, climbing strong, feeling good, and not worried about the quality of his or her protection.

pumped out: When climbers max out their arm muscles (particularly their forearms), making it difficult to grip anything.

rack: The collection of protective gear brought by a climber to safely ascend a wall, such as cams, nuts, and aid climbing gear.

rappel/rap: To descend a rock face or cliff using a rope and belay/rappel device.

runout: A length of a climb that has no way to protect, either with traditional gear or with fixed bolts in the wall. Usually, runout, or R, sections are easier than the rest of the climb to ensure that leaders, when they encounter a 5.7R section, have no problem, because they are coming off of a 5.10 crack, for example. One of the more famous runout climbs in the world is Snake Dike on Half Dome, which demands that leaders go as much as forty or fifty feet on 5.5 terrain before reaching their next anchor.

sharp end: The lead-climber side of the rope. A leader who ties in to the rope and starts up a cliff is said to be on the sharp end of the rope. On a multipitch route, when two partners rotate who is taking the lead on various pitches of the climb, they are also swapping turns on the sharp end.

slackline: A piece of webbing (a one-inch-wide nylon cord) strung between two points and pulled taut. Climbers walk back and forth as well as perform tricks on this line as an entertainment and a way to work on balance. One famous slackline setup in Yosemite National Park is between the Arrowhead Spire and the North Rim next to Yosemite Falls.

sport climbing: Clipping a sequence of bolts for protection while lead climbing a route. Sport climbing can be done in a gym or outdoors and involves using quickdraws (two carabiners slung together with webbing) to clip fixed bolts in the wall and then run the lead rope through those points. Sport climbing is often times the only way to safely ascend an unfeatured face that has enough contours to enable climbing but not enough cracks, horns, pockets, and so on to enable traditional protective gear to be inserted into the rock.

static move: Any move performed with 100 percent control. Climbers generally refer to this style of climbing as "quiet," meaning that when a climber moves from one hold to another, he or she is methodical, slow, deliberate, and not wasting energy on big dynamic moves or grunting and muscling his or her way up a cliff.

static rope: A rope that has none of the elasticity and stretch of a dynamic rope. It is meant primarily for jugging and hauling gear, and should never be used for lead climbing.

talus: Rocks that have broken free from a cliff over eons of time and have collected as a large debris field around the base of the wall. When approaching a rock climb, climbers often need to scramble up large talus fields to reach the actual cliff. Talus fields are also generally an indication of how solid the rock is. The more talus, the less stable the rock may be.

whipper: A significant fall while lead climbing. Once a lead climber on the sharp end of the rope places protection and climbs above that protection, any fall taken doubles the length of the distance climbed above the last protective piece. A particularly scary whipper can result when taking a fall after traversing horizontally or when there are any ledges or hazards that the lead climber could fall into. Ironically, the safest way to take a large whipper is over a roof or overhang. Assuming that the lead climber places protective gear in the ceiling, a fall likely results in the lead climber just falling into free space. This is why most climbing gyms angle their routes with slight overhangs, so that clients consistently fall into open space rather than against the wall.

NOTES & BIBLIOGRAPHY

chapter 4: *the year Jon Scott Glisky crashed* Chris McNamara and Chris Van Leuven, *Yosemite Big Walls* (Mill Valley, CA: SuperTopo, 2011), 173.

chapter 4: *six tons of baled Mexican marijuana* Yosemite and the Sierra Nevada, News and Discussion Forum. "Re: When six tons of pot crashed into Lower Merced Pass Lake," April 21st 2012. <http://yosemitenews.info/forum/read.php?3,53359,53416>

chapter 4: *the quota on hiking Half Dome* National Park Service, "Half Dome Permits for Day Hikers," November 25, 2013, <http://www.nps.gov/yose/planyourvisit/hdpermits.htm>, "A maximum of 300 hikers will be allowed (about 225 day hikers and 75 backpackers) each day on the Half Dome Trail beyond the base of the subdome."

chapter 6: *not allowed to even touch that water* "Hetch Hetchy Valley," National Park Service Handout: Experience Your America, March 2007. "Water Quality: Swimming and boating are prohibited in Hetch Hetchy Reservoir in order to maintain a clean source of drinking water."

chapter 6: *add at least another three pitches to the climb* State of California Resources Agency, Department of Water Resources, and Department of Parks and Recreation, *Hetch Hetchy Restoration Study* (State of California, 2006), 22.

chapter 6: *undiscovered routes right here that deserve attention* Doug Robinson and Bruce Willey, "Resurrection of the Dammed," *Climbing*, September 2006. "This valley everyone had heard of and no one knew. Because it was filled with water. The water was making all the difference - making it noisy and keeping it quiet. Blinding with reflection and scorching with reflected heat. The concrete plug in the throat of the valley was attracting a lot of political heat too. Homeland Security was afraid someone would blow it up, and environmentalists were afraid no one ever would."

chapter 7: *the other few routes up the face* Chris McNamara and Chris Van Leuven, *Yosemite Big Walls* (Mill Valley, CA: SuperTopo, 2011), 166–179.

chapter 9: *The bear bazooka, or "BB gun* Colin M. Gillin, Forrest M Hammond, and Craig M. Peterson, "Evaluation of an Aversive Conditioning Technique used on Female Grizzly Bears in the Yellowstone Ecosystem." Int. Conf. Bear Res. And Manage. 9(1): 503-512, Winter 1995. "The Thumper gun is a Model 267 Smith and Wesson gas and flare gun converted to a 32 mm bore, with a lightly rifled... 55.9 cm barrel.... Projectiles were 602 grain rubber "bullets" made of 31.75 x 76.2 mm plastic bottles filled with 30 cc's of water (Roop and Hunt 1986). The projectile was powered with FF black powder.... In addition to Thumper bullets, factory made plastic "Bear Deterrent Cartridge" projectiles and occasionally "Ferret Soft Slugs" were used...."

chapter 10: *a little plastic contraption with chemical filters* Michael van Gortler, "Sipping the Waters: Techniques for Selecting Untreated Backcountry Water for Drinking," Backpacking Light, last modified September 20, 2006, accessed April 14, 2012, http://www.backpackinglight.com/cgi bin/backpackinglight/sipping_water_drinking_untreated_backcountry_water.html#. UcdRnnZ4RYI.

chapter 10: *Makes you wonder where John took Teddy The National Parks: America's Best Idea*, directed by Ken Burns, aired on PBS September 27, 2009 (Washington, DC: Florentine Films, 2009), DVD.

chapter 10: *the Clif Bar corporates, who dropped sponsorship of soloists* John Branch, "A Sponsor Steps Away From the Edge: Clif Bar Drops Sponsorship of 5 Climbers, Citing Risks," New York Times, November 14, 2014.

chapter 10: *There's a proud history* "The Ascent of Alex Honnold," *60 Minutes* (New York: CBS News), October 2, 2011.

chapter 10: *Some climbers have publicly stated their opposition* Sam Moses, "On the Rocks, Kauk Is It, Ron Kauk, acclaimed as the best there is at going up sheer granite walls, lives as freely as he climbs," *Sports Illustrated, June 1986.* "I'd really like to be able to slow things down and have climbers think about themselves, use climbing for a tool to better themselves, not try to impress people." Ron Kauk also delivers presentations in Yosemite every summer during which he discusses his evolution as a climber and shares with visitors about his organization, "Sacred Rok," which brings incarcerated youth into Yosemite. When asked about free-soloing, he has maintained his position that the ethic of climbing should be more respectful of the wall and the dangers involved and less egocentric.

chapter 10: *National Geo is like any grocery-store tabloid* Mark Jenkins, "Daring. Defiant. Free. A New Generation of Super-climbers Is Pushing the Limits in Yosemite," *National Geographic,* May 2011.

chapter 11: *compliance with federal legislation was ordered by the Supreme Court* Robert W. Righter, *The Battle Over Hetch Hetchy: America's Most Controversial Dam and the Birth of Modern Environmentalism.* (New York: Oxford University Press, 2005).

"On April 22, 1939, Supreme Court Justice Hugo Black delivered the opinion of the court, reversing the circuit court on the basis that, 'Congress clearly intended to require—as a condition of its grant—sale and distribution of Hetch Hetchy power exclusively by San Francisco and municipal agencies directly to consumers in the belief that consumers would thus be afforded power at cheap rates in competition with private power companies, particularly Pacific Gas & Electric Company."

chapter 11: *the State of California Department of Parks and Recreation study in 2006*

State of California Resources Agency, Department of Water Resources, and Department of Parks and Recreation, *Hetch Hetchy Restoration Study* (State of California, 2006).

chapter 12: *Galen moved to the south of Yosemite Valley* Shirley Sargent, *Galen Clark: Yosemite Guardian* (Yosemite, CA: Flying Spur Press, 1981).

chapter 12: *Galen helped to shape and pass the Yosemite Grant* "150th Anniversary, Yosemite Grant, 1864 to 2014," National Park Service, U.S. Department of the Interior, December 16, 2013, www.nps.gov/featurecontent/yose/anniversary.

chapter 13: *that quote from Muir* Greg Barnes, Chris McNamara, Steve Roper, and Todd Snyder. *Tuolumne Free Climbs* (Mill Valley, CA: SuperTopo, 2003), 84.

chapter 15: *people have been free soloing in Yosemite* Susan M. Neider, *Wild Yosemite: Personal Accounts of Adventure, Discovery, and Nature* (New York: Skyhorse Publishing, 2007), 241–252. Yosemite National Park has a long tradition of free soloing, dating back to 1866 when a surveyor by the name of Richard Cotter and a geologist by the name of Clarence King climbed what they called the Merced Obelisk. To gain the summit of what is today known as Mount Clark, Richard and Clarence had to mount massive granite pinnacles "made of immense, broken rocks poised on each other in delicate balance, vast masses threatening to topple over at a touch." They continued up "climbing with the very greatest care . . . making sure of [the] foothold . . . and clinging by the least protruding masses of stone, now and then looking over our shoulders at the wreck of granite, the sloes of ice, and frozen lakes thousands of feet below . . ." Once the intrepid duo was within sight of the summit of the obelisk, the "bold red spike which rose grandly above us," they ran into a chasm that had to be leapt across in order to make the final push for the top. "Summoning nerve, I knew I could make the leap, but the life and death question was whether the debris would give way under my weight and leave me struggling in the smooth recess, sure to fall and be dashed to atoms. Two years had we longed to climb that peak and now within a few yards of the summit, no weak-heartedness could stop us . . . There was no discussion, but planting my foot on the brink, I sprang, my side brushing the rough projecting crag. While in the air I looked down, and a picture stamped itself on my brain never to be forgotten. The debris crumbled and moved. I clutched both sides of the cleft, relieving all possible weight from my feet. The rocks wedged themselves again and I was safe."

Though many parties have since gained the summit of Mount Clark, no one has been able to ascertain exactly where this death-defying chasm leap took place. The lore associated with this first piece of free soloing and the conviction held by both men not to be "weak-hearted" resonates in much of today's climbing community.

chapter 16: *that horror movie...Red Velvet* Dan Noyes, "Father, Daughter Accused of Real Estate Fraud," *ABC7, KGO-TV* (San Francisco, CA), July 6, 2009.

chapter 16: *right-to-vote initiative* Marc Lifsher and Dianne Klein, "PG&E's Customers Vote Down Prop. 16," *Los Angeles Times*, June 10, 2010.

chapter 16: *quoted that dude Hodel* Boyd Sprehn and Marc Picker, "Interview with Secretary of the Interior Donald Hodel." *ENVIRONS,* May 2, 1988.

chapter 18: *the little known Paul Simon song* Paul Simon, "I Know What I Know." *Graceland* Album, General M.D. Shirinda, 1986.

chapter 18: *the firebombing of Vail Ski Resort* "Operation Backfire: Help Find Four Eco-Terrorists," The Federal Bureau of Investigation, last modified November 19, 2008, accessed April 14, 2012, http://www.fbi.gov/news/stories/2008/november/backfire_11908

chapter 19: *the first major killer of people in the Park* Michael P. Ghiglieri and Charles R. Farabee Jr., *Off The Wall: Death in Yosemite* (Flagstaff: Puma Press, 2007), 575.

chapter 28: *shoved his wife, Dolores Gray, off a cliff* Michael P. Ghiglieri and Charles R. Farabee Jr., *Off The Wall: Death in Yosemite* (Flagstaff: Puma Press, 2007), 575.

chapter 30: *Since Operation Backfire* "Operation Backfire: Help Find Four Eco-Terrorists," The Federal Bureau of Investigation, last modified November 19, 2008, accessed April 14, 2012, http://www.fbi.gov/news/stories/2008/november/backfire_11908

chapter 30: *frame one of the founders of Earth First!* Kate Coleman, *The Secret Wars of Judi Bari: A Car Bomb, the Fight for the Redwoods, and the End of Earth First!* (San Francisco: Encounter Books, 2005).

chapter 33: *This little known fact* Michael P. Ghiglieri and Charles R. Farabee Jr., *Off The Wall: Death in Yosemite* (Flagstaff: Puma Press, 2007), 575.

chapter 37: *actually dam a national park* John Warfield Simpson, *Dam!: Water, Power, Politics, and Preservation in Hetch Hetchy and Yosemite National Park* (New York: Pantheon Books, 2005), 174.

chapter 37: *broken gas mains and broken distribution pipes* Kenneth Brower, *Hetch Hetchy: Undoing a Great American Mistake* (Berkeley, CA: Heyday Books, 2013), 40.

chapter 37: *future quake in San Francisco* Robert W. Righter, *The Battle Over Hetch Hetchy: America's Most Controversial Dam and the Birth of Modern Environmentalism* (New York: Oxford University Press, 2005), 58.

chapter 37: *the reason we even have environmentalism* Kenneth Brower, *Hetch Hetchy: Undoing a Great American Mistake* (Berkeley, CA: Heyday Books, 2013), 36. "In a remarkable number of ways, the Hetch Hetchy Valley was the cradle and crucible. The environmental movement as we know it today was forged in the fight against the Hetch Hetchy Dam (as it was then called) in the years just prior to the First World War."

chapter 37: *WP&G couldn't profit from public power* Robert W. Righter, *The Battle Over Hetch Hetchy: America's Most Controversial Dam and the Birth of Modern Environmentalism* (New York: Oxford University Press, 2005), 179.

chapter 37: *stopped enriching the coffers* Ibid., 186.

chapter 39: *Military Contractors Scrutinized After Assassination.* John F. Burns, "Tough Role of Military Contractors Comes Under Scrutiny in Iraq," *New York Times*, September 23, 2007.

chapter 41: *never will be trodden by human foot* John Muir, *The Yosemite* (San Francisco: Sierra Club Books, 1988). In the early 1870s, numerous attempts were made to reach the top. John Muir tells of "John Conway, the master trail-builder of the Valley, and his little sons, who climbed smooth rocks like lizards, [making] a bold effort to reach the top by climbing barefooted up the grand curve with a rope which they fastened at irregular intervals by means of eye-bolts driven into joints of the rock. But finding that the upper part would require laborious drilling, they abandoned the attempt, glad to escape from the dangerous position they had reached, some 300 feet above the Saddle." Finally, during October of 1875, George Anderson picked up where John Conway had left off. He scaled the rock using the old rope left by Conway and then, according to Muir, "resolutely drilled his way to the top, inserting eye-bolts five to six feet apart, and making his rope fast to each in succession, resting his feet on the last bolt while he drilled a hole for the next above." The native spirits of the valley were perhaps none-too-pleased with Anderson for being the first to conquer Tis-se'-yak, for that winter Anderson died mysteriously in his little log cabin. Since that time, many have followed in Anderson's footsteps. The Sierra Club had cables installed in 1919 from near the top down to the saddle. These cables, along with upright steel posts and wooden boards, have become the hallmark of alpine adventure for many tourists and weekend warriors who hike the eight miles from Yosemite Valley to climb the "cables" and then descend the same way after enjoying, for their moment in time, the zenith of the rock that Whitney once described as "perfectly inaccessible."

chapter 45: *Snake Dike is down here* Don Reid, *Rock Climbing: Yosemite Free Climbs* (Helena, MT: Falcon Press Publishing Co., 1998), 216.

chapter 51: *feasibility of the dam removal proposition* State of California Resources Agency, Department of Water Resources, and Department of Parks and Recreation, *Hetch Hetchy Restoration Study* (State of California, 2006).

chapter 51: *lambasted the city of San Francisco* Gerald H. Meral, *Finding the Way Back to Hetch Hetchy Valley: A Vision of Steps to Restore Hetch Hetchy Valley in Yosemite National Park and to Replace Water and Energy Supplies: Feasibility Study 2005* (Sonora, CA: Restore Hetch Hetchy, 2005).

chapter 65: *Muir describes Yosemite Valley* John Muir, *The Yosemite* (San Francisco: Sierra Club Books, 1988).

chapter 66: *they climbed high into the branches of ponderosa pines* Rebecca K. Smith, "Eco-terrorism?: A Critical Analysis of the Vilification of Radical Environmental Activists as Terrorists," *Environmental Law* 38, no. 537 (2008): 537–576.

chapter 69: *power generated by the O'Shaughnessy Dam* Robert W. Righter, *The Battle Over Hetch Hetchy: America's Most Controversial Dam and the Birth of Modern Environmentalism* (New York: Oxford University Press, 2005), 179.

chapter 72: *voilà, San Francisco has abundant clean water* Robert W. Righter, *The Battle Over Hetch Hetchy: America's Most Controversial Dam and the Birth of Modern Environmentalism* (New York: Oxford University Press, 2005), 115.

chapter 72: *for use and profit only by the public* Ibid., 7.

chapter 72: *WP&G purchased power from Hetch Hetchy* Ibid., 168.

chapter 72: *electricity to finally be rerouted to public municipalities* Ibid., 179.

chapter 72: *this federal mandate was still being violated* {Author's note: From this point in the story, *The Elixir of Yosemite* as a novel clearly stands as a work of fiction and not an accurate representation of history. The Supreme Court order was indeed followed by the City of San Francisco and power was rerouted to the Modesto and Turlock Irrigation Districts, with the explicit instruction for it not to be resold or put back onto the larger power grid. As of 1951 the Raker Act has been complied with and PG&E was no longer purchasing surplus power generated at the O'Shaughnessy Dam.} Robert W. Righter, *The Battle Over Hetch Hetchy: America's Most Controversial Dam and the Birth of Modern Environmentalism* (New York: Oxford University Press, 2005), 186.

chapter 76: *But that was back in 2006* "Putting Intel to Work Against ELF and ALF Terrorists," The Federal Bureau of Investigation, last modified June 30, 2008, accessed April 19, 2012, http://www.fbi.gov/news/stories/2008/june/ecoterror_063008

chapter 76: *but against property as well* Rebecca K. Smith, "'Eco-terrorism?: A Critical Analysis of the Vilification of Radical Environmental Activists as Terrorists," *Environmental Law* 38, no. 537 (2008): 537–576.

chapter 76: *same category as murdering a plane full of passengers* If a Tree Falls: A Story of the Earth Liberation Front, directed by Marshall Curry, debuted at the 2011 Sundance Film Festival (Oscilloscope Laboratories, 2011), DVD.

chapter 79: *pulling the gear along the way* John Long and John Middendorf, *How to Climb: Big Walls* (Helena, MT: Falcon Guides, 1994), 105.

chapter 82: *Warren Harding's creative repurposing* Chris McNamara and Chris Van Leuven, *Yosemite Big Walls* (Mill Valley, CA: SuperTopo, 2011), 80. Warren Harding and his team of climbers had anticipated needing to augment their rack of pitons, hooks, and other early climbing technology. Frank Tarver had located some old sections of enameled stovepipe that Harding used in a leapfrogging manner to gradually make it to the top of the two- to three-inch-wide crack.

chapter 89: *divert water into the mountain and canyon tunnels* Gerald H. Meral, *Finding the Way Back to Hetch Hetchy Valley: A Vision of Steps to Restore Hetch Hetchy Valley in Yosemite National Park and to Replace Water and Energy Supplies: Feasibility Study 2005* (Sonora, CA: Restore Hetch Hetchy, 2005), 21.

chapter 89: *O'Shaughnessy Dam had yielded only 0.2 percent of California's energy usage* Ibid., 49.

If you enjoyed this story, please review it on Amazon and sign up for the MC Behm newsletter to get updates and free Tahoe Dad funnies - http://mcbehm.com/newsletter/.

ACKNOWLEDGEMENTS

I'd like to extend a sincere thanks and heartfelt apology to all those friends and family that I've taken out rock climbing over the past five years. I know that sometimes my estimation of difficulty might be slightly warped. If any tears were shed, I was doing research.

This project would not have been possible without the nudges, sighs of exasperation, and resolute badgering of many disparate individuals.

Those people who looked at my earliest iterations of this book, including my brother (whose name I stole for my main character) and my Aunt Kris. Thanks for believing in me. Thanks also to my sister-in-law, Marion Frebourg for all of the stunning black and white illustrations.

And for reading this over my shoulder as a perpetual speller and grammar checker, my lovely, wonderful, gorgeous, athletic, funny, talented, inspirational, and bookclub-gigalo wife. Thank you.

I'd especially like to thank all those climbing buddies, on whom I inflicted whole sections of the book while traveling to and from Yosemite. This group would include Alex Steel, Jason

Welch and his twin Josh, Jason Peterson, as well as our international exchange student Mark Liu from Taiwan and his friends Daniel and Faizan. It would also include Sloan Gordon who provided the necessary nudge for me to by saying, "I don't know that much about mysteries, but you could have been reading to me from a book off of the bestseller list." Michael Habicht who steered me clear of inauthentic gear and route descriptions, and Ryan Goralski, for consistently changing the topic whenever I started to read to him.

At the second draft of my story, before my characters really owned their own skin, I owe a tremendous thanks to the librarian at South Tahoe Public Library Katharine Miller, a book reviewer and friend, Danielle Ledesma-Smith, and, of course, my mother, whom I drug up many climbs in Yosemite, including Cathedral Peak. Way to go, Granny!

Also, I really owe much of the story's flow to the wonderful minds who make up Tahoe Writer's Workshop. You encouraged and inspired me to get out the scalpel and allow my characters to speak for themselves.

Made in the USA
San Bernardino, CA
20 September 2018